G'Day USA

Beach Nut Press

For Dora. She made me a reader.

DISCLAIMER

This is a work of fiction and as such, the characters and situations in this book are entirely fictional.

Except for those characters whose names you recognize. They're real, but the words coming out of their mouths are entirely mine.

Readers familiar with the Venice Beach area may notice some geographic discrepancies. Sorry. I've taken the liberty of adding some apartments and cafes to facilitate the flow of the story.

There really was a *Kevin Pollak's Chat Show*. It is no longer a thing, but the archives are a treasure trove of brilliance.
www.youtube.com/@kevinpollakschatshow

I highly recommend you stop by and visit. It's a blast.

ACKNOWLEDGMENTS

Big thanks to my beta-readers, Gord, Kay, Kelley and Norm for their valuable input.

Chapter One

Kevin Pollak looked into the camera. "If you're just joining us, what the fuck? We started over two hours ago. Fix the clock on your iPhone. We're having a nice chat with Ellie Bourke, one of the stars of the soon-to-be-released *Blood Thunder,* poster girl for Australian beauty and all-around nice girl." He shifted into his impeccable Carson. "And so, Miss Bourke, we come to where you are now. On the precipice of international stardom."

I smiled. I could barely believe it myself. And I was sharing it with Kevin Pollak on his weekly Chat Show.

Such as it was. Four of us in a small studio, a couple of cameras and a table and he *owned* the place.

He continued. "We saw early copies just last week. Loved it." He turned to the two cohorts to my left. "Jaime? Sammy?"

They both started talking at once, and then Samm stopped and let Jaime talk. "I bawled my eyes out at the end. And don't let these guys tell you any different. They did, too."

Samm shrugged. "What can I say? Excellent flick." He held up a finger. "You do know, of course, David Paymer stole another role from me. Once again I lost out to that bastard. I could have been one of those scientists."

I laughed. It was a running gag with Sammy. "Are you serious? We could have been working together in this, too?"

Kevin interrupted. "That's right. How did I miss that? Who did this dossier? They are fucking fired. You guys had two episodes of *Modern Family* together, am I right Samm?"

"Indeed. Ellie was in her second episode as the tutor and they brought my character back for a couple of shows."

I had to pinch myself. Not much more than a year ago I was doing cattle calls and barely scraping by, ready to head back to Australia and now here I was, days away from the premiere of what promised to be as big as *Avatar*.

He tapped the table. "Earth to Ellie. You okay?"

"Hell yeah. I was just thinking about how much has happened in the last, what, sixteen months? Completely different world."

"How different?"

"I had maybe $200 to my name, living in my car because I couldn't go back in the guest house I was living in."

"Because of the..."

He had the decency to not push it. "Yeah. Joel was killed in there.

Killed by the guy who owned it. I was literally packed and ready to go back to Australia."

"And now, I hear, you've got a nice place on…let's not tell everyone, just down the road from Jaime and I."

I nodded. "That whole area is a freak zone. A nice freak zone. Makes me feel normal. Very, very normal. The strangest part of my life now is that I actually own a gun. A cop friend suggested I have one and learn how to use it if I was going to be going out at all hours for movie work." I took a sip of ice water. My bladder was starting to announce its imminent need to void. "What's the longest one of these 'conversations' you've done?"

"Eddie Izzard held the record for quite a long time. What was the date, Sammy?"

"Would have been October 11, 2009. He's an amazing actor. Two hours and thirty one minutes."

"Right you are. And it didn't feel a minute over a flat two hours. His record was smashed by Damon Lindelof."

"Interview 117, 27th of June. Went an astounding two hours and forty-eight minutes." Either Samm had a fantastic memory or he had imdb.com open on his phone.

"Conversation, Sammy, not an interview." Kevin looked up at the clock. "We're sitting at a bit over two-fifteen. Think you can break his time?"

"Only if you let me pee on the floor. I'm going to pop in about ten minutes."

"Ah, well, we can't have that." He steepled his fingers. "The gun. You really think you need one? Jaime won't let me keep one in the house."

I shook my head. "Like I said. Never used it. It's been in the drawer by my bed for the last six months. The last time I took it out was during the shoot. We had gun training and I thought it would be good to get mine out and fire a few off at the range. Almost broke my wrist."

Kevin laughed. "In deference to your bladder, it's probably time to wrap things up. You ready for your Larry King? Do you want me to go over the rules first?"

Jaime interrupted. "Before you get to Larry King, can I ask a question? You don't have to answer if you don't want to."

"No, no. Anything. I'm an open book." I had a feeling I knew where she was going with this.

"It's about Bart Sweeney's trial."

Bingo. "Surprised you took this long to mention it."

"We're nothing, if not sensitive." Jaime smiled. "What do you think of the trial? How it's playing out?"

I shrugged. "I haven't been paying any attention to it. The guy's an asshole, not fit to scrape the dog shit off my shoes. I understand there won't be a death penalty option, unfortunately, because the evidence I provided to the police showed it was an accident. But since he killed Joel in the commission of another crime, drugging him for sex, the penalty should be pretty stiff. You know he actually broke the foot of a fellow actor to get him to limp properly for a role? The man was an absolute psychopath. "

Kevin slipped into his Peter Falk, right eye dancing independently of the left. "Oh, uh, just one more thing, before I forget, how did you nail the bastard?"

I couldn't help but smile. He was dead on. "Found a recording on Joel's phone."

He dropped the Falk bit. "Yeah, I heard. But how did it happen that he was recording at the time? That was never explained. I always thought that was too much of a coincidence."

"Joel kept an audio diary of every day." I sniffed and shook my head. "He wanted to be you, you know."

"Be me? I'm already me."

"You know what I mean. He wanted to emulate your career. The first fifteen minutes of the recording was him bursting with excitement about being on this show." Sad smile. "He never made it." I sniffed. "Bumming me out. Can we change the subject?"

Kevin looked at his cohorts. "Absolutely. Too much good stuff coming up in your life for you to keep it sad. Larry King?"

"Larry King."

"Okay. Gather your thoughts while I explain this for our viewers at home. Here are the rules: Larry King is approaching his second century. Eventually he will reveal something on air we never wanted to hear. You need to do a poor Larry King impression, and I must impress upon you it must be poor, reveal a disturbing fact about Larry King, not yourself, and if you have a good city name to throw to, that's even better. That's your camera. When you're ready."

I leaned my elbows on the table, dropped my head and lowered my voice as much as I could. *"Ya know, mating kangaroos are as disturbing a sight as you would imagine them to be. Woolloomooloo, hit me."*

Kevin slapped the desk. "Put down your pencils, we have a winner. Of course. Kangaroos. Woolloomooloo? That's a place?"

"My dad lives there. It is a place."

He collected his papers. "Fantastic. Now if you'll sit there uncomfortably for a couple of minutes, I'll wrap things up."

"Go for it." I sat back. The bladder was getting insistent. He pulled it all together, announcing the interviewees for the next couple of weeks and then finished with his usual close:

"Thanks for watching, and as always, get outta my face."

After a two-second pause one of the voices behind the cameras said, "Okay, we're clear."

I exhaled a held breath. "Great. That was fun, really. Where's the bathroom?"

Jaime pointed to a door behind the cameras. "Second on the right."

When I got back, at least three pounds lighter Jaime and Kevin were muttering to each other in a corner. They stopped when they saw me. "What is it guys? Something I said? If Sweeney tries to sue for what I said about him, he'll be coming after me, not you. And I know where he hurts. Don't worry about it. Or was it the swearing? We Aussies swear a lot."

"So you haven't heard the news?" Jaime took me by both hands. "No, you couldn't have. It just happened."

"What happened?"

"Sweeney's been released."

"He got bail? Wait, no. That doesn't make sense. The judge denied bail right up front. How? Did he escape?"

"Released. His attorney persuaded the judge to throw out the case this afternoon."

"What? It's a rock-solid case. I should know. I built it."

"That, unfortunately, is part of the reason it's been tossed. They're saying the evidence, most of it, anyway, came from you, and you were pissed off at him for hitting on you so much. Some other reasons also, but that's the main one." Jaime pulled her hands back. "Ouch."

"Shit, sorry. I didn't mean to squeeze. Oh, what the fuck is this place coming to? He better not cross my path." I scratched my head. An ideal day turned to shit in thirty seconds. New record. "I've got to go. Thanks again for letting me do this. I know only a couple of hundred people were watching live, but it was still fun. I've got to get going. Some busy days ahead."

"Well, you didn't reach Sugar Ray Leonard numbers, but you were in the mid-four digits at one point. And the podcast will be watched by thousands more." Kevin surprised me by giving me a hug. I'm at least four inches taller than him. "Did he really break a fellow actor's foot? Would have thought that would have come out at trial."

I pulled away. "I didn't find out until after the trial. Too bad. Would have been good to add a couple of nails to his coffin. He might still be in there."

"Forget about Sweeney. You're at least three tiers above him in this city. After this movie premieres, you're going to be unstoppable. Everyone knows what he did. His career, such as it was, is over. Not only is he not fit to scrape the dog shit off your shoes, he's lower than the shit. Go and be happy. You deserve it."

I nodded, chewed the inside of my mouth and walked out the door into the blinding Sunday afternoon Santa Monica sunlight.

I was of two minds about this. I had achieved my dreams. Hell, I exceeded my dreams. I had never imagined a blockbuster was in my cards, and based on early reviews, this was a proper blockbuster. In two days I'd be doing its red carpet at Grauman's Chinese Theatre.

And I had a heap of things to do before then.

But it royally pissed me off that the man who killed my best mate was out of jail. It sounded like he was going to get away with it. I thumbed the Bluetooth button on my steering wheel. "Call Marty."

He answered after a couple of rings. "Princess. What's going on? You ready for Tuesday night?"

"You know I hate it when you call me princess. What do you know about Sweeney getting out?"

I thought the call dropped. There were about five seconds of silence before he answered. "So you heard?"

"Just. What's this about them cutting him loose because I was the one who brought in the evidence needed to convict him? That's bullshit."

"I know. You know. *He* even knows. Asshole defence attorney. What are you going to do? Ignore him. He doesn't exist."

I pulled onto Rose Avenue from Lincoln. "He exists. He will always be a piece of crap. I'll always be looking over my shoulder for him. Do you know if he's in his place in the Valley?"

"I know you, Ellie. Stay away from him."

I took a breath, then exhaled, puffing my cheeks. "Look, I'd love nothing more than to show up on his doorstep and tell him what I really think of him. Run him out of town, even."

"I have to strongly advise you, as your manager, to stay well away from him."

"Yeah, your job is to give advice, and mine is to consider it. I don't always follow it. You, of all people, should know."

"Ellie, come on."

"Hey, I'm just saying." I paused. "I just finished Pollak's show. It went great, I think. Thanks for asking. Kinda closed the loop, since it was the fact Joel was booked for the same show which convinced me he didn't actually kill himself." I shook my head. "And after the work I did to get Sweeney *in* jail, now he's not."

"Where are you now?"

"Almost home."

"So stay home, get some friends over, grab a bottle of wine and celebrate the last few days of relative solitude."

"How do you mean?"

"When this movie comes out, you are going to be on the receiving end of paparazzi from here to New York. A few of us here in LA know how good you are. After Tuesda,y, the entire country will."

"Oh, Jesus, I hope not. You really think so?"

"What, the paparazzi? Definitely. You are going to be hot property. Stay above the Sweeney shit. You did what you had to do and everyone knows what he did. Consider him dead to you. Because he is."

"I wish."

"Never wish that on anybody. Listen, I've got Tom coming in. I need to let you go. Stay out of trouble, enjoy the life you now have and I'll talk to you tomorrow. Be good."

He disconnected and I turned into the parking garage below my small apartment.

Small, but it overlooked Venice Beach and I was finally back by the ocean.

I loved it here. The nut cases on the beach really did make me feel normal. And some of them were really nice people. I had a regular breakfast date with one of the jugglers. The guy kept a bowling ball, running chainsaw and a bag of flour in the air.

I had two spots in the garage. The spot in front of my regular spot was reserved for my ancient, trusty VW Beetle. It got me through a rough spot in my life. I was slowly restoring the body myself. Very slowly. I hadn't the time to touch it in the last six months.

One day.

The view off the balcony, looking into the setting sun, was spectacular. It was a warm March day. It was going to be another hot summer, by the feel of it, and it started early. The traditional Venice Beach inhabitants were reluctant to leave the warm weather behind. Strings of roller skaters tooled up the boardwalk. The muscle heads were still ripping out reps. T-shirt and chalupa vendors were packing up their stalls for the night as the sun touched the horizon.

A couple of surfers worked the small waves. The ocean calmed as the sun set. They'd be crazy to keep surfing after it got dark. *I* wasn't even that crazy.

I gripped the railing and squeezed. The nervousness was probably just the upcoming premiere, but I couldn't help but feel that Sweeney seeing this same sunlight, breathing this same air was what was putting me off. The bastard should be behind bars for the rest of his sorry life and now he was probably sitting back on his deck with a drink in his hand and a fat cigar in his pie-hole.

I tried to shake it off. He didn't have the right to take my moment from me. I worked my little ass off to get here. And dammit, he wasn't going to spoil it.

The two surfers finally called it a day. Maybe they weren't as dumb as I thought they were. They were about my age, one a beach blond and the other dark hair. Lanky-thin and very fit.

I squinted. The dark haired guy looked like someone I knew, from long ago, in a land on the other side of the world.

Ghosts from my past.

Chapter Two

Kent Williams peeled his wetsuit off, letting it hang from his waist. He finger-combed back his black hair and squinted at the setting sun. "Shit waves, man."

His surfing partner looked up at him as he took his bathing suit off under a towel. "Meh. It's been better. Why this beach? Huntington's better."

"You remember *Beast of Bondi,* Charlie?"

"How could I forget? And so what?"

"Ellie." Kent point to the string of apartments on the other side of the beach, near the skate park. "She lives up there somewhere. Thought we might run in to her."

Charlie squinted back up the beach. "Really? She lives there? How do you know?"

"I was fucking around on the interwebs today and ran across a live podcast with her and that Kevin Pollak guy. She was talking about her movie coming out, how her life has improved over the past year or so and she mentioned she'd moved out of Sweeney's guesthouse to this part of town."

"She was living with Sweeney? What a dog."

"Yeah." Kent slid his board into its case and strapped it to the roof rack. "I don't think they got along well, what with him killing her room-mate and ending up in jail over it."

"Where the fuck do you get this stuff, man?" Charlie tossed his wetsuit into the back of the old Honda Accord and tied his board along side Kent's. "I completely lost track of these guys. So Sweeney's in jail? Not surprised, actually. Karma catches you eventually."

"How do you mean?"

"You know I was AD for him on *Beast*. He treated me like shit."

"He treated everyone like shit." Kent limped to the driver's side of the car. "But yeah, he reserved the special shit for you."

"Lucky me." Charlie hopped in the passenger's side. "So, how long is Sweeney in for?"

"Oh, he's out."

"You just said he went to jail."

"He was sprung today. Some technicality with the evidence."

"You're losing me."

"Ellie's friend was killed and the cops thought it was a suicide. He was some comic. Not bad, I hear. Ellie didn't think it could have been suicide and found enough evidence to get Sweeney locked up. Now it appears the evidence was questionable and his lawyers persuaded the judge to toss the case."

"I should probably pay more attention to the news. So where's Sweeney now?"

"Fucked if I know. Probably back at his place in the Valley."

"So you know where he lives too. You're a regular Google Maps."

A smile slowly spread across Kent's face. "Fuckin' brilliant idea, mate. We should go visit him. Like a bit of a reunion."

"He was an ass. Why in the hell would I want to go visit him?"

"See his place. Say hi. Rub his face in the fact he's now got absolutely no career left."

"Neither do I."

"Well, you've done well for yourself with the cellular stuff."

"I just work there. It's not like it's my company. I could have been a good director."

"Well, there's a vacancy. He's not in the business anymore. Can you imagine anyone hiring him now?"

"They let him go."

"Everyone knows it was a technicality. He did it. There's audio tape floating around of him doing it."

Charlie looked out the window at the passing hills as they drove up the Santa Monica Freeway. "Huh. Maybe I should get back in the saddle. Though, to be honest, I'm not really keen on seeing him again."

"Oh, come on. We'll pick up some pizza on the way. His cupboard is probably empty. And some beer. Come and gloat with me. It'll be fun."

Bart Sweeney climbed out of the taxi, pulling the small bag of possessions with him. He tossed a fifty on the front seat. "Keep the change."

"The fare's $72.50, Mac. You still owe me."

"Get it from the state. I don't have it."

"I'm not leaving until you pay the remaining fare."

Bart leaned down and looked in the window. "Look, you know where you just picked me up. I've been behind bars for the last fourteen months. I don't have it. You can sit out there for the next year if you want, because it'll probably be that long before I get work again."

"Asshole." The cabbie slammed the car into drive and left with a scream of rubber.

"Likewise, my friend." Bart fished through the bag of belongings for the house keys. He walked in the front door to a stale, dusty smell of emptiness. Unlived in for over a year. "Son of a bitch." He strode across the room to the phone in the kitchen. Picked it up and held it to his head. "Dial tone. At least he got that right."

He punched the numbers from memory; the only number he'd been calling the past few months.

"Saul speaking."

"I thought I said I wanted this place cleaned. You assured me this place would be cleaned when I got back."

"I didn't expect the judge to rule until tomorrow. God's honest truth. Cleaner was supposed to be there first thing in the morning. Tomorrow morning."

Bart grunted. "Yeah, okay. Fine. Thanks for pulling this off. Didn't think you could do it. Don't cancel the cleaners for tomorrow.

This place is a shit hole. Talk to you later."

"Wait, don't hang up."

"What?"

"You looking for work?"

"Does the pope shit in the woods? Why?"

"I'm your guardian fucking angel."

Bart sat down, the telephone cord stretching across the room. "What ya got?"

"An indie operation is looking for a director experienced with putting together low-budget pictures. They heard you were out and approached me."

"They asked for me specifically?"

"You bet. Your rep precedes you, buddy."

Bart rubbed his whiskered jaw. "I'm betting not much money, being an indie."

"Hey, work is work. Get this done and the doors will open. Just keep your fucking nose clean."

"Maybe I was being too subtle. How much money are we talking? I don't work for free."

"Hundred up front and take a piece of the backend."

"Wow, that is small. How far along is this?"

"They're ready to start shooting in about a week. They've got some old widow financiers; as far as I know, the principals are in place, and they were ready to start with a rookie director when they heard you were available."

"What's the story? No, stop. Never mind. I don't want to know. Send me the information. Did you get the Internet hooked back up?"

"Yes. All the log in information is under the keyboard. I'll email the details to you now. Give these guys a call."

Bart looked around his barren house. "Look, Saul, friend to friend, since you know I'm going to be getting $100,000 shortly, can you spot me a couple of grand to tide me over? I'm flat."

Saul chuckled on the other end of the phone line. "I'll bring by two thou in the morning. You'll owe me big time, buddy."

"Tomorrow." Bart shrugged. "Okay. Tomorrow it is. I'll live until then."

"So you're going for the Director's thing then?"

"I thought it was implied. Of course. I'll contact them as soon as you send me the info."

"You gave me power of attorney; I can let them know on your behalf and set up a meeting for tomorrow morning."

"Make it tomorrow afternoon. I need a haircut and some new clothes. I lost about twenty pounds behind bars."

"Okay. 2:30 pm. Get a phone, too."

"I will. Do me a favor, will you? See if you can track down Ellie Bourke's number? I want to mend fences. Maybe I can get her a bit part in this indie thing."

"She's bigger than *Ben Hur* right now, buddy. Doubt she'll go for this thing."

"Still. I'd like to apologize, privately, without a horde of media."

"Good luck. I'll email you her contact details.

There was a knock at the front door. "Thanks Saul. Someone's at the door. Gotta go."

Bart hung up and peered out the living room window. Two faces he hadn't seen in over four years were standing on his porch, one with a couple of pizzas and the other with a case of beer. He yanked the door open. "Kent. Charlie. What the fuck, boys? A welcome home party? Someone shoulda told me."

"So you *do* remember us." Charlie cocked an eyebrow. "Thought maybe we were ghosts to you."

"What the fuck? Come in, boys. If you're planning on sharing, that is. Excuse the mess. I've been, well, detained."

"Yeah. We heard." Kent held up the case of beer. "Thought you could use a drink or three. It's been what, fourteen months?"

"Close enough. Appreciate this. What you two been up to?"

Kent placed the beer on the kitchen table. "Bit parts here and there." He slapped his leg. "This fucking limp doesn't help any."

Bart grimaced. "That happened on the Bondi shoot, right? Ever figure out how it happened?"

"You really don't know?"

Bart shrugged. "You just showed up limping one day. Perfect timing." He turned to Charlie. "And you, old boot. You disappeared. Haven't heard a peep out of you. What kind of movies you making these days?"

Charlie looked at Kent then back at Bart. He pulled a bottle out of the case, twisted off the top, and took a long pull. "Really?" He wiped his mouth with his sleeve. "You didn't know? Find it hard to believe."

"What, is it a fucking mystery? I don't keep track of everyone I used to work with. You're here in the States, so you must be doing pretty good."

"I'm a contractor. Working for one of the mobile operators here.

Technical role. I haven't been on a movie set since *Beast*. Thought you, of all people, would know."

"And how in the hell would I know?"

Charlie took a step toward Bart, almost nose to nose. "I'm out because you made it the worst experience of my life."

Kent jumped between them. "Hey, guys, cool it. Let's head out to the balcony and enjoy." He sniffed. "It's a bit stale in here."

Bart took a deep breath, looking Charlie in the eyes. "Forgive me. I *was* an asshole. I've had over a year to realize what a dick I was. Truly sorry, Charlie. You should get back into the business. You really were good. If I can give you any references, just let me know." He took the pizza from the table. "Kent is right. Let's head outside. It's still warm out. Sun's down, but the heat remains." He looked to Kent, then Charlie. "Clocks change next weekend, right? So longer days."

"Same length days. I just have to get up earlier for work." Charlie followed Kent and Bart outside, the three of them taking up three sides of a patio table. He sat facing the guesthouse. He nodded toward it. "That's where it happened?"

"What?" Bart strained to look over his shoulder. "What happened?"

Kent placed his hand on Charlie's arm. "Don't, mate."

He shrugged it off. "You know. The thing you ended up in jail for."

"Guys, ancient history. I made a mistake. Bourke exaggerated the evidence. Hey, I was let go today. It's in the past, okay?" He flipped a pizza box lid. "What have we got here? Pepperoni? Grab a slice guys." He slid the box off the one underneath it. "And Hawaiian? You're too good to me."

Kent caught Charlie's eye and shook his head. He sniffed. "Only the best for our favorite ex-con. What are you going to do now? The movie business is probably not in the cards. Too many bridges burned."

Bart smiled and sipped his beer. "You think?"

"You know, just saying. It was a pretty serious crime." Kent held up his hands. "I know, I know. You were let go. Double jeopardy though, right? You can't be tried for the same crime twice. So you're safe. Did you do it?"

Bart shook his head and pulled a slice of pizza from the web of melted mozzarella. "Some nerve, boy. Some fucking nerve. I'm hosting you in my house, and you've got the nerve to bring that up." He looked at the expression on Kent's face and laughed. "Fucking with you. Eat. It's good."

They sat in silence; the only sounds the light traffic on the street, the odd bird in the trees and the sound of the neighbor's TV.

After fifteen minutes of eating Charlie broke the silence. "You say you enjoyed working with me in Australia, and I'll admit the first few weeks were okay, but after that you were an unholy asshole. What the fuck happened?"

Bart chewed on the crust. He held up a finger, swallowed and said, "I was under considerable stress. We were running out of time and money. It was just pure luck things got on track. Really sorry about the stresses. It wasn't directed at you intentionally. I was an asshole to everyone. Right Kent?"

He grunted. "Especially to me."

Bart laughed. "Look, see? The star of the show. The Beast of

Beast of Bondi copped more shit than anyone else. You're still in the business, right? What have you been in lately?"

Kent shook his head. "Nothing big. Local commercials, small TV bits. This foot has kept me out of the good roles."

"Shame, that. You've got a talent. Well, boys, I'm directing an indie. Meeting the team tomorrow afternoon. If you want I can see if I can get you a part, maybe behind the camera for you, Charlie."

Charlie swallowed his mouthful of beer and carefully placed his bottle on the table. "What was that? The day after you're out of jail and you've got a gig? That's fast. What is it?"

Bart dismissively waved his bottle of beer. "Details aren't important. It's a gig. I'm directing and I can find spots for you. Just say the word."

Charlie looked at Kent and stood. "I've got to get going, mate. You driving or do I need to catch a bus?"

"Was it something I said? Boys, sit. There's more beer. I think I might have a bottle of scotch squirreled away somewhere."

Kent slid his chair back. "Nah, I gotta go too. I'll talk to you later. Welcome back to the free world."

"Well, whatever, boys. More for me. I've wasted way in the slammer." He grabbed another piece of pie. "I'll see about getting you two boys a piece of the action. I'm meeting with them tomorrow afternoon. Drop by around 4:00 and I'll let you know how it went."

Kent followed Charlie around to the front of the house. "Whatever, Bart. I'll call you later."

He unlocked the car and motioned for Charlie to get in. "Back to your place?"

"If you could, I'd appreciate it."

"You free tomorrow morning?"

"I've got a job, mate."

"Pull a sickie. I want to surf Venice again."

"It's shit there."

Kent looked across at his friend. "You're a bit thick. I want to bump into Ellie. *That's* the wagon to hook yourself to."

Charlie thought for a minute. "Yeah. Why not." He drummed his fingers on the dashboard. "Can you believe it? That ass has a job the day he gets out of jail. I had to leave. I was this close to punching him in the neck."

"I could tell. Annoys the hell out of me, too. Especially after what he's done."

"Yeah, I know. Killing that guy."

Kent shook his head. "Not talking about that. You say you left because of what he did to you, but it pales in comparison to what he did to me."

"You were the "star" of that steaming pile of cow shit. He treated you with kid gloves."

"Ha. Not likely." He turned on to the 405 South. "This brilliant stroke of luck he was talking about? The one that broke the stress for him?"

"Yeah. What was that?"

"Me, finally being able to limp."

"It was a stroke of luck that you broke your foot?"

"That's the problem, mate. *I* didn't break it."

"I don't follow."

"Asshole back there broke it."

"Bullshit."

"Not bullshit. Think about it. He tried for two weeks to get me to limp properly. I couldn't. At least not good enough for him."

"No, no, no. Why?"

"Like he said. Running out of time and money. I couldn't do the limp the role called for."

"So he just broke your foot? I find that hard to believe. He's a fat pig. Or he was. And you're in pretty good shape. Don't believe he could do that to you. Not without you letting him."

Kent shook his head. "He invited me out to his place one night. We went nuts. Started with a bottle of Grey Goose, some coke, and it went downhill from there. I have absolutely no recollection of most of that night. And the next morning his problems were solved. I had three broken bones in my foot and he had a leading actor who, suddenly, could limp." He shook his head again. "No, not a coincidence. He knocked me out and broke my foot. Made my part in that movie perfect, and locked me out of almost everything since. What a fuck. I was kinda hoping he spent the rest of his sorry life behind bars." He squeezed the steering wheel. "You really didn't know? I got the impression *I* was the only one who didn't know."

Chapter Three

I woke late. Almost 9:00. I must have been really tired to stay in bed that long. I'm usually up a lot earlier. Kind of a side effect of getting up at 4:00 for six months to get to makeup before very long days of shooting. The lie-in was nice. It would be nothing but hectic for the next few weeks. I rubbed the sleep out of my eyes and turned the shower to hot and steamy.

The water pounded my neck and upper back, and I just stood there, the massage head trying to beat away the tension. I was starting to get nerves. Working on a movie was one thing; going to a premiere with the press watching every move was something else all together. I took a deep breath and calmed myself and smiled. As far back as I could remember, this was what I wanted. And it was here.

It wasn't the fame I wanted, and for damned sure not the paps. Those were side effects to success. I was making real money now, although that wasn't my dream either. But with the money came the freedom to choose roles I wanted - good roles in sometimes-small movies. The opportunity to pick and choose instead of beg and steal.

I lathered my hair. It was getting too long to manage. I had to leave it that length, at least for the premiere, since that's how long my character's hair was in the movie. After, though, I was going to cut it. It was more work than I wanted.

Finally out, dried, dressed and hungry, I stepped on to my balcony and looked out over the ocean. It was gray and a bit foggy. It was a book day, which suited me fine. A down day before the madness sounded perfect.

I tied my hair back into a damp ponytail, grabbed my iPad and made a beeline to the cafe just outside my apartment. I had no food, and even if there was something in the kitchen, I was too lazy today to cook.

Emily and Henry ran a little six-table cafe on the beach. Four inside and two outside under an awning. They were perpetually smiling, always adding a bit more to my sandwich than seemed physically possible and generally taking good care of me. Henry cooked, and Emily prepared. It was a match and, apparently, a marriage made in heaven.

"Hey, Ellie. You're up late. Thought you weren't coming by today. What will you have?" Emily was about a foot shorter than me and Chinese. As was Henry. She looked up, expectant smile on her face.

"I've got to be good. Big premiere tomorrow night and I need to fit into the dress or my manager will kill me. So a bowl of fruit, wheat toast and a black coffee, okay? I'll be sitting outside. Looks like this might be a good day to crawl inside a book."

Emily laughed. "You, maybe. We'll be feeding people all day. No time for books."

"You love it."

"We do. Go have a seat. I'll bring it out to you."

"Thanks."

The sun was trying to poke through the cloud and fog with little success. Fortunately it was warm. Spring was here and the cold winter nights seemed to be behind us for now. Well, cold compared to Australia. I had Canadian friends who thought January here was pure heaven.

I had just opened up the Sydney Morning Herald app on my iPad to catch up on news from home when I heard a voice I hadn't in years.

"Watch what you're doing or I'll slice you from ear to ear."

I grinned and replied: *"You've got to catch me first, you miserable fuck."* I turned and saw Kent Williams, my co-star in *Beast of Bondi*. He was the Beast, a psychotic killer stalking the skate parks of Sydney while living in a storm drain off Bondi Beach. I was his last victim. That was the dialogue just before the big fight scene at the end. Pretty bad.

"Kent. When did you get into town? And Charlie? Jeeze, this is almost a reunion."

Kent sat across from me. "Yeah. All we need now is butt-fuck Bart."

I shuddered. "No thanks." Charlie was still standing. "Sit, man. What have you guys been up to? When did you get here?"

"Almost two years now. I think we got here not long after you did." Kent fiddled with a menu. "Charlie a few months after me."

"And you didn't look me up?"

Kent waved at Emily to come and take his order. "Kinda busy. Didn't think you'd be that interested in catching up anyway. But I'm glad we bumped into each other. You're on fire now."

I nodded. "Not doing too bad. Have you been acting? I haven't run into you anywhere. And I can't even tell you've got an Australian accent."

"Small parts here and there. Nothing like *Modern Family* or that movie you're in. What's the name?"

"*Blood Thunder*."

"Right. Congrats."

"Thanks." Charlie sat very quietly, almost invisible. "What about you. Directing anything?"

He shook his head. "I've been out of the business since *Beast*. That was enough for me. Sweeney did a great job of turning me off the whole industry."

"That's too bad. You were great. Any time Sweeney was in trouble it was you who fixed things up. And when he gave you the Second Unit stuff, hell, some of the best footage in the movie."

"Bullshit."

"Seriously. You should think about getting back in."

He furrowed his brow and looked at me intently. "How is it that Sweeney is now out of jail? He said something about you planting evidence. Is that true?"

"No, it's not. When did he say that?"

Kent folded the menu and looked up. "Dropped by his place last night. He's lost a bunch of weight in there. It looks like prison has actually done him well."

"Why would you go to his place? Especially after what he did to you."

"Come on now. Relax. I - we - just went by to welcome the man back to the land of freedom." He grinned. "Right Charlie?"

"He said you fabricated evidence, or something, and that's why the case was tossed. I don't like the guy any more than you do, but why would you do that? Are you saying he didn't kill your roommate, whatever his name was?"

Before I could answer, Kent interrupted. "And you knew about what he did to my foot? And you didn't tell me?"

"Whoa, whoa. Guys. You're ambushing me. Charlie, no. I didn't fabricate any evidence. I just took what I had to the police. His slime-bag lawyer got him off. And yes he did kill my roommate. His name was Joel." I looked closely at him, making sure he caught everything I said. "He absolutely killed Joel. His lawyer, apparently, convinced the judge that I was pissed off at him because he was hitting on me. Neither was true. I wasn't pissed off with him until after he killed Joel, and he never really hit on me."

Emily came to the table. "Food, gentlemen?"

"I'm paying for this, Em. My treat. These are old friends from Australia."

"It was sounding a bit loud. You okay?"

"Just friends catching up. We're okay. Boys, get whatever you want. Her husband is a fantastic cook."

"You sure, dear? I can get Henry out here to straighten these two out."

Kent laughed. "It's like she said - we're old friends. Can I get some pancakes?"

Charlie chimed in. "Me too. And coffee, if you could. Thanks Ell."

Emily cocked and eyebrow and looked at the two shaggy surfer types. "Yeah, okay. If I hear anything untoward from you lot, I'll have Henry out here with a cleaver to sort you out. Don't mess with Ellie." She looked at Charlie then Kent. "Your pancakes will be ready in a couple of minutes."

Kent watched her walk back in to the cafe. "She your bodyguard or something?"

"Something like that. Kind of adopted me when I moved in. It's nice to know they've got my back." I leaned back in my seat. "Let's dial it back a notch guys. We had fun on the movie. Best of buddies. Sweeney is history. Ancient history. I've decided I'm going to enjoy my life. Sweeney can go fuck himself. The odds of me ever crossing his path again are slim to none."

"Not likely you'll cross our paths, either," said Charlie.

"Crazy talk. Serious, Charlie, you should get back in the business." I looked at Kent. "I didn't know about your foot until way later. Thought it was a surfing accident or something. You shouldn't let your foot slow you down. Despite the *Beast* reviews, you were - are - good."

Kent took a deep breath and seemed to think about what to say. "Let's say for a minute you didn't know what Sweeney did, and I'm not convinced yet, there's still no way I'm going to be able to get any serious roles with a foot that still hurts like hell if I'm on it for more than an hour or so. It even cuts in to my surfing." He shook his head. "I'll be bit parts. Nice of you to say otherwise, but I'll deal."

I scratched my head. "What did he do, exactly?"

"Third, fourth and fifth metatarsi. Fractured all three of them. They didn't set right because the ass forced me to do the role or he'd sue me for breach."

"You mean it's going to hurt all your life?"

"Unless I get surgery I can't afford because my insurance is calling it a pre-existing condition."

"And how much would surgery cost?"

"Don't even. I don't need your help."

I sighed. "I'm obviously not going to force it on you, but think about it. I really want to help. And I can. Money isn't as much of a problem."

"Don't rub it in." Charlie looked like he was getting steamed, and I really didn't need that aggravation.

"Hey, mate. It's your decision to get out of the business. I can only suggest you get back in. You were good. I'd love to see you making movies again."

Charlie pushed back his plate. "Nice seeing you again Ellie, but we've got to go."

"Hang on a sec, Chaz. Ellie here is just trying to be friendly. Right Ellie? Listen, while we're in the neighborhood, why don't you show us your digs? Never seen a movie star's place before."

I didn't want to come across like a dick. Dickette? Whatever.

"Sure. Not long though. I've got heaps of stuff to get done before the premiere tomorrow."

Kent stood. "So when did you buy the place?"

"Six months ago. I'm leasing though. Might buy something bigger up in Malibu later." I caught Charlie throw Kent a glance. "Hey, boys, don't make me feel bad for doing well. I had to work hard to get here, and I'm going to enjoy it. Come on up. It's not much, but the view is great." I stood and left a fifty under the edge of my plate. "Were you two surfing here last night? I thought I might have seen you. Or I saw someone who looked familiar."

"Charlie and I caught a couple waves."

Charlie pushed his chair in. "Not very good here. Not compared to Huntington, anyway."

He had a point there. "And Huntington isn't even close to North Narrabeen. Am I right boys?"

"You ever miss home?"

I opened the building door and stepped to one side to let them in. "Sometimes. But the opportunities are much better here. What about you?"

Charlie shrugged. "Sure. It's nice there. But like you said, there's more business here."

I locked the front door. "What is it you do?"

"Telecomms engineer, working for a couple of different companies as a contractor. On and off work, but when it's on, it's pretty good money." He followed me into my apartment. "But sure as hell not this good. This is nice."

I smiled and waited for Kent to come in before locking *that* door.

"Yeah. It is. Beats the hell out of the guesthouse in the Valley."

Kent plopped onto the sofa. "So were you doing something with him?"

"Who, Sweeney?" I opened the doors to the balcony. "Are you kidding me? No. He was like a father to me. A smelly, overweight father." I shuddered. "Gah. I think he was just trying to help out."

Charlie stepped out on the balcony. "Great view. Must have spectacular sunsets out here."

Kent bounced up. "Hey, where's the loo?"

I pointed down the hall. "Second on the left."

Charlie called from the balcony. "Ellie?"

"What? Everything okay?" I joined him on the balcony. "What's up?"

"Sorry if I came across like a dick. Wasn't called for. You have done well. And it was kind, but unnecessary for you to say I was a good director."

"It wasn't bullshit, Charlie. Bart has only ever succeeded when he's had a strong AD with him, and you were the best. You should look around for some small stuff, make your name, and go for it. If I can help, I will. We Aussies need to stick together."

"Thanks."

"So where did this telecoms stuff come from?"

"Got a TAFE diploma way back. Information and Communications Technology. Finally putting it to good use."

"What are you talking about?" Kent pushed onto the small balcony. "What are we sticking together against?"

Charlie turned away. "Nothing, mate. Don't worry about it."

"I was telling Charlie here he was the one who kept Bart from totally screwing the pooch in *Beast*. Don't you think?"

Kent shrugged. "Yeah, he was good. So were you. And despite the foot, so was I. Sweeney knows how to make good dreck. You're not doing too bad. Was that the new MacBook Pro on your desk I passed?"

I don't generally like visitors for exactly this reason. They tend to be snoops. "Picked it up a few weeks ago."

"Nice." He rubbed his hands on his thighs and tucked a bit of the front of his shirt in, then pulled it out again. "So, Sweeney. You think he's going to continue his love affair with C-Grade horror?"

I chuckled. "Not anymore. I doubt he'll be making anything now. I wouldn't be surprised if I ran into him pushing a squeegee at an intersection in Compton. If I ever went to Compton, that is."

"I live in Compton."

"Shit, Charlie. Didn't mean anything by it."

"Sure. Anyway, you're wrong."

"About Sweeney?"

"About him working, yeah. Kent and I are going to talk to him this afternoon about stuff. He might have something for us. Giving it some serious consideration."

"No, no, no. Don't give him any money. You can't trust him."

Kent laughed. "Like I have money to give. Not that at all. He's been asked to direct an indie. Asked. He didn't go looking for it, and he wasn't asked to put any money in. They've got the financing. He thinks there's work there for both of us, so I guess he isn't dead. Yet."

That took my breath away. Karma certainly wasn't pulling her weight. "How does a sack of shit like him manage to come out of this smelling like roses? Un-fucking believable." I dry-scrubbed my face. "What an asshole." I looked at my two guests. "Shit. Sorry. I know this is good for you two, but it really pisses me off. He killed my best friend. He shouldn't be out of jail, and he sure as hell shouldn't be working." I ushered them off the balcony. "Sorry, but you gotta go, guys. I've got a ton to do. Keep in touch, okay? You know where I live."

I closed the door behind them and dropped on the sofa. Took a deep breath. Tried to remind myself that my success didn't depend on his failure.

I was having a hard time convincing myself.

Chapter Four

Charlie stood on the sidewalk outside Ellie's apartment and looked at his vibrating phone. "Shit."

"What?"

"Boss is looking for me."

"You told him you were sick, right?"

"Yeah. He's a fucking wanker." He turned off the phone. "Fuck him. I'm sick." He rubbed the back of his neck. "Remind me to call him later, or I'll be out of work." Charlie grinned. "But I'm going to have to go in tomorrow and make my resignation official if Sweeney actually comes up with the goods. I don't feel like burning too many bridges."

"So let's go see the man."

Charlie looked at his watch. "Too early. He said this afternoon."

Bart woke to insistent hammering on his front door. He threw on the now too large bathrobe and padded barefoot to the front door and peered through the side glass. He grunted and pulled open the door. "Saul. What's the fucking emergency?"

"Okay. You're alive." The short, balding middle-aged man, perpetually sweating, wiped his brow with a handkerchief.

"Why in the hell wouldn't I be?"

"The cleaning guys were by here at 9:00 and nobody answered the door. I thought - I was afraid, maybe something happened to you." The lawyer pushed in to the house and wrinkled his nose. "I'll call them and tell them to come back."

"9:00? What time is it?"

"A bit after 11:00. You sleep well?"

"First time in fourteen months I wasn't worried about getting corn-holed. I slept like a baby. You have money for me?"

Saul pulled an envelope from his inside suit pocket. "Two grand, as promised. I'll add it to my bill."

Bart opened the envelope and fanned the bills. "You're a lifesaver. I'm running out of J&B." He looked at Saul. "And food, of course. And I need a haircut and a new set of clothes. I can actually see my dick now."

"Lucky you. Have you called them?"

"Who?" Bart peeled five hundred off the pile and slid it into his wallet. The remaining he placed inside an unread copy of Keith Richard's 'My Life'.

"The backers for the indie. I talked to them last night and told them you were interested, but they'd like to talk to you directly."

"I need a haircut and some clothes. Like I said. You drive me to Northridge Plaza and I can be ready by 2:00, at the latest. Call them and confirm while I shower."

Saul watched his client walk to the bathroom, wondering when he became his manager. "Prison didn't change him. He's still a motherfucking dick."

The man the media would soon be calling "The Killer" smiled to himself. His heart pounded with the excitement. Years of plans not brought to fruition, and today the puzzle pieces all fell in to place. Well and truly fell. It couldn't get any better. It was the perfect vengeance storm. Means and opportunity were handed to him. Motive was years old. And a fall guy dropped in his lap. A firm believer in the adage that the more prepared you are, the luckier you get, the Killer silently thanked himself for his obsessive preparation.

It was time. It started today.

Marty dialed Ellie's number again. "Come on, girl. I need to talk to you." He looked at the desk phone while the speaker *burred* the ringtone on an unanswered phone. Then to voicemail. *"This is Ellie. The beep is your cue."*

Marty punched a button and lifted the handset. "Ell, it's Marty, your ever faithful and extremely concerned manager. You're not trying to duck me are you? I want to talk to you. I know Sweeney's release has freaked you out. Don't let it. You've got a huge day tomorrow.

Your success, if I may be frank, is of huge interest for me, since fifteen percent of your success ends up in my bank account. Call me. It's really, really important."

He dropped the handset in the cradle and leaned back in his chair. "Chloe?"

His PA stuck her head in his office. "What's up, boss?"

"Try and track Ellie down will you? I can't reach her. Make sure she's okay."

Kent and Charlie spent three hours killing time along the Venice boardwalk.

Charlie's stomach rumbled. "Need food, mate. And I'm on rationed cash. Any ideas?"

"I do. Follow me." Kent led them back to the breakfast cafe. "Go with whatever I say, okay?" He stepped up to the counter. "Emily, right?"

She looked at the two. The cafe was empty, the lunch hour finished. "Ellie's friends, right?"

"Exactly. I'm Kent and this is Charlie. We are Ellie's good friends. Haven't seen her in a long time. It was great catching up with her this morning. Do you have anything left to eat?"

"Ellie must be the smart one of you three musketeers. Why wouldn't we have food? Do they regularly run out of food in Australia? What would you like?"

"I'll have a BLT on toasted wheat. What would you like Charlie?"

"Chicken Caesar salad?"

Emily raised an eyebrow. "Are you asking if we have any, or are you asking for a bowl for lunch?"

"Lunch."

"Anything to drink?"

"Ice lemon tea for me."

"Me too," said Charlie.

"Sitting in here or outside?"

"Outside. We need to talk business." Kent nudged Charlie to the door. "You'll bring it out?"

"I'll bring it out. Go sit, Ellie's friends."

Charlie swung the chair around backwards and straddled it, leaning his chin on the back. "So that's the super plan? Ordering food?"

"You got it. Brilliant, right? I miss craft services."

"What? Yeah." Charlie scratched his chin. "To tell the truth, I miss most of the movie business. The money was pretty good, and it didn't seem like work. Most times." He tilted his head. "Why are we hooking up with Sweeney when he so royally screwed us over?"

Kent looked over his shoulder and leaned in close so no one could overhear. "I'm going to use him to get better opportunities. No loyalties with that ass. Just go along with it. We can have some fun, make a few bucks and network a bit. I've hardly had any work this year, and it's March already."

"Maybe we go along with him and sabotage him from within. While pretending to be his best pals."

Kent laughed. "You're a devious little fucker."

Charlie scowled. "Except he should be in jail."

"Or dead."

Charlie nodded. "That would be justice."

Emily came out with a tray bearing food and drinks. "BLT for the tall and dark one and chicken Caesar for surfer boy." She gave them their drinks. "That'll be $35.00 for the pair of you."

Kent winked at Charlie. "Ellie told us to tell you she would take care of it." He beamed a big smile up at her. "She's great, isn't she?"

Emily shook her head. "She would have mentioned that. I better give her a call." She took a cordless phone from her apron pocket and dialed a number. She held it to her ear for a few minutes before dropping it back in to her pocket. "She's not answering. You two worry me. I haven't seen you before and you were not being nice this morning. I think you should pay. I'll apologize to Ellie if I'm wrong."

Kent shrugged. "So you don't believe us. Doesn't make it less true." He recited Ellie's number and address. "She's doing a dress fitting this afternoon for her premiere tomorrow night. Hair and makeup tomorrow morning, then the world gets to see who she really is. Trust me when I tell you we are close like this." He held up crossed fingers. "I think she'll be offended if you make us pay. We're her best friends from Australia, and her guests. You, of all people, should know how generous she is."

Emily looked at the two of them. "I don't believe you. But I'm going to give you the benefit of the doubt. If I find out you're pulling a swift one on me it'll be the last time you ever eat here."

Kent smiled. "Yeah, sure. Whatever. Give her a call later and see that we're right. Thanks for the food, Em." He turned to Charlie. "So, mate, how's the salad?"

Emily shook her head and walked back to the cafe muttering about freeloading assholes and too generous *ingénues*.

Charlie watched her leave. "Well done, mate. Would have ordered cake if I knew what was up."

"There's a lot more of that coming."

Bart looked at himself in the changing room mirror. JC Penney's would have to do for now. He stepped out to where Saul waited like an impatient husband. "Full wardrobe for under three hundred smackers. Not bad stuff, too."

"Are you fucking finished? Or do you want your nails done too?"

Bart looked at his fingers. "Nah, they'll do. Just one thing left, and you're going to have to help me with that one."

"Bart, we've got to be in Reseda in thirty minutes. Quit fucking around here."

"I need a phone. I can't get anything on contract right now so I need a prepay. I don't have a valid driver's license for ID. It expired six months ago. I'll give you the money, but you've got to set it up, okay?"

"I don't think they ask for identification, but we'll grab one on the way. I don't want you to be late, since I'm now apparently your manager."

Marty's PA intercepted him as he came back into the office from a late lunch. "I talked to her, boss. She's fine. Surfing at Huntington. Not easy taking a call when you're on a board, she said."

"Surfing? Shit, I hope she doesn't kill herself. Did you tell her we needed to talk?"

"She said you could catch up tomorrow. Said she was going to be out of touch for the rest of the day."

"Doing what? She's a hot commodity. I can't have one of my top clients out of touch for a whole day."

"She turned off her phone just after she told me, so yes you can."

Marty grumbled under his breath. "Okay. I can't control her. Double confirm the limo I arranged for tomorrow and make damn sure there's flowers in the back this time, okay?"

Chloe smiled. "You're stressing over the premiere, aren't you?"

"No, that's bull." He paused. "Well, maybe a little. Her first big movie, and she asked me to go with her."

"Rumors abound."

"We're not a thing. I'm her manager, and ten years older than her."

"Just the right age difference." Chloe's eye's twinkled. "And I think she likes you."

"How about you squash that rumor like a bug, okay? If you talk to her again today, remind her the limo picks her up at three. I'll be with it. She better not be late."

"Consider it done. Now go take a Xanax."

Kent and Charlie pulled up outside Bart's house just as Bart and Saul arrived from their movie meeting.

Charlie hopped out of car. "Perfect timing."

Kent stretched. "You going to move away from this place Bart? It's got a lot of history. I know I'd certainly get out of here."

Saul and Bart walked down the drive toward the visitors. "Boys, you came back. Did you bring pizza and beer again?"

"Sorry, not this time, boss. Can we call you boss? *Should* we call you boss?"

Bart looked at Kent and cocked an eyebrow. "Eager, aren't you?"

Kent and Charlie walked up the drive to meet them. "We had some fun on *Beast*, didn't we? Mostly. Except for the breaking my foot bit, and you demeaning Charlie every time you opened your mouth, it was a laugh a minute."

Saul looked at Bart. "What the fuck's he talking about?"

"History. Ancient history. Right boys? All behind us. I'm a changed man." He looked closely at Kent. "How long have you known?"

"As long as Ellie has."

Bart's face darkened. "Let's not mention her name. She's not taking my calls, did you know that? It's because of her I lost the last year of my life."

"I thought it was because of what you…." Charlie trailed off. "Never mind. Like you said. Ancient history. What's the deal with the movie? What's it about?"

"You, in a minute." He turned to Kent. "What do you mean you knew as long as Ellie has? She knew?"

"You said we weren't talking about her."

"When did she know? When did she tell you?"

"Right after it happened. She didn't tell me until yesterday. I think she was afraid of you. I *know* she's really pissed at you now."

"Why are you even talking with her? If you sign up for this deal you have to exclude her from your life. Come in. I've got something cold to drink."

Charlie followed him up the steps. "You're all over the place about her, mate. Let's just drop it. You haven't told us about this alleged deal and what roles you may have for us in it."

"You kids have no sense of timing. Patience, ass." He opened the fridge and pulled a beer out for each of them. "Back deck. Too hot in here." He looked around. "But at least it's clean now."

Saul opened his attaché case and pulled out some legal documents. "You probably should hear what the project is before you commit to anything."

"Does it pay well?" Charlie sat back in his chair.

Saul waggled his hand. "It's relative. It's an independent movie. Bart has negotiated, with the help of his manager, his deal up by 50% with a smaller cut on the back end, so we know the money is there." He leaned forward and pointed at Kent with his pen. "There's a part in the movie not yet filled and on Bart's recommendation they're willing to give it to you." He shifted is gaze. "And AD and Second Unit is yours if you want it. The pay is scale with a cut of the profits, but the backers are well known and well connected. Impress here and there's plenty of work in the pipeline."

"You still haven't told Charlie and me what the hell it is."

"Hitting the high points, it's about a military guy in the Philippines post-World War Two trying to get over the death of his wife from malaria while falling in love with a teacher at the international school his nine-year-old boy goes to."

"So I'm the military guy?"

"No. That's cast. Jeff Donovan. You're one of the teachers at the school, a rival for Jeff's character."

"I like his stuff. Smiles too much though. Script any good?"

Bart laughed. "Since when did you care? It will be re-written half a dozen times before the movie is in the can."

"I don't know if I can work you with you again." Charlie sat back and took a long pull on his beer. "You were such an absolute dick."

Saul shrugged. "Bart went to bat for you. Extolled your virtues. Told the folks you were the best new young director he's ever seen. It's your call. It would get you out of the shit you're doing now."

"That shit pays better than scale."

"But it's hard work, and you're not going to get much better in the dollar area than you're doing now. Directing, on the other hand, the sky's the limit."

"I'm a fucking genius in the telecom space, mate. You'd be surprised how much money I could make if I wanted to. And not one client has treated me like this guy has."

Bart pointed the neck of his beer bottle at Charlie. "Told you yesterday, I was under a ton of time and money stress. Those days are behind me. You'll have free rein on all the Second Unit stuff and your input as AD will be considered very seriously."

"But you know I don't like you."

"I like your work."

Saul pushed two contracts across the table at Kent and Charlie. "Standard management contracts - I'm assuming neither of you have managers right now."

Charlie took the paper and picked up the proffered pen. "Why am I doing this?"

"You just quit your job mate. You need the rent money."

"Haven't quit yet. How much? Fifteen percent?"

"Standard in the industry. You know that." Saul licked his lips, snaring his second and third client in his burgeoning management career.

Charlie signed. He tapped the pen on the table. "I know I'm going to regret this." He passed the pen to Kent. "You on board?"

His friend grabbed the pen and scrawled his signature across the bottom of the contract without pausing to read it. "Hell, yes. I'm hitching my wagon to Bart. Anyone who can land a job so soon after getting out of the pen gets my vote."

"Glad to hear that, gentlemen." Saul removed two more contracts from his attaché case. "The deal for the movie."

Kent took the folio and flipped through to the section on remuneration. "And you get 15% of this, right? Well, at least I'm not going to be paying you much." He flipped through the pages. "Dates?"

"You'll get a script delivered to you tomorrow and rehearsals start on Friday. Two weeks of that and we start shooting. The shooting schedule is a very fast four weeks." Bart smiled. "So that small amount of money is only, really, two months work. Less, actually. Doesn't look that small now, does it?"

Charlie checked his numbers. "About the same as I'd make contracting for the telcos. Hardly worth the risk."

"This is the first step of many, and if you don't enjoy it, you can always go back to the drudge of working 9:00 to 5:00."

"The drudge of dawn to dusk is better?"

"It's a hell of a lot more fun, boy, and you know it."

Charlie thought for a second, smiled a half smile and signed. "I'm in. No rehearsals needed for me. I'm going to need to see the storyboards and script breakdown to set up the Second Unit stuff."

Bart stood and held out his hand. "Charlie Bates, I've got to hand it to you; you're as pro as they come. I promise this will be a different experience for you."

Charlie looked at Bart's hand and remained seated. "If it's all right with you, mate, I will do this on my own. We'll discuss and agree, but I would prefer not to be known as your lackey."

He stood. "Kent, I've got some things to do around here. There are a couple of friends I'd like to catch up with here in the Valley. I'll call you later, okay?" He passed the papers back to Saul. "Can you send me copies? My contact details are on the last page. Thanks."

Bart watched him walk out, sucked air between his teeth and clapped Kent on the back. "He'll be fine, if he doesn't try to torpedo me. You keep your friend in line, okay?"

Kent shrugged. "I'll do what I can. Now, tell me more about the story. Any sex scenes for me?"

Chapter Five

I woke with a start. A vaguely nebulous dream lingered in my subconscious, hints of home, and danger and old friends drifting apart, then faded as the message to pee pushed to the front.

I satisfied the bladder urges and stepped out on the balcony. At just a bit after 6:00 the sky was a pre-dawn gray. The Pacific was gray also, but calm. Perfect for a morning swim.

Gulls scattered along the beach as I jogged past the empty skate park bowl and across the sand to the water. It was a lonely beach. A few homeless people combed for bottles or loose change left behind in the sand. A regular gave me a wave and a decayed toothy smile and turned back to her task at hand. She was mid-fifties or so, shape almost impossible to determine. She always wore a wool hat and many layers of jackets and coats. I made it a point to stay upwind of her.

I stripped down to my suit and ran into the water. The cold caught my breath, but it was a momentary pause. I put my head down and swam. Sometimes, you just needed to bury yourself in an activity that did not need brains. Swimming fit the bill perfectly. It was as automatic for me as breathing. I swam out about a hundred yards, then turned right and followed the beach. My stroke was strong. It had been a few months since I last went out, but, again, it was like breathing. The ocean was really flat this morning, like swimming in a giant, slowly rolling pool.

With the swimming on autopilot I had a chance to think. I *was* remarkably lucky. The ascension from getting by week-to-week not even two years ago to where I was now was, by most standards, meteoric. Granted, I had paid a price. I lost a good friend to a senseless murder. That hurt the most. And my social life was non-existent. The hours put in when making a movie as grand in scope as *Blood Thunder* made a 9:00 to 5:00 job look like a vacation. Not that I'm complaining. But add to that the semi-regular spot on *Modern Family* and the occasional soft drink commercials, and whatever free time I had left was reserved for me and me alone. And even that was sparse. I've had time to read only three books in the past year, and none of them were huge. I'm not a slow reader. There just weren't enough down days. I was mentally exhausted.

And as an Australian it shocks me to say this, but my drinking had dropped way off. Try getting up at 3:00 in the morning for a 4:00 a.m.

makeup session when you've had a drop or two the night before. It just wasn't worth it. And I estimate I had spent more time in the air than on the ground in the last month doing the rounds for this movie. I'd hit every talk show from Conan down to the local cable show run out of the owner's garage in Boise. At least on the Boise trip I caught up with Joel's parents.

After tonight's premiere I had a break for a day, then it would be red carpets for the next few weeks. The last one in Sydney. I was looking forward to going home.

I groaned. I realized I was sounding like a spoiled brat. I had done everything I wanted to do. I was making more money than I knew how to spend. And if the early reviews held, it was a pretty good movie. If anyone overheard my whining they'd laugh in my face. Any actor who says they have a difficult job needs a good slap up the head, Gibbs style.

I reached the north end of the beach and turned back. I was about halfway through. My shoulders were loose, and my breath still easy. And I was feeling good, physically. The sun was up, and the air was getting warmer. It was going to be a scorcher.

So here I was, doing better than I could ever imagine myself doing, and living a life I didn't dare dream of, and I wasn't satisfied. With all the people I'd worked with over the last fourteen months, I was actually lonely. I was raking in the big bucks, face plastered on half the billboards in town and I was eating alone, sleeping alone and one of my regular non-business, social contacts was currently digging through the sand for lost loose change. The other was a juggler. The last time I saw him work it was a machete, a loaf of bread and a bottle of scotch. Cheap scotch, I hope.

Aside from those two, my contacts outside the business were sporadic. Regular cafe visits made me friends with the lovely Emily and her husband, but that was based on the money I brought in. I had no illusions.

I mulled over my prospects for a while. Bumping into Charlie and Kent was a nice surprise. I'd known them for years. They were like brothers. Or cousins. The kind you hear about at family dinners after they'd spent the night in jail for wrecking a club in a drunken brawl. I didn't need that. Not now. I'd managed to avoid bad press so far.

If it weren't a criteria of my job, I'd be happy with *no* press. I wasn't doing this to get on *Entertainment Tonight*. And while it was great, I wasn't doing it for the money. I was doing this because I loved telling stories.

I was back to where I started swimming, almost. I turned left and almost body-surfed back to the beach. My towels and flip-flops were where I had left them. I pulled the towel over my shoulders and carried the flip-flops as I walked back across the sand. Emily and Henry would be cooking up a storm. Hopefully, they kept a table for me.

As I passed the fence backing the skatepark, I was assaulted by the vermin who made everybody's life miserable. As if appearing from nowhere, at least fifteen assholes with cameras jumped in front of my face yelling things I couldn't make out, even if I wanted to. And trust me, I didn't want to. One of them, a middle-aged, fat and greasy son of a bitch I'd run into on more than one occasion stuck his foot out and tried to trip me. Nothing like a picture of me falling flat on my face under a 'Drunk at 7:00 in the morning' headline.

I wasn't an idiot. I stepped over the foot, giving him a kick as I did. "Watch yourself mate. You're going to hurt yourself." I wasn't going to pull a Sean Penn. Just below the falling down drunk picture, from a value perspective, was the 'Brittany beating on a car with an umbrella' picture. I wouldn't give them anything.

They didn't like that.

The cameras pressed closer. I started making out sentence fragments. "Sweeney out of jail - fucking him? - What are you going to do? - Comment on the story - what about the dead kid? - Are you fucking him again?"

I clenched my jaw. I tried to ignore the comments and pressed through the crowd. I'm skinny, but I'm strong. The most exercise these guys ever got was reattaching lenses to their cameras. I just spent a year in weapons and unarmed combat training with some very tough guys.

Then it went over the line.

"So if Sweeney didn't kill the faggot, he must have killed himself then, right? Why'd you try to set up Sweeney?"

I popped.

"Who said that?" I picked out the questioner. A younger slime-ball, shaggy hair, a shaggy beard and really foul body odor. I reached out and grabbed a fist full of beard and immediately regretted it. It was greasy. I had to wrap my fingers around it to keep a grip.

But a grip I kept.

I yanked hard and pulled his face close to mine, regretting that also. He clearly couldn't afford any oral hygiene. "Listen, you smelly, half-assed piece of shit. You don't know what you're talking about. I swear to God, if I see you anywhere near me again, I will pop you in the fucking eye. You like Sweeney so much, go ask him what I fight like." I gave the beard an extra hard yank and released him. "You smell worse than the bag lady on the beach. Have you no pride?"

That only seemed to spur them on. I tried to push through them, but the beard yanking seemed to have triggered some sort of bloodlust, like chum to a shark. It was frightening. I was getting manhandled.

I snugged the towel tighter. Hands tugged at it, trying to pull it from around me. "Back off. Let me through before I call the police."

"You don't have a phone, bitch."

I was looking for the owner of that voice, to deliver a punch to the neck when some of the paps on the east side of the group started dropping. A couple more dropped before anyone noticed. I pushed through in that direction and met Henry taking a swing at the kidneys of the really fat, greasy guy.

To the rescue.

I had to stifle a laugh. As frightening as that experience was, the sight of a middle-aged Asian man in a cook's apron wielding a rolling pin was classic. Five of the paps were on the ground holding a leg or their back. I tucked in behind him like he was my bodyguard

The fat guy looked up at the two of us and started yelling. "That asshole hit me with his stick." Murmurs of painful agreement followed from the others on the ground. Those remaining on their feet backed off a bit but had their cameras at the ready.

"Pics or it didn't happen boys." Henry looked around. "But I've got video of you assaulting Ellie and if any pictures of this encounter show up anywhere, I'm sending the clip to Perez, TMZ, *Entertainment Tonight* and every TV station in the LA area. I got most of it. Don't try me."

"Who gives a fuck what you do with the video?"

"I've got close-ups of all of you. The public distaste for the shit you guys peddle is high, and now they'll have faces to put to your work." Henry smiled. "Such as it is. This is just the beginning, weasel faces. You'll be as well-known as the people you photograph. Fucking pariahs."

"What, like the fish?" The bearded wonder was also a moron.

"Get lost assholes." Henry poked the closest one in the sternum with a roller pin jab hard enough to *thunk*. "Or I'll finish a couple more of you."

He took me by the arm and escorted me out of the mob. "You okay?"

I nodded. "More frightened than anything else. Thanks for stepping in. I could have taken out a couple of them, but fifteen is a bit more than even I could handle." I took a deep breath and looked back at the beach. The paps had disappeared to whence they came. The homeless lady was standing halfway between the surf and the skate park, watching me. "Who is she?"

"Huh?" Henry looked in the direction I was pointing. "Oh. That's Ann. A pretty regular fixture around here for a couple of years now. We help her out from time to time, but it's not often. Very independent. Why?"

"She always gives me a wave. From a distance, though. Whenever I try to talk to her, she mutters something, laughs, and walks away."

"At least she waves at you. She ignores me. Emily manages to elicit a smile once in a while. Mostly she just grabs whatever food we give her and waddles off down the beach." He stopped near the entrance to their cafe. "Hungry?"

"I'm starving. Hold a table and I'll be back in a minute. I need to rinse the salt off and I'll be damned if I do it in front of those ass-hats with cameras."

Henry smiled. "I understand. Usual?"

"Usual dress-fitting day food. Fruit, wheat toast and some pink grapefruit juice."

"And no strawberries. Once of these days I'll get you to taste my cooking. Inside table I think."

"Unfortunately. It's a beautiful day. Those guys had to ruin it."

"Tonight's a big night. I'm sure you've got a long day ahead of you. Go shower and relax. Don't let them dictate your mood. Take a deep breath and be one with the universe." His eyes smiled when he said this.

"Okay Master Po. But you better let Emily know about this."

"I usually do. Why?"

"You're going to be on the cover of half the tabloids in town, identified as my new boyfriend." I smiled and hugged him, and went back to my apartment.

I stepped out on the balcony. The gray sky and vacant beach had transformed into a hot blue sky and a bustling marketplace. The vendors had set up, ready to foist t-shirts and sunglasses and hats on unsuspecting tourists. Muscle-bound narcissists applied liberal coats of oil before their flex-fest. Roller-skaters, and roller bladers, already populated the boardwalk. It was going to be one of those Southern California days Katy Perry sings about.

I showered off the salt and pulled on some Capris and a golf shirt. Tied my hair in a pony-tail and once again thought about getting it cut. After all the publicity, of course. The part of the job I liked the least. But the studio insisted on it. They invested the money in the movie so I guess it was their right to parade me like a trained chimp trying to flog the movie.

Henry had a table reserved for me inside, away from the window. My chilled crystal bowl of sliced fruit - no strawberries - was waiting for me. The crystal bowl wasn't my idea, honest. Henry thought it was a nice touch and I had to agree, but it made me look a diva.

Emily sat across from me. "Henry told me what happened. That's terrible. You used to be anonymous around here." She placed a hand on my arm. "In a good way, of course. If you ever need refuge, come on in. We reserve the right to turn away anyone, and all of those paparazzi assholes will get turned away." She shook her head. "I'm upsetting you. I'm upsetting myself. Enjoy your breakfast. It will be the last peaceful one you get for some time."

"You're a champ Emily. I'll try to keep you and Henry out of the messes I get myself in. I appreciate the offer of refuge, even though my apartment is only ten feet from here." I smiled. "Maybe I should be offering you two refuge. Those guys are going to haunt this place."

Chapter Six

The nineteen-year-old kid hammered on the front door again. "Breakfast. Mister, it's getting cold, and if you try to stiff me because it's late, I'll be really pissed." He knocked once more and rattled the doorknob. It turned, and the door opened. The kid took a step in. "Buddy, if you don't pay for this, I have to, and I'm trying to save money for stunt school. You in here?" He slid the thermal carrier onto a table and looked around. The floor down the hallway was wet. The sound of running water in the back of the house seemed to indicate someone was home. He tip-toed through the water and knocked on the bathroom door. "Mister, can you hear me? Food's here and I need to get paid." He looked down. Water slowly seeped across the floor. The door swung open to a body floating in the overflowing tub. "Fuck,

fuck, fuck.”

He stumbled backwards and reached for his mobile phone in his back pocket. He punched 9-1-1 and backed out of the front door.

“9-1-1 operator. What is your emergency?”

“I - I - I just found a dead dude in a tub.”

“Is he breathing?”

“He’s *dead*. Didn’t you hear me? D-e-a-d.”

“What is your location?”

The delivery guy gave the operator the address in the Valley. “You gotta get out here.”

“An ambulance has been dispatched. How are you certain he’s dead?”

“There’s a fucking hole in his head and he’s face down in an overflowing bathtub. Trust me, the ambulance will have nothing to do. Send the cops.”

“Dispatching police. What is your name sir?”

“Rod Worthington. Look, I’ve gotta deliver breakfasts. It’s my job.”

“The police will be there shortly. They will want to ask you questions. I suggest you call your boss and tell him you’ll be detained.”

“I could just leave.”

“We have your mobile number and name. I wouldn’t.”

Rod heard sirens approaching. “Yeah, okay. They’re almost here.”

He sat on the front step and waited for the cops to arrive.

The ambulance got there first.

He hiked a thumb over his shoulder. “In the bathroom guys. Take your time.” He slid to one side to let them through. “It’s not pretty.”

A plainclothes car pulled up to the curb, stripped of all decoration. "Obvious cop car. Why do they bother?"

A suit got out of the driver's seat and approached him. "My name is Detective Jacob Sampson. You discovered the body?"

"Um, yeah. I'm Rod Worthington." He rubbed his hands on his pants and shook the Detective's hand. "Delivering breakfast for the guy. I knocked three times and the door was unlocked. I just wanted to get paid, man. I wasn't trespassing or anything."

Detective Sampson smiled. "Relax. You're not going to be charged with anything. What time did you arrive?"

Rod looked at his watch. "Oh, about ten minutes ago. A few minutes after 8:00."

"Is this the first time he's ordered breakfast from your company?"

Rod shrugged. "First time I delivered here. Maybe he ordered before and someone else delivered."

"You got a menu?"

Rod pulled one out of his pocket. "Yeah, sure. Hungry? This guy's not going to need his food."

"No, son. I want the company name, phone number and address. This is the easiest way for both of us." He took the tri-fold and slipped it in the back of his notebook. "Do you know what time this morning he ordered?"

Rod scratched his head. "It wasn't this morning. Look, if you call the number on the menu and ask for a guy named Rick, he's the manager, he can tell you. It was late yesterday sometime. Pre-ordered for a morning delivery. A lot of people do it. Delivery can take up to an hour on some mornings. Makes better sense to order it ahead of time and have it delivered when you wake up."

"How many deliveries do you do in a morning?"

"It's a Tuesday. Pretty slow. Maybe ten all up. I've got two more in the car getting cold."

Detective Sampson handed Rod a business card. "I'll let you get back to work. Call me if you think of anything else." He handed Rod his pen and his notebook. "Write your address and phone number here, just in case I need to talk to you." He smiled when Rod hesitated. "Scout's honor, you're not going to be charged with anything."

Rod scribbled his details and handed the pad and pen back to the detective. "I can go?"

"Go. Hungry people need their food. Thanks for hanging around."

"Yeah, well the dispatcher kinda intimated I'd be arrested if I didn't. Gotta go, man."

Sampson walked in the house and back to the bath. "What ya got?"

One of the paramedics looked up from her clipboard. "Dead. Have you called the ME? Nothing for us to do."

"Thanks for stopping by." He walked out on the front porch and called the dispatcher to send the meat wagon. An unmarked car rolled up at the curb and plainclothes police got out.

"Hey boys. We got a floater in a tub. ME is on the way." Sampson looked closer at the older of the two. "Perkins? Long time, pal. When did you get the sergeant stripes?"

"Almost a year now." He checked some notes in his ever-present notepad. "I've been here before."

"As have I, my friend. Bart Sweeney's place. It's been almost year and a half."

"I'm really pissed he got let off. What's her name?" he snapped his fingers.

"Ellie Bourke?"

"Yeah. She dropped the evidence on my desk."

Sampson smiled. "I was there, Perkins. Remember?"

Perkins nodded. "I do. He was as guilty as sin. Shouldn't have been let go. Goddamn lefty-lawyers. And judges." He adjusted his shoulder holster. "So the deceased - is it Bart himself?"

"Couldn't say. I haven't been here long and just finished first responder duties. What took you so long? Frozen yogurt sale?"

The Medical Examiner's wagon stopped in the driveway, interrupting their conversation.

"Where's the body?" The portly, young ME levered himself from the front seat. "Paras said they thought suicide. Have you had a look yet?"

"Gerry, I'm surprised. No conclusions without evidence, right? You tell us. And no I haven't had a look yet. Perkins and I were just about to go in."

The police followed the ME. Forensic techs had also just arrived and the photographer took shots of the body *in situ*.

"What do you see, Sergeant?" Sampson crossed his arms and surveyed the scene.

"Can't tell how long the water's been running, what with the drain in the floor. Could be an hour or it could be a day." He looked to the ME. "You got a time of death, Gerry?"

"This is going to be tough to judge, boys. The water is warm.

Check what kind of water heater he's got, will you? If it's a tank, it can help set the time. The running water was still hot. If it was one of those infinity ones, it's no good to us at all."

Sampson nodded to one of the techs who went in search of the source.

"The death was most definitely caused by this close range shot to the head, right temple. Small calibre, probably .22. No exit wound, so the bullet is in there somewhere, among the scrambled brains. The body has bloated and there's rigor. My bet - and it's a really rough estimate until we can look at stomach contents and internal organ decay - is 12 hours. 8:00 last night. Give or take a broad three hours."

Samson checked his notes. "Last night he called in a food delivery for this morning. The restaurant will have the time."

"If he made the call."

"Always the conspiracy theorist, Perkins."

Sergeant Perkins smiled. "Love a good conspiracy. Any sign of the weapon?"

The ME pointed in the tub under the body. "In the water. Probably no prints after being in there, but that's not my problem." He stood. "I'm finished with him if you want to drain the water. I'll have him in the morgue and tell you what I find in an hour or so."

Sampson leaned over and reached for the chain attached to the stopper.

Perkins grabbed his arm. "Hang on. There might be something in there. Wait until the body's out."

"Good point. I'm taking a look around. Let me know when it's all clear." He pulled on a pair of latex gloves and moved into the kitchen.

Two old pizza boxes sat on the counter. He lifted the lids and looked. A slice of Hawaiian and two of a pepperoni and cheese mess. "Christ. If he hadn't shot himself, his heart would have done itself in within the year." The number of plates indicated either four people were there the night before or he was a very sloppy person. "Perkins?"

The Sergeant wandered into the kitchen from the living room, notepad in hand, penciling notes. "Yeah?"

"Find anything? Looks like maybe he had visitors here last night. We'll need prints off the bottles." He button-holed one of the younger crime scene techs. "Make sure you check these. Looks like there may have been someone here last night."

Perkins flipped his notepad closed. "The place was recently scrubbed clean. Looks like the guy killed himself though. Not sure why the prints have any bearing on this." He stopped as if he just realized something. "Why is the dog squad here anyway?"

"I was on my way in and heard the call. Seemed like something I should check out."

"You really want these glasses dusted?"

"Better safe than sorry."

"You've got a vested interest in this."

"I do. I suppose we should tell her."

"Make sure it's him first."

Sampson nodded. "By-the-book Perkins. Okay. I'll do it your way." A gurney with the remains rolled down the hall past the kitchen. "Looks like we can head back in there."

The tub was emptied and the gun sat on the bottom in a shallow pool of water. Perkins lifted it out using a pencil in the trigger-guard. A tech held open a plastic bag.

"Damn, this is a cute piece of iron." He hefted it a bit. "Though I doubt there's much iron in it. It can't be more than 10 or 12 ounces. Ruger lady gun. Not like something this guy would own."

"At the range he was from himself, a .22 would have done the job."

Perkins nodded. "Find a note?"

"Less than twenty percent -"

"Yeah, I know the drill. No note is not an indicator of no suicide. Seems pretty clear." He dropped the gun into the waiting evidence bag.

The tech hefted the bag. "Looks to be the same calibre as the hole in his head. Lines up, roughly for a shot in the right temple if he was sitting in that end of the tub. Ballistics will confirm it in a day or so if there's anything left of the slug. And there's a very legible serial number on this piece so ownership shouldn't be a problem."

"Find the casing?" asked Sampson.

"It was in the tub. Under the body."

"How did it get under?"

"Brass doesn't float, fat, gassy bodies do. Look, gents, we've got everything we need here. I'm not the final authority, but I'd call it a suicide."

"Tape the door. Were out of here too." Perkins followed the detective out of the house into a phalanx of media.

"Is it true Bart Sweeney was involved in a shooting?" "Can you tell us who shot who?" "Will you be making an arrest?" "Do you think this may have something to do with his acquittal based on tainted evidence?"

"People, back up, please. My name is Detective Jacob Sampson. I can't tell you much right now. We just got here. I wonder how you all knew to get here so fast. I'm still amazed at the network you guys have. You should use it for good once in a while."

He took a breath. "So where to start? Yes, this is the residence of Bart Sweeney. Yes, there was a shooting in this residence. No, it doesn't appear to be a homicide. No, we haven't positively identified the body, but if it's Sweeney, then his prints are obviously on file, and we'll know shortly."

"Excuse me, detective, what do you mean there was a shooting but not a homicide? Did he commit suicide?"

Perkins shook his head. "Sergeant Larry Perkins. P-e-r-k-i-n-s. It's too soon to make any definitive statements at this time. The cause of death is not 100% confirmed. The identity of the body is not 100% confirmed. Making unfounded speculative statements at this time would be reckless. We'll have a statement for the media by the end of the day with any additional information we may have at that time."

"Detective, or Sergeant, whoever will answer me, did Bart Sweeney receive any death threats since his release?"

"Can't comment any further than we already have. Listen, people, I'm surprised at the interest. This guy was, on his best day, a D-grade director. He's been released on a flawed technicality and apparently felt remorse. I don't get it. Is there no other news in LA today?"

Sampson looked over the crowd of faces. A year ago, he was running the dog squad in Boise. In his past life, he would talk to maybe one reporter a year. The media blitzkrieg he experienced in Los Angeles was one thing he couldn't get used to.

He leaned in to Perkins. "We're staying here until these jackals leave. Wouldn't put it past them to break in and take pictures of the inside. They're as bad as the paparazzi."

"The threat angle is a valid one."

Sampson shook his head. "He didn't report any. At least none I'm aware of. You know this guy; he'd be crying like a baby if anyone so much as looked at him the wrong way." He clapped his hands. "Head back. I'll wait here for a bit longer and make sure none of the parasites come back. Like every other case, we investigate until it's verified by the evidence and autopsy to be a suicide."

Perkins looked up the drive at the guesthouse. "I was in a similar situation a year and a half or so ago. Strangely similar. Bathtub involved then too. Turned out I assumed wrong. It looks like suicide. No argument there. But we need to make sure the same mistakes aren't made."

Sampson followed his gaze to the guesthouse. "You've got memory loss problems, Perkins. I swear. It was my brother in that tub. That's what brought me out to LA." He shook his head. "Don't worry. The same mistakes won't be made."

Chapter Seven

The butterflies in my stomach were as bad as the first day I stepped on stage.

But it felt great.

It was a feeling I wanted to have again and again, as nerve-wracking as it was. Like grabbing a wave and hanging on the edge. A thrill, but never sure how it would end.

My phone warbled a Kylie song. It was the alarm. Time to go. Final dress fitting, then a marathon hair and makeup session, after which I was untouchable until the night was complete.

I took the elevator down to the parking garage. My almost brand new VW Beetle sat behind the old-school Beetle I'd owned since I moved to LA. I was restoring it, slowly, to pristine condition. Almost pristine. The bullet hole in the back, just above the engine compartment, *that* was going to stay. A reminder to myself I could make it through anything. I took a cleansing breath and got in the new car. Sweeney couldn't get rid of me then, and I vowed to not let his release from jail affect me now. "He has no control over me. He has no control over me. Damn. If I keep repeating myself, he *does* have control over me."

I backed out of the spot as one of my favorite songs came on. *"Till I Met Your Sister"*, by Nathan Bishop. Brilliant. I smiled. Things were looking up. The mess with the paps had almost receded from my memory. It was good to have a short-term memory problem.

The song ended, and the station started a news break. I reached to change the station but was stopped by the first words:

"Bart Sweeney, schlock horror movie director and recently acquitted of murder charges was found dead in his Northridge home this morning by a food delivery person. Suicide is suspected, though investigations are ongoing. Sweeney was recently on trial for the aggravated manslaughter of young, up and coming comic Joel Sampson. Recent revelations by his defense team that some of the evidence against him may have been fabricated by a former lover has resulted in his case being thrown out. He'd been out of jail for less than forty-eight hours when his body was found. It's believed he killed himself the night before his discovery."

I turned off the radio. Former lover? Over his dead body. Well, actually, not even then. Dead? Suicide?

What a bizarre feeling. He was maligning me after his death, but he *was* dead. Gone. Never to bother me again. I certainly didn't need to worry about him crossing paths with him. But 'former lover'?

I thumbed the voice activation button on my steering wheel. "Call Marty."

"Dialing"

Halfway through the first ring, he answered with: "I just heard. How do you feel?"

"Strange. Shouldn't feel happy about this, but it's about time."

"Strange he killed himself just after he finally got out."

"Either the guilt got to him, or one of the many people he's pissed off in his past got to him. Does it really matter? I'm rid of that ass. Finally."

"Didn't realize he had that kind of enemy."

"Oh, trust me. He could bring the worse out in people. Take it from one who knows all too well."

"Yeah. It's behind you now. Look forward. New challenges and rewards and all that stuff."

"Exactly." I took a deep breath. "I'm getting freaky excited about tonight."

"As well you should. Golden Globe performance. No bullshit. I'm looking forward to seeing the final product up on the screen."

"I am too, but I've done this before a couple of times. Why am I freaking out?"

"Probably because this movie cost more to make than all of the others combined. All of them. And, if I can brag, the money you're making for this movie - and you'll be making it as long as DVDs are sold - completely dwarfs the money you've made in the past."

I smiled. "Yeah, you're a fantastic negotiator. As you should be since you get 15%."

"There is that. What are you up to?"

"Final dress fitting. After that, I'm not allowed to even look at food until tonight is over. Then hair and makeup, back home to change, and you pick me up in a not ostentatious limo - Marty, it better not be a pink Hummer - and we go off to the night of my life."

"It will certainly be the highlight of your life so far. And after this you will be on fire. Everyone will be talking about you. Then you'll make more money than you know how to spend and I'll be following you around, siphoning off my 15%."

"If it's too much we can reduce it. Half, say?"

"No, no. That's okay. Have fun this afternoon. Just make sure the whole package is ready by 3:30. And it will be a classy limo. Don't worry."

I laughed and disconnected the call.

Still felt weird. Sweeney was dead. The cloud which had creeped in on me - emphasis on the word creep - had suddenly dissipated. Which was good. I smiled again. It was behind me. A chapter of my life was closed with a finality only brought by a coffin.

He never struck me as suicidal though. Too arrogant for that. At least he was the last time I talked to him. Must have had a personality transplant in jail.

Happier thoughts. A dress was waiting for me. A beautiful open-backed red thing. I'm not much of a girly-girl. I grew up around surfers at North Narrabeen. Fought off a lot of them. I was most comfortable in a pair of jeans and t-shirt. Make-up was something I only wore on set. And this was the longest my hair had even been.

Today that all changed for me. At least for today. The red Gucci dress was form-fitting. I'd be going commando tonight. I smirked at what Marty would think if he knew. I was convinced the dress was ready last week when we had what I *thought* was the final fitting, but apparently the few ounces I might have added or removed from my frame since then were critical. The lunch I just had could be last food I was allowed to have until the premiere was over.

I pulled into the parking lot, turned off the engine, sat back and took a breath. Only six hours to go.

Forty-five minutes later and I was putting a dress box with the nicest piece of girl-clothes I'd ever owned in the back of my little car. I punched the button on my steering wheel. "Call Cathy".

It rang through to voicemail. *"Sorry. Can't take your call. Hit me after the beep."*

"Cath, Ellie here. You ducking me? Been trying to reach you all week. Big night tonight. Was hoping I could get you to tag along. I've got a couple of extra tickets. Thought you and Bernie might like to join me." I drummed the steering wheel. "Look, I'll leave the tickets at the cashier under your name." I hung up. I had some ugly history with Bernie and didn't really like that my best girlfriend had gone back to him, but it was her life. And I had my life and was determined to enjoy it.

Hair and makeup for tonight was being done by the same lady who took care of me in the movie. Appropriate, I guess.

Jane was an old pro. Really old. She must have been fifty, at least. She had unflagging energy, like a force of nature. She had invited me to her house in Glendale, where I was just arriving. She met me at the door with a smile and a glass of sparkling water with a slice of lime.

"Ellie, dear. Right on time."

"Thank the GPS. I had no idea where I was going."

"You do your dress yet?"

"It's in a box in the car. It looks fantastic."

"Let's see it. I need to do a makeup match. A subtle touch, but it could go awfully wrong if I don't do it right. You better bring it in to the studio."

"I'd rather not put it on until the last minute."

"Oh, honey, you don't need to wear it. I just need to see it. To see the color, specifically."

"It's red."

"Red?" She smiled. "Would that be carnation? Cardinal? Cerise? Amaranth? I need my eyeballs on it. Takes just a minute and I'll have it locked in my head. You go grab it, and I'll get the stuff ready in the studio. And you need to think about what you'd like done to your hair. Go. I'll be waiting."

I said a force of nature, right?

I showed her the dress. She gently lifted it out of the box and held it against my skin at my chest, my arms and my face.

"This is a beautiful dress. Interesting counterpoint between your tan and this color. I hardly need to do anything. It's almost embarrassing charging you. Almost. But not quite." She handed the dress back. "Spectacular. You're going to be beautiful. You already *are* beautiful. So I have a big challenge. Put it down over there and sit."

She had a setup identical to the one she had on set and, like on set,

I zoned out to my surroundings. She asked a few questions about what I wanted to do with my hair. I resisted telling her to cut it all off, even though the maintenance of it was becoming a huge time-waster.

When the hair was finished (thin braids along the sides tied back in a cluster - very Topanga Canyon-ish) she spun the chair around to get my attention.

"Are you thirsty? I'd ask if you're hungry, but that dress is going to be snug enough without any more food."

"Not really, why?"

"Nothing touches your lips after I'm finished. Not until *after* the media *after* the premiere. Understand?"

"Yeah, yeah. I understand. Apply the paint."

"I *am* an artist. Sit still."

Fifteen minutes or so later - it's difficult to judge time when you're sitting in a chair with your eyes closed while a woman paints your face - she stepped back.

"Beautiful." She turned the chair to face the lit mirror. "What do you think?"

I opened my eyes. I looked like I had a fresh summer tan, a beach glow that looked real. "How do you do that? It doesn't look like I'm wearing makeup, but I know I am. It's like you Photoshopped my actual face." I moved a hand toward my cheek and had it slapped down faster than a Sergio Leone gunfight.

"No. Do not touch. Do whatever you want later tonight but right now, do not touch." She held out a hand and helped me out of the chair. "Have a fantastic night tonight. You're going to be fine. The movie is going to do great, and one day soon, I'll be pointing at you on TV and telling my grandkids, "I used to make up her face". Go have a bunch of fun, and don't forget the dress. I'm too short and fat for it. And red doesn't look good on me."

I thanked her, was rebuffed when I tried to kiss her on the cheek and laughed as she scolded me for forgetting already. Now it was home and change and hope Marty wasn't in a prankster mood with the limo.

From Glendale back to my apartment was about thirty minutes. Marty would be showing up in a bit over an hour. Cutting it close. I pushed it a little on the I-10 and was edging Culver City when my phone rang.

"Ellie speaking."

"Hi, Ell. Cathy here. I got your message. Wow. The première's tonight?"

"Where the hell have you been? I've been trying to reach you for ages. The tickets will be there. Can you make it?"

"I'd really love to, but we're in Branson."

"Missouri?"

"I don't think there's another one. We're flying in late tonight. Back in LA in the morning. We need to catch up. It's been too long."

"It has. Still with dipshit?"

"Come on, Ellie. Bernie made a mistake. He apologized a hundred times. Let him be, okay? When are you free to come by for a barbecue? Just like old times. Eat a little food, get a little drunk, have a lot of fun."

I thought about my schedule. "Not trying to blow you off, Cath, but I'm completely booked with publicity gigs all over the US for the next two - almost three - weeks. It's 'G'Day LA' tonight and 'G'Day

USA' for the rest of the month. If it's any consolation, I'm not going to be having any fun doing it."

"Right. Flying first class, best suites, pampered like a princess." She chuckled. "I'd hate it too."

"Oh, you know what I mean. No time is mine. It's like a three-week long choreographed play with no intermissions. Tons o' fun. Hey, you want to come along? I could use a friend by my side."

"Shit, that would be awesome, but no. Rehearsals start next Monday at the Los Angeles Shakespeare Theatre. You know, the one in Topanga Canyon. I'm Beatrice in *Much Ado* and Bernie is stage managing. You'll have to come see it. It runs for a couple of months."

"Yup. I can see you as a Beatrice, never shutting up. Suits you." I swung on to the PCH. Two minutes to home. "I really miss hanging with you, Cath. Damn shame you can't make it. We could play sisters again. We had them convinced before."

"We're almost identical twins, except I've got about twenty pounds on you." Cathy paused. "What a shame. Our lives are too busy."

"I bet you wouldn't want to change anything."

"You're right. I've got to take it while it's being handed to me. I've got to get going Ellie. We'll catch up soon."

She hung up before I could reply. I really missed her. It had been too long. But I had to shake it off. Marty and his ride would be by in far too little time, and I had a movie to go see.

Tonight would be an event that would alter the course of my life.

Chapter Eight

Perkins leaned back in his chair, scratching his head. "Dog-show, this is troubling me."

Sampson dropped the magazine he was reading. "Something is always troubling you, Perk. What this time?"

The Sergeant slid the ME's file on his desk. "Time of death narrowed down to closer to 8:00pm."

"Yeah, I read that."

"Make any sense to you? The cook at the restaurant told me the order for breakfast was placed just after he arrived, a bit after 6:00 p.m."

"Got that too. Where's the conspiracy this time?"

"Why would someone bother killing themselves less than two

hours after pre-ordering a breakfast for the next morning?"

Sampson shrugged. "Who knows? Manic-depressive ordered food in a manic state then slipped to a deep depression."

"Seems pretty pat." He lifted an evidence bag. "And what about this? Pretty pansy gun for a man his size. His finger would barely fit the trigger guard."

"And it's cheap and the guy didn't have much money. Anything on the serial number?"

"Shit. Knew I forgot something." Perkins turned on his computer. He held up an earring in another plastic evidence bag. "And this. Lady's earring found on the bathroom floor."

"He had a guest. Prints will be in sometime later today. Maybe tomorrow. Look, Perk. This is your case. I've got other things to do. I only stopped by the house on the call because I was just around the corner. If you don't think it's a suicide, by all means investigate it. It's got all the markers, but you need to be satisfied."

"I want to bounce some ideas off you once in a while."

Sampson pulled on his suit jacket. "Sure thing. I'm heading out for a coffee. Want one?"

"We've got a machine here. I'm good."

"That dog piss? I'll bring you something."

Perkins absent-mindedly waved him off. "Yeah, thanks. Whatever." He returned his focus to the files. He made a mistake before, assuming a murder was suicide. It defined his attitude after that. Never assume. Never guess. Always dig as deep as possible, and one inch more.

Something didn't smell right with this one.

"What the fuck is it with this?" He made notes in his ever-present pad. "Timing is all wrong. A guy doesn't order food then kill himself. Out of character. And the gun. Too small." His computer prompted for login credentials. He looked to the back page of his notebook and entered the user name and password. Following the instructions in his book he navigated to the firearms database.

He lifted the gun out of the evidence bag and tried to read the serial number. "Dammit. Fucking eyes are going." He put the handgun to one side for the moment and concentrated on the ME's report.

The entry angle of the gunshot, according to the report, matched the expected angle of a right-handed person shooting himself in the side of the head. Powder burns on the skin around the entry wound showed the barrel was either contacting the skin, or was very, very close. He flipped the page, scanned through the rest of the examination and sat back in his chair. "No powder on the hand. I wonder."

He called the ME's office.

"Morgue. What?"

"What?"

"What. What do you want? What can I help you with? What the fuck is it now, Perkins?"

"Hey, Gerry. Good to hear your voice. I've got a question about the Bart Sweeney report."

"The suicide?"

"Maybe a suicide. I can see some inconsistencies. Things which could maybe point the case away from suicide and right into the foul play pile."

"Oh for God's sake. Sometimes suicide is just suicide."

"Follow me here. Stippling at the entry wound."

"You can still read. *Bueno*. I'd say lightly pressed to the skull when he pulled the trigger."

"Okay, fine. I accept your expertise in the matter."

"That all?"

"Not by half. So where was the GSR on the hand? You don't mention it."

The silence on the phone spoke volumes. "Wait."

"I'm waiting. You missed that?"

"Yeah, I did. Good point."

"Any chance it could have come off after soaking in the tub for twelve hours?"

Ben snorted. "No, pops. It takes a pretty good scrubbing to remove it. Highly unlikely. This is peculiar. What was the handgun?"

"Ruger LCP. Small girl's gun. Very narrow, very light. At the angle he'd have to hold it I'd expect to see a little bruising in the thumb webbing." Perkins flipped the pages in the report. "Don't see anything about it in here either." He dropped the handset in the cradle, stood and called across the room. "Stanfield, come with me."

"Fantastic. Need to get out. What's on?"

"Canvassing."

"For what, exactly?"

"Sweeney's death. Need to see if anyone saw anything there last night at 8:00 or so. Time's wasting."

"Not again. It was a suicide. He shot himself in the head, in the tub. It was pretty fucking clear, Perks. Ka-*pow* in the skull."

"No GSR on his hand."

"Twelve hours in the tub, maybe?"

"ME says no. Doesn't scan. Need to talk to some of the neighbors."

"There were fingerprints on the bottles picked up, right? Should talk to the owners of them, too."

Perkins walked out to the front steps of the Devonshire Street squad room. "Warm and sunny. As usually. Those prints will be on my desk by 5:00 I'm told. We've got time to knock on a couple of doors before then."

"So suicide's completely off the table?"

"Until I can prove conclusively it's not murder."

The Killer stood in his apartment, too hyped to sit. One down. "So many more to go." He did a little soft-shoe shuffle step and turned on the TV. "Five hundred and twenty-three channels and not one is doing local news?" He left it on a local cable channel and checked his watch. Almost 5:00 p.m. He paced. Waiting was the hardest part. And the best part. Building the anticipation, savoring the rush. The play was unfolding exactly as he wanted. First the suicide. It had to look like a suicide, but not too convincingly.

He stopped the pacing and frowned. It had to be discovered for what it was. Or for what he wanted it to be. It had to. He picked up his phone and thought. There might be a way to ensure that.

Perkins and Stanfield left the last house on their canvas. A couple of people mentioned visitors earlier in the night, around 4:00 or 5:00, but the three visitors had left by 6:00. An older, short and slightly overweight gentleman in a BMW, a younger, tall dark-haired guy in an old Honda Accord and a young, shorter blond guy, looking like a "surfer-dude" according to one, who left on foot. All well before the time of death.

"Blanks, Perks. Nobody saw nuttin'."

"Not in that time frame. The killer was there later. A couple of hours later."

"So you're 100% on the no suicide thing now." It wasn't a question.

"If there's a single piece of evidence pointing away from suicide I assume foul play. Thought you'd have adopted that stance also."

"There could be an explanation."

"For a shooter to have no GSR on his hand, or bruise? You ever shoot one of those Rugers? Tiny little thing. Truly a woman's gun. Really light, and while it only fires a .22 calibre round, because it's light it kicks like a son of a bitch. And the grip is thin. That kick with the small grip in a hand as big as Sweeney's he would have had a bruise." Perkins slid in to the front seat of the car. "And the gun wouldn't have ended up in the tub."

"How do you figure?" Stanfield got behind the wheel of the car.

"Physics. The bullet hits your brain and you immediately lose all muscle control. Newton's Third law is still in effect, pushing your hand away from your head. The right hand was on the outside of the tub and the Ruger would have ended up somewhere near the toilet."

Stanfield nodded. "Makes sense. So there's a killer out there."

Perkins scrolled through the numbers on his phone. "And we need to act like it. We need to review the trace evidence a little better." He dialed.

"And we need to establish means, motive and opportunity."

"We've got all three. Hang on." Stanfield turned his attention to the phone. "Perkins here. Do me a favor, will you? I'm heading back to the station and need to see the evidence collected at the Sweeney residence. Can you have it delivered to my desk?" He listened. "Yes all of it. And no, it wasn't suicide. If you guys think the place needs another sweep, by all means come out here and do it. As a matter of fact, send some uniforms out here to lock the place down until you do. Thanks."

He looked at his partner. "You got anything planned tonight?"

"It's Tuesday. Must see TV is recording as we speak. I'm all yours."

"I bet you say that to all the guys."

Stanfield laughed. "What did you mean, we've got all three?"

"Means is the gun, opportunity is the apparently otherwise empty house after 6:00 and motive? Well, half this town had motive to kill him."

"True. We need to talk to the people who shared a beer and pizza with him last night. Last people and all that." Stanfield parked. The station was less than a mile from the crime scene.

"The results from the prints should be back by now. I'll buy you food and we'll go visit."

He hung up the phone. It took some coercion. Some threats. Some promises of very nice drugs. But she'd do it. And once she did, he had her for anything else he needed her to do.

The Killer sat on his sofa, feet twitching with nervous energy. The adrenaline coursing through his system rivaled that of anything he'd done before. "Fuck, if I'd known this was so much fun I would have started earlier."

He wasn't finished. There were others on his list. Some deserved it more than others, but none more than Sweeney. Soon stage two would kick off. This was the best spectator sport. Especially when you were the only one who knew what was going on.

Perkins tossed the results of the AFIS search on Stanfield's desk. "Three people other than the victim: Saul Green, 57, lawyer for the victim. Lives in Reseda. We'll stop by and see him later. Kent Williams, 27, a small time actor with unfulfilled dreams. I believe he's worked with Sweeney before. He looks like the lead in that Sweeney horror flick based in Australia. Can't remember the name. His address is an apartment in Encino. Not the nicer part. Charles Bates, 26. Works, as far as we can tell, as a contractor in the telecoms industry. He doesn't appear to have any connection to the victim or the other two visitors. He lives in an apartment in Compton."

"Their prints were all on file?"

"They've all been on international flights since the fingerprinting started."

Stanfield nodded. "Shylock first?"

"That's an unfair characterization of a man we've never met. He might be a nice guy." Perkins smiled.

"He's Sweeney's lawyer. Or he was. I think that takes him off the nice list." Stanfield handed the file back to Perkins. "Think he's home?"

"Let's find out." He stood and headed for the door. "You're driving again."

"Yeah sure. You ever run the serial number of the murder weapon?"

"Ah, shit. I'm getting forgetful in my advancing years, young pup." He slid into the car and pulled his phone from his shirt pocket and called a colleague. "You haven't left. Excellent. Need one more quick favor. I started but didn't have time to finish. Have you determined ownership of the murder weapon? No? Can you run the serial number and text me the results? Fantastic. Thanks." He looked at Stanfield. "Done. Should know in half an hour or so."

"That'll be another question answered. Lawyer's place is around here somewhere." He pulled up alongside a moderately well-kept yard surrounding a modest two story house. "Not the most expensive lawyer, by the looks of it."

"Sweeney probably owed him a ton." Perkins grunted as he opened the door. "Let's go ruin his dinner."

Saul opened the door as they walked up the steps. "Cops?"

"Did our fashionable haircuts give us away? Are you Saul Green?"

"I am. I've been expecting this visit. It's about Bart, isn't it?"

"May we come in?"

"Certainly. Something to drink?"

"We're fine. Thanks." Perkins opened his notebook. "You were Mr. Sweeney's defense attorney, correct?"

"Yes. His suicide was a complete shock to me. Things were turning around for him."

"How's that? He was just released from jail. Hadn't been out for two days before he was killed. What was looking up?"

"Killed? I thought it was suicide. It was announced on the radio it was suicide."

"Don't believe everything you hear. New evidence has come to light which is leading us in a different direction. I understand you were with him late yesterday afternoon.

Saul nodded. "I was. That makes a bit more sense then."

"How's that?" Perkins waited with pen poised over paper.

"He had no reason to suicide. I just signed him to a directing job. Not a lot of money, but more than he's made in the last year." He smiled. "A lot more. Work was going to start in a day or so. Rehearsals were starting next Monday." Saul shook his head. "No. This makes more sense."

"If it makes more sense, could you tell me who you think may have had enough of a grudge with him to kill him?"

Saul sighed and smiled. "Who didn't, really? He wasn't the most loveable of men."

"Who had he been talking to recently?"

"Aside from me, that I know of, Kent Williams and Charlie Bates - they were over last night - and the financial backers of the project earlier in the day. None of them would gain by killing him. Certainly not the backers. This is going to delay the movie. And Kent and Charlie had parts in the piece."

"I thought Charlie was in the telecoms business. He acts on the side?"

"No. He's been Assistant Director for Bart a couple of times. Bart asked him to come back. Signed him up as AD and Second Unit. He seemed keen to get back in the saddle."

"So with Bart out of the picture this Bates kid would slide in to the spot?"

Saul frowned. "Possible. I'd have to talk to the backers, but he'd be the logical choice."

Stanfield leaned forward. "How well do you know Mr. Bates?"

"Just met him. Seemed a quiet guy. Definitely the quieter of the two. Looked like your typical surfer dude."

"So you don't know if he was talking to anyone else?"

"Who, Sweeney? No. Check his phone records."

"PacBell is sending us the records of his house phone. We'll certainly look at that."

"Check his mobile also."

Perkins looked at Stanfield. "Do you remember seeing a mobile phone in the personal effects inventory?"

"No. Strange in this day and age, but I put it down to his recent release from prison."

"I picked up a pre-pay for him. I don't have any of the paperwork. I don't even think I took it with me."

"Where?"

"The Alltel shop in Northridge Plaza. Check with them. It would have been under my name. Wonder where it is?"

Perkins took his phone out to arrange for the sales records from Alltel when an incoming message vibrated his phone. He opened it and swore.

"What is it, pops?"

Perkins frowned. "First, what have I said about calling me that in front of others? And second, they just sent me the name and address of the registered owner of the murder weapon." He held the phone up so Stanfield could read it.

"Shit. We better go." To Saul he said, "Thanks for your time Mr. Green. If we need anything else we'll give you a call."

Perkins clenched his jaw. "I hope there's a mistake with this. I kinda liked her."

Chapter Nine

I knew how the scene, and the movie, ended, but the emotional hit was still strong. I blinked back tears and looked around me. Wet cheeks reflected the explosion on the screen as the music swelled and the movie came to an end. Credits crawled up the screen and there was a sudden explosion of applause as the theatre stood as one.

Now *that* was freaky.

Marty took my hand and lifted me gently to my feet. I looked around. Everyone was facing me as they applauded. I knew the movie was good; I was part of it. But I had no idea it was *that* good.

He leaned close to my ear. "Wow. That was incredible."

"*This* is incredible. They're being awfully nice, aren't they?"

"This response isn't because they're nice. It's because you, and the

Hanks made an incredible movie. This is going to break all records. When this hits the rest of the country on Thursday there isn't going to be an empty theatre seat in America." He gave me a squeeze. "And you won't have to audition for anything again, if you don't want to."

Tom Hanks reached across a couple of seats, took my hand and smiled. "You nailed it. So glad you were part of this. It wouldn't have been even half of the movie without you. And man am I glad my name is attached. Makes me look even smarter than I am. When all this hoopla dies down we need to meet, you and I and Marty, and decide what next you're going to do. If you'll excuse a slightly inappropriate turn of phrase, I'm going to milk you for all you're worth." He gave my hand a pat. "Damn fine working with you. Now where did my son go?"

We made our way to the lobby. The champagne flowed and press who were at the screening waited for their opportunity to ask questions.

A sea of other supporters took turns poking a nose in to offer congratulations. I'm cynical for my young age, but this seemed to me to be people wanting to rub against success, hoping some of it comes off on them. But hell it was fun.

"You look stunning tonight. That dress is fabulous." Colin's wife, the delightful Sam Bryant, had a smile on her face, her red hair pulled up and offset with a brilliant jade floor-length dress. "Gucci, right?"

"You know it. You look fantastic yourself. And your husband is a doll."

She squeezed Colin. "I know. And quite the hero in this. I like the way he buffed up. Inspired me to get fit too. If I was eight inches taller I might fit in your dress."

She probably could.

I buzzed *without* the champagne. Taking the offered glass was probably not a good idea. My tolerance was low. I had hardly touched a drop since we started filming, and that abstinence had continued through post. My system was no longer accustomed to alcohol.

Jon Favreau caught my eye from across the lobby and waved me over. Pecking order had been established. Probably subconscious on his part, but there it was. I smiled and excused myself from the discussion I was in and met him a quiet corner.

"You beckoned?"

"Oh, don't make it sound like that. I would have come over there, but it was too noisy and it's nice and quiet here. And I want to talk to you."

"Well I'm a huge fan, so this is even more exciting than the premiere. Did you like the movie?"

He nodded. "I had to see you up close, too, because you look so frail, but that fight scene, where you had to carry Colin's unconscious body back to the hospital, how did you do that? You did that, right? That wasn't your face slapped on someone else's body?"

"No, that was me." I flexed a tiny little bicep. "I'm stronger than I look."

"Clearly. So what's your schedule look like for the next few months?"

I gestured back to the larger crowd. "Tom wants to sit down with me and Marty and decide that in a couple of weeks when the wild and crazy wears off."

"Makes sense. You're golden right now. I'll chat with them and see if I can horn in on that action."

"It's a bit overwhelming. The attention has ratcheted. I came out of the water this morning to a crowd of paps who almost physically assaulted me."

"At the swimming pool?"

"No. Swam off Venice for about an hour this morning. Very refreshing. I was trying to relax and those knobs killed it. I wasn't very nice."

"Wait. You had it out with the scum of the planet and there's nothing in the press? You really are golden."

"A friendly cook helped me out. Long story."

"One you'll have to tell me someday." He looked over at the crowd surrounding the Hanks and Paymer. "You've got a hell of a hit on your hands and it's going to be a non-stop rocket ride for the next few years. If I could give you any advice it would be to take it all with a sense of humor. It will all end, and in three years you'll act in something that makes *Juwanna Man* look like Golden Globe material. You'll look back at these days with disbelief, like this is a dream. It happens to everyone in the business. Marty should have told you already. Where is Marty? You're going to be making that man very rich. He should taking care of your every need right now."

I shook my head. "Not sure. He was talking to Tom and got a phone call. Haven't seen him since."

"Probably his broker called and he's in his counting house, counting all his money. I'll get some of my upcoming projects in front of him and let him sort out the logistics. That's not something you should be worrying about anyway, right?"

"I guess not."

Jon took his phone out. "Let me give you my number, and you can call me if your schedule changes."

"Are you hitting on me?"

"Oh, God no. Joya would kill me."

I laughed. I entered his number in my phone and called him. "Now you have mine. I would love to talk to you, but more to pick your brains about how you've made it. You started out in indie works early on, and moved on to big stuff. Huge stuff acting, huge stuff directing. I just loved *Cowboys and Aliens*. And you're still a really nice guy."

He laughed. "You forgot writing." He scratched his head. "I can't teach you to be nice. You're born nice. I've heard the stories. You just need to stay you. Don't get too big. It's really easy to get too big. The limos, obscene amounts of money, the pampering hand and foot. Enjoy it, but don't take it for granted."

"Sounds easy, but I've met a lot of dicks in this town. Wait, not like that. You know what I mean."

He smiled. "I do. I've got to mingle or people will start talking and Joya will stab me in my sleep. Enjoy your night."

He gave me the industry-standard cheek kiss, which I returned. Makeup was less of an issue now. The night was almost over.

The voices reduced to a murmur, and I noticed people were starting to look at me a little differently. I surreptitiously checked for obvious wardrobe malfunctions, un-ladylike drops of drink on my dress or food on my face. All clear. My phone vibrated with an incoming message and rang at the same time. Marty was calling.

"Where'd you go, Mar? You abandoned me. Find a better pay

check?"

"What do you know about Bart Sweeney?"

"Why are you spoiling this night bringing up that ass-hat? He sat in his tub and killed himself yesterday, in a piece of incredibly appropriate karma. Why are you calling me about him?"

"He didn't commit suicide."

"Sure he did. It was on the radio yesterday. We talked about it. By the sounds of it, it was a head wound no one could survive. Don't tell me he's alive. Although I doubt anyone would notice the lack of brain."

"He's not alive, and he didn't commit suicide. He was shot in the head in an attempt to make it look like suicide."

This didn't make sense. "Okay. Again, why are you calling me?"

"You don't know anything about this?"

"Just what I heard on the radio, which apparently was wrong. What the hell is going on?"

"I'm outside the theatre with Sergeants Perkins and Stanfield who would like to talk to you about the killing."

"Yeah, sure. Why all the mystery?"

"The murder weapon is registered to you."

"What? No. Not possible. It's in the table by my bed. And I haven't seen the guy in almost two years. It must be some mistake."

"I'm sure it is. Come on out, and we'll have a chat with these guys and get it all settled."

"Yeah, absolutely."

I hung up. The news must have spread. The faces looking at me weren't the faces of people who just enjoyed a movie. They were the carnivorous faces of people starved for scandal. Looks like I was on the menu. I check the text message I'd received when Marty called. It was from a number I didn't know, but a person I did.

"Ellie, it's Kent. I heard about the cops looking for you. You need to call me asap. It's worse than you think."

What the hell was that supposed to mean? I slipped through a side door to the backstage area where the noise levels were a lot lower and I could get some privacy. I called Kent.

"Ellie? Thank God you called me. Have you talked to the police yet?"

"No. I just had a chat with my manager. Apparently my gun was found at the scene of Sweeney's murder. It wasn't a suicide after all."

"Oh, it's worse. I've got an old girlfriend who works in the station and she's told me the evidence they have against you is slam dunk level."

"How? I wasn't there."

"Right. They have your gun, registered to you, with your prints on it. You were known to be pissed off Sweeney was out. An earring was found at the scene which apparently matches one found in your apartment."

"They were in my apartment? Why in the hell were they in my apartment?"

"You're a murder suspect. You need to face the fact they're ready to throw away the key."

"But I wasn't there. Shit, the closest I've been to Northridge was when I got my hair done today in Glendale. I haven't been in his neck of the woods since he was initially arrested."

"But they have a witness who saw you there."

"Impossible. Fuck. What's going on?"

"I'm not sure. I think it's best for you to stay below the radar until you figure out what's going on. I'll help. This is bullshit."

"You mean run? From the cops? No way. They're outside the theatre. I'm going out and turning myself in and sorting this shit out. I didn't do it."

"Who's the cop on the case?"

"Sergeant Perkins."

"Is he a good cop? Does he dig for the truth and make sure everything makes sense?"

I thought about the whitewash he gave Joel's death until I found the evidence proving Sweeney killed him. Now he was going to whitewash me. "No. He rushes to judgment. He had Joel down as a suicide until I intervened. Now he's going to make sure I go to jail." I paced. "But I didn't fucking do it. Jesus Christ, this is so much bullshit."

"Can you get out of where you are without being noticed?"

I looked down at my $2,000 dress. "Yeah, I'm not really all that subtle. Bright red open-back dress, pimped out for the premiere."

"Oh yeah. How'd it go?"

"Focus, Kent. Cops, remember?"

"Sure, sure. You've got money on you, right?"

"A bit."

"Sneak out the back and take a cab to your place, get changed and hide out in a cheap motel somewhere. There's a city-wide bulletin out for you, so stay really far below the radar. Maybe even get out of town while you figure things out."

"How in the hell can I figure things out if I'm out of town? And who in the hell is this witness?"

"I don't know. Some woman said she saw someone who looked like you in the neighborhood. So they have the means, motive and opportunity. Where were you last night?"

"Zoning out at home. Nobody saw me." I deflated. "Oh, fuck, this can't really be happening." My phone beeped an incoming call in my ear. I pulled it and looked at the display. "Marty's calling me, wondering where I am."

"Answer it and stall him. Tell him you're in the bathroom and you'll be out in five minutes, then get the fuck out."

"It doesn't feel right."

"It's that or jail, Ellie, and they have the death penalty for premeditated murders in California."

He hung up on that cheery note.

I took a deep breath in and exhaled slowly. He was probably right. I was screwed. For some inexplicable reason the universe didn't feel like giving me a break. I called Marty. "Sorry, Marty. Having a pee. I'll be out in five minutes, okay? We need to get this straightened out."

I hung up before he could answer and looked for the exit sign. I cracked the door open and checked the alley. It was clear. I stood in the doorway. If I went through it I would be committing myself to running. If I went through the front doors, though, I'd be wrapped up in a mess I doubt I'd ever get out of. I at least owed myself some time to try and figure out how Perkins had screwed this one up.

I stepped through.

I walked down the alley to the next main road. To my left was the front of the theatre and a huge crowd of waiting fans. And Perkins. Good for him he finally made Sergeant, but I wasn't about to trust him with my life. I turned to my right, then right again. A tall, thin and well dressed blonde in LA does not wait for a taxi. I barely raised my hand when two cabbies were fighting for my fare. I took the one who seemed to have the cleaner car. "Venice. Take your time. The fish pier."

"You sure?"

"Positive."

I sat back and planned. There would be paps and cops at my place. I needed to keep my distance until it was clear. The parks were well lit, but the pier would be closed down by now.

If I wanted to stay out of jail until I figured this out, I'd have to be invisible.

Chapter Ten

Sergeant Perkins looked at his watch. "I'm not liking this. She's given you the slip."

Marty sighed. "She's given us both the slip. Shit. She's a smart girl. I didn't expect this."

"I'm not surprised. She *is* a smart girl. She knows what's up. I'll send a squad car to her house. No way she's going to get around town in a fancy gown." He poised a pen. "What did it look like?"

Marty rubbed his hand over his forehead. "Look, boys, I've got to find out what she's up to." He looked at Perkins. "It's a red open-backed Gucci. Full-length. She didn't do this, guys. Someone is setting her up."

"Sir, harboring a fugitive is a felony. You must call us

immediately when you find her."

"No shit, Sherlock. Keep an open mind."

Marty called Ellie's number. It rang out to voicemail. "Ell, hon, this isn't the smart thing to do. I know this is a set up, but you running just makes it look worse. Call me and we can sit down and sort things out. You're a smart girl. Don't mess up your future, okay?"

He walked back in the theatre with Perkins and Stanfield in his wake. "This night certainly isn't turning out like I thought it would." A phalanx of media shoved microphones in his face. He held up his hands in an attempt to stem the flood of questioning.

One voice rose above the rest: "Where is Ellie Bourke? What is her response to the allegations made by the LAPD? Did she kill Bart Sweeney in self-defense or was it premeditated?"

"You guys are quick. And why are the only two options self-defense and premeditation? Miss Bourke categorically denies these allegations. She was not involved in Sweeney's death in any way. She will be turning herself in to the police later tonight, once she gets out of that gorgeous gown. I'd appreciate a bit of restraint on the part of the press, but I'm not so naive to expect it. I'm not going to answer any more questions, so save your collective breaths."

Kent checked his watch and muttered to himself. "She should be clear by now." He redialed her number.

"Kent?" Ellie's voice was hushed.

"You clear?"

"I'm out of the theatre, if that's what you mean. I'm under the pier. There's a uniform in front of my house and a ton of paps."

"It'll do you no good to get nabbed now. I didn't get a chance to tell you earlier. It was more important you get out of that place. You stay in the dark as long as you need to. The cops were by to see me and Charlie. They got our prints from Sweeney's place. They must have questioned me for about half an hour, probably because I was arrested when I was a kid for shoplifting. Like that's anything like plugging a guy in the head."

"Sorry man. Could you tell then they were looking for me?"

"They asked a lot of questions about you, like how you knew Bart and if I'd seen you around. Guess they asked Charlie the same thing. I haven't talked to him yet. I'll give him a call after this. So how are you doing?"

"I'm sitting in a really expensive dress I'm supposed to return, surrounded by seaweed and what I hope are clumps of mud. It doesn't smell too good. I'm hoping the tide is high and I won't get wetter, but my luck hasn't been the best lately. This dress is a one of a kind and it's a write-off."

"I think you should be a bit more concerned about the charges against you and less on the dress."

"The dress is real, mate. These charges are a bad dream fueled by too little food and too much stress."

"Oh, they're real. Want me to come out to your place and give you a hand?"

"No. You'll just draw attention to yourself."

Kent listen to the silence and was about to break in when she talked again.

"So, that visit you and Charlie made to Sweeney, he really had a project?"

"He really did. And as far as I know, the project still exists. He signed me on in a supporting role and Charlie as both AD and Second Unit Director."

"And then someone killed him. Is the project a contentious one? Something that might piss some people off enough to get rid of the director?"

"Not really. Filipino war story. We were supposed to get back together again with Bart and Saul and the backers and go through the details, but I doubt it gets more contentious than that."

"Who's Saul?"

"Sweeney's lawyer and business manager. Hey, he's my manager now, too. You're asking a lot of questions."

"Because I haven't found the answer yet. Why is someone framing me?"

"You really didn't do it?"

"How long have you known me, asshole? You ever, even once, get the inkling I'd kill someone? Fuck no, I didn't do it."

There was another pause in the conversation.

"So, where did you and Charlie go after seeing Bart?"

"I went back home. Not sure where Charlie went. He said he was going to visit someone in the Valley and left on foot. Very atypical of him. To walk, I mean."

"And you don't know where?"

"What are you, a cop?"

"I may as well be. *They're* not going to help me."

"So young to be such a cynic. Don't take any chances, okay? I think I believe you about not doing it."

"What?"

"Just kidding, Ell. I *do* believe you. You didn't do it. Let me call my contact inside the department and see what I can find out. Stay safe."

He terminated the call and dropped into the sofa. "I wonder what Charlie is up to?"

Marty sat in the back of his limo heading to his cliff-side house in Malibu. His phone had been planted to the side of his head since he left the theatre. "Ellie, quit ducking my calls. This is not going to just go away. What the hell is going on? Where are you? Call me."

He terminated the call and threw the phone on the seat beside him. It started ringing before the first bounce. Ellie's face was on the screen.

"Shit, Ellie. Where are you?"

"Not in jail for now. You need to stop calling me. It's going to kill my battery."

"I am completely stumped. Why in the hell are you running? I know you didn't do this. And you're doing a piss-poor job of convincing anyone else you didn't do this. Let me pick you up wherever you are and we can talk this out."

"Talk about what? Perkins has no imagination. If he is spoon-fed facts pointing to me, he's going to run with it. And there's pretty damning evidence there, too. My gun, which I've never shot outside of the firing range. And one of my earrings and apparently a witness who saw me there. An impossibility since I spent the night sitting on my balcony, watching the sun go down, reading a relatively good book."

"Did—"

"No. I know what you're going to ask. Nobody saw me. I didn't talk to anybody. I didn't bump into anyone in the hall. I have absolutely no alibi."

Marty took a deep breath. "That may be good."

"In what universe is not having an alibi good?"

"If you were planning to kill someone you'd have made yourself an alibi."

"I'd yell at you right now, but I don't want to draw attention to the fancy-dressed lady hiding in the shadows. Don't worry about me, Marty. You've got plenty of other clients you *can* help."

Marty looked at the phone, call disconnected. His driver waited for the gate to open before entering the long drive. Marty slid down the partition window. "Hey, you know Ellie, right?"

"Drove her around an awful lot for about six months. Lovely girl."

"Yeah, I thought so too. She's got herself into a big mess. Very unlike her."

"I heard. It's been on the radio."

"They named her?"

"Every chance they could."

Marty held his head in his hands. "Fuck. Wonderful. Well, I guess that was inevitable." He slid out of the car. "There are days the fifteen percent doesn't come to anywhere near enough money."

Henry closed up the restaurant and nodded at the police car. "Em, you heard the news, right? About Ellie?"

"Doesn't sound like her." Emily followed his gaze to the black and white.

"She told some unbelievable stories about this Sweeney guy. It could be possible. I know I'd probably snap." He locked the door and pocketed the keys. "And where in the hell did the paparazzi come from all of a sudden? She's been doing movie publicity for the past few weeks and there's been nothing. All of a sudden, wham. Dozens of the parasites."

"And they're still parked out there at this time of night."

"There's more than this morning. I guess the news has drawn them. As if she'd come back here."

"You've got her number, right?"

"I'm sure she's got more to worry about without me calling her and warning her about the paps outside her place. She's probably talking to the police right now anyway." He held the car door for his wife. "Doesn't have time to talk to me."

Emily shook her head and waited until he got in and closed the door. "You haven't been paying attention. She's not talking to the cops. She's gone. Took off. The police are looking for her. She's on the lam."

Henry laughed. "You're kidding, right? Ellie? Goody-two-shoes Ellie?" He sobered at the look on his wife's face. "Oh, that's bad. You think she might have actually killed the guy?"

"No way. You said it yourself: goody-two-shoes. We need to get a message to her that we believe in her."

"And implicate ourselves in this mess?"

"Give me your phone. Don't be such an ass. She's always supported us and we need to support her. Or don't you believe in her?"

"I do. I just don't want to get involved."

Emily composed and sent a text with a ferocity Henry hadn't seen in years. She tossed the phone back on his lap. "You're involved."

"What did you send?"

"A message of support." She crossed her arms and promised a silent ride.

Marty paced in his back yard, looking at the reflections of the full moon on the black Pacific. He wasn't used to feeling this impotent. He dialed her number again.

"What?"

"Where are you? I'm very worried for your safety. And your mental health, if I'm honest."

"I'm not crazy."

"Then why are you hiding in the shadows, afraid someone will recognize you? You must be freezing. You didn't have a wrap tonight and it's down into the fifties."

"I'm not outside."

"The hell you're not. I can hear the waves in the background, there's a shiver in your voice, and you're whispering. Why whisper if you're not hiding from at least one person?"

In a diametrically-opposed neighborhood to Marty's, income-wise, Kent hung up the phone and tapped his coffee table. How to proceed? He had called Ellie's number and received a "waiting" message on the display. She was talking to someone else.

"No time to wait." He sent a text message.

"Where are you? I need to talk to you asap. See you in person, preferably."

He dropped the phone on the table and looked at his watch. A few more productive hours left in him. He turned back to his laptop.

Marty was in full negotiator mode. "This is a tough city, Ell. You're not safe on your own."

"I'll be fine."

Marty heard a beep. "What was that?"

"I got a text message. I've been getting a lot of very supportive messages. None from you, of course. Let me read it."

Marty waited. He could hear her muttering in the background. He did hear waves before, and he could still hear them. She was somewhere near the ocean, obviously, and hadn't moved since the last time they talked.

"I've got a pretty good idea where you are, Ell. The waves, the fact you haven't moved." There was a slight electronic click and all the background noise disappeared. He looked at the phone's display. She had terminated the call. "Shit."

He re-called her number, and went directly to voicemail. She had shut off her phone.

The Killer mentally moved another chess piece on the board. His board. He controlled the game. He controlled the behavior of each party. If there was an Olympics for manipulative behavior, he'd get the Gold and convince Silver to hand over their medal.

There would be sacrifices. There always were. Nobody won a chess match without giving up some pieces. On occasion the Queen was even surrendered in return for better board position.

So far everything had fallen into place. The players in their parts had reacted as he programmed them to. The second act was well under way now. Confusion was king. And when confusion reigned, misdirection was the weapon of choice. Tomorrow morning a second piece would be sacrificed. And the game would progress.

Perkins turned off his computer. "Stanfield, I'm calling it a night. She's with the wind. There's a BOLO out for her and I'll get a call as soon as she's found. So will you. There's nothing to be gained staying here."

"We haven't even touched all the evidence bags yet. And we still need to interview this Charlie Bates guy."

"It can wait until tomorrow. She's not a serial killer. We've both met the victim before. The world actually is a better place with him gone. I'm not going to lose sleep. She's young, pampered and frail. All public transport avenues are being watched. We'll catch her at a Starbucks in the next day or so. I'll even give you odds."

"You've got a short memory. She's going to fight this with everything she's got. Just like she fought about the so-called suicide over a year ago. You're living in a dream if you think otherwise. Am I right?"

Perkins sighed. "Oh, Jesus, I hope not. This is cut and dried. The evidence is a mountain beside her molehill of protestations of innocence. We already figured out the killing wasn't a suicide. It's clear she set it up to *look* like a suicide and did a very poor job of it.

That's as premeditated as it gets. She knows what she's done and she knows the consequences of getting caught. No wonder she's taken off. I probably would too."

Chapter Eleven

The last lights of the LA County Life Guard building turned off. Finally. I'd been in the shadows of the fishing pier for a couple of hours. The dress was ruined. It was soaked with salt water from the waist down. I guess I owned it now.

To get to my apartment I needed to move undetected up the beach almost a mile under a full moon, get through an ever increasing mob of smelly paps and a couple of cops sitting outside the front entrance.

At least that's the way they *expected* me to get to my apartment. They must think I'm an idiot.

The last truck drove out of the Life Guard parking lot. I stepped out from the shadows of the pier and looked across the expanse of empty sand.

I walked to the south side of the life guard building, awkward in the long dress. The building shielded me from the crowd in front of my building. My face would show up on the security camera footage, but it wouldn't be noticed for a couple of days, at least. But now I had half a mile in the open with the full moon shining in a clear sky. Half a mile to cover undetected to get to the guys who were looking for me. Nope. I'm not an idiot.

The black-and-white sat on N. Venice right up at Ocean Front Walk. The paps were hanging out by the skate park. They may as well have had spotlights on them. I looked around the south-east corner of the life guard's car lot. I could go east a block on twenty-fourth and approach the apartment from the back. Except I was still in a ruined $2000 gown. Even in the capital of Southern Californian weird I'd stand out.

I needed to tramp it up a bit.

And to do that I needed something sharp. It was impossible to keep a beach as large as this one clean. An almost empty bottle of beer rested in the sand by the walkway. I squatted, turned my head to protect my eyes and tapped it on the concrete walkway. And then I hit harder. The damned thing wouldn't break. I hauled my hand back to hit with all I had when someone grabbed my wrist.

"What the fuck?" I turned, landing on my ass, looking up at Ann, the crazy bag-lady.

"Why are you doing that? Kids will cut their feet on the glass."

I crab-walked back a couple of steps. "What? I'll clean up the mess. Be quiet, okay? I don't need the attention. "

"That doesn't make any sense. Why would you beak it if you're just going to clean it up?"

I struggled to my feet. My dress was hugely impractical when running from the law. "Look, Ann, please keep it down. There's a bunch of people over there looking for me, and they're not nice." She seemed puzzled. Best to change the subject. "I need something sharp to cut down this dress. I can't get around in it like this." I hefted the bottle. "So if you'll excuse me I've got some breaking to do."

"Wait." She dug through her jacket pockets and pulled out a blue-handled paring knife. "Will this work?"

I looked at it, and at her, my unlikely co-conspirator. "This is perfect." I accepted the knife and started cutting at about mid-thigh.

She nodded and gently took the knife from my hand. "Let me do this." And she did. Much better than I could.

I stepped out of the ring of red cloth. "Ann, you're a genius."

She slipped the knife into her pocket and picked the bottom half of the dress off the ground. "Thanks. Can I have this?"

"Sure." Then I had a thought. "Wait. Let me have it for half an hour, and I'll get it back to you, as well as the rest of it. Do you trust me?"

She smiled. She really needed urgent dental care. "Of course I do. Will I meet you here?"

I looked around. I didn't feel like exposing myself on the beach again tonight. I took the bottom half of the dress from Ann and tied my hair in a bun, letting the ends drape across my shoulders. "Walk with me. There's a nice bench you can rest on until I'm finished doing what I need to do."

She shook her head. "You go. I can't wait around. I don't belong out there." She pointed up 24th. "You'll see me around again. Give it to me then."

She smiled, turned and walked into the night.

Well, it was now or never. Getting close to midnight and the crowds were dissipating. I went with the theory that if you looked like you belonged, people would believe you belonged. I just needed to get in my place without getting tagged.

I strolled up 24th, trying to keep a balance between casual and slutty. With my luck, I'd be propositioned or pulled up for soliciting. I tried blending in. I was too tall in high school and spent a good deal of time in the early years trying to blend in with the wall. It wasn't until I discovered tall could get me money as a model, early in Year 12, that my confidence took over and I was paid to *not* blend in. Now here I was trying to undo all that.

It was like I was back in Year 11, trying to disappear in the middle of a crowd. In the middle of an empty street.

But after I turned left on Speedway I *was* in the middle of a crowd. I walked in the same direction as the traffic on the one way street. And I would walk that way until I reached N. Venice and the far corner of my apartment building.

So far so good.

But it was not to last.

About halfway up Speedway, right across from Virginia Court, a little crap car pulled up beside me in a cloud of exhaust. The driver tapped his horn and leaned out the window.

"Ellie, what the hell's going on?"

I closed my eyes and swore. "Jesus, Charlie, what are you doing out here?"

"Looking for you. What about the bullshit this afternoon? It's true bullshit too. I heard you were evading the police and figured you'd come by here."

"Who else knows?"

"Nobody. I came on my own."

"What about Kent?"

Charlie shook his head. "Haven't talked to him since last night. We had beer and pizza at Bart's place then split up."

"He's called me a couple of times. Warned me about the police, actually. Now they're sitting in front of my apartment, as are about two dozen paps. And you're drawing attention to me, which isn't healthy. Don't get yourself involved, mate. Go and pretend you've never seen me, okay? If you want to help, let it be known I was seen in Oxnard. Or Simi." I picked up the pace and kept my eye on the apartment building in front of me.

He cruised along side. "Seriously, Ellie. Let me help."

"*Seriously*, Charlie. Fuck off and get out of here. You're going to get me picked up."

"Why don't you just go in to the police and tell them what happened?"

"Because I don't know what happened. I was framed."

Charlie laughed.

"Shut it. I'm not joking. Get out of here and tell the cops you saw me in Santa Barbara."

He shook his head, rolled up his window and pulled ahead, turning right on S. Venice.

The entrance to the car park, and my way in, sat on N. Venice, about thirty or forty feet behind the cop car. I stood at the corner, partially covered by a mail box. An old guy sat in the stairwell behind me, smelling of cheap wine and urine. He didn't appear to notice I was standing there, not even five feet from him.

The driveway was lit—a coded keypad provided entrance to the basement car park. Once in there I was in the clear.

I stepped out from behind the mailbox and a pair of bicycle police spun by on Ocean Walk. I almost broke an ankle turning. I tried to be casual walking back toward Speedway. Without looking trampy. Damn this acting was hard.

I gave it a couple of seconds and turned back toward the parking garage. Coast clear. The six-digit code raised the door. I ran in as soon as I could and punched the button to close the door.

I took a deep breath. The elevators ran up the center of the building. Top floor was my place. I took the stairs. Nobody else did and I really didn't feel like meeting neighbors in the elevator.

My apartment felt different, like I hadn't been there forever. Hardly six hours had passed since a limo picked me up.

Six hours and a lifetime.

The street lights would have to provide illumination. I couldn't risk turning on lights or moving near the windows. I got down on my hands and knees and crawled below the window line to my bedroom. The drapes in there were closed. I stood and took stock. No time for a shower, but I had to change cloths. Denims, button down shirt and deck shoes would do. I grabbed a ball cap and attempted to stuff my hair under it. The damned stuff was too long. I took a pair of scissors and was about to do a quickie cut, and stopped.

They'd see the hair in my apartment; no matter how hard I tried to get it all in the cleanup, I'd miss some. Then they'd know I cut it. I tapped the scissors on the bathroom sink for a minute, thinking. My old Beetle was in the garage. Still in running order. Nobody knew it, and I could use it to get away for a little while until I could sort things out.

So I tossed the scissors on the counter, grabbed my ATM card and the money I had in the apartment - around $500 - and then stopped again. My ATM card would be like a tap on the cops' shoulder. So only the cash. I tossed the card on my dresser. Just the cash and my phone. And I had to keep my phone off to preserve the battery.

Like a caveman.

A wry smile was better than no smile at all. Enough money in the bank to live comfortably for years, and I couldn't access it. One of the best phones on the market, and I couldn't turn it on.

I took the stairs back to the basement. My new Beetle was blocking in the old girl. The police would probably have broadcast the make, model and tag number. I couldn't even drive my new car.

I moved the cars around, an exercise in vehicular ballet, and sat behind the wheel of my old VW Beetle.

The car park exit was on the south side of the building, exiting on S. Venice. The opposite side of the building. I should be clear. I plugged my phone into the cig charger and pulled up to the security keypad. I entered the six-digit code, but before I touched the 'enter' key the door started to raise. I threw the Beetle into reverse and backed up as a pair of cops walked in. Shit.

One of them recognized me through the car window, placed his hand on his holster and started running toward me. "Miss Bourke. Stop the car and keep your hands where we can see them."

As if.

I looked over my shoulder, backing though the maze of pathways in the garage, the young cops keeping pretty close. I drew them well into the garage before shifting back into first gear and flooring it. "Sorry boys." I hope they were quick on their feet. They split, one of them diving to the floor. "Not necessary, buddy. I was nowhere near you."

I glanced in the rear view mirror. The one on the ground had drawn his gun. Doubt he would use it, but it wasn't worth the risk. I shifted into second, yanked the car around a corner and made a beeline for the garage door.

There were no shots. I bounced on to S. Venice and headed inland. My plan of taking off in the Beetle was shot. The description and license plate would be on every cop's dashboard computer within five minutes. In addition to the money I couldn't access and the phone I couldn't turn on, I had a car I couldn't drive. Two cars I couldn't drive. Happy days.

I had to get rid of the old girl quick, before it was seen. The last thing I wanted was a high-speed chase. Not in this car. I might be able to outrun cops on foot, but not their cars. A couple of blocks down the road, sirens in the distance, I saw the perfect spot. The Venice Farmers Market had a huge tree-lined parking lot. The gate was closed, but there were gaps between the trees wide enough to accommodate my little car.

I carefully navigated the curb, wincing at the scraping noises that didn't sound good at all. I turned off the headlights and navigated by the full moon. A nice dark corner, far from the adjacent roads, became its home. I locked her up, gave her a gentle pat on the hood and slipped between the trees.

I was tired and I had nowhere to go for the night. I looked at my phone. I couldn't call Cathy. She wasn't back yet and besides, I didn't want to get her involved with this. And my luck I'd be located just by turning it on. I wasn't sure how that worked.

There was a cheap hotel about a mile up the beach. Far enough from home, nobody would know me. With my face on half the billboards in town, I still had the risk that *someone* might recognize me. I had to get rid of the hair. A pair of sunglasses, scissors and an Angels ball cap at a 7-11 would have to do the trick.

I walked a few feet down a walkway by the canal, took a deep breath and started butchering the hair that had made me the poster girl for *Blood Thunder*. It was a crude job. I didn't care at that point. Each fistful of hair I removed went into the canal. I cut it short enough so the ball cap would completely cover it. I could make it presentable in the motel.

I had to waste a fifty over the room charge to get in. I had no identification and the kid was a little bit of a stickler for the rules. Very little bit, since the fifty shut him up.

The TV was on, the news playing in the background while I attempted to fix my hair. It was a never-ending battle of attrition. By the time I was finished, I looked like a tall, flat-chested Anne Heche.

It had been a long day. The shower was refreshing. And toweling my now short hair, I wondered why I didn't cut it earlier.

Probably because I wasn't running from the police earlier.

I dropped on the bed and turned up the volume on the news channel. My face was on the screen. The talking head was in mid-sentence:

" - bizarre twist in the Bart Sweeney acquittal, suicide and then murder case. Sources inside the police department who wish to remain unnamed are telling us the case against actress Ellie Bourke, former lover turned accuser, has become very strong. Evidence at the scene, as well as her actions when approached by the authorities, put her at the top of the list of suspects. If you see her please do not approach her. Call your local police authorities or 9-1-1 immediately. She is considered dangerous."

Fuck.

I turned off the TV. This was probably on every channel. The kid downstairs, odds on, just saw this also. Staying here would be worse than stupid. And I was just digging myself a deeper hole.

I stuck my nose out the door to the walkway along the second floor of the motel. Quiet still. I grabbed my jacket, made sure I had my phone and slipped down the stairs. I jogged past the office and saw the kid from the front desk talking on the phone. He saw me and started talking more animatedly.

Double fuck.

I hopped across the street, hat pulled down on my head and headed as far from the motel as possible. It was midnight, I was wanted and had nowhere to stay. The news report made it sound like the street was crawling with cops looking for me.

Fifteen minutes of walking later I leaned against a back-alley wall. The only thing that made sense was to do what they least expected me to do. I'd walk back to Venice and live in the shadows for now. The crowds would be my cover. I wasn't the girl in that picture. She was a glamour girl. I would be a surfer girl again, living on the beach and evading the cops.

Until I figured out what in the hell was going on.

Chapter Twelve

"Oh, sweet Jesus those guys can be stupid." Perkins clicked off the TV and dropped back in his recliner. He took a sip of his drink and rubbed his forehead. "She was never his lover. She'd kill him first." He grunted and took another sip. "Well, looks like she really did it this time."

"What was that, dear?" His wife of thirty-seven years came out of the kitchen with a cup of tea. "Were you talking to me?"

"No. Don't worry about it. I'm going to have to crash soon."

"Is it about that case? The suicide that wasn't?"

He nodded. "The reporters are having a field day. They've got most of the facts twisted and would have the public believe she's a threat to everyone around her." He sipped, winced and swallowed.

"She's a scared girl who killed a man because she thought justice wasn't served. And I agree with her - justice wasn't. Sweeney should have been in jail for at least ten years for what he did. His release was a travesty." He rubbed his forehead. "A lot of people were upset he was released. I know his victim's brother was upset." He looked to his wife. "He's a cop too, you know. Transferred down here from Boise after Sweeney killed his brother. I think he thought he might hook up with Miss Bourke." He shook his head. "She's not going to kill again. I can feel it in my gut. She's running scared. Hopefully no citizen tries to be a hero and take her out."

"You like her."

Perkins smiled at his wife. "Don't worry, sweetie. She's way too young for me. I do like her though. Very down to earth, very tough. Very independent. And very funny in the things I've seen her in. Shame she had to let the hate go to her head."

The Killer paced his living room, muted news as his backdrop. The waiting was worse than he thought it would be. "One down, many, many more to go."

The plan was fool-proof. The cops bought the sloppy fake suicide and the planted clues. Almost better than killing Bart was watching Ellie squirm. He wanted to watch her squirm, though, not imagine it. And he always got what he wanted.

"Where are you, bitch? Where are you hiding?"

The news on the TV rolled around to the top of the hour. 1:00 a.m. There was no tired. There was only doing. He would have plenty of time to sleep when he was dead. "But I'm going to live forever."

He grabbed his jacket and ran out of the apartment. He'd find her. He couldn't not find her. He had to watch her squirm.

Detective Jacob Sampson was exhausted. "It was never this hard in Boise." His dog looked at him and cocked an ear. He leaned down and scratched the Golden Lab behind the left ear. "Not talking to you, Lisa. Why aren't you asleep?"

Lisa's soft woof and shuffle toward the back door was a clear message.

"Sorry I'm late, pooch. Helluva day." He opened the back door and let her out to the fenced-in yard. "Starting to get cool. Don't be long, dog." The full moon lit up the small yard, the yellow lab casting a sharp shadow.

Jacob left the door open and went back into the living room, and turned on the TV, catching the last half of the news report. He watched with a combination of amusement and dismay.

Lisa padded into the room and dropped on the floor beside his chair with a grunt.

"You close the door behind you?"

The dog looked up and him and woofed softly and lay her head back on her paws. He smiled, reached down and gave her head a pat. "Good girl. You were the smartest one of the lot." He gestured at the TV. "Did you see that? Ellie is a dangerous fugitive from justice. My ass. I can sort of understand why she did what she did, but I can't really believe she did it." He shook his head. "That's not the Ellie I know."

Lisa lifted her head at the sound of Ellie's name and looked up at Jacob.

"Yeah. Ellie's in trouble again. Big this time." He gave Lisa a pat. "But there's nothing we can do about it tonight. Time to hit the sack."

The Killer cruised the streets of Venice. 2:00 a.m. and there was still enough traffic he had to pay attention to what he was doing. "Where are you, you little bitch?" A flutter of self-doubt grazed his conscious and he snarled. "Fuck no. No doubt. I'm looking in the right place. I know I'm looking in the right place."

His cheeks were heavy and his eyes were starting to burn. He looked at the clock on the dash and did some mental math. He had to do it three times before he trusted the answer. "Forty-two hours awake. I can go another twelve, easy." He grabbed an Altoids tin from the glove compartment and popped a couple of pills. "Dead easy."

Angles weren't straight and the colors a diffuse brilliant, but he was still conscious. Judgment started to slip a bit, to be expected in this situation. He spotted a tall girl ahead of him walking briskly away up the street, Ellie's height and build. He pulled over, two wheels on the sidewalk, in front of her.

"Marty, honey, what's going on with Ellie? I liked her so much."

Marty looked up from his iPad and frowned. "I don't have the foggiest fucking idea. She's off the ranch. I've had a couple of talks with the police, and they've got enough evidence to lock her up for a very long time."

"All the times we've had her over for dinner I didn't once get that vibe from her."

"Yeah, well, Sweeney was in jail then. He was out of her life. She was satisfied knowing, in large part due to her efforts, he was paying the price for killing her friend. Things were right with the world. I think she snapped when his lawyer got him released. For her, he was the epitome of all that was wrong with this industry and him back on the streets must have been too much for her."

His wife snapped shut her paper with finality. "We need to reach out to her and let her know we care about her predicament."

He cocked an eyebrow. "I'm all for helping friends in need, but we're entering felony territory. Aiding and abetting after the fact, or something like that." He closed the iPad case and stood. "If she turns herself in I'll make sure she's got the best lawyer her money can buy. But this isn't a trivial matter. We're talking premeditated murder." He walked through the glass doors from the lounge room to the back pool area. "I know she's a tough girl, but I never would have thought she'd have that in her." He looked back into the lounge room. "Hon, get out here. This is the most brilliant full moon I've seen in a long time."

He jumped out of his car. "Ellie. Fancy running into you here."

The girl lifted her head. "You looking to party, mister?"

The Killer narrowed his eyes. "Tramp. You're not Ellie. Move off before I gut you."

She flipped him her middle finger. "Get fucked, pal."

She received a punch, a right cross, for her efforts and fell on her ass. "Jesus, you prick. That wasn't called for."

The Killer kicked her in the ribs. "Fuck off." He spat on her and got back in his car. He glanced at the hooker in his rear view mirror as he drove away. She had her eyes closed and was she was muttering something.

Then he forgot about her completely.

"Come out, come out wherever you are." He scanned the road. Logic would dictate she wouldn't be walking around on the street at 2:00 in the morning, but the logic part of his brain hadn't functioned normally in a long time.

"Fuck, fuck, fuck, fuck, fuck." His heart fluttered and palpitated. He coughed and punched himself in the chest. "Not now. Definitely not now."

He blurred a bit and glanced his car off the curb. "Okay. Time to rein it in. Time to stop it, time to pack it in for the night. Forty-three hours. Is that Keith Richard's record? Whatever. It's good."

He pulled off the surface streets onto the I-10 and made his way back toward his home. He'd get her tomorrow. He had a way of locating her.

The plans were starting to gel. The list was long, but doable. The order wasn't yet defined, other than the keystone. Sweeney had to be first, of that there was no question. Number two was just out of his reach.

But there would be a death tomorrow.

Another one.

Marty's wife took him by the arm and led him back into the house. "It's past two. You've got a meeting with Hanks and Favreau tomorrow morning."

He waved her off. "The meeting is at 10:00. Here. I can sleep until 9:00 and be ready. At my age, six hours is more than enough sleep. Not that I'm going to sleep."

"Why, Marty. What do you have in mind?"

He laughed. "If you're up for it, I am. I was talking about Ellie though. I can't get her out of my mind."

"I'm jealous."

"You know what I mean. Where is she? What is she doing? What in the hell is she expecting to accomplish? Argh, fuck, you women can be frustrating. Your collective logic escapes me, most times."

"So much for you getting lucky tonight."

"No, seriously. What in the hell is she thinking?" He peeled off his clothes and tossed them into the laundry hamper. "She actually thinks she can outrun the cops?" He brushed his teeth and slipped under the covers. "Does any of this make sense to you?"

"She's scared, she's pissed off and she doesn't trust the cops. Can you blame her? The last time the police were certain about something she had to ram evidence down their throats to convince them of the truth. Now she knows they're on the wrong track again. Except this time it's against her. She has nobody to help her. So she has to help herself."

Marty groaned and shoved his head under his pillow. "You're going to want me to help, aren't you?"

"Stay out of the felonious territory. I kind of like this lifestyle. But yes, Marty, I want you to help her as much as you can without going to jail yourself."

The Killer snapped his head forward with a snort, drool flying off his mouth onto his steering wheel. "Oh, my fucking head." He'd fallen asleep in his car on the side of the road, about half a block from his apartment building. "Not good."

He yawned and scrubbed his scalp with his finger tips. "Fuck, fuck, fuck." He felt like shit. A thick layer of sweat coated his body. He rubbed the back of his neck and it felt like he'd just been in a sauna. He climbed out of his car, gripping the open door to steady himself.

"Shit."

He held on to the roof while he closed the door and locked it. He leaned back against the car and closed his eyes. "So fucking tired." He took a deep breath, clenched his jaw and stood upright. "Fuck tired. There is no tired." He inhaled deep through his nose and walked the half block with as steady a step he could muster.

Three attempts required to get the key in the lock of the main door. Four attempts to get the key in his apartment door. He threw the key ring on the floor and dropped into the chair in front of his laptop. He consulted a piece of paper on the desk and logged into the site. After a minute of searching a message appeared telling him the mobile was offline. "Fuck." He ticked the box to get an email when the device was located.

"You can run, bitch. But you can't hide."

Chapter Thirteen

Bizarre swirling dreams of *The Little Mermaid* and the old woman selling food to birds collided with cold water on my feet and a foul stench.

I went from lying in the sand to sitting upright fast enough to get head rush. I put out my hands to steady myself and smashed poor Ann in the face. She rolled away and sat up. So the source of the smell was clear now.

The sparkly red vision dissipated and I could see where I was. The cold water on my feet was the tide coming in under the Venice Fish Pier. I was well under it, and Ann was sitting beside me with a brown toothy smile on her face.

"You slept well? You snore, you know." She tried to pull a ratty, no doubt lice-infested, blanket over my shoulders. "You'll catch your death of cold.

I struggled to shrug it off. "No, no. That's okay. Leave me alone. Just - just - just keep your distance, okay?" I brushed sand off my hands and scrubbed my scalp with my finger tips. Shit. It was short. I forgot. I brushed my hand over it, getting used to the feel. It was okay. I could get used to this.

I yawned. "Where do you pee around here? I'm busting."

She pointed up the hill toward the boardwalk. "Public toilets. Or under here. Nobody can see."

"Yech. No thanks. I'll chance it." I crouched as I walked out from under the pier, dusting damp sand off my ass. "Hey, if I'd known I was going to bump in to you so soon I would have brought that cloth back with me."

She gave me a clumsy wave of dismissal. "No, it's okay."

It didn't feel real. It was an age ago I walked the red carpet at the premiere of my movie, and it was only twelve hours later. Shit, what had I gotten myself into? I walked up the beach watching for any signs of attention. Muscle heads were oiling themselves in the early morning sun. I really shouldn't laugh. They were as dedicated to their goals as I was to mine. It just seemed like a really silly goal, building muscle. And then not using it to move stuff. Just showing it off.

A couple of bike cops pedaled down the beach walk, slowly taking in the early starters. I steeled myself for a run. If I could get to the water before they got me, I could out swim them.

But they didn't give me a second glance.

Sure woke me up though. Forget about caffeine, a surge of

adrenaline perks you right up.

I finished my pee and headed back under the pier. Ann had left. I looked up and down the beach; there was no sign of her. It was a pretty open landscape. Almost impossible for normal person to disappear, and this was shaggy looking lady in six coats. If I saw her again - when I saw her again - I'd have to find out how she did that.

I sat back against one of the pilings under the pier and took stock of my situation. I think I may have fucked myself over. In the cold, but warming, light of day some of my actions last night seemed reckless and ill-advised. Maybe the best thing would be to grab a bite and find Perkins and talk it out. I'd convinced him before. He knew me to be a straight-shooter. I'm sure I could convince him again. But I needed food first.

And I didn't have to worry about what I ate. I felt like a good old bacon and egg roll. Screw it. I didn't need to get in a fancy gown tonight and it would be weeks before all this got sorted out.

I kept to the 'look like you belong' adage and rolled up the cuffs of my jeans and carried my shoes while I walked back up the beach. Dozens of little cafes were open for the early tourist business and until I found Perkins I'd keep a low profile and be one of the thousands who showed up here for the weirdness.

I bought a bacon and fried egg on a roll, a large skinny cap and sat at one of the outdoor tables. The muscles preened. I'm sorry. I really think it's silly. Some of the guys were pretty good looking but had way too much muscle. I mean, really. If the muscle prevents you from bending your arm enough to touch your shoulder, there's too much muscle. Most of these guys had larger chests than I did. I squinted and looked closer. One of them was a woman. Shit. She was bigger than some of the guys. I smiled and shook my head. It took all kinds, and all kinds were definitely here.

The bacon and egg roll disappeared in short order, not surprising when you consider the last meal I ate was a fruit bowl for breakfast yesterday. It hit the spot. I sat back and sipped on the coffee, relaxing into my situation. I was never afraid of a fight and I always faced my problems head on.

But on my terms.

And if I wasn't careful I'd forfeit those terms.

A familiar face was setting up for a day of busking. Danny Flynn moved from Boston three years ago, a year from finishing a law degree and as far as I know has spent every day on the beach since then.

Juggling.

And for the last six months, having breakfast with me.

Shit. I pulled the cap farther down over my face. But it didn't do any good.

"Hey, Ell. What the hell you doing down this end of the beach? You move?" He pulled out the chair opposite and sat. "What you having?"

It was possible he hadn't heard. Danny was almost perpetually in a state of semi-stonedness. If the audience knew how baked he was when he was tossing the bowling ball, bag of flour and running chainsaw, they'd be standing a little bit further back. "I ate already, mate. What brings you down here? You're a bit out of your area."

He shrugged. "Felt like I needed a bit of a change. We can still breakfast together, right?"

I chuckled. "What do you want?"

He ordered a plate of pancakes and pork sausages and a massive tumbler of grapefruit juice. His usual.

I paid. As usual.

"So, Danny boy, what's new in your world?"

"Hey, you cut your hair."

I lifted the cap for a minute and let him look. "You like?"

"Kinda Anne Heche-y. You have a lesbian role next?" He smiled.

"You'd like that wouldn't you?" He was the biggest hands-off perv I knew.

"It would make me go to a movie for the first time in five years, that's for sure." He shoveled pancake in his mouth. "Saw some weird shit on the news last night about you. Or maybe I imagined it."

I shook my head. "You didn't imagine it. It's not true though."

He dismissed me with a wave from a fork dripping with syrup. "Of course it's not. Just more media bullshit. This is why I left law school. Did you know that?"

"You never told me, actually. I thought maybe you got caught with a really big bag of pot and got tossed out."

"Nah. Didn't start smoking until I got down here. As far away from that place as possible without having to use a passport." He gulped grapefruit. "I got talking to some of the kids who graduated a couple of years before me. They were associates in various law firms in the area. All smart guys and girls. The girls were actually smarter, for some reason."

"I'm not surprised."

"Of course you aren't." He worried something from his teeth with his tongue. "So anyway, to a person, every one of them hated what they were doing. Those who chose the defense side of the coin told me about defending people who they absolutely knew were guilty of something. Sure, everyone is guaranteed a fair trial and a competent defense, but some of these things - how do you defend them? On the prosecution side they told me about the pressure to get the conviction. If a case was dodgy and they thought they didn't have the evidence to convict, they'd bargain it down, even if there was doubt in their minds the perp was actually guilty."

"You could have gone corporate. Lots of money in that."

He shook his head. "I went into law because of *Legal Eagles* and *LA Law* and *The Practice*. Turns out none of that shit was real."

I had to laugh. "Of course it's not. This is the land of make-believe. Even the reality shows aren't real. There are as many writers on them as *Modern Family*. So you're happy doing what you're doing?"

He waggled a sausage on the end of his fork. "Hell ya. I haven't paid a cent of taxes in the last three years. I am completely off the grid. No driver's license, no passport, no mobile phone. I pay cash rent to my very appreciative landlord and these guys," he jerked his thumb in the direction of the muscle-heads, "know where all the good pot is."

"And I give you free breakfast every day."

"Everyday you're in town. You've been away a lot the last few months."

"I'll tell Marty to have our breakfast written into my next contract."

He tilted his head at me. "I never know when you're fucking with me." He wiped the last of the syrup with the last of his pancake. "So what's this bullshit all about? Why do they think you offed this Sweeney dude?"

"Jesus, mate. Keep your voice down."

"Ah, right. You're on the lam. Apologies." He paused. "So?"

"I don't know. I was sitting on my balcony watching the sunset and reading Gaiman when it allegedly happened."

"Oh, there's no allegedly about it. It happened."

"Okay, when I allegedly did it."

"That's better. So what are you going to do? What to join my show? You fund me to Hawaii and we can live a life of felonious leisure on the North Shore of the Big Island."

I shook my head. "I'm going to see the cop behind all this. Today. As soon as I finish this coffee."

"You're nuts."

"What about my nuts?"

"No, I said it with the apostrophe. And I've seen you in a bikini. No nuts. A bit if the toe of a camel, but no nuts."

I reached across the table and smacked him on the arm. "You're horrible. And I'm not nuts. I can't run from this forever. I shouldn't have run last night."

"So why did you?"

"I don't know. Freaked out. Marty called me to tell me the cops were waiting outside the theatre to talk to me and then a friend called to tell me it was worse than I thought it was."

"And how would he know?"

"His ex- works at the station and she told him about the evidence they had. Pretty damning, but on reflection this morning, it can't be real, because I didn't do it."

"For what it's worth, I believe you. But good luck getting the cops on your side. They have a philosophical bent to prosecution. I think you're crazy to walk into the lion's den."

"Maybe I'll change my name to Daniel first."

"Huh?"

"Never mind."

He wiped his face and hands with a paper napkin and balled it into his empty juice glass. "Off to work then. I have so much fun doing this. Yesterday I made a black guy from Mississippi take my chainsaw and chase a white guy from some conservative bastion of preppiness while I videotaped it. Near pissed myself laughing." He stood. "Stay safe, sweet cakes, and trust no one. Not even me."

I waved good-bye. The pot was making him even more paranoid than usual.

I turned on my phone and checked the contacts. I was sure I still had Perkin's number. Three messages came in, one after another.

The first was from Marty:

"What the hell, Ell? What are you thinking? This is going to be hard on your career. Mel Gibson hard. If you did it, if you didn't do it, it doesn't matter. Turn yourself in. Call me first though, but then turn yourself in."

What? *If* I did it? Jesus.

The next was from Cathy. I hadn't seen her in too long.

"Now I wish I'd been at the premiere. I would have protected you from yourself. I know you didn't do it. Can't possibly believe you did,

so they're wrong. You've dealt with wrong cops before. Do it again. I'm back in LA. Call me and let's figure this out."

Always reliable Cathy. And she was right. Perkins *did* run down the wrong track with my roommate's death. I convinced him it wasn't a suicide and he ended up arresting the right person: Bart Sweeney. I'd have to convince him he was wrong again.

The third one was from Charlie. Considering I'd only seen him a couple of times in the last three years, it surprised me.

"It's me, Charlie Bates. Not sure if you've got my number in your phone. I know it's been a while, but I thought you were smarter than this. Unless you're trying to get yourself killed. Suicide by cop is stupid. But hey, what do I know? Killing Sweeney did a lot of us a favor. If you need somewhere to lay low, let me know."

Another vote from the peanut gallery. I contemplated a rude reply when the phone rang, startling me enough to drop it on the table.

"Hello?"

"Ellie, it's Kent. What the hell is going on? Where are you?"

"How long have you been calling me? I just turned on my phone."

"Lucked out. Where are you?"

"Not important for you to know right now. Why did you call?"

There was silence on the line save for keys clicking. Then he was back on the line. "I'm worried about you. You need to get somewhere safe."

"I'll be somewhere safe in about thirty minutes."

"Great. Where?"

"Police station on Devonshire, where I'll have a nice long chat with Sergeant Perkins about this mess and hopefully get it all sorted out."

"Hell no. That would be the worst thing you could do."

"I don't think so. I can talk to the guy."

"No, no, no. My friend in the station is telling me about the case they're building. The fact you hit one of the cops with your car last night isn't helping your cause. They've added assault of a law enforcement officer to your charges. It's not looking good, Ell. Not even Perkins will be able to help you out. I understand he's leading the charge anyway."

"How do you know I hit the cop? And I didn't. Just missed him."

"It was in the news. And in the tabloids. And TMZ. You're a star."

"Lovely. And what do you mean, Perkins is leading the charge? Really? Hard to believe Perkins leading anything."

"Hey, I'm just repeating what I'm told. Let me snoop around. I'll take my friend out for coffee and see what she knows. I'll call you back at noon, okay? Leave your phone on in case I find something out earlier."

"I'll shut it off. You call me at noon. I'll turn it on then."

"Yeah, but what if I find something out earlier?"

I thought about that. If he could get me information that could help, every minute would count. "Okay. Just make it fast, okay? I'm on half battery right now."

"Will do. Stay safe for me."

This wasn't being done on my terms. I opened the settings on my phone, turned off Wi-Fi, turned off location services and turned off cellular data. I might get a couple of extra hours out of it.

And now I needed to figure out what to do with myself for the next three or four hours. I could only wander the boardwalk for so long. I was a wanted crim.

Chapter Fourteen

Perkins called his partner over. "What have you found so far?"

Stanfield scratched his chin. "I've had all of her haunts checked and nobody's seen her. The bank account hasn't been touched, but it's early yet. I've got a warrant for the phone records and they've been asked to triangulate her position."

"When did it go in?"

"I was just approved. Technically we should get something from them in about half an hour."

Perkins stood. "Good. Hate that it's come to this, but she's gone off her stick. Sweeney should never have been let out."

A voice responded behind him. "You're right. He shouldn't have."

Detective Sampson poured a coffee from a glass urn and sat across from Stanfield. "What have you found that implicates her?"

"Aside from the gun, matched by ballistics, an earring matching one in her apartment, and her hair at the scene, a witness placing her in the neighborhood in the time window of Sweeney's death, nothing." Perkins smile was sad. "Got her dead cold."

"I know her, and she wouldn't do this. She's strong, but she's not psychotic. Has anyone verified the witness sighting?"

"Anonymous tip line. Haven't confirmed anything yet. It's a suburban neighborhood at 8:00 at night. We were lucky to get one witness."

"Exactly." Sampson sipped the coffee and winced. "Shit, this is worse than usual."

"'Exactly' what?" Perkins crossed his arms. "What do you mean?"

"It's too easy, don't you think? A clumsy attempt at faking a suicide, one we both saw through in less than fifteen minutes, followed by a slam dunk case against a person with no alibi? If she did it, don't you think she'd make sure she had an alibi?"

Perkins dropped in his chair with a barked laugh. "Right. Using those criteria I'll have to reopen over half my cases. Sometimes it's not an episode of *Castle*. Sometimes it's just a straightforward murder." He scratched his nose. "And I've got no idea if she's got an alibi. She ran. Almost killed a cop. Sure sign of guilt."

Samson sighed. "Didn't even touch him. And if he was in a bit better shape, he could have gotten well out of the way."

Perkins shrugged. "It's a pattern of behavior. Hey, I like the kid too. She made a fool of me back then, but I'm a big enough man to admit when I'm wrong."

Stanfield snickered. "I'll say you're big enough."

"Shut up kid or you'll see what my fist feels like."

"'See' what it 'feels' like? That makes absolutely no sense. How am I going to see what something feels like?" Stanfield redirected his attention to his computer. "Incoming from the telco." He printed a couple of copies of the pages and tossed a copy on Perkins" desk.

The Sergeant put on his glasses and looked at the call log handed to him. "What do we have here? Incoming call, text message, outgoing call all around the time we were at the theatre. A few more incoming, one from the agent - I was beside him when he made that call - and another one from Kent Williams." He looked at his junior partner. "Get his particulars. I think we need to have a chat with him."

He scanned down the page. "A couple more incoming and a mess of text messages. Why don't we have the contents of the text messages?"

"Can't get the contents with this warrant. Did you look at the triangulation?"

Perkins looked at the second page, Sampson looking over his shoulder. "Is she crazy?" He flipped the page over. "Is this the most current location?"

The green dot on the map turned gray and the Killer kicked back his chair and swore. "Fucking bitch. Motherfucking stuck-up bitch."

He took a deep breath. "Calm yourself. This is merely a simple, small setback." He drummed his fingers on the arms of the chair and thought about next steps. That was the corporate lingo, he heard. Next steps and synergistic blah blah blah.

No matter.

He dialed the number. "Now is the time. You need to do it now. Go into the station. Tell them your story. Ask specifically for Perkins."

"But I've already told them what I saw."

"It was on an anonymous tip line. You need to put a face to it." The Killer took a deep breath. "Remember what's in it for you if you do what I tell you. And remember what happens if you don't."

The Killer heard a sigh, then, "You don't have to tell me. Okay. I'll do it."

"This morning."

"This morning? I'm at work."

"Make up something. You feel sick. Your kid is ill. It's that time of the month. I don't fucking care, just do it." He hung up without waiting for an answer. She'd do it. She had no choice. Nobody defied him.

He needed to find Ellie. She needed to die. And it needed to look like she killed herself out of anguish or guilt or some other plausible excuse. Guilt was winning by a nose.

The dot on the screen had turned from green to grey at the Venice Fish Pier. She had no car. The old one had been found in the Farmer's Market parking lot that morning, and the new one was in her parking garage. Everyone knew it. So she was on foot. "Her legs are long, but she can't make up that much distance."

He checked his appearance in the hall mirror by the front door. He thought he looked fine. The sheen of sweat, the pallor of his skin and the dilated pupils didn't register. "Looking good, man." He popped another pill, dry swallowed it and left for her rendezvous with death. "Grandiose. At all times. The dominos are teetering."

Perkins looked up from his notes. "Could you spell your name please?"

"I-n-d-r-a-n-i G-u-p-t-a. Indrani Gupta. It's not difficult, Sergeant."

"And could you tell me again what you saw?"

"It's the same thing I said on the phone."

"Ma'am, I didn't hear the recording. I'd like to hear it from you, now."

"Where do you want me to start?"

"Why were you in the neighborhood? Your address is on the other side of the Valley."

"I was visiting a friend. She lives a block over. I was walking to the bus stop."

"So you walked past this address?" He slid a paper with Bart Sweeney's address on it across the desk.

"Yeah, I would have."

"And when you were near that address, what did you see?"

"A tall woman with long blonde hair was leaving the house. She got in a new VW Beetle and drove off in a hurry."

Perkins placed a sheet of paper on his desk. There were six photos on it. "Can you pick out the person you saw leaving the house?"

Indrani took a quick look and pointed at Ellie's photo. "Her. No question."

Perkins made a mark on the paper. "And what time was this?"

"I was going to catch the 8:30 bus, so somewhere near 8:15."

"We're going to need you to testify in court."

Indrani swallowed and shifted in her seat. "That will be necessary?

Can I can sign an affidavit or something instead?"

Perkins shook his head. "You're going to need to be in the courtroom, I'm afraid. You're the linchpin of our case. It's all circumstantial otherwise. But you putting her at the scene clinches it."

"Really? Oh." She stood to leave.

"No, not yet. Please sit down Miss Gupta. I've got a couple of more questions."

She sat, and took a deep breath. "Yes?"

"Why now?"

"Excuse me?"

"You left the anonymous tip yesterday. Most people would leave it at that. But you decided to come in today to retell your story. Why?"

"It seemed unfair he should be released from jail and then killed by the person who fabricated the evidence to put him in there in the first place. I couldn't let it happen."

"So you know Mr. Sweeney?"

Indrani pulled the cuffs of her sleeves down to her palms absent-mindedly as she talked. "Oh, no. I never knew the guy. I heard about him, though. He came up with that *Blood Thunder* movie, then that Ellie girl framed him for murder and killed him after he was acquitted."

"He wasn't acquitted. His lawyer got him released on a technicality. He really did kill that young man, and there was enough evidence to convict him. Unfortunately for us, and fortunately for him, he had a very liberal judge who believe the stream of crap fed to him by Sweeney's lawyer. If he hadn't been killed we'd be in the middle of appealing his release." He closed the file and stood. "Thanks for your time. I've got your contact details. We'll be in touch in the lead up to the trial if we need you."

The best place to hide is right in front of the people looking for you. Ellie's a smart cat. Who would think she'd go back to Venice? The cops are probably scouring the Valley for her. "They'll find her when I want them to find her. She'll be floating facedown in the LA River." He downshifted. "But she's got to suffer as bad as I did." He squinted, believing himself to be channeling Eastwood. "If only I could figure out how to make her suffer as long as I have."

He parked in a public lot at the north end of Venice and started strolling up the boardwalk toward the fishing pier. No way she'd still be there, but it was a place to start. He was getting distracted. The bikinis and the roller skates and the tight asses and the...he took a deep breath.

He pivoted and walked backwards watching a bikini bottom skate away from him. He licked his lips. "I should come down here more often." He sucked air through his teeth. "You, my sweet cheeks, will live." He turned back around and continued to walk, trying to pick out a tall blonde in the crowd of tall blondes. "Fuck. Like looking for a particular tree in the fucking forest. Tempted to cut down the entire lot of them."

He sidestepped a panhandler and spit at his feet. "Get fucked, butt-wad." He shook his head. "Not worth the effort." He leaned down and looked the man in the eye. "You're a lucky son of a bitch, you know that?"

The colors were bright and the sun hot. The skate park was full of kids. More BMX bikes than boards in the skate park today. He got in the face of a boy on a bike. "Shouldn't you be in school, punk?"

The kid rolled up the inside of the bowl. "Fuck off asshole or I'll fucking smash you."

The Killer's hand snapped out and grabbed the kid's front wheel as it stopped on the upswing. The kid fell backwards, smashing the back of his head. He slid to the bottom, trailing a streak of blood.

He hopped in the bowl after his victim. "Smash me? You're going to fucking smash me?" He kick the prone kid in the ribs. "Get up ass-hat."

He leaned over the prone body and grabbed him by the hair and lifted. "I said get up so I can knock you down again." He pulled hard, removing clumps of hair as the mostly stoned kid tried to get to his feet.

"What the fuck man? What did I do to you?"

The Killer looked at his victim's friends, standing around the edge of the bowl watching. "Your friends are pussies. You're all pussies." He grabbed the kid by the throat and punched him hard in the face. The impact jarred loose his grip on his neck and the kid dropped like a rag.

That roused the other three who came at him in unison.

"Oh, goody. A fight." He held up his hands and said, "Whoa, stop, stop, stop. There's three of you and one of me. Not a really fair fight. You want to go get some more guys?" He laughed at the look on their faces. " 'More guys'. See what I did? Said it wasn't fair and you'd assume I meant because I was outnumbered, but it's because," he lashed out and punched the closest one in the throat, "you're going to need more people if you think you've got even half a chance of coming out of this unscathed."

The remaining two attacked at the same time, from either side, trying to double-team him. He laughed and elbowed the first one in the jaw and followed through with a punch to the other's solar plexus, doubling him over.

He stood and looked at the four, three down and one struggling for air, and laughed. "I can not be defeated. By anyone."

The one skater still standing took a swing at him. He shrugged off the feeble attack, elbowing the young skater in the head. He looked around. The crowd was thick. There were dozens of witnesses, iPhones and smart phones capturing video of the event. "Fuck off the lot of you. He asked for it." He flipped them the bird and ran down one of the side alleys.

"Well, that was fun." Adrenaline coursed through his veins. He looked back at the scene he left. The crowd was still focused on the mess in the skate park bowl. Sirens were approaching, ambulance and police. "Time to be elsewhere." He rolled his shoulders and flexed his hands. "That felt great." He stretched out his neck. "Now where's that bitch?" He turned another corner and used the app on his phone to log in to her account and selected 'find my mobile'. After a minute of searching the application reported that the phone was offline.

"Shit. The fucking thing is still off."

Emily held a napkin to the young man's head. "Henry, get me some ice." She patted the young man on the back and pulled her hand back as she winced. "Sorry. You'll be fine. The ambulance is not far away. Did you know that man? Why did he do this?" She took the ice from her husband, wrapped the cloth around it and held it to the young man's head.

He winced. "Some bat-shit crazy dude I've never seen before. What the hell was his problem?"

"He seemed crazed."

"Yeah, that's what I mean by bat-shit crazy. He took out four of us. Dude's doped up. And he's not even that big." He looked up at Emily. "Did you see it?"

She shook her head. "I was in the kitchen. I heard the ruckus, but by the time I came out he was just leaving, hightailing it down the lane."

"So you saw him? You could identify him?"

"There were enough videos of the fight. I'm sure the police will be able to identify him. Do you have anyone you should call?"

"Nah. I'm good. My folks are going to kill me as it is."

A pair of medics took over from Emily. She walked back to the entrance of the cafe shaken and concerned. "Henry, it didn't used to be like this."

He shook his head. "This wasn't normal. I've seen the odd push and shove in the park and an occasional mugging, but that was psycho. Is the boy all right?"

"He seemed lucid. No blurred vision. He wanted to leave. I think he should be in school and is in for a bit of trouble at home."

"Parents who don't know where their kids are, are probably too thick to notice the young man has a gash on his head. He was the worse, right?"

"Bumps and bruises for the rest. Surprised four of them couldn't defend themselves against a single attacker. They were big kids."

Henry smiled. "I didn't see it, but I can guess. These kids in the park are more likely to smoke weed than anything else. Fighting is the last thing they would want to do." He hugged his wife. "Relax. You're tense. The guy is gone. I don't think we'll see him again."

She looked up at him. "You didn't get a look at him, did you?"

"No. Why?"

"I didn't see him from the front, just the back, but I got the feeling I knew him from somewhere."

Chapter Fifteen

I was getting too hot. A couple of people had glanced at me over the past couple of hours like they thought they knew me. I disguised my hair, had picked up a horribly-priced pair of sunglasses from one of the carts along the boardwalk and had my hat pulled down low. But I couldn't disguise my height.

I had turned my phone off to conserve battery about half an hour after talking to Kent. Marty would be wondering about me. What in the hell was I going to do? Someone else killed - *killed* - Bart and I needed to figure out who. I needed to exploit Kent's friend on the inside. If I knew what the police knew, I could better understand why they found the case so compelling. Kent said he was going to call at noon. My source of time was the thing I had turned off. I went up to a hot dog vendor and ordered a dog and a drink.

"Buddy, have you got the time?"

He glanced at the sun. "About noon."

"You don't have a watch?"

"Sure do. It says about noon too. You want sauerkraut on this?"

"No, that's good." I paid him and took my *not* A-list food to the beach wall and sat looking at the ocean. Still hiding in plain sight. Like a tree. I turned on my phone and waited for the flood of text messages imploring me to turn myself in.

The first one through was from a number I didn't recognize.

"Your running, but your not hiding very well. We'll find U"

Hard to take a threat seriously when they can't distinguish "your" from "you're".

There were two more from Marty, each more desperate than the previous. One from Cathy telling me to call her and that she'd help and one from her asshole boyfriend Bernie. I didn't bother reading that one.

Cathy would help. Of that I had no doubt. We hadn't talked much, but she had my back 100% when Sweeney was trying to kill me a year and a half ago. I was stupid. If I'd pressed *those* charges, instead of just going for the case of Joel's murder, he'd still be in jail, I wouldn't be on the run, and I'd be having lunch right now with Favreau and Tom Hanks. A lunch a hell of a lot better than this.

Someone sat beside me. I avoided looking over in case they recognized me.

Wasn't necessary. It was Danny.

"Hey, Elle. What's shaking?"

"Jesus, mate. Lower your voice, okay? I'm on the lam,

remember?"

"Sure do. That's why I'm sitting beside you. Nothing sticks out more than a beautiful girl eating alone. That stuff you're eating will kill you, you know that, right?"

"We all die, Danny."

"Only crazy people want to accelerate the process."

"Maybe I'm crazy."

He laughed and shook his head. "No one in this entire fucking city is saner. Hey, did you see the new thing I put in my gig?"

I shook my head. "Been kinda distracted. What is it?"

"I've got this new puppy. A gorgeous black lab. I call him Damien which is funny because he's the sweetest, cuddliest animal you've ever met. So I hold him up and show the audience, walking around and letting the kiddies pet him. And some of the hot girls because, hey, guys and puppies, right? And then when I reach in my bag of tricks to pull out the bowling ball, I swap him for a very real looking stuffed dog. Nobody ever notices the switch because, you know, I'm fucking amazing. Then I juggle the puppy, bowling ball and running chainsaw and the crowd absolutely looses it. I finish by picking out a middle-aged woman and throwing the puppy at her. More than one thinks it's dead. I have had to pull the real deal out of the bag a couple of times now to stop a riot." He laughed. "Brilliant, no?"

I groaned and shook my head. "You're going to get arrested one of these days. The bag big enough for the puppy?"

"It is for now. This will only work for the next couple of months and then he's going to be too big. He loves it in there, though." He shifted on the wall, moving a smidgen closer. "So, I've got to get going back and earn some coin. What are you doing for the rest of the day, besides keeping your gorgeous head down?"

"I'm waiting for a call from that friend who has a friend in the police department in the Valley. He's trying to find out as much about the case as he can. If I know as much as the cops do, then maybe I can figure out why they're so damned intent on only looking at me for this."

"You trust him?"

"We worked together before and both of us suffered under Sweeney. He's a fellow Australian I've known for years."

"You didn't answer the question."

I thought about Kent. All he'd been through, still acting where he could and doing the best he could, and nodded. "Yeah, I do."

"Okay then. Have your phone call and come and see my puppy act." He reached over and gave me a side to side, brother type hug, hopped off the wall and wandered back to his setup.

And on cue, my phone rang. But it wasn't Kent.

"Hey, Charlie. I can't talk. I'm expecting a call."

"What? Where are you?"

"Seriously Charlie. I'm in the wild with no charger and limited talk time. I've got to go." I terminated the call and impatiently kicked at the wall with my heels, waiting for Kent.

The time on my phone was 12:17 when it rang.

"Ellie?"

"Kent, did you find out what I asked?"

"Wow. You charging that thing somewhere? I've got a ton of news."

"No, I turned off all the non-phone stuff. No Wi-Fi, location services, even turned off the mobile data. Voice only. And then I turned it off after I talked to you last. So give it up. What did you find out?"

"Stevie works in the homicide department as a records clerk. She's a good friend. I know what she tells me is true. And it doesn't look good."

I slid off the wall and sat in the sand, leaning back against it. "Tell me."

"Apparently Perkins is very conscious about the mistake he made with Joel's death, thinking it was a suicide when it wasn't. They discounted the suicide angle very quickly. They have your gun. You had a gun?"

"I've never had to really use it. It's more of a security blanket."

"Well they have it now, and ballistics match it to the bullet in Sweeney's head."

"So someone stole my gun."

"There's also the earring, a couple strands of long blonde hair and a witness who saw you leaving Bart's place the night he was killed."

"No." I closed my eyes and leaned my head against the wall. "Not possible. I was here. I was home."

"You're home now? Are you crazy?"

"No, I'm not home now." I chewed my lip. "Tell me about the witness."

"An Indian lady visiting a friend walked past the house on the way to the bus stop and saw you. She picked you out of a photo line-up."

"She's mistaken. My face is on half the billboards in town. Of course she picked me out. Casino Indian or Dell tech support Indian?"

"Dell."

"Okay. We all look alike, right?"

Kent laughed. "I'm just repeating what I heard. But it doesn't sound good, does it?"

"Shit, Kent." I looked at my phone. There was a new text message. "I've got to go. This battery isn't going to last forever. Thanks for all your help. I need to hunker down somewhere and think."

"No problem. Hey, you're not the only one fucked over by this. Charlie and I had a deal in this new movie he was making."

"They're still going to make it, right?"

"I don't know. Charlie's talking to them today about taking the director's role. I guess if he gets it I'm still in. If they go for someone else though, I'm pretty sure we're out."

"In the grand scheme of things in my life, that doesn't rate. Sorry. I've got to go." I hung up and looked at the text. It was from Cathy again. I sighed and called her

"Oh my God, Ellie?"

"Hey, Cathy. What's new?"

"Jesus, girl. What the hell have you gotten yourself into? The news on TV is getting worse."

"Deep shit, it would appear."

"Anything I can do to help?"

"I don't want to get you involved in this. I'm sure they're looking at my phone records and they'll be by to talk to you shortly. I don't want you to have to lie for me, so I'm not going to tell you where I am."

"You can't survive out there on your own. They're going to find you eventually."

"You're probably right. I've got a friend who is helping me out. For now, anyway. I'm sure the cops will be sitting on him soon."

"Who is he?"

"An old Australian mate. He's got a friend inside the police. A Stevie someone who works as records clerk. She's feeding him what the cops have and he's relaying it on to me. At least we'll be on a level playing field."

"Until they catch on. You trust him?"

"Second time in fifteen minutes I've been asked. Yes I do."

"But you don't trust me."

"I trust you more, but I'm not going to get you involved in this."

"You already have. Hang up Ellie. And tell me you're in Oxnard."

"I'll tell you first, then I'll hang up. I'm in Oxnard."

"Cool. I won't be lying when I tell them that you told me you were in Oxnard."

I laughed. "Cath, I love you. Too bad you're stuck with Bernie. I'd be by more often."

"Discussion for another day. Stay safe."

She hung up. I looked at the beach and considered my next steps. I needed to get the witness's name and contact her somehow. Clearly she really didn't see me at Bernie's place. I hadn't been there. I texted Kent, asking for the lady's name. I needed to meet her face to face.

I left the phone on for five minutes waiting for a reply, then turned it off. He had it or he didn't. Maybe he had to go through Stevie to find it out. That could take hours.

Someone had to break into my place to get my gun and some of my hair and an earring. The number of cameras at the entrances and exits of my apartment building rivaled a movie set. But I couldn't just walk in and ask security for a copy.

Plus, the cameras would prove I never left the place. I needed someone to get a copy for me, legitimately.

Henry and Emily's cafe was right beside the main entrance to my apartment building. Might be some help there.

Like a tree.

I walked in the cafe and tapped on the counter. Emily looked up from the cash register and smiled a work smile. "How may I help you?" She squinted. "Ellie? God, what are you doing here?"

"You have a place in the back we can talk? I don't really want to be noticed." Trade was light. She lifted the partition on the counter and ushered me through. Henry stepped to one side and opened the storeroom door, waited until we passed through and closed it behind us.

Emily hugged hard.

"Damn, you're going to crack a rib. Good to see you too." I extricate myself. "I don't dare stay long. I just need you to do one thing for me."

"Sure. Anything."

"I need to see the video from the security cameras on the front of my building. I can't ask the security people at the building, but maybe you can help."

"I can ask, but why?"

"Someone took things from my apartment. They needed those things to frame me. I need the cops to see if someone else went in there."

"How will they know who did it?"

"It would be anyone coming in who didn't live there."

She nodded. "I can do that. Not sure how, but we'll think of something."

"Easy. Tell them you had a break in. Nothing was taken, but someone broke in."

She shook her head. "I'll see what I can do. When would this have happened, though? It would have been while you were out, which makes it daytime, and honey, we're open every day. Would be kind of hard to have a break-in while we're here."

I deflated. "Shit. Sorry to bug you."

"No, no. Hon. We'll think of something. Anything. Anything for you. This whole thing is a crock of bullshit."

"Did you by any chance see me on my balcony the night before last?"

"No. I could say I did."

"I'm not going to get you in trouble. Appreciate the thought though."

"So what do I do with the video when I get it?"

I smiled and took her hands. "You won't get it. The police will get it and I have a friend working inside the police station. Or a friend of a friend. She can get a look at it and maybe feed some info to the cop leading this investigation. I've got to try something."

"We'll figure it out. Henry is good at this kind of thing. Where are you going to stay tonight?"

I looked around. "Is there a back way out of here? I shouldn't put you in any more danger. Harboring a fugitive is a felony."

Emily took me to the service door. "I don't care about harboring a fugitive. You're innocent."

"That's very kind of you, but the cops don't think so, and that's all that counts right now." I opened the door to the back and looked out, poking an eye around the corner. "If anyone asks if you know where I am, tell them I told you I was going to Oxnard."

"Why are you going to Oxnard?"

I smiled. "Em, You just tell them what I told you. Where I end up could be anywhere."

"Ah, gotcha. Oxnard. Lovely this time of year. The strawberries are delightful."

"I'm allergic. Be safe. Be careful and text me when you get the video thing sorted out, okay?"

"I will. Be careful."

"Thanks. You too. But seriously be careful. Perkins has a bee in his bonnet. And once he gets an idea, he never lets it go."

Chapter Sixteen

Emily came out of the storeroom alone. Henry looked in as she exited. "Where'd Ellie go?"

"Oxnard." She laughed. "Or so she said. Although I think she'll stay away from the strawberries."

"What was that all about?" He wiped his hands on his apron and locked the storeroom door. "She okay?"

"I don't think so." Emily patted her husband on the arm. "She wants us to get the security footage from the apartment building in the cop's hands."

"There's a good reason for this, I expect."

"Things at the scene of Bart's murder came from her place and it had to be taken when she wasn't there."

"And she wants us to look at the video? Why us?"

"No, just get it to the cops. She says she's got a contact inside the department who can get it in front of the right people. They can check who came in while she wasn't there against the residents of the place."

"She's got a contact inside the police department? Seriously?" Henry shook his head and turned to serve the two customers who just walked in.

"Who has contacts? That wouldn't be Ellie Bourke, would it?" The man held out his badge. "I'm Sergeant Perkins and this is Sergeant Stanfield."

"Ellie who?"

Perkins smiled. "She has breakfast here most mornings. She lives next door. You know who I'm talking about. Have you seen her lately?"

Henry hesitated and Emily jumped in. "Sure. Lots of times. Like you said, she's around her all the time. She was here for breakfast yesterday. If you can call it that. Small bowl of fruit and a piece of dry toast. Is that any meal for a growing young girl?"

"Her mobile phone was located in this general area this morning. Have you seen her today?"

Henry looked at Emily and cleared his throat.

Emily jumped in again. "Yes. She stopped by to say she was heading north. A friend in Oxnard, I think."

Perkins opened his notebook. "Oxnard you say?" He scribbled a note. "And when did she say that?"

"She stopped by this morning. About an hour ago." Emily hoped they couldn't tell she was lying. She hoped Ellie was far enough away right now that they wouldn't bump into her by mistake.

And maybe two birds could be killed with one stone. "Listen, officers, we've been having problems around here for the last week or so and some punks have been harassing customers. There's a security video on the apartment building next door. Could I get you to have a look at it and we can see if the guys show up on it?"

Perkins looked out the door at the apartment next door, then flipped through some pages in his book. "That would be the apartment Ellie Bourke lives in, correct?"

"I believe it might be."

"Well, ma'am, if you've been having problems with the local teens, I'd suggest you call your local police department. The closest station is in Marina del Rey." He pointed at his partner. "Stanfield and I are from the Devonshire precinct in the Valley."

"Oh. Well, okay."

Perkins fished a card from his shirt pocket and handed it to Henry who handed it to Emily. "If you see Ellie, or hear from her, please give us a call, okay? Remember it's a felony to aid a fugitive." He nodded at Henry and Emily and made his exit.

Henry waited until the two policemen were well out of the cafe and had moved down the boardwalk. "Is she still in the storeroom?"

Emily shook her head. "She made it out the back about five minutes before they showed up. I told her we'd get the security footage to the police, but if they're in the Valley I'm not sure how we can pull that off."

"You think she actually went to Oxnard?" Perkins walked along the boardwalk looking at tall blondes.

"I think she told everyone she was going to Oxnard so they'd tell *us* she was going to Oxnard. Ten bucks she's nowhere near Oxnard."

"No bet, kiddo."

"So we going to walk along the beach for the rest of the morning?"

Perkins watched a bikini skate by. "For a bit, maybe. Keep an eye peeled for a tall blonde."

Stanfield laughed. "That's like saying keep an eye peeled for sand. The place is polluted with them."

"This kind of pollution I can live with.

The Killer sat on the beach wall watching the police leave the cafe. "The noose is tightening, bitch. Better hope they find you before I do." He slid off the wall and followed the police as they walked along the beach. "Piggy one and piggy two. You better hope I find her before you do," he muttered. "Because if you fuck up my plans, you're both next on the list."

He followed about fifteen yards behind the plainclothes police as they looked for Ellie. "You boys really think she's going to be out in the open like this? I've been down here almost an hour and I haven't seen hide nor hair of her." He snorted. "Fucking lazy twats."

He walked closer until he was no more than a couple of steps behind them. He sniffed. He could smell their piggy-ness. And it fueled a rage. He bounced his jaw muscles, clenching and unclenching them in rapid succession. He was within reach of them. It would take less than a second to knock the fat one on the ground, get his gun and shoot them both.

He almost walked into their backs as they stopped to talk to a juggler. He blinked, took a deep breath and peeled off.

"Calm down, old boy. You almost fucked up the whole plan." He stood back, leaning against a palm tree as the cops talked.

Perkins held out a picture of Ellie. "Have you seen this woman, sir?"

"Dude, you're driving away business. I've got a right to make a living, man."

Stanfield looked around. The thinnish crowd walked by with no intention of stopping and the juggler wasn't even set up. "What's your name?"

"I don't have to tell you."

"No, you don't. But if we think you're obstructing our investigation we can arrest you and take you into custody at our station. In the Valley. It could take hours to get through all this, so why don't you just help out a bit and get this over with. What's your name?"

He looked at the two cops, weighing his options. "Gerald. Gerald Fitzpatrick."

"Can I see your ID?"

Danny shook his head. "I don't have any ID. I don't need any. Haven't for years."

Perkins shook his head. "Right. Have you seen this girl around here today?"

"You're fucking with me, right?" He pointed to a billboard on the side of a building. "She's on every billboard in sight. Ellie Bourke. Australian goddess. Of course I've seen her. I see her every day."

"I think the funny man wants a trip into the Valley, Perk. Do you want to cuff him, or should I?"

"Wait, wait, wait. Gents. Sorry. I have a natural distrust of authority. Comes from spending so many hours on this beach. Look around you. This is about as anti-establishment as you can get."

"So, about Ellie? When was the last time you saw her?"

Danny looked up and down the boardwalk. Others who weren't friends of hers would speak the truth. He couldn't protect her this way and he couldn't keep an eye out for her while in jail. "I had breakfast with her. This morning."

"Where?"

Danny pointed to the cafe. "Over there. But don't bother wasting your time looking for her around here. She's left."

"Gone to Oxnard, right?" Perkins flipped his book closed.

"You're psychic, dude. How did you know?"

"Miss Bourke has a remarkable circle of friends who are willing, it would appear, to do anything to help her evade detection. She's not in Oxnard, on the way to Oxnard, or planning to go to Oxnard. Although I do admire you all for sticking up for her. Listen to me carefully. This is how it's going to go. If you see, smell, hear or in any other way interact with Miss Bourke you will notify me immediately." Perkins handed Danny his card. "And immediately means you drop whatever outlandish props you happen to be juggling at the time, pull out your phone and call me without hesitation."

Danny shook his head. "No way dude." He held up his hands. "Don't arrest me or nothing, but I don't actually have a mobile phone. And I don't have a phone in my apartment. Don't believe in them."

"Don't believe in phones? It's not like we're talking about

vampires, or alien abduction. It's just a fucking phone."

Danny shook his head. "No way. Can eavesdrop, track location, all kinds of things. I don't have one."

"So, smart guy, drop a quarter in the pay-phone over at the corner and call me from there. Because if I find out you're keeping her below the radar, you'll be going to jail."

"Chillax, man. Got it." He stuffed the card in his back pocket. "You'll be the first I call."

"Right you will, Mr. Fitzpatrick."

"My friends call me Fitzie." Danny smiled. You found fun where you could.

"Well, Fitzie, be smart, okay?"

Danny watched them walk away, showing Ellie's picture and taking notes. "Fitzie. I like Fitzie."

"Your name isn't Fitzie though. Isn't it Danny something? Hey, I'm looking for Ellie. You seen her around?" Kent stuck out his hand. "Kent Williams. An acting friend of the tall lady."

Danny slowly stood and took his hand. "An acting friend standing in until the real friend comes along?"

"Funny guy. You seen her today?"

"Oh, yeah. I saw you with her yesterday morning. Breakfast. You and another smaller guy."

"Yeah. Charlie Bates. Anyway, nice meeting you and all, and have you seen Ellie around?"

Danny looked at the receding backs of the two cops. "This morning. She said she was going to Oxnard, but just to throw the fuzz off her tracks. I think. She doesn't have her car and her face is plastered everywhere, so I don't see how she can get anywhere."

"Kinda hard to miss a tall, thin long-haired piece of work like her."

"Actually, that describes half the girls around here. They're all from the same cookie-cutter. It's short now."

"Short? She's not short. Too much pot man. You're making no sense."

"No, her hair is short. Cut it almost all off. Really butch looking."

"Damn. Really? Shame. Loved it long." He cocked his head. "Really? When did she cut it? It was long last night at the premiere. When would she have had time?"

"So like it had to be between the premiere thing and breakfast this morning and it's really, *really* short now. Didn't recognize her."

"She color it too?"

"Nah, I don't think so. What was left was still blonde."

Kent looked up and down the boardwalk, as if he might suddenly spot her. "So she's *not* going to Oxnard, or she *is* going to Oxnard? You weren't too clear on that."

Danny sniffed and shrugged and started looking at his juggling paraphernalia. He had work to get to. This guy was holding him up. "Look, Kenny."

"Kent."

"Right. She told me to say she was going to Oxnard. Maybe it's a double twist, telling everyone where she's going so no one will believe she's going there, but then going anyway. Or maybe she's hanging out locally, sleeping on a park bench and living it rough. Why do you care?"

"Why? Why do I care? I've known her since we both acted

together in Australia. She's a very good friend. I'm concerned for her well-being. How the hell do you know her? You just mooch off her, caging free breakfasts whenever you can."

Danny took a step back. "Whoa, dude. Dial it back a bit. Appreciate you're a good friend. I've only known her for three months and yeah, she feeds me on occasion. But we're still close. Like brother and sister close. I'm concerned about her too, but she's not a baby. She's smart, she's strong and she knows what she's doing."

"Really doubt that."

"What?"

"That she's strong or knows what she's doing."

"Trust me. She's strong. All that training for the movie? She was telling me about the hand-to-hand combat training she got from some ex-Navy Seal. She's hard as a rock." He cleared his throat. "And I've got to assume she knows what she's doing. There's no other reason for her to be out here and not talking to the cops about this bullshit."

"What, you don't think she did it?"

Danny shook his head. "I thought you said you knew her. No fucking way, man. You think she did?"

Kent shrugged. "I assumed so. Sweeney *was* a dick, and he screwed her over big time. With him getting out of the slammer I figured she just snapped and did him. Wouldn't put it past her."

"You really don't know her, man."

"We have been out of touch for a while. If you see her, let her know I'm looking for her. Just want to help."

"Okay, I gotta get set up here. People expect me to do a show at 1:00 and I'm running a little late."

Kent shook his hand again and Danny watched him walk up the boardwalk in the same direction the cops had gone about fifteen minutes earlier. "Ellie, hon, you better keep your head really low." He reached into his satchel and scratched his puppy on the crown of its head, getting a lick as a reward. "Damien, dude. You ready to freak out some nice little old ladies?"

The Killer's frustration level reached dangerous levels. He needed to vent or the pressure would cause internal damage. He was sure of it. He watched the cops looking for Ellie and cursed her for going off grid. He had a fool-proof way of tracking her. Had it locked. Could dial her in to within thirty feet, easy. And she somehow found out and neutralized it.

"You'll pay, bitch, when the time comes. You'll pay."

An old, shabby bag-lady in about six jackets approached him for something and the smell was overpowering. "Back off, slag. Get a fucking job."

She muttered something he couldn't hear, spat at his feet and turned to walk away.

He grabbed her by the arm, held her close to him and spoke in a low growl. "Hey, bitch. Big mistake. Fuck off and get out of my sight. Next time you see me you'll be looking up through water."

He pushed her away and continued his search for Ellie.

Chapter Seventeen

I knew I was only three or four blocks from Marina del Rey, the marina of the moderately wealthy, but my surroundings didn't reflect that at all. I wandered inland from Venice Beach. The streets were narrow and the quality of the neighborhood diminished rapidly. I saw more homeless people than I expected to see this close to affluence. It was disturbing. I had no idea.

But there was nothing I could do about it now. I had to find out what was going on. I ducked into a back alley off Pacific and sat against a wall. An old guy scavenged through trash bins looking for either bottles to return for money for food, or for food. I had almost $300 in my pocket. I could give some of it to him, but I had no idea how long I was going to be on the street.

I turned on my phone. More battery was dead than alive. I needed to get this charged soon. Or something.

I called Kent. An update on the goings on would be good. He answered almost immediately.

"Ellie, that you? You in Oxnard?"

I smiled. "If that's what people are saying, it must be true. I called to ask you about your contact in the police department. Is she reliable?"

"Yeah. Why?"

"The witness thing. No way a person saw me there. I wasn't there."

"Well, that's what she said. The witness, I mean. Stevie told me she read the witness statement and it was unequivocal. Saw you, identified you from a photo line up without hesitation. You tell me you're not there, then I guess I have to believe you, but someone looking very much like you was there. Close enough the witness thought it was you."

"But it wasn't me. It's like they're hanging all of this on a single witness." I slumped against the wall and batted away some flies. "I need to meet her."

"Yeah, I saw your text, but no way. You'd have to turn yourself in. Let me find out more."

"Can you get her address?"

He paused before answering. "That would be considered tampering with a witness. Not really a good idea."

"What the hell have I got to lose? They're stringing me up as it is. It can't get any worse. Might actually help, for all you know."

"You're right, it couldn't get much worse." He exhaled. "Okay.

I'll see what I can do. No guarantees though, and if you go ahead with this, my name isn't attached."

"Yeah, sure. Just find her for me, okay?" I hung up. I was getting nowhere. Every step I took put me in a worse situation. I had to find a way out of this.

I was about to turn off my phone to save battery when it rang, startling me. I dropped it. "Shit." I scrambled and retrieved it from the sandy ground. It was like an inland beach here. I looked at the number. It looked familiar. "Hello?"

"It's Charlie, Ellie. Thank God I caught you. Where are you?"

"Oxnard."

There was a pause. "I don't think so. A warrant has been served against the phone company. I had to turn over all your call records and triangulate your location. You've been clever, haven't you, keeping your phone off? The last time I triangulated you, you were near the Venice Fish Pier. I'm looking at my call details right now and the cell site you took this call on is the one northwest of Marina del Rey. You're still in the general area. You're being foolish. They're going to come asking me to triangulate you again. I can't refuse; someone else will do it if I don't, anyway. And if I do catch the task, I can't feed them false information. They *will* find you. You're much better off turning yourself in and dealing with it straight up."

"I think I'm too far gone now. But thanks for the phone tip. I'll have to do something about that. Thanks for the call and the concern, Charlie, but I've got to go." I hung up.

Shit. I needed to get a new number.

Still no chance to turn off my phone. Marty called.

"Hey, Marty. What's new?"

"Jesus. I've had cops here three times now. They think I'm hiding you somewhere. Call them and tell them I've had nothing to do with this, would you? My wife is actually starting to think I've spirited you away somewhere to avoid the police."

"Are you kidding? Sorry Mar. This is out of control now. Get them to polygraph you or something. I can't talk long. The police are tracking my phone." I had a thought. "Wait, Marty, before you go, can you get me a shitload of money?"

"No. Wait, why? How much is a shitload?"

"Hundred grand or so. I need to get out of the country. I can't fly and I can't use anything needing identification. But if I can sneak into Mexico I should be able to get a flight back to Australia. Once I'm there I'm clear."

"Oh, that would be monumentally stupid. Not only can I not get you any money, I wouldn't if I could. Turn yourself in. I can't stress strongly enough how important it is for you to turn yourself in. If Perkins and his what's-his-name partner come by again I swear I'm divorced. And I can't afford to give her half of everything. If for no other reason than my financial security, turn yourself in."

I laughed. "She's not going to divorce you. You take too good care of her."

"Don't bet on it. If the cops talk to me again, and the odds are heavily in favor of that, what do I tell them? Oxnard?"

"Why not. Maybe they'll really believe it. Or maybe they'll think I'm trying to fake them out and discount it, and then I'll go there, free in the knowledge nobody is looking for me there."

"Don't tell me anything."

"Tell them I'm going to Tustin. Tustin is a beautiful place. Might stop at Disneyland on the way."

"Take care of yourself Ellie, and stop being a dummy. I've got to go. A cop car just rolled up the driveway."

"And I've been talking too long. They're triangulating me. Did you know that? I've got to shut this off and get a new number. It's been great knowing you Marty. Sorry to put you through this. Talk to you later. Or maybe not."

I hung up just as he answered. But there wasn't much he could do for me now. And there was no point dragging him further into the quagmire I was in. I needed to get some cash out of the bank and then I'd do like I told him. In to New Mexico, sneak in to the *old* Mexico, see if I could get home from there. No idea how I'd do it, but there was no way I was going to be nailed for Sweeney's murder.

But once again, as I was turning off my phone, another call came in.

"I can't talk long Jacob. You guys are triangulating me and I really don't want to be found right now."

"Not now? When then? What is it you actually think you're accomplishing? Every minute you're not talking to the police voluntarily the hunt ratchets up. I like you Ellie. I really like you. And I know you're smarter than this. Go to the nearest police station and tell them to call me. I'll make sure you are treated very fairly. I'm sure a self-defense defense could be used here."

"Jacob, I didn't do it. I wasn't anywhere near there. Read my fucking lips. I. Didn't. Kill. Sweeney. I had nothing to do with killing

Sweeney. Get the security video from my apartment and see who came in while I was away and doesn't live there. The place has cameras at the doors and each lift lobby. I'm sure you'll find someone who doesn't belong, but attached somehow to Sweeney, in there when I wasn't. Trust me, Jacob. I'm not bullshitting you."

I heard him sigh on the other end of the phone. "The evidence says you did it. I'm not on this case. I can suggest the homicide boys look at the video, but they really don't have any reason too. The evidence is just that strong."

"We're getting nowhere. I've got to go. I've talked too long and stayed in the same place too long. I appreciate your friendship, but wish you believed in me a bit more. Good-bye Jacob."

I leaned my head against the wall and closed my eyes. I was hungry and thirsty. I needed to go out in the open again, something I really didn't want to do. The sun beat on the small section of wall warming me up. My eyes were heavy. I had almost no sleep last night and it was catching up to me. So was the stress.

The 10% battery life warning popped up on my screen. Kent called back as I was turning it off.

"Did you get the witness's name?"

"Which one? There are two now. A second person has come forward saying they saw you there."

Oh, crap. "I wasn't. Seriously. Unless I'm sleep walking and driving and killing, and that's unprecedented."

"Good defense, though."

"Jesus, Kent. I didn't do it. I did not do it. Don't tell me you believe the cops too?"

"Well, Charlie and I were talking and you've got a perfect motive for it. God knows there are enough people who hated the guy, but yours was a special kind of hate."

"I didn't hate him. I despised him. I loathed him. And maybe I felt a tiny bit sorry for him being such a loser, but hate is a word I don't use often."

"I hated him. That broken foot trick really fucked me up, so I completely understand if you did it. And if there's anything I can do to help you, let me know."

"I gotta go, Kent. You're pissing me off right now, sorry. Can't talk anymore. They're going to find me."

" 'They'? Who?"

"I'm being triangulated. Talked to Charlie a few minutes ago and he said the cops have a warrant to triangulate me. Could be happening right now, so I've got to shut off my phone. Battery is almost dead anyway."

"Get one of those battery life extenders. Takes AAA batteries and plugs into the charging socket on the bottom. Works a treat. And Charlie can do that?"

"The techs at his company can. Don't know how he does it. And I don't care. I have to hang up."

And I did.

The battery extender was a good idea. And I needed to find a place where I could get a pre-pay phone.

And my phone rang again.

"Jesus, Kent. What now?"

"You didn't give me a chance to finish. There's more evidence.

Against you."

"What? What possible evidence could be worse than what they have now?"

"Stevie tells me there was evidence under Sweeney's fingernails. Skin tissue matching yours under his nails."

"Oh now that's completely impossible. I haven't seen him in over a year."

"Hey, I'm just telling you what Stevie told me, and she's reading it from the case file."

I shook my head and stood. "That makes absolutely no sense. Now I really do have to go. Don't call me again, okay? I'll call you if I need anything."

And I hung up and turned off the phone before it rang again.

When I was a kid, playing hide-and-seek with my friends, I almost always won by doubling back and hiding in places they already looked. It would probably work again. They triangulated me to the beach and I wasn't there when they looked, so I'd head back there. There were a dozen different mobile phone shops along the beach, too. One of them would have this battery life extender Kent talked about, surely.

I walked down 24th toward the beach with a combination of confidence and caution. Not an easy trick.

But I think I pulled it off. I wasn't catching any untoward attention. The smell of sausages and sauerkraut started an autonomous stomach growl and salivation. I had to eat, right?

"Could I get a Polish sausage with mustard and hot sauce? And a diet cola." I gave the guy a twenty, took the change and my food and made my way to the wall to sit. Again.

And I had a visitor in less than one bite.

Danny leaned in and whispered. "Ellie. What in the fuck are you doing here? Are you crazy?"

"Like a fox. The cops have been by here, right?"

"Yeah." He laughed. "I told them my name was Gerald Fitzpatrick. And you were in Oxnard. I don't think they believed me."

"You certainly look like a Fitzpatrick."

"I don't think they believed you went to Oxnard."

I smiled and leaned in close. "So maybe that's where I should go."

He nodded and cocked an eyebrow. "Hang on here a sec."

He ran back to the juggling set up and grabbed something out of his kit bag and ran back. He dropped the something - a small Black Lab puppy - in my lap. "Say hi to Damien."

The dog stood on my lap with his back legs and tried to crawl up my front as I held the bunned sausage out of his reach. "Hi Damien. Piss off. Danny, get this mutt off my lap. I'm trying to eat here."

He scooped the puppy and held him in his lap, scratching him behind his left ear. "Mutt? Hell no. No mutt. This is a beautiful purebred dog. Aren't you, Damien?"

"Fine. I'll admit he's a beautiful dog. Just keep him away from my food or his life is in danger."

"You just came back for the sausage? It's not that good."

"I need a couple of things for my phone. And maybe you can help me out."

"Anything I can do, you know that."

I gave him $100. "Can you get me one of those battery extender things for an iPhone, and enough batteries to fill it? And I need a pre-pay phone."

He pocketed the money and handed me Damien. "Deal."

He strode off with purpose while Damien fought for my food. "I say you're a mutt with poor manners and no finesse." I leaned down as I scolded him and he licked the end of my nose. "Great. A cute, lovable mutt. Don't get any ideas. This is mine." It didn't take long before I relented, sharing a piece with him and tearing off a piece for me.

I was down to a nubbin and a piece of bun when Danny came back with a smile and a plastic bag. "You made friends?"

"Damien and I are best of buddies, as long as I have food to share with him. He's going to be way too big for your act, he keeps eating this way."

"Oh, what have you fed the poor pup? He's going to be farting all day."

I laughed. A nice change of pace. "Any luck?"

He pulled a box out of the bag with some flourish. "Battery extender. Adds about ten hours to the life of your phone. Batteries are in the bag."

"Excellent." I rubbed my hands on my pant legs. "Pre-pay?"

He smiled and pulled a small box out of the bag. "Pre-loaded with about $40 credit. Am I good, or what?"

"Double-excellent. You were great, Danny. I'll be seeing you later."

"Next time I'm in Oxnard I'll look you up."

I grinned and pecked him on the cheek. "Take your fucking dog off my lap, Danny, before I steal it."

He scooped Damien. "Make sure the battery thing works, okay?

Hate for you to be out in the wild and find out when you go to use it it's a piece of shit."

"Good point." I took the cigarette pack sized battery pack out of the box and populated it with the AAA batteries. I plugged the cable in the base of my iPhone and turned it on. The battery showed it was charging and the display on the battery pack read 99%.

"Looks good, Danny. Thanks." A text message came through from a three digit number. I showed the phone to Danny. "You ever see a message from a number like this?"

"I haven't had a phone in three years. I've got no idea what it is."

I opened the message and read:

"You need to turn yourself in now. You may be in danger yourself. If you've got a shred of sense, go to your nearest police station and turn yourself in."

Chapter Eighteen

Cathy pushed her empty plate back. "As usual. Delicious. You're trying to fatten me up."

Bernie, her long time boyfriend, smiled and looked up from the paper. "Got to get you ready to be a mommy."

"Not for a while yet. And when it happens I'll be getting fat enough all on my own. What are you reading?"

"There's a thing here about the Sweeney case. The prosecution are laying out all their evidence. I don't know what their deal is, but it looks bad for your friend."

"Let me see." Cathy grabbed the paper and pulled it across the table. "What are they saying about my Ellie?"

She read for a couple of minutes, then swore.

"What did I tell you?" Bernie sipped at his glass of white. "Not good."

The Killer giggled. He had her on the ropes. And he knew how to find her when he needed to. "You can run, but you can't hide. I am the cat and you are the mouse." He looked at his watch. He was a little bit behind schedule.

The sun was low on the Pacific. He remembered days when he played in the ocean, when the only concern in his life was whether or not the waves would be good. He grit his teeth and inhaled through his nose. But it would be right again. He had to get the problems out of his life. That's what he was told. Remove the problems from his life and his life would return to whole. That's what he was told.

Sweeney, by far the largest problem. The shit Sweeney did to him was beyond bad. It made his stomach turn, thinking of that conflict.

And he just took it.

No more.

Ellie was complicit, and she had to be next. The fun and games were just starting with her. They started with her years ago, but he just realized it in the last day or so.

He rubbed his eyes. He'd lost count of the hours he'd gone without sleep. "But it doesn't fucking matter." He popped a pill and chewed down hard, crushing it between molars. He worked up some saliva and swallowed the paste.

He looked at the Altoids case from whence that pill came. There were enough left.

He blinked hard and scrubbed his face and looked out over the

Pacific. The sun was low on the horizon, bathing the beach-goers in a golden suffused light. "The magic hour. My ass." He looked around at the skaters and skateboarders, the muscle-heads and the buskers. All of them sunny and sweaty and happy. "Fuck them. Fuck them all."

A skater rolled past in a ponytail and white bikini top and cut-off jeans and yelled back, "Lighten up, man."

His nostrils flared and he started to stand then checked himself. "Priorities. Happy, happy. Joy-fucking-joy."

The same shabby, over-dressed homeless slag approached him. "Are you all right?"

"Of course not. Why, do I look all right? Fuck off and leave me alone."

She looked at him, narrowed her eyes and opened her mouth to speak.

"I said fuck off so fuck yourself right off before I add you to the list you scabby piece of shit."

She shook head and muttered something under her breath and went back to patrolling the beach for bottles and lost valuables.

A few skaters passing him at the time turned and watched the interaction.

"You all can fuck off." He stood and stared after them and forced himself to remember what he was doing on the beach. He took a deep breath and shook his head. "Ah, fuck." He looked around. She wasn't there. Not obviously anyway. He knew for a fact she was around here not long ago. He needed to flush her out.

Cathy closed the paper. "No way. She didn't do it."

"Admittedly, you're biased."

"No, this isn't just a feeling. I know she didn't do it. No possible way."

Bernie pointed at the paper with his glass of wine. "You can read, right? Her gun, her hair, a witness placing her at the scene."

Cathy nodded. "And the earring, described as a - oh where is it." She opened the paper and scanned for the paragraph. "Here it is. '...*a large hoop earring with feathers hanging from the bottom of the hoop.*' " She looked up at her boyfriend and smiled. "Let's hope her phone is turned on."

Ellie picked up on the first ring. "Cathy? I can't really talk. I'm on a bus to Oxnard."

Cathy laughed. "I can hear gulls behind you. I can prove you didn't do it."

"How?"

"The earring they found at the scene of the crime. Did you ever hear which one was planted there?" Cathy was leaning forward, elbows on her knees, talking low.

"Just that it was one of mine."

"The big hoop with the dangly feathers."

"Really?"

"The ones you hate."

"Oh, Cathy, I wouldn't say I *hated* them."

"You hated them. You wore them the day I gave them to you and you never wore them again. A girl notices things like that."

"I'm not sure how much it can help, but thanks."

"Ellie, listen to me. There are no circumstances in which I could imagine you killing Sweeney, as much as you probably wanted to."

"I've never wanted to kill anybody. Look, sweetie, I appreciate this, but I can't talk long. I'm on my way to Tustin."

"What happened to Oxnard?"

"Allergic to strawberries."

"Ah, that. Seriously, you wouldn't have worn those earrings for any reason. I am more than willing to testify to that in your defense."

"I don't think there's going to be a trial."

Cathy put her phone on speaker and waved Bernie over. "What was that?"

"I appreciate the efforts, Cath, but I've got to get out of town. For whatever reason, someone has locked this case against me up tight. Somebody hates me for reasons I can't understand and has set me up for Sweeney's death. Makes sense they would hate Sweeney and have tied me to him. Whatever, whoever, I'm screwed. I've got to hang up now. They're triangulating my calls."

Cathy looked at the phone. "She hung up. I'm worried for her."

Bernie shook his head. "Nothing more we can do."

"Sure there is. I'm going to make some calls and see if I can help sort this out."

"You'll just make it worse."

She snorted. "Thanks for your confidence. If you don't want to help, don't."

Charlie looked at the time and cursed the fact he was working the night shift. A fax came through on the legal intercept machine. He pulled it and cursed again. Another request to locate Ellie's phone. He recognized the number. It was an easy task. He'd done it so often that a job which would take a green engineer ten minutes, he could do in one.

He looked at the results on the screen, printed them and turned to fax the results back to the police department.

Then hesitated.

His phone rang, and he placed the paper on the machine and answered. "Bates."

"Master Bates, how the hell are you. Where are you? There's things to see, people to do. You heard back from Saul yet?"

"Kent? I'm working nights."

"Still working? Really? I figured you'd be grabbing the director's job out from under Sweeney's still warm carcass. What are you thinking with, mate?"

"Hey, I just did a locate on Ellie. I hate that I'm helping the cops."

"Yeah, but at least you can give her a heads up."

Charlie nodded. "True. Not much of one, though, and I'm fucked if anyone makes a connection between us."

"Tell me, I'll put a word in her ear so there's no electronic trail back to you."

"Hey, not a bad idea. Get her moving." He picked up the paper. "She's somewhere in the Venice area. Still. You'd think she'd learn."

"Somewhere? Anything more specific, mate?"

"She's serving off the sector facing the beach, due south, on the site on top of Gold's Gym on the corner of Hampton and Sunset."

"Dude, really? That's the best you can do?"

Charlie smiled. "With the technology on hand, yeah. Not that big of an area. And she can't be that hard to find." He looked up at the clock. "Look, I can't hold off sending this to the police any longer. Do what you can. I'll catch up with you later."

Kent opened the map on his phone and looked at the area Charlie described. He was right. It wasn't large, but it was large enough. It would take hours to find her, and he didn't have hours. The cops would be there soon and they had more manpower than he did. He was well south of that area, still on the beach, but closer to the fishing pier. He started jogging north along Ocean Front Walk, the boardwalk. He passed the cafe he had breakfast at with Charlie and Ellie and passed the skate park. In his minds eye he was starting to get into the rough geographical area served by that site. His foot hurt. He slowed to a fast walk and started paying more attention to the people around him. Still too many tall blondes, but, he noted, not many with really short hair. He opened his phone and called her number. It went directly to voicemail.

"Shit. Where are you Ellie? Where the hell are you?" He continued walking as far north as the site would cover, at least in his estimation. He started zigzagging across the streets zeroing in on Gold's Gym.

Nothing and nobody. He scrubbed his face and made his way back to the beach.

Perkins looked at the received fax. "What in the hell is she doing? So much for Oxnard. The berries are great this time of year."

"Why? What's she doing?"

"Back in Venice. Or still in Venice. Hard to say if she actually left."

Stanfield picked up is notebook and phone and stood. "Let's go. Flush her out."

Perkins looked at his young partner. "We pick up a bite on the way. I was going to send uniforms for this. I haven't eaten since lunch."

Stanfield looked at Perkins gut. "You'll live. I'm sure you can live off that for days."

"We're stopping for food, kid. Pollo Loco maybe. Chicken and biscuits."

Stanfield shook his head. "Give me the keys. The last time you tried to eat while you were driving you almost killed the both of us and a fat lady walking a Chihuahua."

Perkins tossed him the keys and stood. "Then let's go."

"Call the locals?"

"I'm thinking we keep this low-key for now. I don't want an army looking for her. She'll spook. You ever heard the story of the old bull and the young bull?"

"Another fucking story?"

Perkins retrieved his gun from his top drawer and slid it into his shoulder holster and pulled on his suit coat. "Yeah. Another fucking story. New bull is placed in a pasture with an old bull and about fifty cows. The old bull is standing on the top of the hill looking over his harem. The young bull trots up the hill and joins him. 'Hey, look at all those cows,' says the young bull. 'Why don't we run down the hill and screw one of them?' The old bull snorted and replied, 'Why don't we *walk* down the hill and fuck *all* of them?' " Perkins looked at Stanfield as he slid into the passenger seat. "Let's not spook her. I doubt she's a real risk to society. We walk in there and take it easy, no uniforms, no brass bands."

"Your call. Hope this doesn't turn into a shit fight. Your career is almost over. It'll stain the rest of mine for many, many years if you're wrong."

"You're assuming you'll have a career if I'm wrong." Perkins laughed. "You worry too much, kiddo. Let life unfold and embrace the strangeness."

"You been down in Topanga getting a contact high?"

Perkins looked over at his partner. "And I've got the munchies. Pull in here. Go through the drive-through. Get me a couple of chicken breasts and a light lemonade. Extra napkins."

Stanfield drove as Perkins ate, washing the skinless chicken down with the sugar-free lemonade. "Is that your idea of a diet?"

"Shut up and drive. It's getting dark. I want at least a little bit of daylight left when we get there."

The darkness enveloped the Killer like a warm cape, making him as invisible as his prey. He thought he spotted her twice now, slowly walking along the back streets. He lost her, if it was her, on a corner both times.

His nerves thrummed like a telephone line in a high wind. He had to resist from thinking beyond the kill. She was next. She was the only thing he should be thinking about. He bit his lip hard enough to draw blood. He licked it, tasting the salty warmth and sensing, more than feeling, the sharp pain. It kept an edge on. Kept him alert more than any pill could.

The cat and mouse game had to end. It was going on too long. He'd been exposed too long. Someone would eventually notice him wandering in an apparently random pattern around the same streets since before noon. He needed to wrap things up quickly.

Or he needed to stop and sleep.

But sleep would just reset the hunt, and he didn't want a reset. He was close. He could smell her. He was sure he could smell her. The meds sharpened his senses. The reduced visibility in the dark amped up the smell and hearing.

He could smell her around the next corner and could hear her talking with her fucking put-on Australian accent.

But she was never around the corner.

"Time for a drastic step." He blinked and sniffed. The street light's reflection off the face of his recently purchased pre-pay phone betrayed his tremor, almost strobe light in frequency.

He considered his approach for a few seconds, then typed. Ambiguity was the enemy. Directness was favored. His English teacher would have been proud:

"Ellie, why are you still alive? I should have killed you by now. But I haven't, which is, I guess, a testament to your Aussie toughness. Unless you want this to be your last sleep, I'd advise you finding a better hiding place than Venice Beach. The muscle-heads aren't going to save you. But it doesn't matter where you go, I can find you. Keep loking over you shoulder all you want, you won't see me coming. You'll be dead before you know what hit you."

He smiled and pressed the send button. "That should get the bitch moving. Just like hunting: Flush them out of the thicket and pick them off while they're running."

Chapter Nineteen

"...Keep loking over you shoulder all you want, you won't see me coming. You'll be dead before you know what hit you."

Seriously?

I'm looking around for a quiet place to spend the night before heading out of town and I get a message telling me to turn myself in, and then this one. "Keep loking over your shoulder". I'm supposed to take a death threat seriously when the twat can't even spell "looking"?

I sat down on a piece of cardboard in a lane near some dumpsters. Nothing smelled bad anymore. Remarkable how quickly I adapted to my surroundings. I caught a reflection of myself in the phone screen. I looked like hell. I bore absolutely no resemblance to the girl on the red carpet twenty-four hours earlier.

I looked at the message again. I couldn't resist. I replied with *"loking? Sorry, I don't understand what you're saying. Did you mean looking? How did you get this number?"*

I needed to shut down the phone. I was too exposed.

And I think I had a plan to get some cash. Marty needed to co-operate, but that was Marty. Mr. Nice Guy.

I was considering how best to word the request when I received another text.

"Fuck with me and your death will be long and slow. But trust me when I tell you you won't live out the night. Doesn't matter if you stay in Venice or go to Oxnard or Tustin, your dead."

Oh, Jesus. I replied:

"My dead what?"

He wouldn't get it, whoever it was. Then it dawned on me. Whoever this was they knew where I was, and where I had been telling people I was going.

Fuck.

I received a reply.

"That's going to earn you additional pain points. Framing you for Sweeney's suicide was a piece of piss. Making your death look like a legit suicide, including confession, will be fun."

Oh my God.

My phone rang and I jumped. "Shit, Kent. What the fuck?"

"You okay?"

"Scared the crap out of me. How did you know my phone was on?"

"What?"

"I just turned in a couple of minutes ago."

"Oh, I've been trying every fifteen minutes or so. You've got to ditch the phone. B-bad mojo hanging on to it."

"I've got a new one. Haven't got it out of the box yet."

"Get it done quickly and text me so we can stay in touch."

"What's the point in getting a new number if I give it to everyone? I'm trying to get out of the country. I don't want anyone attached to that. Shit I shouldn't even have told you that."

"What in the hell would you want get out of the country? You, running away? That's not the Ellie I know."

I cursed myself for opening my mouth. "Just idle thoughts Kent. I'll send you a postcard from Helsinki."

"Norway? Why would you go to Norway?"

I sighed. "Just kidding around, mate. Finland, by the way. And you're right. I'm not a runner. But I don't know how to fight this."

"Let me know how I can help."

"I don't think you can. I need to do this myself. Thanks for the updates. I don't need them anymore. I know I was framed."

"You can prove it? That's great news."

I had talked long enough. This was dangerous. "I've got to dump this call. Talking too long."

"What difference does it make if you can prove you've been framed? Let them find you."

"Prove might be a little too strong. And I've got another asshole looking for me now. No, don't ask. I don't want to get anyone else involved. I can sort it. Hope to catch up with you when all this is over."

I hung up before he could answer and turned off my phone.

Okay.

Assuming the wing-nut who texted me was on the level, the cops were definitely barking up the wrong tree.

Of course, he could just be some insane asshole wanting to make my life more miserable.

"Whatever-the-fuck. I'm getting tired." I stood and turned and almost ran into Ann. "Jesus, girl. You scared the crap out of me."

She had the remnants of my dress around her neck like a scarf. It didn't look too bad, actually.

She moved in to give me a hug. An awkward, uncomfortable hug.

"Thanks hon. How you been?"

She looked very concerned. "Did I hear you say someone besides the police was looking for you?"

"It's nothing. Some crazy thinks they can threaten me and I'd take it seriously."

"Crazy like me?"

"You're not crazy."

Ann smiled and hugged me again. "You're very nice to say that. You're in the minority. I'm worried about you. You're too good to be living on the streets."

I took her by the shoulders. "Honey, *no*body should be living on the streets. Why are you? No, forget I asked. It's your business, not mine."

She took me by the hand and led me into an alcove, a hidey hole about a block away. It was a space about twice the size of my bathroom with a couple of thin mattresses on the floor. Light filtered in through a high window from an outside streetlight. "Spend the night here. You'll be safe from whoever is looking for you."

The place was remarkably clean. I sat on one of the mattresses and leaned back against the wall. "What is this place?"

Ann sat on the other and leaned against the opposite wall facing me. "It's an old storage room. When they renovated this building a few years ago, it was left over. Too small for an apartment and they had a new storage room somewhere else. The owner is an old friend and lets me bunk here, as long as I keep it clean. It's clean, right?"

"Spotless. I don't know how you do it with all the sand."

She smiled. "You're too kind."

I had to ask. "Why are you living in a place like this? You are one of the most lucid people I've met in this city."

She laughed. "You're catching me on a good day. I don't know what it's called. I can't remember the name. But I have episodes. Unpredictable episodes. I start feeling very irritable and it's like a blind slides over my thoughts. I can't formulate coherent sentences. I'm lucky to remember my name some days. When it's really bad I just stay in here."

"Surely you can get medical help for that."

"The insurance only covered treatment for twelve months. I can't afford the meds."

"You're not crazy. Very intelligent. What were you doing before all this happened?"

"Finance. I was in the accounts department at one of the chain department stores."

"And they wouldn't help you out?"

She shrugged. "Business, not a charity."

I shook my head. "Doesn't seem fair. Would have thought they'd take care of you."

"Such is life. Play the hand you're dealt."

"You don't have family who can help?"

"I'm a loner just like you. Had a horrendous fight at Thanksgiving about three years ago. Punched my brother in the face so hard I broke his nose. Kicked my dad in the balls and threw his laptop through the plate glass window in the living room. The window didn't open, by the way. Really *through* the window." She grimaced. "Not one of my better days. Haven't talked to any of them since."

I was laughing. "Oh, I'm sorry, but that sounds like a good Australian party. I would have paid money to be there." I caught the look on her face. "Oh, Ann, so sorry. I know it hurts. You've never tried to contact them? Where do they live?"

She was shaking her head before I was finished talking. "Forget about my family. I have. What was this I was hearing you say about someone looking for you? The police?"

Awkward conversation for 200, Alex. "The police are looking for me, yes. They think I did something I didn't do."

"They think you killed Bart Sweeney."

"Exactly. You've been following the news."

"I know you didn't. Wish I could help you. But I'm talking about 'the someone else'. Who else is looking for you?"

"You don't need to get involved ."

"I already am. Technically I'm harboring a fugitive and obstructing by not telling the police you're here. So spill it before I lose my cognitive abilities. Maybe I can help."

I told her about the threatening text messages, bad spelling and all and how I wasn't sure it the guy was for real or not. "Except he knew my fake plans to go to Oxnard and Tustin."

"Better safe than sorry. At least he can't find you here. You should get rid of the phone."

"Oh can't ditch the phone. I've reached high scores in Angry Birds." I laughed at the look on her face. "I'll show you later. I do have a new number, though. A friend got it and loaded credit on it."

I turned on the new phone and sent a text to Marty. *Need you to front me some money. You can take it back from my earnings. Talk to the money guy. $100,000 should be good. If you can do more that would be even better. By the way, this is my new number.*

Ten seconds after I pressed send, the phone rang.

"Marty, is that you?"

"Ellie? Did you just send this text?"

"About the money, yeah. Can you do it?"

There was nothing but breathing on the phone for almost a minute. I could picture him holding his forehead like it was going to pop off. "I don't know. That would drag me right into the middle of it and I could end up spending the next ten years of my life in a prison, missing the pampered existence I currently have."

"You change the contract so it says you get 20%. Maybe 25%. Pre-date it. Bring it with you when you bring the money and I sign it. It's all legit and no way to trace my bag of cash back to you."

"I gotta think about this. I'm not comfortable helping you run when you should be turning yourself into the police."

I looked at Ann. She shifted her position and leaned forward. I held up my hand to keep her from talking. "I can't go to the police until I understand why I was set up."

"You think someone intentionally set you up." It wasn't a question. "You'll need proof."

"Of course someone set me up. My gun, my hair, my prints. How could it be anything else? You going to do the money or not?"

"I've got your number. I'll let you know tonight. I need to talk this over with financial people to see the best way to do it."

Well it wasn't an outright "no". "Thanks Marty. Appreciate it."

He hung up without answering.

"Marty is a friend of yours?"

"My manager-agent. I guess you could call him a friend. He's a great guy. Always helping. Hopefully he can pull through this time."

"That's a lot of money."

"I know. I feel embarrassed sometime how much they pay me to make believe. And then there are people like you and millions others who can't make ends meet."

"That's the way of the world, Ellie. You can't change it. You entertain millions of people, allowing them to escape their boring humdrum world for a couple of hours."

Ann had removed most of her coats. She was wearing a polyester pair of slacks and a Led Zeppelin t-shirt.

"Kind of you to say, Ann. Close to three hours of entertainment, by the way. Listen, what's the deal with all the jackets? You gotta be dying in the heat."

She looked embarrassed for the first time since I'd met her. "I do get hot. And when I'm in mental shape like I am right now, it's very uncomfortable. But when I fade I need them on. Gives me a sense of safety. I learned a long time ago to wear them all the time I'm not in this room. The shift happens at unpredictable times. I'm a blubbering mess if I shift to the crazies and don't have the jackets on. Better to be uncomfortable some of the time than a gibbering idiot most of the time."

I leaned over and gave her a hug. "Oh, dear. I'm so sorry. I had no idea. I wish I could do something."

"Your problems are a lot worse than mine, Ellie."

I didn't answer her as my phone vibrated with an incoming message. "Hey, maybe something from Marty."

It wasn't. It came from the same number I'd received the earlier threatening message.

"Changing the phone number isn't enough to hide from me. You need to change the phone too. But even then I can find you. I know where you are now. Do you know where you'll be this time tomorrow? I'm dead sure I do."

Freaking me out was becoming a habit with this guy.

Ann sensed something I guess because she scooted over and sat beside me. "What's it say?"

I gave her the phone. I was trembling a little. I took a deep breath and tried to calm myself. There's no way he could find me. Was there?

Ann handed the phone back. "That's freaky. That's a brand new number."

I shuddered. It felt like a cold breeze blew across the fine hairs on the back of my neck. Shit. I re-dialed Marty's number.

He answered quickly. "The cops are here. I told you I'd call you back."

"How long have they been there?"

"Since we hung up last time."

"Did you give anyone my new number?"

The tone of his voice changed. "No problem, and I'll see you tomorrow. Oh, and the answer to your question is no." He hung up. Someone must have been close to him and he didn't want them to overhear.

"He didn't give anyone the number." I looked at Ann. "And he said the police have been there since he hung up last time."

"So he wouldn't have had the opportunity to text you."

"Exactly. What the fuck?"

"So turn the phone off, and get some sleep. You look exhausted. You're safe here. Relax."

"Fucking hell, Ann. Some freak out there is saying they are going to kill me and they're sending a message to a number I JUST GOT. How in the hell am I supposed to relax?" Ann backed away from me. I had frightened her. "Oh, jeez, I'm sorry. You're right. I'm exhausted. It's not even 8:00 and I'm falling asleep. Thank you very, very much for your hospitality. I'll take you up on your offer."

I turned off my phone. Looked around the little nook and rested my head on a small pillow. I was asleep before I counted a single sheep.

Chapter Twenty

Perkins accepted the glass of ice water from Lily. "Thanks. But I still need you to answer my questions. When was the last time you saw Ellie Bourke, and where?"

Marty rubbed his forehead, worry lines etched on his face. "I've told you a thousand times, the night of the premiere. I haven't seen her since then. The last time I saw her was just before you and I were standing outside the theatre and she didn't show. I take it you're having problems picking her up."

"She's wily. She's been telling people she's been going to Oxnard or Tustin, but her phone's been located in Venice, close to home, twice."

"Yet you still can't find her."

"It's only a matter of time. I've put another request in to locate her mobile. Odds are high she'll still be in the area."

"Ever wonder why she hasn't moved from there?"

"It's comfortable. She's familiar with the area. There are people there who will help her, even at the risk of being charged with obstruction." He looked close at Marty. "I sense you are also one of those people."

"Sense? What are you, Jedi?" He caught the look from his wife. "Okay, yes. I'd help her if I could do it and not get in trouble. But clearly, I'm going to get into trouble if I do anything at all to assist her."

"Sir, you'll be in trouble if she contacts you and you don't notify us. Don't even think about helping her." Perkins looked through his notebook, like a habit; something he did while he was thinking. "We believe Ellie may try and leave the city." He looked up. "Not Oxnard or Tustin. Those were intentional misdirections. I think she's planning to sneak into Canada or Mexico and head back to Australia. She would need money to run. You, as her manager, would be the most logical place for her to turn. If she does, you need to inform us immediately. Understand?"

Marty was left-coast liberal and rankled at being told by authorities to do anything. "I've already cut ties with her. I seriously doubt I'll hear from her again."

His wife opened her mouth to say something and he walked on it. "If you'll excuse us officers, or sergeants or whatever you are, my wife and I have a late dinner to get ready for." He looked at his wife and shook his head slightly. "You ready yet, dear?"

Perkins gestured to Stanfield. "Let's go partner. I didn't get an invite to any Hollywood shindig. Think we should call it a day anyway."

Stanfield held up his phone. "Perkins, message back from the last trace request. No joy."

"What do you mean?"

"It's coming back empty. No activity."

"Since when?"

"Since the last triangulation a couple of hours ago."

"So she's got her phone turned off. She'll turn it on again. Tell them to keep watching for her number."

Stanfield nodded and placed the call, following Perkins out of the house to the large parking area.

Perkins stood on the front step, shook Marty's hand and nodded at his wife. "Thanks for your time. Apologies again for disturbing you so late. Call me if she contacts you." He handed Marty a card.

He handed it back. "You already gave me one of these. Thanks. The gates open automatically when you approach them." He closed the door and turned to his wife. "Say nothing, okay?" He watched on the security monitor as the car left the gate and is closed behind them.

"Marty, you watch what you're doing."

"Those assholes can't tell me what to do."

"Marty."

"Oh, relax. I'm not going to get caught. I can be as subversive as the best of them. I'll pick up a pre-pay and we're clear."

"They're watching Ellie's number."

He held up his phone. "She's got a new number. Brand new, I think. They'll be looking somewhere else."

She shook her head. "I don't like it."

"So have nothing to do with it. Leave it to me. You go about your daily whatevers and leave. It. To. Me."

She shook her head and turned on her heel. "I am NOT visiting you in jail."

Charlie looked at the request. It was the third one in fifteen minutes for Ellie's phone. He smiled. "They have no idea she changed her number."

Kent slapped him on the back. "Don't let them know, pal."

"Hey, keep it down. You're not supposed to be in here. Supposed to be a secure area."

Kent lowered his voice. "Sorry. No problem. I still don't get how you found her new number, though."

"That's because you're a mouth breather and can't hold a coherent thought. Dude, speaking of which, what's with the hygiene? When's the last time you had a shower?"

"Corporate flunky. Just because *you* have to shower doesn't mean everyone does. I'm between things, remember? So how'd you find the number?"

Charlie laughed. "It's pretty easy. The cops are asking me to track her phone number. I've been logging the numbers she's been calling and watching them, too. Her number disappeared and her agent - I'm assuming that's who it is, given the address for the account - called a newly activated phone just seconds after he received a text from the same number."

"Easy for you to say."

"And that, my friend, is what an education will get you."

"So where is she now?"

Charlie looked over at his friend. "Where's your warrant?" He chuckled. "Moved south a bit. No longer on the Gold's Gym site. Hanging off the Marina del Rey site - the sector facing west." He pulled out his phone. "I've got to let her know we've got her number."

Kent held out his hand. "Wait, you think we should?"

"Why not?"

"I don't know. Just a feeling."

Charlie started typing a message. "No, she needs to know she's got friends. She's in some pretty deep shit right now."

"Okay. Fine. Good point. What are you telling her?"

"I have her number and she can call us any time."

Kent nodded. "Fair enough. Let her know I've got it too." He folded the scrap of paper with her number and put in his wallet. "And let her know she can call me any time. I don't have a full time job like you, you poor schlep."

Charlie looked at his watch. "I'm out of here in a couple of minutes too. Grab a beer?"

Kent shook his head. "Things to do, mate. Catch you later." He slipped out the door of the office building in Century City and into the night.

Cathy dialed Ellie's number again, got voicemail again and hung up again. "Something's wrong Bernie. She never keeps her phone off this long."

"Keep your nose out of it. You're going to have the cops around here, you keep calling her number. They track those kinds of things, you know."

Cathy slumped back on the sofa. "She's in big trouble." She picked up the remote and turned on the TV. The 9:00pm news was just starting. On the screen was a picture of Ellie on the red carpet.

"Police are asking our viewers to be on the lookout for up and coming actress Ellie Bourke, currently a fugitive wanted for the murder of Bart Sweeney. Regular viewers will recall the sensational trial and recent release of Bart Sweeney and will remember Miss Bourke was instrumental in his arrest. She is rumored to have been his lover while living in the guesthouse on his Valley property."

"Oh fucking hell, they never get it right. Bernie. Bring me a drink."

"Police are now saying Miss Bourke is planning on fleeing the country. Our contacts are telling us evidence of her complicity in Sweeney's murder is overwhelming. A witness has placed her at the scene, and a gun registered in her name was the murder weapon. The police wish to advise the public if they see Miss Bourke they are not to approach her. If you do see her, please call 9-1-1 immediately."

"Doesn't look too good for your friend." Bernie handed Cathy a glass of wine. "She's got herself in some serious shit now."

She pushed the glass to one side. "Try her again."

He tossed her the phone. "You. I know what's going to happen. Voice mail again."

He was right. She left a message asking her to call her back.

"We need to go to Venice and see if we can find her."

Bernie pulled on his beer and wiped his chin. "No. The cops can't find her, there's no way in hell I'm going to wander around freaks-ville looking for her."

"Oh there are days you really piss me off. Where are the keys? I'm going."

"No you're not."

"To hell I'm not." She grabbed the keys from the coffee table and made her way to the door. "Don't wait up. Seriously. You'll be wasting your time."

The Killer laughed when he heard the news about Ellie leaving the country. He giggled and slapped his steering wheel. "Like fuck. Maybe in a box, in pieces, back to Australia." His smile dimmed. He was still no closer to finding her. He knew generally where she was, but the specificity - he giggled and tried to say that out loud: "Specisifity. Fuck." - of her location was missing. His contacts had gotten him her number though. He could harass her. And he would.

He pulled on to the PCH and dialed her number on his throw-away phone. It went to voicemail. He started to talk and saw red and blue lights flashing in his rear-view mirror. The police siren let off a whoop. He pulled the phone away from his head. "Oh, fuck. Fucking cops." He hung up and tossed the phone on the passenger's seat and pulled over.

He rolled down the window as the cop approach.

"License and registration, please."

"Right. Hang on a sec." He took out his wallet and handed the constable the documents. *"Officer,"* he leaned out the window and read the name tag, *"Morris, what have I been pulled over for?"*

"Talking on your mobile phone while driving and," he looked pointedly at the driver, *"driving without a seatbelt."* He opened his ticket book. *"There's a $50 fine for the first and $142 for the second. There will also be court costs."* Constable Morris copied the driver information on the ticket pad, noted the infractions and gave the book to the driver to sign. *"You will be notified of the court date."*

"I can't just pay the fine?"

"Afraid not."

"What if I don't sign?"

"You'll still have to show up in court. Signing is not an admission of guilt. It's just validating what I wrote on the ticket. Your choice whether you sign or not."

The Killer grunted. *"Fine."* He signed the ticket. *"You've been fantastic. I was wondering how I could keep fueling the rage and you've just added the perfect ingredient. Like lemon for chicken or hot sauce on wings. Just. Fucking. Awesome."* He shoved the ticket book out the window. *"Have an absolutely fucking wonderful evening."* The book bounced off the ground.

Constable Morris unclipped the restraining strap on his holster and kicked the book away from in front of the door. *"Step out of the car, sir."*

"Why?"

"Because I told you to. You are now going to be required to perform a roadside sobriety test, and, if you fail, you will be arrested

for driving under the influence and taken to the station. Get out. Now."

"Oh, sweet fuck. My tax dollars at work." He opened the car door, got out and stood facing the officer. "Fine. I'm out. What tests would you like me to perform?"

The constable took out his pen and held it about a foot in front of the killer's nose. "I want you to continue to look at the pen while I move it back and forth." He moved it to the left about two feet, then back past the center point to the right two feet, and back to the center.

"Was it supposed to disappear or something? That's like the worst fucking magic trick ever."

Morris ignored him. "Stand with your heels together, hands down to your side, and lift your left foot six inches off the ground. Count until I tell you to stop."

"Bullshit. You won't say 'stop' until I tip over. You do it first."

"Are you refusing?"

"I am. Don't think there's much you can do about it either. Do you smell alcohol on my breath?" He blew in the officer's face. "No? I'm not drunk, inebriated or under the influence. My sister is waiting for me to help her change a flat and you are unnecessarily holding me up because you don't like my attitude. Well tough fucking luck. Give me my fucking ticket and let me go on my way."

Morris clenched his jaw. He couldn't compel the driver to continue with the field sobriety tests and he had no evidence of inebriation. He tore the ticket off the pad and handed it to him. "Make sure your seatbelt is fastened before you pull off the shoulder."

"Get fucked." The Killer got back in the car and pulled away, his left hand out the window, middle finger extended.

And a traffic ticket on the passenger seat which would set him back over $200 once the fucking court costs add up.

"And it's her fault." He turned right on N. Venice and made toward the ocean. It was only 10:30. The night was young. She couldn't run while she was sleeping and she was doing it rough, somewhere around here.

Cathy eased up in the accelerator until she passed the police car on the side of the road giving some poor schmuck a sobriety test. She turned right on N. Venice and headed toward the beach. She tried the number again. Again the voicemail. "Ellie, it's Cath. I'm in the neighborhood. Thought you might like to get together for coffee or something."

She hung up and continued west. The gate at the parking lot on the beach was locked. She pulled in behind a store on the corner of N. Venice and Ocean Walk and parked her car. "Okay, honey. Come out, come out, wherever you are."

She locked the car, kept her keys in her hand, individual keys sticking between the fingers of her fist, and started strolling the boardwalk. It wasn't dead yet. There was still night traffic, kinda rowdy and definitely loud.

She brushed off a couple of propositions. She wasn't dressed for that role, and she wasn't in the mood for bullshit. They backed off pretty quick.

She had passed the skate park when someone grabbed her arm and spun her around. "Ellie?"

She looked at the man in front of her. "No. Ellie who? Who did you think I am? Who are you?"

"Sorry. Thought you were someone else."

"I *am* someone else. And I don't look anything like Ellie. Were you looking for Ellie Bourke?"

"Who are you?"

"I asked first."

Kent held out his hand. "I'm Kent Williams. I'm an old friend of Ellie. You know her too?"

Cathy looked around. The population on the beach was thinning. There were no police to be seen. "Good friend for the last few years. So you know what's going on with her?"

Kent shook his head. "She's got herself into some pile of shit, that's for damn sure."

"She didn't kill him."

"There are witnesses who say different."

"Wait, are you the friend who has contacts in the police department? You've been a big help. Thanks."

Kent nodded. "Why are you looking down here? This would seem to be the last place she'd be."

"I've got a gut feeling. But she's going to the wind soon."

"She told me she was planning on leaving the country. Not a wise move."

Cathy frowned. "Very bad idea. When did she tell you?"

"Earlier this evening."

"So you've been talking to her today. Excellent. I thought maybe she was hurt or her phone had died completely."

Kent considered for a moment. "You know Ellie well?"

"Best girlfriend. Maybe not as long as you, but we split costs for a few months after Sweeney was arrested. And I had left my boyfriend."

"She's got a new phone number. You should probably have it too."

"How did you get it?"

"She - I have a friend who had it. Another one of her friends. Here." He displayed the number on his phone and showed it to Cathy who copied it to her contacts.

"Thanks a lot. Do you want to look for her with me?"

Kent had other plans. "Sorry, Cathy. I've got to go. Other things I need to tend to right now. Sorry." He stuck his hands in his pockets and limped away from her.

"Weird." She continued walking down the beach, scanning faces, listening for a familiar voice. It was promising to be a very long, frustrating night.

Chapter Twenty-One

Ann woke me with a poke to my back. "You need to go."

"Wha?" I rolled away from the wall and looked through squinted eyes at my hostess who had an almost feral look.

"Best you go. Not good right now. Just get out." She had all of her coats on, her knit hat perched on her head and the remains of my dress wrapped around her neck.

I nodded. "Sure. Whatever you want, Ann. Thanks for letting me stay here."

"Just go." She sighed and lay down, facing the wall. "Please."

I collected my small amount of belongings and leaned down and gave her a kiss on the cheek. "Thanks again. See you around the beach."

She muttered and pulled her coats tighter.

I slipped out the door into the back alley. The early morning sun baked the sand dusting the street. There was no wind. I was sticky from one end to the other. Almost three days without a shower was unprecedented. For me, anyway. My stomach growled and I felt like I just slept on a bag of rocks.

I turned on my phone. I needed an answer from Marty. It was a reasonable request, as far as I was concerned. A couple of hundred grand in return for a much larger share of the earnings in the movie. And they'd be huge once DVD sales were factored in.

I came out on the beach south of the pier. I was in a large parking lot, closer to the Marina than I was to my apartment along side a couple of large RVs. Two bike cops pedaled by, paying me no notice. Really, if this was the best they could muster for a manhunt I had nothing to worry about.

My phone vibrated with four messages. Two missed calls and two text messages.

"What the fuck?" One missed call was from a number I was pretty sure belonged to Cathy. I dialed it.

Cathy answered after half a ring. "Ellie? Where are you?"

I took the phone from my head. I could hear Cathy. Not just on the phone; for real. Couldn't see her, but I could definitely hear her.

I lowered my voice. "Doesn't matter, Cath. How in the hell did you get this number?"

"Ran into a friend of your. Aussie guy."

"Tall and dark or short and blond?"

"Tall. Kent someone. Said he got it from another friend."

"Jesus. I got this number to stay below the radar and now everyone has it. Where did you say you were?"

"I didn't. I'm near the Venice Fish Pier, looking for you. Am I getting warm?"

Shit. I definitely didn't want to see her. Well, I did, but I didn't want her getting caught up in all this. "Cath, hon, go home. Don't get dragged down in my mess. Please. And delete this number from your phone and stop calling it. The cops will eventually catch up with what's going on." I walked closer to the pier, keeping covered, mostly, by the parked cars. I sidled along the edges of the public toilets until I was as close to the pier as I thought safe.

"Ellie? What are you doing? Where are you?"

"It doesn't matter. As soon as I rustle up some cash I'm out of here. Nice knowing you. Where'd you park?"

"Behind a store. Why?"

Because I didn't want her to come up here and find me. "Because you should probably move it before it gets towed. Have you been out all night?"

"Pretty much."

I had a panic attack. "With Bernie?" I looked around for 6'-6" Bernie.

"No. Left his sorry ass at home. Wouldn't come with me. I hope he's freaking out."

Typical Cathy. "Go home and rest. You're a great friend and I don't want you to end up in a jail cell. Tell Kent, if you see him again, he's a bell-end for giving you the number."

"I probably won't see him again. He was off in a hurry last night going somewhere. He's not that big of a dick-head. He's getting information from the police department for you."

"It hasn't helped much, but yeah. I guess." I closed my eyes and rubbed the back of my neck. "Ditch me, Cath. Forget you ever knew me."

"Oh shut up, Ell. I can't forget ever knowing you. You've been the biggest positive influence in my life since I was a kid. You're innocent and there's no reason for you to run."

"Ah, if only it were that easy. I'm going to hang up. Don't want you nabbed."

I terminated the call. I had to forget about her. I stood by the showers and watched her walk back along the boardwalk toward the skate park and N. Venice Avenue.

The public shower was tempting. If I had a swimsuit on I wouldn't stand out. But standing under one with all my clothes on would draw a bit of a crowd, even down here. Standing under it naked, an even bigger crowd.

I walked under the pier. It was evident someone had been hanging out here by the trash scattered across the ground. Maybe Ann.

But it was vacant now. I peeled off my jeans. My underwear was more conservative than most of the bikinis on the beach. I wasn't wearing a bra - didn't really need one - so I kept my golf shirt on. I folded the pants and lay my shoes and phone in the folds. Put the sunglasses and cap on top. The swim would be refreshing. I might even feel a bit cleaner after, saltwater not withstanding.

The swim was an echo of the one I took, what, only two days ago? Hard to believe. Felt like a life-time.

The knots worked out of my shoulders in the first five minutes. The water was a little bit rough, but not too bad. I swam past a couple of guys on boards waiting to catch a good one. They said something to me about seeing a mermaid or something, but I ignored them. Maybe another day.

I turned after my brain had told me I had swum for about thirty minutes. The swim back passed in a haze. I zoned out.

I body surfed in, slaloming around the pier's piles. Not the safest of tricks, but not impossible for someone who had been swimming as long as I had.

I stood when the water was about waist deep and slowly waded to shore. I felt good. Muscles a little sore, breath a little short, I knew I had just had a work out.

The day wasn't going to be all good, though. Some snot-nosed little punk was going through my stuff under the pier.

"Hey. Asshole. Hey. Get back here."

He grabbed my mobile phones and ran.

Big mistake. I grabbed a beer bottle and ran after him.

I'd just spent close to eighteen months in an almost non-stop fitness program. The stunt coordinator had me doing as many of my own stunts as the insurance would allow. I was in better shape than I had ever been.

And I was a good foot taller than the punk running with my stuff. He didn't have a chance.

I caught up to him after less than fifty steps. I grabbed him by the hair on the back of his head and yanked. His feet flew out in front of him and he landed on his ass.

I pushed the base of the beer bottle against his left eye. "Give them back or I'll break this over your skull."

"Give what? You're assaulting me. Help. Police!"

"Shut up. The police come over here and you'll be explaining to them why one of my phones is in your front pocket and the other one is in your hand." I kicked at his leg. "Unless you know the pin code to the iPhone, then I'll apologize and walk away."

"It's a trick so you get to know my pin code."

"Listen, shorty. Hand them over before I rearrange your skull." Two bike cops approached from about a hundred yards away. Shit-tastic.

I dropped the bottle and squatted. "Look, kid. I'm not going to press charges. You just give me my phones back and I won't tell those cops over there anything."

He twisted and looked over his shoulder. "Aw, shit." He dug my phone out of his pocket and hand me it and the pre-pay. "Take them. For fuck's sake, put some pants on. You're really distracting me. And Jesus, how do you run so fast?"

I inspected them for damage, found them okay and mentally dismissed him. I kept an eye on the cops as I walked back to the pier. They continued on toward the skate park. Crisis averted, as they say.

I re-dressed and went for a slow walk in the sun, drying my shirt. I looked at the pre-pay. There were two text messages I hadn't opened yet.

"Charlie here. You should stop phoning your old contacts. That's how I got your number. I can still keep an eye on your location, but the cops haven't caught on yet. They're still looking for your old number.

But if they wise up, there's nothing I can do about it. I'll have to give them your location."

Trust Charlie to find me. He must have given my number to Kent who gave it to Cathy. God only knew who else had it.

The second message chilled me.

"No, no, no. Changing your number won't help. Changing your phone won't help. I will find you. It doesn't matter what you do. And I'm thinking a suicide in the LA River would be appropriate. Don't make any plans for tonight."

Sweet Jesus, my stalker still had a bead on me. I had plans for tonight, and they included getting out of town.

Plans change. Enough is enough.

I dialed Marty's number from memory. His wife, Lily, answered. "Hello? This is Marty's phone. He's kind of indisposed right now. May I help you?"

"Lily? This is Ellie. Is Marty around?"

"Oh, dear. Marty is, um, biologically indisposed, if you know what I mean. Too many burritos I think."

"Ouch. Don't tell him I called. I don't want him getting into trouble. I'll try him later."

"Don't hang up. He's only going to be a few more minutes. I want to talk to you anyway. He mentioned something to me about money for you to disappear."

"I wish he hadn't."

"He did. How many times have I fed you at my house? A couple of dozen over the last year and a bit?"

I sighed. She wasn't going to shut up. "At least. Always excellent food, too. Why? What does that have to do with anything?"

"In all those times you broke bread with me, did you ever, even once, take me for an idiot?"

"Of course not. And I don't think I've ever *called* you an idiot. Silly question. I thought we were best of pals."

"I've got a pretty level head on my shoulders. You're buried in this too deep. You're not seeing the facts. Running is absolutely the wrong thing to do."

I sighed. "I know."

"What?"

"I've received a couple of text messages from someone who has claimed to have set up Sweeney's death to look like a faked suicide and ultimately fingering me as the killer. He, or possibly she, has threatened to kill me now and make *that* look like a suicide, complete with a note expressing remorse for killing Bart. I've changed my mind. I'm not going anywhere. I'm going to find that asshole and drop him."

Silence. For almost ten seconds, then Lily exhaled a deep breath. "My, but don't you live an interesting life. You're obviously going to the police with this."

Ah, the $64,000 question. "Not yet."

"Hang on, I'm putting you on speaker. Marty's here."

There was a click and the unmistakable sound of Marty huffing and puffing. "Who is it Lil?"

"It's me, Marty. Just telling your wife not to worry about the money. I've got bigger problems."

Lilly interjected. "She just told me the person who killed Sweeney has contacted her, admitted to it and has threatened to kill her now."

"Ellie, call the police right now. Hang up and call the police and tell them this."

"No, not yet."

"Why in hell not?"

I didn't know if I could explain it correctly. I wasn't sure myself. "The police aren't going to believe me. I ran. That was stupid, but I did it. Then the evidence kept piling up making it look even worse for me. They aren't going to believe me unless I can get some concrete evidence."

"You've got the messages, don't you?"

"Probably from a throw away phone like the one I've got. I could have got a second phone and sent myself the messages. I need to find this person and get them to admit something only the killer would know."

"No, no, no, no. This is insanity. You're not VI Warshawski. Although that would be a great remake for you. Remind me once all this is sorted."

"Marty." Lily's voice could cut glass. I smiled. He was always trying to make a deal.

"Sorry. Look young miss, I'll get some private detectives on this. I know some guys."

"Marty, you're a helluva nice guy. I'm calling you to tell you I don't need your help. I do not want you to help me. Is that understood? As far as the police are concerned I'm still a fugitive and you'll be both obstructing justice and aiding and abetting and probably something else, too. I'm hanging up now. I'll call you in a couple of days when I've got things figured out. Don't call me, promise?"

"How can I promise that?"

"You've got to. I need to go." I hung up before they had a chance to reply. Good old Marty. Knowing him he'd be on the phone right now calling some private detective and getting them on the case. Like a boss.

I had to get to work on this. Tracking the number would be a good start. Charlie said he was working at a mobile phone company. If he was still there.

I went back to the message he sent and called him.

"Charlie speaking."

"Mate, Ellie here. Are you still at the phone company?"

"That's how I got your number. Looking for a job?" He sounded tense.

"Is everything okay?"

"As well as can be expected. I thought I was finally out of the rat race. Sweeney had a good deal for me and now he's dead and I don't know what the hell's going on. What can I do for you?"

"Are you at the office?" I slid into a walkway, out of sight of most of the passing foot traffic.

"Working evenings this week Ell. You actually woke me. Why?"

"I'm sorry. I'll call you later."

"Hey, I'm awake now. What's up?"

"I received a threatening message from someone who said they killed Sweeney. I wonder of you could find out who owns the number."

He hesitated. I could almost hear him thinking. "I can log in remotely and have a look, but no guarantees."

"Can I give you the number and you get back to me?"

"This is unofficial, okay? I'm not supposed to access these records without a legal request. Under the table stuff, okay?"

"Absolutely." I recited the number from the text message. "Let me know what you find out when you can. Thanks. I really appreciate this."

"Don't thank me yet." He hung up.

Fingers crossed.

Something about that number seemed familiar. Like I'd seen it somewhere else before. I scrolled to the missed calls list and there it was. Late last night. So the bastard had called me. I was sleeping at Ann's. Too bad. I'd love to talk to this guy.

So I dialed the number. It rang once then went to a generic voicemail prompt. "The person you have called is unavailable. Leave a message after the tone." I didn't bother.

He dumped me. He knew I was calling and rather than talk to me he chose to dump the call to voicemail.

I jumped as a text message arrived. From him.

"You don't control your life. I do. I'll talk to you when I choose to talk to you. And it will be a very short conversation. Enjoy your last day on earth."

What a fucking asshole.

Chapter Twenty-Two

Stanfield placed a large coffee on Perkins' desk. "We need to find Bourke today. It's going on too long and we - our - asses are going to be in a sling." He looked pointedly at Perkins' chair. "And in your case a very large sling."

"Thanks for the coffee partner. And point noted. About Ellie. Not about my ass. That was harsh."

Samson walked in the middle of the conversation. "He after your ass already? Stanfield, want to transfer to West Hollywood?"

"If it isn't dog-squad. What brings you up here?"

"What's the latest on our mutual felonious friend?"

Perkins flipped open the file on his desk. "According to the phone geeks her number hasn't surface in a long time. She might still be at the beach, she might have hopped a rail car to Canada. Hard to say."

"You've got to have more intelligence than that."

"Excuse me?"

"Not personal intelligence, Perkins. I'm sure you're a smart guy. Situational intelligence. You checked on her friends?"

"Not too many to pick from."

"You're kidding, right? Cathy and Bernie. Emily and Henry. Marty and Lily."

"Isn't he her manager?"

"And friend."

"We talked to all of them. They know *nuthink*."

"Thanks Schultz. They're going to lie to you. Or at least withhold information. When Ellie makes a friend they tend to be very loyal." He scratched his chin. "I consider her a good friend. And while I wouldn't lie for her, I'll help her on this anyway I can."

Perkins stood and squared off with Sampson. "So you think she didn't do this."

"I don't. I'd bet a good chunk of my annual salary she didn't."

Perkins shook his head. Hands on his hips he cocked his head and smiled a half smile. "Thinking with your dick, dog-squad. For you to be right, someone would have had to steal her gun, earring and some strands of hair, determine a time when she had no alibi, kill Sweeney in a poorly staged fake suicide, and leave enough evidence to point us in her direction. This is mastermind type of stuff."

"Hardly mastermind. Clever, maybe, and certainly not beyond the realm of possibility."

"Are you familiar with the principle of Occam's razor, Sampson?"

"Who isn't? Lazy man's way of looking at things."

"The simplest solution is usually the right solution."

"And that's my problem with it, right there. Usually. Not 100%, not always, not every time. Usually. That leaves open a very wide door for it not being the right solution." He put up his hands. "Look, if I was just looking at the evidence I'd be with you on this. But it's more than the evidence. I know Ellie. I know her quite well. Well enough to know she didn't kill Bart." He crossed his arms and strolled around the office. "That means, obviously, your far-fetched idea is what actually happened. Who else are you looking at for this?"

Perkins shook his head. "Were you not paying attention, dog-squad? I'm not looking at anyone else. This has Bourke written all over it."

Sampson nodded. "Sure. But you might want to expand your horizons a bit. Someone out there, not Ellie, has done this. And they might be looking at other targets now, what with the success they've had deflecting suspicion from themselves."

"You're building an alternative case out of fog and smoke. I'm not sure I can trust you, Sampson. You've got emotional ties to this case. You can't be objective."

Sampson stepped closer, nose to nose. "Really?"

Stanfield jumped out of his chair and wedged himself between the two. "Whoa, boys. Relax. You're disturbing the rest of the inmates." He looked at the other cops in the room and smiled. "Nothing to see. Move along."

Sampson smiled and clapped Stanfield on the back. "Okay, okay. Lots of conjecture, but not outside the realm, right?" He pointed at

Perkins. "Think about it. You're going to run into a dead end with the Ellie angle sooner or later."

Charlie poured a cup of black coffee and sat at the desk in his bedroom, laptop booted. He connected to the company systems through corporate VPN and logged into the billing records with a generic login. He had his own, but he didn't want his digital fingerprints on this. He would use one of the group accounts. A smart audit would track his IP address, but he'd worry about that later.

He read the number Ellie gave him off the scrap of paper and entered it in the search field. A second's pause to access the database and the screen filled with generic billing information. The name of one of the many retail shops, the sales agent's name and the shop address. It was a pre-pay consigned to the shop, and the billing data not updated. Yet. It might take a day or so for that to happen.

He closed the billing system and opened the Legal Intercept engine. He entered the number again and let the tool search the cell sites the phone had been on recently.

Knowledge was power.

Marty and Lily sat on the back patio by their pool overlooking the Pacific.

"Lil, if I have fruit for breakfast one more time I'm going to turn into Carmen Miranda." He tossed the pineapple ladened fork on the table. "I want fucking steak and eggs for breakfast."

"Your blood pressure is in the medium to high range and your bad cholesterol is very bad. You know better."

"Hey. I'm going to be spending the rest of my life in jail eating slop. I should at least be able to eat what I want until then."

Lily put her spoon in her bowl of oatmeal and fruit. "What have you done?"

He wiped the corners of his mouth. "You know the guy who caught George with the cheerleader? I've got him sniffing around, on the down-low."

"What do you mean, caught George with the cheerleader? When did that happen?"

"Oh, shit." He held his face in his hands. He peered between fingers. "You didn't know?"

"What did this happen? Oh, poor Daphne."

Marty looked up and bark a laugh. "Poor Daphne? She was *schtupping* the pool guy. I'd say pool *boy*, but he's 51. I'm in better shape than he is."

Lily laughed. "Good for her."

"What? You were ready to string George up by the balls not thirty seconds ago. Talk about double standards."

"Exactly. You think it's fine for George to have some fluff, but not for Daphne?"

"Did I say that? How did we get on this subject, anyway? The private dick, what's his name, Lennie, is doing some snooping around for me. He's got the contacts to help track down Ellie. Then we'll get that excellent lawyer," he snapped his fingers, "Levin. Ira Levin. He'll have the cops so tied up in knots this won't go to trial for decades."

"I don't think that's what she wants. Didn't you listen to her? There's some guy trying to kill her."

"Yeah, so we bring her in, keep her safe and out of trouble."

"Genius, why don't you have Lennie looking for the killer instead of Ellie."

He shrugged. "Not a bad idea. I'll give him a call, see what he can do."

"You better let Perkins know what you're up to."

Marty stood and shook his head. "Not in a million years. I don't trust those guys as far as I can throw them. You know what they did to her the last time. No. I'll let Lennie dig some stuff up before I get the police involved." He pointed his finger at his wife. "And don't you get any ideas about talking to Perkins about this. Good idea, though, having the PI looking for the black hat. Did Ellie tell you what his number was? Can do some tracing."

Lily shook her head and retrieved her husbands phone from the table. "I'll ask her." She sent a text message to Ellie asking what number the threatening message came from and placed the phone back on he table. "Lennie is discreet enough?"

He nodded. "He dislikes the police almost as much as he likes his fees, so he should be okay. You worried?"

"You know me. Don't like going off the reservation very often. Prefer it nice and safe and sound at home." She looked over the Pacific, another sunny day in Southern California. "Would hate to jeopardize this lifestyle we've come to enjoy so much."

"Bah, you worry too much. Let me handle it. It'll be okay." He picked up his phone. "Need to sort Lennie out."

Stanfield looked at his partner. "Can't say I mind this case too much.

I've been to the beach more in the last couple of days than I have in the last couple of years."

"Keep your eyes on the road."

"Yes, boss."

"And don't get lippy." He clicked his pen for a few seconds. "So how much credence do you put in Sampson's theory?"

"What, that she was set up?" Stanfield drummed his fingers on the steering wheel. "Really?"

"I asked, didn't I?"

"It's a possibility. Nothing's impossible."

"That would mean she's actually a target and a potential victim, and not a suspect."

Stanfield nodded. "If he's right."

"And how could we test that?"

"Talk to her, obviously."

"Obviously. Except we can't find her."

"Because she thinks we want to arrest her for killing someone she may not have actually killed."

Perkins sat in silence, thinking about options and past mistakes. "So we get her to stop running." He called the desk Sergeant. "Claire, Perkins here. You doing well?" He nodded while he listened to the long-winded response. "Yeah, fine. Good. I've got a request. Scale back the hunt for Ellie Bourke, okay? I want to try a gently-gently approach. Want her to stop running long enough for us to actually catch her. I'm getting slow in my old age, you know?"

He chuckled at the response. "That's very kind of you. I appreciate if you could make that an immediate command to the boys and girls on the street, okay?" He nodded again. "Thanks. Much appreciated. I'll talk to you later."

He hung up and blew a big breath through puffed cheeks. "God, what a lot of words that woman has."

"She wants you."

"What? No. I'm old and overweight."

"And married. Yet you still have some kind of hold on her. She hardly gives me the time of day, and I'd spend every penny of my pay-check to try and change that. You, you're old and arthritic and married and she wants to set up camp in your pants. Daddy issues."

Perkins dismissed him. "Whatever. So the cops are dialed back. How do we let Ellie know?"

"Sky writing?" Stanfield turned on to N. Venice and headed to the beach.

"How did you get promoted again? Got a better idea. All those friends who were telling us she was on her way to Oxnard."

"What about them?"

"We tell them we think she's been set up and want to help her."

Stanfield was shaking his head before his partner finished. "They'll never believe us."

"We tell enough of them, often enough, it'll trickle through to her. We know she's ditched her phone. If she has a pre-pay the odds of us finding out what the new number is, is almost zero." He slapped the dash. "So it's worth a try. Find a nice place to park and let's start walking and talking."

Emily looked north on the boardwalk and signaled her husband. "The cops are on their way back."

He took off his apron and moved to the front of the shop. "You go to the back. I'll handle this." He stepped out on his small patio as Perkins and Stanfield approached. "Gentlemen, what can I do for you?"

"We're still looking for Miss Bourke."

"Of course you are. That's what you do."

Perkins paused and looked at Henry in the eye for a minute. "You're not going to help us, are you?"

Henry smiled. "You need help? What can I do to help?"

"We're looking for Ellie Bourke."

Henry tapped the side of his head. "*Déjà vu*. I could have sworn you just said that."

Stanfield stood a little to the back of Perkins, a small smile on his face.

Perkins took a small step forward and checked himself when he felt Stanfield's hand on his arm. "Would you know where she is?"

"You guys are Valley cops, right?"

Perkins shook his head. "It doesn't matter what precinct we work out of, our case has taken us here. So do you know where she is?"

"You check Oxnard?"

Stanfield stepped forward. "We're pretty sure Ellie is in danger. We think she was framed and the person who did it might be targeting her next. We really need to talk to her."

Henry nodded and flicked them a salute. "Nice try guys. You're pretty transparent. I've got to get back to work, okay? In the unlikely event I run in to Ellie, I'll pass on your message." He turned back into the cafe and put on his apron.

His wife stopped him. "What did they say?"

"They want me to believe they think she's in danger and should turn herself in." He snorted. "Pretty sincere looking too."

"It's La-La-Land. Everyone's an actor." Emily frowned. "Unless they were telling the truth. That's what's Ellie's been saying. Do you think they were telling the truth?"

Henry shrugged. "Maybe. You've got her number, right? Let her know. Send her a text."

"Come on Perkins." Stanfield threw his suit jacket over his shoulder and strolled south along the boardwalk. "He'll tell her, and even if he tells her and discounts it as bullshit, he'll tell her. Let's find the juggler."

"He's so stoned he's not going to remember his own name." Perkins slid his hands in his pockets and walked along side his younger partner,

"He'll pass on the information. He pressed the Oxnard story the hardest."

Perkins loosened his tie and undid the top button of his shirt. "You're probably right. He's plying his trade up there. Let's take in the show and have a chat with Potsy."

"Who?"

"Never mind. What the fuck is he doing with that puppy?"

Stanfield started laughing as he watched the juggler with the chainsaw, bowling ball and stuffed dog proceeded to freak out the females in the crowd. "You didn't catch that, did you?"

"Catch what? That asshole is juggling a puppy." Perkins pressed forward.

"Hang on, partner. He switched the real one with a toy. Very real looking toy." He smiled. "Pretty fucking hilarious."

Perkins grunted. "Right. A riot."

They watched as the juggler finished his act by tossing the stuffed dog to a matronly woman protesting the loudest in the front.

He calmed the crowd and passed the hat, getting almost nothing from the women but overcompensated by the offerings from the men.

Perkins walked up with his badge out, Stanfield along side doing a slow clap.

"That was good. Loved it." Stanfield gave him a little bow. "I'm impressed."

"What can I do for you guys?"

"Excuse me, Mr. - " Perkins flipped through his notepad.

"Patrick Fitzgerald."

"Hmm. My notes say it's Gerald Fitzpatrick."

"Ah, that would be me gay lover." Danny laughed at his own poor Irish accent. "What do you want this time? I think Ellie's gone to Boise."

"She hasn't gone to Boise, Tustin or Oxnard." He cleared his throat. "I know you're in contact with Ellie."

"How, cop? I don't have a phone, mobile or otherwise."

"You'll see her and you'll talk to her. We know she's staying in this area for some reason. I'd like you to give her a message. We believe she was set up and may be in danger. It's important she contact us as soon as she can and come in to the station."

"Bullshit. You expect me to believe that? You got anything better than that?"

Perkins sighed. "Tell her. This is not bullshit, it's dead serious." He nodded at Stanfield. "Let's go talk to her manager."

Ann started at the banging on the door. She rolled off her mattress and pulled her hat snug on her head. She closed her eyes tight and took a deep breath and laid back down. She wasn't feeling good. Maybe it would go away.

The hammering continued. "Hey, anyone in here? I'm not leaving until someone answers the door." The banging continued.

Ann groaned.

She shuffled to the door and cracked it open. "Go away."

The man pushed her into the room and slammed the door shut. "You know Ellie, right?"

Ann fell back on the bed. "Who are you?"

"Where's Ellie?"

"Who?"

The man leaned in close and yelled. "Where the fuck is Ellie?" Spittle sprayed on Ann's face. "Where the FUCK is she?"

"I'm confused. Who are you? Why are you in my place? You need to leave."

The man's voice lowered, a menacing growl. "Listen you crazy fucking bitch, you tell me where Ellie is or I'll kill you."

Perkins and Stanfield pulled into the drive in Santa Monica, the gates swinging shut behind them. "Perks, what a place, eh?"

"Every time we come here I get the feeling I know this place. I've seen it in a movie."

"Probably. It's massive and you *know* a location manager would have picked the exteriors for something."

The walked up the front steps. As Perkins raised his hand to knock, the door opened.

"Gents. This is becoming a regular occurrence. What can I do for you?"

"May we come in?"

"No point really. This is going to be a quick conversation. I have a busy day ahead." He placed his feet shoulder width and crossed his arms, his body language screaming "Fuck off".

Chapter Twenty-Three

I looked around the corner of the apartment building about three down from mine. Perkins and his partner were grilling Danny. Danny, as was his usual approach to authority, appeared to be frustrating the hell out of them. He was smiling and Perkins looked like he was going to pop a vein. His partner seemed to be enjoying himself.

I waited a few minutes after they left and casually walked over, a typical tourist chatting up the talent. "What did they want?"

He was squatting on the blanket, scratching his puppy behind the ears. "What? Oh, hi. They're looking for you."

"Still. They seemed to be giving you a hard time."

"The old dude was. Young guy said he really liked the puppy act. Didn't he Damien?" Hat patted the blanket beside him. "Pull up a seat.

Say hi to my co-conspirator."

I sat cross-legged on the blanket. Damien hopped over and crawled on my lap, put his paws on my shoulders and licked the end of my nose. I picked him up and sat him back on my lap and scratched his head. "Cute pooch. I think he loves me. What did Perkins say?"

"You were set up, you're probably in danger. You should march your ass right down to the nearest police station right now and turn yourself in. For your safety, of course."

"Really? That's weird. Because I was set up, and my life probably is in danger." I scratched the dog's back. "But I think Perkins is just fishing. There's no way he could know. He's just trying to lure me in. Bastards."

"Yeah, well I told them you were in Boise. Don't think they believed me."

I laughed and hugged him. "You're my hero. What city is next?"

He smiled and shrugged. "Whatever the mood tells me. Might be Boston, might be Moose Jaw."

"Don't tell me. Make it a surprise." I handed back Damien. "You get the feeling he was bullshitting, or was he legit?"

He shrugged. "Who the hell knows? Go with your gut. You know I don't trust those fuckers."

"I do. Thanks again Danny. I'll let you get on with your day. I think I'll give Perkie a call."

"You think that's wise?"

"Why not? He wants to talk to me. I'll talk to him."

"He'll get your number."

"Oh, shit. Close call. Thanks. I'll figure it out. Maybe from a pay-phone. No matter. Take it easy mate, and give Damien a few extra kibbles for me."

I turned tourist and walked the boardwalk. I was tired. Almost slipped up and called Perkins from my phone. But the fact was, I did want to talk to him. I believed his story as much as I believed in the tooth fairy. If it was Sampson telling me, maybe, but not Perkins.

My phone vibrated, which was disconcerting. Far too many people knew this number, already. And nobody was programmed in my directory, so I was never completely sure who it was.

"Hello?"

"Hi, Ellie. It's Lily. Just wanted to make sure you were okay."

"Oh, you're going to get yourself in trouble. You shouldn't have called."

"I'm relaying a message from Perkins."

"He gets around. Let me guess. My life is in danger, I've been set up and I should hustle my ass to the nearest police station before I get myself killed."

"Spot on."

"When was he there?"

"He and his young partner are driving out of the gate right now. They seemed sincere."

"It's Hollywood. He had no explanation for this sudden reversal, did he?"

"Not that I could tell. Kind of strange, isn't it?"

"What?" I stood in a doorway and watched a police car drive down Speedway.

"You really are being set up and that guy has threatened you. So

Perkins is right."

"He's just trying to get me to turn myself in. Look, Lily, I don't want to be rude, but I've got to go."

"Before you hang up, Marty has hired a PI to try and find the ass who set you up. Can you tell me the number he used? This guy has contacts and might be able to get more information about him."

"Got a pen?" I recited the number from the text I'd received, thanked her, and shut down the call. I didn't like other people risking their freedom on my account.

Torn between wanting to believe Perkins and not trusting a single fucking thing coming out of his mouth was distracting me from what I had to do. I took a deep breath and called the number which sent me the threatening text. It went to a generic voice mail box again.

"Coward. Answer the phone and face me like a man. Bitch."

I hung up. I needed to control the situation. I needed to make sure the asshole didn't get to me before I had a chance to set the stage.

And I wasn't ready yet. I needed to lay low.

This Perkins angle was intriguing. He didn't strike me as the type of person who'd resort to trickery. But Kent had an inside source. Maybe he'd be able to dig up the truth.

He answered out of breath. "Ellie. What's going on?"

"Perkins is going around telling anyone who knows me he fears for my safety, that he knows I was set up. And he wants me to turn myself in."

"No, I don't buy it. Too risky. Let me talk to Shelley and get the scoop."

"I thought her name was Stevie."

"Yeah. Stevie. I'll call her and get back to you shortly. Don't do anything stupid." He grunted and hung up.

Sounded like he was weight lifting.

And here I was waiting again. But I didn't have to do *nothing*. Charlie might have more information.

He answered with a groan. "What felony do you want me to commit this morning?"

"Good morning, Charlie. You still have the number, right? The one I gave you - "

"What, you think I'm disorganized?"

"Can you check the location for me? I don't want that fuck sneaking up on me."

"You're going to get me fired, mate."

"Only for another day or so Charlie. Appreciate it." I listened to keys clicking for a very long, nervous minute.

"The number is located very close to you. You just called it, right?"

"Yeah, I did. Define close to me?"

"Different sectors of the same site. Like rock throwing distance from each other."

"Oh, fuck." I pulled myself into the doorway and tried to make myself smaller.

"Fuck, indeed." There was a bit more clicking of keys. "There's been nothing since then, but it wasn't very long ago so he can't be far. Watch your ass, right?"

"I will. Thanks again. I promise not to bother you too much."

I slipped the phone into my pocket. What does a psycho look like?

If Charlie was right, and he knew this stuff pretty well, Mr. Nutbags was within a mile of me. Looking for me. Wanting to do me physical harm.

Not if I could help it.

I felt like everyone was looking at me, now. Fuck, I hated feeling like this. All eyes seemed to be accusing me. I wanted to leave the anonymity of the crowds on Venice Beach and head to a hidey hole.

My ass vibrated.

I squeezed out the phone. It was him.

Calling, this time.

"Hey, nutbags. You looking for me? You'll never find me."

"I know where you are right now. I saw you pull that phone from your very tight back pocket." The voice was a deep "I'm Batman" kind of voice. It was either electronically disguised or the guy was good at doing voices.

I spun around and looked into the crowd. There were more than a dozen people on their phones. One of them could be Sweeney's killer. Or not. There were plenty of windows he could be looking from.

"So why are you keeping your distance, asshole? You promised grievous bodily harm. You going to break your promise?"

"I'm not stupid. There are crowds. When I get you, I'm going to get you alone. It's just going to be you and me, for an extended visit."

"Candlelight and wine?"

His voice dropped a key and evoked menace. "You're not going to enjoy this visit."

"You have halitosis?"

"Bitch, I will make you *wish* you could die. And I'm going to tell you exactly how it's going to happen." He took a deep, shuddering breath.

"I'll make sure you can't make any noise loud enough to be heard outside the room. And then I'm going to start hurting you. I'm going to make you feel pain in places you never thought pain would be felt. You will think it can't get any worse, and then it will. You'll plead for me to kill you to put you out of your misery.

"But I won't. That will be stage one. You'll soon long for stage one. Because stage two will be ten times worse. The horror you experience will make you regret every self-serving action you've ever taken. You'll realize every person you trod on to get you to where you are now is getting their collective payback.

"And then, when it's beyond what you can humanly bear you will become the apparent victim of self-immolation."

I swallowed and slipped back in the doorway. "I thought you were going to make it look like a suicide."

"Didn't you catch the 'self' part of 'self-immolation'? I thought I knew you, Ellie. I guess I was wrong. Selfish, I understand. I didn't think you were stupid."

"You know me?"

"You're not random."

"Where am I now?"

"Why, are you lost? You're not far from me. I'll keep an eye on you until it's dark, and then you're all mine. I suggest you enjoy the sunset tonight. It'll be your last."

"Fuck you."

"Eloquent."

"If you know me, tell me your name. This impending doom is apparently inevitable. Telling me who you are shouldn't make any difference."

His laugh sounded like gravel in a galvanized tub. "I want to see the look on your face when you find out."

"How did you find me so fast?"

"You're not exactly hiding. You haven't gone more than a few miles from your home. I'm surprised the police haven't picked you up already."

"So you're a cop?"

He laughed again. "God, no."

"So how did you find me so fast? Tell me."

"You can thank your friend, the crazy bag lady for her assistance. Once I got her going, she wouldn't shut the fuck up."

I gripped the phone so tight I was afraid I was going to crack the screen. "What did you do to Ann?"

"A bit fragile upstairs, isn't she? I'm sure she'll be fine. Eventually. Barely a mark on her frumpy body, but her mind may be scarred for the rest of her very short life."

"Listen, you f-"

"Shut up." Heavy hoarse breathing filled my ear. "It's not all about you, bitch. You're just one on a line of victims. Number two. Sweeney was one. Setting you up was almost as fun as seeing the look on his face just as I shot him in his fat fucking head." He took a breath. "No, there will be many more after you. This is the best fun I've had in a very, very long time."

I heard his shoes, or boots, clicking across a floor. "You're a sick fuck."

"Of course I am. That's what makes me so fun to be around. It's not even noon yet. Barely past 11:00. You've got seven hours to sort your shit out. I'll be keeping a very close eye on you for those seven hours, so don't think you'll escape."

The call dropped. I peered out from the corner of the doorway. He could see me, I couldn't see him.

Lovely.

Chapter Twenty-Four

Ann groaned and held her face as she slowly regained a sense of where she was. She opened one eye and checked if her unwelcome visitor was still there.

She sat up, a bit too quick for the pain in her head. "Oh, my goodness. What have I done?" She wiggled a tooth with her tongue and winced. "Ouch." Her hand came away from her mouth sticky with partially congealed blood and her lip felt like it was twice its normal size.

She knew the man from somewhere. She'd seen him on the beach before and she thought she'd seen him with Ellie, but she wasn't sure. Her thoughts were hard to pin to reality. The fog was getting thicker and she fought against it, but inevitably surrendered to the confusion.

Marty struggled in the backseat against the handcuffs. "I have the right to call my attorney."

Perkins looked up from the confiscated mobile phone and half turned in his seat. "Wrong. You have the right to *have* an attorney. The phone call - at the station, by the way - is a courtesy." He turned back to the phone and logged on to his onboard terminal. "Watch the potholes, kiddo. I have a hard enough time typing on this thing as it is."

Marty slumped back in his eat. Lily had called him names he hadn't heard her use in years. "Hey, these things are really uncomfortable. Are they necessary?" He leaned forward and tried to relieve the pressure on his wrists.

"Serious crimes you've been charged with. Obstructing justice, harboring a felon, resisting arrest." Stanfield laughed. "You're in pretty good shape for an old guy."

"I haven't actually been *charged* with anything yet, and after my attorney is finished with you, you won't be arresting anyone for anything ever again."

Stanfield looked at Perkins. "Is he threatening us?"

"Watch the road, kid. I don't think it qualifies as a threat if he can't back it up." He clicked a couple more keys and dropped Marty's mobile in a plastic evidence bag. "Okay. The phone company should get the call details from this phone shortly. But I noticed a single number with no name attached, incoming and outgoing and at the top of a couple of interesting text messages. They're going to geolocate that number first."

Marty banged his head against the window. "Fuck. Really? You guys need to leave her alone. She didn't kill him."

"We know, sir. We've already told you on many occasions. That's what make's this so tragic. If you made the effort to get her to turn herself in you wouldn't be in the backseat of my car and Ellie's life wouldn't be in danger. But you had to be all anti-establishment and now look where the both of you are."

Marty grunted and sat lower in his seat. "Can't you take me to the station in Malibu? I really don't want to go to the Valley."

"Hey, Perkins, the rich man doesn't like the Valley. What's wrong? Not good enough for you?"

"Leave it kiddo." Perkins looked over his shoulder. "We're the station handling the case, that's the station we take the suspects to. Do yourself a favor and keep it shut."

Charlie looked at the incoming request and swore. They'd found Ellie's new number. Now they'd find Ellie. He didn't want them to find Ellie.

He sat back in his chair and contemplated losing the request. It would buy her some time. His company had a commitment to provide location information within fifteen minutes. Losing it wouldn't buy her very much time and it's likely he'd be taken off the legal intercept desk. All in all, a bad trade-off.

But he could warn her before he informed the cops and try and keep her out of their clutches. He used an online messaging service.

"Your number has been discovered. Geolocation will start shortly. Turn it off, find a new phone and keep your head down."

He pressed enter and turned back to his task. On an average day he could do it and report back to the police in less than two minutes. Today, for this one job, it would take the full fifteen.

Lily paced beside the pool, phone to her head, waiting for their attorney to pick up. "Hurry up you piece of - "

"Lily? Is that very nice?"

"Sorry, I'm a bit upset and you know how much I hate waiting."

"What's Marty done this time?"

"He's gotten himself arrested."

"Where is he and what has he done?"

"It's a long story. They're taking him to the Devonshire station."

"The Valley? He's being taken to the Valley?"

"So what?"

"Traffic is a bitch today." He sighed down the phone. "Okay. I'll head out there now. Do you know why he's been arrested?"

"Obstructing justice, harboring a felon and resisting arrest."

"The resisting part I get. What's this about?"

Lily sighed and sat at the outdoor table. "You know Ellie?"

"Oh, shit. Is he hiding her somewhere?"

"Not quite. We know her new mobile number and have talked to her a couple of times and he wouldn't cooperate with the police when they came around. Got kind of belligerent." She smiled. "It was like when we were first dating in the late seventies and went to all those political rallies."

"Why? For God's sake, why? And the Valley? Christ. Marty didn't like Sweeney either, but there's no cause to hide a killer."

"She didn't do it."

"Oh, they never do, Lily."

"No, really. I've had a good talk with her. She didn't. There's someone else who killed Sweeney, set her up and now is trying to get her. I wish she *would* come in."

"Irrelevant at this point. I need to get going. I'm going to miss my lunch for this."

"You can afford to miss a couple of lunches. Call me when you know when he can come home, okay? But don't rush it. He needs to cool off and I can't think of a better place."

The lawyer terminated the call and Lily sat back and tried to remember the name of the private detective. She had to call him off. There were enough problems already.

The Killer bided his time. Sunset was in six or so hours, and he had her corralled. General area, anyway. He wanted her on her toes, not sure where he was going to be next. Time to juice her.

He dialed her number. The new number. It went directly to voicemail.

"Shit." And he was away from his computer. He couldn't track her online. He had to rely on his wits.

He backtracked to the cubbyhole where he found the homeless bag lady. He raised his fist to hammer on the door when a toothless scrawny guy somewhere north of thirty, but not yet in his sixties interrupted him.

"She ain't there."

"Who the fuck are you and why should I care?"

"You looking for Ann?"

"Baggy lady with way too many coats and a black eye?"

The old guy pushed himself off the wall. "You did that to her?" He did the two right steps followed by a left step stagger most drunks were familiar with and balled up his fists like a bare-knuckled fighter from a century ago. "She's a friend. And a lady. Nobody hurts one of my friends. And a lady." He feebly flung his fist.

The Killer casually batted it away and slapped him on the side of the face. "Get stuffed, before I rearrange your boney old body." He gave him a shove, landing him on his ass in the alley. He squatted down and looked at the bum in the eyes. "So if she's not there, where can I find the hag?"

The old drew a deep breath and let loose a wad of phlegm an alpaca would be proud of, catching the Killer on the right cheek, just below his eye.

He staggered back and wiped his face with his sleeve. "Cocksucker, I'll kill you." He swung a boot into his ribs, smiling at the cracking sound on impact. "I'll be back for you, bones."

The old guy, Ann's friend, groaned and rolled into a fetal position. The Killer stood over him, unzipped his fly and urinated. "This should improve the smell. Now if you'll excuse me, I've got a bitch to find and kill."

Marty hammered on the one-way glass. "What the fuck is taking so long? Did you all go home?" He cupped his hands around his eyes and pressed against the glass in a vain attempt to see the other side.

On the other side, Stanfield elbowed Perkins in the ribs. "How long are you going to make him stew?"

"Until he shuts up and sits down, or his over-priced attorney shows up. Whichever is first."

Sampson walked into the viewing area. "The attorney wins. He just got here. Looks like he pays more for shoes than I do in rent." He flicked the business card with his nail and handed it to Perkins. "Nigel Hopkins. Your case. You can deal with the guy. Only non-Jewish lawyer in LA, I think." He handed him the card, smiled and walked out.

Stanfield went and retrieved the lawyer and joined Perkins and Marty in the interrogation room.

"Have you been talking to my client without me present?"

"Idle chat, the weather, Angels, LA Kings. Nothing related to the case. Although I don't think you have anything to worry about. It was a one-way conversation. Your client is as mute as Marcel Marceau."

"Officers,"

"Sergeants," corrected Perkins.

"Sergeants, what are you charging my client with?"

"He's been obstructing justice and harboring a fugitive, both charges related to an ongoing case, and resisting arrest, which is not related to any specific case. It's a result of us attempting to place your client in the squad car and being met with moderate physical resistance and an incessant yelling."

"Yelling? Yelling what?"

"I believe it was 'Attica', at the top of his lungs. Doesn't make much sense to me."

"Attica refers to a riot in the Attica Correctional Facility in Attica, New York in, I believe, 1971."

"I know what it refers to counselor. What doesn't make sense is the riot was triggered by poor living conditions. Have you seen your client's house? Of course you have. It's palatial."

"Which of your fugitives is he harboring? What case is he obstructing?

Perkins filled open a case file, spun it to face the other side of the table and pushed it toward the lawyer. "A Miss Ellie Bourke. She currently is a suspect in the murder of Bart Sweeney."

Marty leaned forward. "Hey. You told me in the car you thought she was set up."

Perkins held up his hand. "You're supposed to tell your client to not speak without your consent." He took a deep breath. "Until we can speak to Miss Bourke, she is still the prime suspect. Now, there may be information she can provide which would change our view, but we need to talk to her first." He pointed at Marty. "Your client has talked to Miss Bourke a number of times. When we asked your client what was said in those conversations he refused. He's also warned Miss Bourke, we believe, when we've been in the general area she's in. Harboring and obstructing."

"Ridiculous. It's not harboring if she's not under his protective care."

"I think we can convince the District attorney a virtual harboring occurred."

Nigel took off his glasses and wiped the bridge of his nose. "What do you want to make this go away?"

"Where is she, what has she said, and he contacts her and tells her to come in."

"That'll get rid of all the charges?"

Perkins pulled the file back and closed it. "Obstruction and harboring go away. Not sure about resisting."

Stanfield chuckled. "He's kinda soft, partner. Wasn't *really* resisting. I mean, I've definitely had worse."

"Good point." He looked at Marty and then at his attorney. "Cooperate with helping us track down Ellie and I'll drop the resisting."

Marty leaned close to Nigel and whispered. "No guarantees, Nigel. I talked to her a couple time and we texted, but I don't really know where she is. I already told her the cops thought she was set up. Don't think she believed me."

"You didn't try very hard to convince her, did you?"

"Oh, hell no. I still don't believe them. Him. Whatever."

Nigel nodded and sat up straight. "Gentlemen, We agree to the premise of your deal, but I have a slight concern with the details."

"Of course. You get paid by the six minutes. What's concerning you?"

"He can certainly tell you what was said in the conversation, but he's no surer of her location than you are, by the sound of it, and he's not comfortable telling her to turn herself in when he believes it to be nothing more than a trap."

Perkins stood and collected the file. "Okay. The bail hearing will be tomorrow. Your client will be spending the night." He opened the door and motioned for the constable on the other side to take Marty to the holding cell. "Process this guy." He handed him the file. "It's all in here." He and Stanfield left before Nigel had a chance to counter-offer.

"Why are you just sitting there? I'm paying you an obscene

amount of money to keep things like this from happening." Marty struggled a bit when the constable lifted him from the chair and cuffed him. "Come on, Nigel. I don't want to spend the night here."

"Then cooperate. It's easy."

"It goes against my better judgment."

"If this is your better judgment, you cuffed and heading for fingerprinting and a cell for the night, I'd hate to see the not so better judgment." He placed his glasses on, down near the end of his nose and smiled up at his client. "Just do it, Marty. You know what you have to do."

The Killer walked south on the boardwalk along Venice Beach for the third time in the last hour. He'd circled the geographical area he was told she was in and hadn't seen her since he saw her hiding in the alcove.

He scrubbed his face with his hands. His whiskers were getting soft. It had been a couple of days. Fished the Altoids tin from his pocket and popped two more pills. He dry swallowed and suppressed a retch. The brights were getting brighter and the sounds echoed like his head was in a fifteen gallon plastic bucket.

Anger, no, rage fueled him. The threads were slipping through his fingers and he never lost control. "Never." But it felt like he was in danger of losing it this time.

He reached the end of the beach, past the fishing pier and all the way to via Marina at the entrance to Marina del Rey. He wiped the sweat from his neck and walked up via Marina until he reached Pacific Avenue, where he turned left again and headed north. "I'm probably too far south. Fuck." He stepped up his pace until he passed the end of the lagoon. "This is closer to her location. Her last location." He debated having her checked again, but that was something he couldn't do forever without getting caught. He looked at his watch. He still had four hours before it was critical.

He was moving on instinct now. Left on Hurricane then right on Speedway. A few more blocks and he was near the hole in the wall where he slammed the bag lady.

He discounted going after her again. "She's a waste of air." He was about a block away and ready to get back on the beach when a movement caught the corner of his eye. He took a step back and watched Ellie step out of a doorway.

"Luck of the fucking Irish. You're mine."

He shadowed her, a bit more than a half a block behind. He wouldn't lose her again.

Chapter Twenty-Five

I felt like I was in the cross-hairs of a sniper's scope, eyes on me all the time. Shadows flitted past the corners of my eyes. I couldn't place any one person tailing me, but the feeling was unsettling.

Almost as unsettling as the message from Charlie. The police had my number. I needed a new one. I was running low on cash, but the alternative was broadcasting my location to the cops every step I took.

I dropped in to the same phone shop on the boardwalk Danny had visited and got another pre-pay phone.

What the asshole said about Ann worried me. I took a mazy route back to her place. She had nothing to do with this and I really didn't like him getting her involved.

I paused by the door and looked around. Nobody appeared to be paying me any attention. I knocked gently on the door and slipped into the old storage room.

Ann was curled up on her mattress, back to the door, face to the wall. Her snores sounded wet, like she was choking on phlegm. I gently rolled her over and stepped back. "Shit." Her upper lip was split and blood caked her cheek.

She moaned and pulled back. "Lemme alone."

"Ann. It's me. Jesus, girl. Are you okay?"

She pulled her coats tighter and grunted something I couldn't understand. She needed a stitch or two in her lip and a good cleaning, but I couldn't help her in the state she was in right now. And the longer I stayed here, the more likely I'd be on the receiving end of a battle I didn't want to have around her.

I gave her shoulder a squeeze. "I'll be back, Ann. Take it easy. Lock the door and don't let anyone in. Remember, lock the door."

If he was following me, I'd make sure he followed me far away from here. Ann had enough.

And I'd make sure he'd have to work for it.

I turned on the newest phone and looked at the compromised pre-pay phone. I stuffed it in the front pocket of my pants.

A cold gust of wind swept in off the Pacific. I looked west and saw a bank of dark clouds moving in at a good clip. It was going to get wet before it got dark.

I debated sending a message to Charlie thanking him but discarded that idea pretty quickly. My number was going to stay very private until all of this was finished.

I slid it in my back pocket and slowly scanned the full 360

degrees. I was just south of the fish pier. The population on the beach was light to start with on a Thursday, and the approaching cold front quickly dispersed those who remained. Harder for me to hide, but harder for ass-hat to sneak up on me. And if he wanted to keep an eye on me he was going to have to work for it.

It was little over two and a half miles between the Venice Fish Pier and the Santa Monica pier. I used to run it frequently, two or three times a week, before the training intensified for the movie. Then I got enough exercise with the hand to hand combat training - I needed a five mile run like I needed a second head.

I started off with an easy stride. I was confident I couldn't be tracked through my phone meaning this guy would have to keep up if he was going to keep an eye on me like he said he would.

The beauty of it was jogging in Southern California was as natural as bottled water and spray tans. I fit right in. Not sure if he would.

Jogging up the beach walk was easy. Keeping an eye behind me to see if someone was following, not so much. I'd slow and rotate the full 360 every few hundred meters, and there *were* others jogging along behind me, but none looked like homicidal maniacs.

Whatever that looked like.

The crowd thinned. The wind picked up and the temperature dropped.

The crowd on the beach were pussies. This was perfect running weather. It had cooled to the low seventies and working up a sweat was no longer a concern. I hit a rhythm. At this point I didn't care if I was being followed; endorphins had kicked in and I was feeling excellent.

I wound around the Venice Beach Rec Centre and took a glance over my shoulder. Nobody. Not a single soul was jogging behind me, which was disconcerting. Either I had lost the guy, or he had other plans. I eased up on the pace to a coast. I was half way to the Santa Monica Pier. The plan didn't really work. There was no point doing the full run. I turned around and started jogging back.

I felt like those Secret Service guys you see running beside the Presidential motorcade, hyper-alert and ready to take down anyone even slightly suspicious.

But there was no one.

Sitting on the edge of the skate park bowl was a face I hadn't expected to see. "Kent?" He looked like shit. "You okay?"

He rubbed his face. "So there you are. I've been looking for you."

"Why? I'm trying to keep a low profile here, mate."

"I've been trying to call you and it's been going to voice mail. Thought the worst might have happened to you."

I stood in front of him, arms spread wide. "I'm just fine. You shouldn't be down here. The cops are still looking for me and you're a known associate. If they're following you around they'll find me, and I don't want them to find me."

"So you're okay?"

"I'm fine." I looked around. Was anyone watching us? The crowd was thin. I stuck out a bit. "Where are the kids? This place is never empty."

He nodded toward the ocean. "Probably the crap weather coming in. So you're sure you're okay?"

"Don't I look it?"

"You look like you've been living rough for a couple of days.

Where you been hanging out?"

I shook my head. "Doesn't matter. It's ending tonight."

A small smile crossed his face so fast I almost missed it. "Turning yourself in?"

"Eventually. Things I've got to finish first."

"What in the hell are you hoping to accomplish?"

I sat down beside him. "I can't go talk to Perkins and their crowd until I have enough information to convince them somebody set me up and is now trying to kill me."

"So the cops are right? Someone's trying to kill you? Who?"

"Some Batman-voiced asshole calling me. And texting me. He's already admitted to killing Sweeney and has promised tonight will be my last sunset."

"And you're not going to the cops?"

"Like they'd believe me. No, I'm going to draw this asshole out and finish him off myself."

He laughed.

"What's so funny?"

Kent wiped his face and tried to compose himself. "Look, I'm all for female independence and all that, but if there's a guy threatening to kill you, don't you think you should take him a bit more seriously? You're not a muscle-bound athlete. You're scrawny." He got a silly serious look on his face. "Look, Ellie, you've got to take this seriously. You don't want to end up dead over this when you could avoid it."

"Avoiding things just puts it off. This guy is a whack-job. He said I'm just one on a list and when he's finished with me he's got more to go through. I just avoid it and someone else is targeted. You know me.

I can't do that. I need to find the fucker."

He put his hands up in surrender. "Hey, crazy lady, you're on your own. Don't let me get in front of you and your crusade. You're just going to get yourself killed."

I stood and dusted the sand off my ass.

"Where you going?"

"You don't need to know. I don't want any of my friends dragged into this. Too many people getting hurt already. I don't want to add you to the list." I took off my cap, scratched my scalp and tugged it back on. "So bugger off and let me finish this. Don't follow me. There's already someone out there saying they're following me and I don't want to get confused." I turned to leave. Then thought of something. "Hey, just one thing. Can you check with Stevie, or whatever her name is to see what Perkins and his cohort are really up to? I don't buy this angle they believe I was set up. I think it's just a trap. Can you sass it out? I'll be by here tomorrow at noon. Gives you a day to find out for me."

"Noon tomorrow? I thought tonight was going to be your last sunset." He had a mocking grin on his face.

"Don't piss me off or I'll show you how strong I am. You check with Stevie, okay?" I continued jogging south, keeping an eye for whoever was following me.

I scratched my scalp though my hat. I was getting itchy. No, check that. I *was* itchy. This lack of personal hygiene did not suit me.

The beach was almost vacant. I hadn't been paying attention to the news, let alone the weather. The storm must be a big one. The onshore wind picked up. The caps ripped off the top of the swells, but they were big. Some boys on boards stuck some nice ones. I envied them. I would love nothing more than to take my old board out and submerge myself in the waves. It had been too long.

And it had been too long since I had a shower. I felt like Ann looked. I jogged south past the Venice Fish Pier and cut closer to the surf.

And almost ran into Ann.

I caught myself and took her by the hand. "Ann? It's me, Ellie. You okay?"

"You mean am I lucid right now? I am." She winced as she licked her lips. "A bit sore, but I'm lucid."

A held her head gently and leaned down to look at her face. "Oh, honey, so sorry. This is because of me. Someone chasing me somehow linked you to me and because of that you got hurt. I never meant that to happen."

"Of course you didn't. That's just stupid talk. I've had worse, believe me." She snugged her coat. "We're in for a biggie. Who was that guy?"

"Which one?"

She pointed at her face. "Which one do you think I'm talking about? The one who punched me. He knew you and wasn't very nice."

"I don't know his name, but he's the guy who killed the man I've been accused of killing, and now wants to kill me."

"Young lady, you need to go to the police."

"You sound like my mom." I smiled. "What she sounded like. Before she died."

"I'm sorry."

"No, it's been over ten years now." I took off my hat and scrubbed my scalp. "I need to get clean. I can't go to the police. They still think I killed a guy and unless and until I can prove different, going to them will just guarantee me a life in jail, or the death penalty if they still do that."

She stood there shaking her head until I thought she was slipping into a fugue state again.

"You okay?"

"Too much death. Too much death." She started walking south, the surf lapping at her feet. "Too much death."

I ran up along side and stopped her. "No more." I took her by the hand. "Now you wouldn't happen to have any soap or shampoo in one of those pockets would you?"

She sniffed, squeezed my hand and looked up at me. "Sure. And you need it. You stink." She took a small bar of soap from one of her many pockets. "Biodegradable, safe for the planet."

"You're a life saver. Where can I go?"

"What do you mean?"

"Where can I go to wash? I can't just lather up in the ocean, they'll freak."

"Who?"

I pointed to the life guard shack down the beach. "Them."

"They closed the beach early, about half an hour ago. Big storm coming in." She smiled. "The pretty boys left ten minutes ago."

"Just us pretty girls, then. I'm going in."

I took off my shoes, jeans and top and folded them in a pile under the pier.

"Um, Ellie, you're topless."

I crossed my arms across my chest. "Sure. I know. But hardly." I leaned down and picked the soap up from the pocket of my jeans. "I'll get under quick. I'm going to be staying under the pier anyway."

"Oh, I don't know. It doesn't seem very safe. The waves are getting big and those pilings are concrete."

"I'm a big girl. I've swum in much worse conditions than this. You should see some of the surf we get in Australia. And I'm not even going out very deep. Just need to wash off. You coming out too?"

"Oh, no. I got a place I can go to every once in a while. YWCA just up the road. You could have gone there."

I shook my head as I started to wade into the cold water. "No, the police would have sent my picture around there, probably. If you're not coming in could you keep an eye on my stuff? Thanks"

I waded into the water, up past my waist, threading through the pilings. The waves were building in strength, pushing me against them a couple of times. I got up to my armpits in the water, waves crashing off the pilings and then off me, bouncing me around a bit.

I caught a shadow in the other side and stopped and looked. Nothing. I turned my back to the beach and started lathering. I was probably going to get busted for this so I moved fast. There was no way I'd feel fully clean with the salt water, but this was much better than nothing. I lathered all the sweaty bits then submerged my head.

God, the water was cold. I returned to the surface and soaped my hair. The short hair felt funny, but good. I was going to keep it that way for a while. I ducked under to rinse off the lather and I didn't think I was ever going to make it back to the surface.

Chapter Twenty-Six

The Killer sat in the sand a short distance north of the pier and watched as Ellie undressed. He smiled and licked his lips. This might be better. It wasn't the plan, but when opportunities like this presented themselves he had to take them. There was no question.

This opportunity he couldn't pass up.

From where he sat the pilings were a disorganized stand of concrete tree trunks, but if shifted a little bit, either toward the water or away from it, they lined up forming a diagonal grove of pillars.

He didn't have the cover of darkness like he wanted to, but the darkness under the pier and the cover provided by the pilings almost made up for it.

This scenario also prevented him from torturing her as much as he wanted to, and he had anticipated that part of the mission the most. But death by drowning could still be a very horrible way to go, especially if he didn't actually kill her, but incapacitated her somehow and left her to drown.

He laughed. He promised her a death by self-immolation, the 'self', of course being involuntary. Now he was on the opposite end of the spectrum, trading fire for water, contemplating drowning her.

He shook his head. "No, not contemplating, doing."

Once he was done with her he could leave a scrawled suicide note, crumpled and damp from the rain, stuffed in a pant pocket.

He watched her fold her clothes and stack them under the pier. Perfect. Then as she walked into the water she disappeared among the mess of the pilings. Occasional and brief glimpses between them marked her progress into the ocean.

Disorganization was his friend. He stood and slowly approached the pier. He needed to use the angles for concealment. As he approached he could hear her humming. This was even better than he expected. Her guard was down. She wasn't expecting anything during the day and it was a couple of hours before it got dark.

Perfect.

Roughly ten feet separated the pilings, three across the width of the pier and extending well out into the ocean. He walked down toward the water on the north side of the pier, peeking between pilings to ensure he wasn't spotted.

A large wave surged up the beach and between the concrete pillars, swirling seaweed and foam in a dizzying and loud mess.

The noise covered his stumbling approach through the water.

He stopped in knee-deep water and look down.

His shoes, his clothes, his wallet and his watch. He hadn't thought this through.

But there was no time for thinking. It would all work out. It always did.

The water squished though his shoes and socks, weighing down his legs. His jeans pulled down on his ass as the water wicked up to his crotch. Another wave swept up the beach and he had to hold on to a piling to stay on his feet. He inched a little closer and peered around the column and saw Ellie, short hair full of suds, humming while she scrubbed. Her back was three-quarters to him. He could see the slight swell of her right breast.

"Small-titted bitch."

She stopped scrubbing and looked around. He pulled back out of sight and waited for her to duck her head under for a rinse.

Cathy picked up her phone and put it down on the table.

Bernie made a tick mark on a piece of paper by his chair. "That's ten."

"Ten what?"

"Ten times now you've gone to call someone and thought better of it. What's going on?"

She rubbed her nose with the back of her hand and shook her head. "Nothing."

"Horseshit nothing. It's something. What is it?"

She sighed. "You know Ellie mentioned someone was framing her and she had a friend who had a friend in the police station who was helping her out?"

"The friend's name was Kent Williams."

"Not him. What was the name of the person inside the police station?"

Bernie closed his eyes and thought. "Different name. Guy's and girl's. Sammy? Shelly? Not that's not a guy's name, just a girl's name."

Cathy snapped her fingers. "Stevie."

"Yup. That's it. Why?"

"I'm calling the station and talking to her."

"She's not going to talk to you."

"She's talking to an actor about Ellie. I'm Ellie's best friend. Surely this Stevie will talk to me."

"The actor's her friend, but what the hell, go for it. Maybe you'll get lucky."

The killer looked around the pillar to see Ellie submerge herself to rinse the soap out of her hair. He seized the opportunity and pushed through the swirling water as fast as he could. Less than three seconds after she went under he was near her. Behind her.

He placed his hand above her head. As she came up to breathe he let her get to nose level then pushed down with all of his strength. He leaned into it. Her hands breached the surface and started grabbing at his, but he had a full handful of her short hair.

He braced himself and pulled up, hard.

His voice deepened. "Too bad, no fire to end your life. I'm sure you were anticipating that. No, today you drown. Repeatedly."

She struggled to turn around to see him. He smiled and shook his head. "No dice." He grabbed her by the back of the neck and held her steady. "Got your breath? Hope so 'cause you're going under again." He chuckled, deep and hoarse. He was doing his throat in with this. He looked forward to killing her and stopping with the stupid voice.

He relaxed his attention a bit too much.

Wool gathering, his grandmother used to call it.

A pointy fist to the side of the head would be his new name for it. "Hey, bitch," he growled. "The more you fight, the longer I'm going to keep you alive, suffering in one contrived torture session after another."

She struggled again, trying to turn.

He grabbed her by the back of the neck again and squeezed. "Bitch." He leaned his head close to hers. "Get used to being owned, bitch."

Ellie snapped her head back, catching him on the nose and left cheek, cracking both. "Ungh. Fuck you asshole." She lunged forward and glanced off a piling, wiping soap from her eyes.

The Killer held his face and swore. He struggled forward against the waves and dove under the water, catching her by the ankle. He pulled her under and stood on her back with one foot, feeling her struggle. He leaned against a column for support and waited until she stopped. He held his face with one hand, blood pouring out of his nose.

When she stopped moving he reached down to grab her by the hair and was met by a flurry of fists and kicks. A wave surged around the pilings knocking them both off their feet. Clumps of seaweed covered them, like slimy fishnets pulling them under. The Killer kept his head averted and staggered around behind Ellie, grabbing her by the throat from behind.

She struggled to stand, grabbing his pinky fingers and twisting them outwards with a grunt. She rolled her left shoulder and swung her elbow back glancing off his jaw, knocking him backwards into the surf.

He fought through the increasing waves and the seaweed. He leaned against a piling and peeled a clump of seaweed from his face. Ellie was cursing and yelling something, fighting against the waves to get to the beach.

"Like fuck, bitch." The two of them fought against a rising surge. The wind increased and the heavens opened, a sheet of rain coming from the sky.

The Killer wiped the rain from his eyes and lurched forward, grabbing Ellie by the arm and dragging her back, careening off one piling and smashing her into another. The wind whipped the caps off the waves, blinding them with the spray. His rage grew. This wasn't supposed to be so difficult. He stumbled, falling more than he was walking and fell on top of Ellie. He pushed her face into the water and wiped the spray off his face with the other hand. "Fuck, you fucking bitch." She struggled, flailing with both arms, then kicked out with her feet catching him in the groin.

He double over, releasing her head and cursing. She pushed up, sucked in a lungful of air and screamed something the Killer couldn't make out. She kicked at him again, missing and ran up the beach. A wave caught her, slamming her into one of the pilings. She slumped and grabbed on to it. The Killer struggled to get to his feet and pushed through the water to reach her when the crazy bag lady waded into the water. She looked at him, narrowed her eyes and helped Ellie get to the beach.

The Killer weighed his options. She was tougher than he thought she was. He needed a plan B. He couldn't do her now, and there was a witness. He didn't want witnesses. She saw his face, but he knew where she lived.

He staggered to the north side of the pier and pushed through to the beach. It was vacant. The surfers had surrendered to the weather. Not even the insane would be out in this. He wiped the water off his face and winced when he touched his nose. "Shit. Fuck, that hurts." He looked at his hand and watched the rain wash away the blood. "Oh, she's gonna pay."

He was drenched and it felt like he had a broken nose. "There will be blood. Lots of blood."

It looked like Ellie was staying with the old lady. Tonight was going to be a two-fer.

Cathy hung up.

"What did you find out?"

"I was on hold the first time so long my battery almost died. The second time I called I got shunted between homicide, robbery, and someone who had an accent so thick I couldn't understand a word they were saying. This last time I was on hold again. Gave up waiting." She looked at her watch. "And pretty soon all the office schleps will be gone."

Bernie snatched the phone from the table. "Let me try."

He waded through a veritable IVR hell before he got a person.

"Ah, fantastic. My name is Steve Austin with the Valley Free Press. I'm doing a story on the proposed State initiative to halt all pay increases for the next two years. Can I talk to your media relations person?" He winked at Cathy while he waited for a pissed off media rep.

"What are you doing?"

"Just wait." He returned his attention to the phone. "Good afternoon. What was your name again? Miss Wilson? Oh, Nancy. So would you care to comment on the proposed initiative to cap salaries in the police departments around the state for the next two calendar years?"

He listened with a concerned look on his face. Cathy tried hard to stifle a laugh.

"My name? Steven Austin of the Valley Free Press. I just read about this initiative on the wire so I'm not too surprised you haven't heard about it yet. Apparently the Governor is pulling out all stops to balance the budget, or at least appear to, before the next state election. A bit harsh on the public servants, but the polls seem to support his actions."

He nodded and listened. "Yes. Yes. Interesting view. May I quote you? Your official title?" He nodded and pretended to scribble. "Thank you very much. I appreciate your time."

He listened for a couple of more seconds before interrupting her. "Hey, listen, can you help me out here? Took me a dog's age to get through to you and I've got to talk to a girl in the evidence room. I tried calling her mobile, but it's off, or the coverage in there is as bad as it's always been. Can you put me through to her? Transfer me or something? We met last weekend and were supposed to get together tonight for drinks."

He listened, frowning. He put his hand over the phone. "It's Stevie, right?"

Cathy nodded. "Why?"

He held up a finger and returned to the phone. "No, it's not Wally I'm looking for. Her name is Stevie. Works in the evidence locker area. Really? Wally? Maybe Stevie has transferred to a different department?"

He shook his head while he listened. "So Wally has been there for the last two years and will be until he retires in six months. So no Stevie? This is Devonshire, right?"

Cathy whispered. "What's going on?"

He shrugged and talked to the phone. "No Stevie of any sort there? Huh. I guess I was stood up. Well, Nancy, I apologize for taking your time, and thanks for talking to me about the Governor's initiatives. I'll be sure to send you a draft before it goes to press on Monday."

He hung up and sat back. "Weird."

"That was slick, and possibly illegal. What was that all about? Wally? Who's Wally?"

"Ellie told you her buddy, what's his name, Kent had an inside track with the cops, right? A Stevie in the evidence area, right?"

"Records clerk."

"Same difference. There's nobody at the station by the name of Stevie unless you count Steve Hanson, the dude who washes the cars."

"Wally?"

"The guy at the evidence locker. Overweight dude putting in time until he can cashier out on full pension."

"Very weird."

"Ellie's under a lot of stress. She probably heard the name wrong."

Cathy snorted. "How much stress do you have to be under to mistake "Wally" for "Stevie"? No, something's fishy about this. I'm going to call her."

"Really? Over an incorrect name?"

"She's got the right to know." Cathy dialed the number and went straight to voicemail. "Ellie, it's just me. Call me when it's safe. Tried to reach Kent's contact at the police station, Stevie. There is no Stevie there in any job. How well do you know Kent? Watch your back, Ellie. I've got a bad feeling about this." She closed her phone and took a deep breath. "Don't like this, Bern."

"What? The guy got the name wrong?"

"I don't think he got the name wrong. I think he's feeding her a line of bullshit."

"Why in the hell would he do that?"

"How the hell should I know? You're too trusting, Bernie. My best friend is running around trying to keep from getting killed and one of the guys supposed to be helping her has been lying to her. What am I supposed to think about that? Shit. Where the hell is she?"

Chapter Twenty-Seven

I ran out of the water with Ann holding my arm, fighting to fill my lungs and keep my balance. The rain and the spray cut visibility to a few hundred feet and I had no idea where the asshole was.

"Ann, thank you." I stooped and grabbed my clothes and kept running. "You're a sight for sore eyes."

"You better put a shirt on before you get arrested."

"I'll take a cop, right now. Can you see the guy?"

"Who?"

"The guy who just tried to kill me. Is he still behind us?"

Ann looked back and shook her head. "I don't see him. Are you okay?"

"I thought I was dead there for a minute. But I got a few good licks in. Did you see him?"

Ann nodded and kept running, pulling me with her.

"Hang on, putting on the shirt." I put the pants and the shoes on the wet beach and struggled with my polo short over wet skin. "I'm incredibly uncomfortable right now." I scooped the pants and shoes and kept running. "Where are we going? Back to your place?"

"No good. He was there already. He knows the place."

I nodded. Smart. "So where?"

She took my arm and ran between two buildings and turned an abrupt left.

"Ann, I'm shocked. You're in pretty good shape."

"Spend a lot of my time on my feet. Keep up, will you?" She slowed a bit. "He was bleeding. Did you see him?"

"Didn't see his face, no. Did I get him in the nose?"

"Seems so. He wasn't happy. Do you know who this crazy person is?"

"Like I said, I didn't get a look at him. He talked like Batman all the time so I don't recognize his voice and I have no idea why he's doing this. But he certainly knows me. My fucking luck."

She tsked me.

"What?"

"Young lady shouldn't talk like that."

I smiled. "Okay mom." A gust of wind swamped us with a wave of rain. "Dam - Darn it, I'm soaked. Where are we going?"

"Just around the corner."

"That's what you said last time."

"What's wrong, getting tired? I thought you were fit."

"I just had the stuffing beat out of me, ma'am. If you don't mind, I'd like to sit a spell."

She laughed. "In here." She pulled open the door of a container sitting on a construction site.

"What is this?"

"They haven't worked on this site for six months. A friend broke the lock off this a couple of months ago. Not many people know about it and it's not very comfortable. But it's safe."

She closed the door behind us.

"It's dark in here, Ann."

"I haven't been able to convince DWP to hook anything up."

I couldn't see her face so I couldn't tell if she was kidding or delusional. But I wasn't going to argue the point. "Thank you very much. I owe you my life."

"I've been bored lately anyway. You've added a bit of spice to my life."

"You're better than this, you know that, right?"

I heard her sigh and adjust herself. "It's just too hard to try and keep it on an even keel. I gave up a couple of years ago."

"Surely you have friends or family who can help you."

She didn't reply. I heard a sniffle and then nothing.

"You okay?"

Nothing.

It was going to be a long night. And it was starting to cool off. Wind blew sheets of rain against the side of the metal container, sounding like nails against the metal sides.

I felt around on the floor for my jeans. I heard a thunk as I picked them up. "Shit. My phones." I pulled the wet pants on my wet legs. Better than nothing. Body heat would help them dry. I felt around until I found the phones. The pre-pays were flip phones. I couldn't tell in the dark which was which. I turned them both on and check the call records and turned the busy one off and left the new one on. The light from the display was weak, but it allowed me to see the inside of the container. Shelves lined the far end. Blankets, burlap sacks and other scraps of cloth lined the half the floor they were on. The other half was bare metal, empty food containers scattered around the floor.

"It's not going to work in here." She was awake.

"Excuse me?"

"It's a metal building. The signal in here is too weak. It's not going to work in here."

She was right. I was flickering between no service and a single bar. I stood and moved toward the door. "I'll have to go outside then."

"It's pouring out. You'll get drenched."

"I'm already wet, Ann. It's not going to make any difference." I cracked open the door and quickly closed it behind me and ducked around to the lee side of the container. I needed to talk to a friend.

I leaned against the wall and hugged myself. I dialed Cathy's number from memory. This meant she'd have my number now, but frankly I didn't care. I was cold, wet, alone and some jerk-wad had just tried to kill me. And I was hanging with a lady who all of a sudden wouldn't let me fucking swear.

She answered almost before it rang.

"Is this...?"

"Cathy, Ellie here. Thanks for answering. I needed to hear a friendly voice. I've had a hell of a day."

"Where are you? I'll come and get you. We can hang in that Super-8 we shared a room in a lifetime ago."

I smiled. Good memories. "I can't get you wrapped up in this. I just needed to hear a friendly voice. You been hassled by the cops much?"

"Not really. They've come by a couple of times. Perkins and his kid partner. Reminds me of Josh Hartnett."

"Perkins?"

"His partner. Bernie ever pushes my last button I may track this cop down and make him an offer he can't refuse."

I laughed. I could hear Bernie yelling something in the background. "Why wait?" A clatter of rain drowned out the conversation for a second as a gust swept through from the ocean.

"Are you out in this? Ellie, you've got to get under cover. This is a hell of a storm and it's just going to get worse."

Good old Cathy, mother-hen from the first time I met her. "I'm cool. Got a place I can go to get out of this mess. Just standing outside right now so I don't disturb my roommate while she sleeps." I sniffed. "It's getting cold."

"Are you okay? You don't sound okay."

"Well, aside from the fact I've been framed for killing someone I wanted dead, been threatened myself and not half an hour ago fought off some asshole who tried to drown me, yeah, I'm peachy."

"So you're still near the beach. Someone try to pick you up and got a bit too aggressive?"

"No. The same guy who killed Sweeney tried to get me."

"Shit."

"Exactly."

"Did you get my voicemail?"

I was momentarily confused. "You didn't have this number. How did you get it?"

"I called in the last number I knew. You must have just changed it."

"I was getting too many creepy messages and now apparently the cops have it. Marty was arrested for not cooperating with the police and they, I guess, got the number from his phone."

"So what now?"

The thought of a warm hotel room, a pizza and a couple of beer with my best friend was very tempting. "You're wearing me down."

"Tell me where you are and I'll be there as fast as I can."

"I can't. Really. Look, this is coming to a head. The whack-job tried to drown me and he'll be looking for me to finish me off. I've got to get him and the cops in the same room and end this once and for all."

"Did you get my voicemail?"

"You asked that already. I didn't know the prepay had voicemail. So no. What was it?"

"I called the station - sorry, I tried to call the station. Bernie called the station and asked to talk to Stevie. We wanted to find out what they knew."

I closed my eyes and swore. "Jesus, Cathy. You're going to get yourself in serious trouble. I appreciate the thought, but don't help, okay? This is serious stuff."

"No, that's what I'm trying to tell you. There is no Stevie there, in the records room or the evidence locker or anywhere else. Not a female Stevie, anyway."

I stood up straight. "You called the right station?"

"Devonshire."

"Yeah. That's the one." I twirled some hair. Some nervous tics held on from my early teen years. "Kent must have got the name wrong. Or maybe she's in a different station and has contacts in Devonshire."

"Or maybe Kent's full of shit."

"What would he gain from that?"

"Trying to get into your pants, maybe? You known him long?"

"Since we filmed *Beast of Bondi* in Australia some four years ago. No. He's never shown any interest in anything like that."

Cathy laughed. "You are a blind girl when it comes to the opposite sex, honey. He could be crawling all over you and you wouldn't get it."

"Am not." God it felt good talking to a friend. "This is nice. I'm glad I called. I've got to get going, though. I need to get inside before the jack-hole finds me."

"You need to talk to the police about this. He's going to kill you."

I shook my head. "No fucking way. He got the drop on me and he had no success. I'm not going to be that stupid again. I know he's coming after me and he won't catch me by surprise. Don't worry about me. I'm a lot tougher than I look. And whoever he is, he's going to find that out once and for all."

"You're not going to go looking for him in this weather are you?"

"I'm not crazy. No, I'll hole up where I can keep my back covered tonight. Tomorrow I'll finish him once and for all. I'll talk to you tomorrow, Cath. And fingers crossed I'll be clear of this shit."

"Be careful. I feel like I should be helping you."

"I'll talk to you tomorrow." I hung up and walked out from behind the container. The rain was pelting down, in waves. Global warming, my ass. I was freezing. I slipped into the container, careful not to disturb Ann. I closed the door behind me and sat against the wall, an old blanket around my shoulders.

I couldn't sleep. A few things Cathy said kept running through my head. I didn't know these prepay cards had voicemail. I had a couple of missed calls earlier from her and on from the person who had been threatening me. His voice mail, if he left one, might shed some additional light on what was going on.

Other than the light from my phone, though, it was pitch black in the container. I fished my old pre-pay phone from my pocket. Hopefully it hadn't been damaged in all the crap I'd just gone through.

I cycled the power on the phone and when it came back up I had no service. I had to go outside again. Shit. And I was just starting to warm up.

I slipped out, pounded by the weather and scooted to the relative calm of the lee side of the box. The phone vibrated with four new messages: Cathy's missed call and assumed voice mail, two missed calls from Marty's phone and one indicating an unheard voice message.

The pre-pay phones were with the same provider as my iPhone so I dialed the same retrieval number and got through to a recording informing me I had four messages.

The newest one was from Perkins. He must have used Marty's phone to call me, expecting me to pick up.

"Miss Bourke, I'm calling again in the hope you listen to this and take yourself to the nearest police station, for your own safety. I understand you believe this to be some sort of trick. It's not. You would be well advised to follow these instructions as soon as you hear this message."

Blah, blah, blah.

The messages were in reverse chronological order. The next one was also from Perkins:

"Miss Bourke, Sergeant Perkins calling you from your manager's phone. He is currently in custody for resisting arrest, harboring a fugitive and obstructing justice. Do him and yourself a favor and contact me as quickly as possible and let us help you sort this problem out."

I smiled. Marty in jail would be a treat to listen to. Ann wouldn't like it. Marty had some of the most colorful swearing I've ever heard a non-Australian use.

The third message was from Cathy:

"Ellie, it's just me. Call me when it's safe. Tried to reach Kent's contact at the police station, Stevie. There is no Stevie there in any job. How well do you know Kent? Watch your back, Ellie. I've got a bad feeling about this."

She sounded more concerned on that call than she did while I was talking to her.

The fourth message was brief. It was from the asshole trying to kill me, or at least scare me. There was a lot of background noise on the message and at the end the voice was faint, like the phone was held a distance from his head. There was the whoop of a police siren and then some words. The voice was vaguely familiar.

The rain beating against the metal box behind me didn't help any. I shivered and turned the volume all the way up and replayed the message as I pressed the phone hard to my ear and plugged the other one. The first few words were in his bad Batman imitation:

"Hey bitch, you think you can hide - "

And then it stopped. I could hear the police siren. It almost blew my eardrum out. Then his voice, un-Batmanned:

"Oh, fuck. Fucking cops."

Shit. Four words. I had to be sure. I played it back again, eyes squeezed shut in concentration, listening to those four words. I recognized the voice.

But it couldn't be.

Chapter Twenty-Eight

Rain pelted the beach as the Killer sat under the Venice Fish Pier and weathered the storm. He felt his nose and winced. The bleeding had stopped, and it was very tender and swollen, but he didn't think it was broken. The cut under his left eye had stopped bleeding, probably because of the amount of sand packed in it.

He closed his eyes and took a few deep breaths through his mouth. His heart was pounding. He rolled on to his knees and crawled out from under the top end of the pier. Sheets of rain, ocean spray and blown wet sand covered him almost immediately. He shoved his hands in his pockets and tucked his head and quickly walked up the beach.

He stopped on the pedestrian walkway on the 24th and took his bearings. He turned in a full circle, almost losing his balance and landing on his ass. "Oops." He sniffed, and tilted his head, closed one eye and tried to remember where he had punched the bag lady.

"In the face, of course." He giggled. "But where the fuck was I?"

He turned right at the next lane and headed south. Exhaustion robbed him of what little coherent thought he still had. He remembered it was on this street. He remembered the door was a little off the street and opened to a storage room. He had no idea which building it was in. He walked south, holding his face and pushing on doors as he passed them. A couple of yells from inside spurred him on. They weren't the correct doors. He'd know it when he saw it. He had perfect memory.

He hoped.

Almost two blocks down the road and the door appeared in front of him as if by magic. He gave it a push and stood back as it slowly swung open. "Hey bitches. You in here?"

He peered around the corner, walked around the door jamb and into the room. "Yeah, this is the place."

The two mattresses looked untouched. This may have been the place, but they weren't here now.

He sniffed. "Stinks in here. But not enough."

He lowered his fly and urinated on both mattresses and the floor between them. "Where. The fuck. Are you?"

Perkins rapped on the cell bars with the ring on his ring finger. "You awake in there?"

Marty rolled over. "Ah, Sergeant. Do you have room service? I'd like a BLT and a nice cold beer, if I could. On multigrain. Toasted."

Perkins smiled. "Your sense of humor has returned."

"I'm just absolutely delighted at the money I'm going to get out of the county for this unreasonable arrest and restraint and whatever else my expensive lawyer can think of. Can I leave now?"

"Well, you've been such a great guest, I don't see why not." He motioned for the constable to unlock the cell. "Plus, your attorney has made bail, so we really can't keep you anyway."

Marty swung his legs off the cot and stood. "Excellent. This bed leaves a lot to be desired. To whom do I lodge a complaint?"

Perkins snickered. "Your attorney has the details for the court appearance. Don't be late."

Marty held out his hand and Perkins shook it.

He pulled his hand back. "No, I wasn't offering to shake your hand. I want my phone back."

Perkins held the phone between his thumb and forefinger. "We've got everything we need from it. But I caution you to play it straight with us going forward. You're lucky I haven't insisted on the obstruction charges. Had a strong case."

"I don't believe it for a second, but," he took his phone and held his hands up in surrender, "I'm not going to fight it. It really is an uncomfortable bed and I'm glad to be out. Which way do I go?"

The constable led him out of the station and left him with his lawyer.

"Nigel, my boy, what the fuck took you so long? The most uncomfortable cell I've ever been in."

Nigel unfurled an umbrella and held it above the both of them. "Really? I've seen you in worse."

Marty leaned into the wind and aimed for the car. "In my youth, yeah. I was younger in my youth. I was tougher." He rubbed his stomach. "I'm getting old and fat now and this jail shit isn't as much fun as it used to be." He hopped in the passenger seat of his attorney's car. "I'd ask you to take me to Venice, but you'd end up telling Lily, so take me home. I'll head out later."

His lawyer laughed. "I'll go with you. Used to be my stomping ground as a kid. You got any ideas where in that mess she might be hanging out?"

"That's the problem. Not the slightest."

Nigel laughed. "So where do we start?"

"Skate park, then head south. I don't know why, but she seems to be hanging around where she lives, which is stupid on the face of it, but there you go."

"You going to call Lily?"

Marty drummed his fingers on the armrest. "I probably should. But I'm not going to. She can think I'm behind bars for a couple of more hours."

"I won't tell if you won't." He pulled on to the Pacific highway and pointed south, toward Venice.

His nose throbbed and the heat coming off the cut on his cheek felt like a small furnace. Sand migrated down the crack of his ass making walking uncomfortable. His clothes were still wet, but the pounding rain wasn't going to let them dry. Wet was wet.

He stood in the middle of the skate bowl at Venice Skate Park and tilted his face up to the rain. "Let it come, bitch." The water pounded off his face, driven by the wind, striking him like needles. He grit his teeth, closed his eyes and roared. "BRING IT YOU FUCKING BITCH."

He spread his arms, crucifix style and absorbed the power of the elements. "You can't hide. You can't hide. You can't fucking hide."

He shook his head, spraying water into the rain, like it was nothing. His shirt and pants were drenched, sticking to his skin like wet tissue. A shiver travelled from his shoulders, through his chest and down to his abdomen. Intellectually he knew he was losing body heat and needed to find cover, but intellectual wasn't winning the race right now. Limbic was in the lead, and the limbic-fueled rage was telling him to find Ellie and get done what needed to get done. He was already almost a day behind schedule and that was intolerable.

He turned the points of the compass, slowly, sniffing the air like some deranged bloodhound. Despite his misguided intentions he couldn't smell her, but he felt drawn to the south, toward del Rey.

Limbic was in charge. He scrambled up the side of the skate bowl. It was slippery concrete. He barked his shins twice attempting to get over the lip, then tore a strip off his shirt as he squeezed through the tear in the fence around the park. "Fucker." The rip left his skin exposed to the rain. He felt nothing.

He alternated between a brisk walk and a light jog toward Ocean Front walk, the vendors all shuttered for the storm. "It's like a fucking ghost town." He stopped and turned the points of the compass again, trying to pick something - anything - up. Back in the direction he came, north on Ocean Front Walk, two men were approaching, umbrella up, canted into the onshore wind. He laughed. It looked like it was doing absolutely no good at all.

He turned and started walking south when he heard them call out to him.

Marty squinted into the rain. "There's another crazy asshole out in this."

"I'm billing you double for this. Plus a new suit. This one is garbage."

"Yea, whatever." He stepped up his pace. "Hey, you. Yeah, you. Hang up a minute, would you? Want to ask you a question."

The other person on the walk stopped, but didn't turn. He dropped his head and shoulders.

"Doesn't look that impressed," said Nigel.

"Who would be? Absolutely crap to be caught in. Step up the pace."

As they approached the third man slowly turned. He was face to face with them by the time they had caught up. "Yes?"

"Jesus, pal. You okay?" Danny peered at the damage on his face. "You look like hell."

"Oh, great. Fantastic, because I'd hate to feel like I do and look *good*." He touch the end of his nose and winced. "Fell off my bike. What are you guys doing out in this shit? You don't look like you belong around here."

Danny frowned. "So where's your bike?"

"Oh, it's trashed, man. I'm going to have to get a new one when all this is over. You guys lost? Need directions?"

Marty opened the photo album on his phone. "Looking for a friend who we believe is down here in a bit of trouble. Maybe you've seen her." He held up a picture of Ellie. "You see anyone looking like her around here? Her name is Ellie Bourke. Maybe you've heard of her."

He took the phone from Marty and held it closer.

Marty grabbed him by the wrist. "Keep it under the umbrella, man. I don't want that thing getting wet."

The looked up as if he was just noticing it was raining out. "Oh yeah. Sorry." He leaned closer to the phone, getting uncomfortably close. "Ellie Bourke? Of course I've heard of her. Killed some dude in the Valley. Old boyfriend or something. She still on the run? Didn't think she was smart enough to stay away from the cops." He stepped back as a thought occurred to him. "Hang on, are you cops?"

"No. I'm her manager, and this guy's my lawyer. What did you say your name was?"

"I didn't. Look, guys, if she's an escaped felon then I need to stay clear of her. I don't want to get wrapped up in any police business."

Marty squinted. "Have we met before?"

"I don't think so, man. You guys look like you travel in circles with a bit more money than I have."

Marty snapped his fingers. "No, I know you. I recognize the face. I never forget a face. I forget names like you wouldn't believe. I called this guy Darrel yesterday, and he's been my lawyer for twenty-three years now. But faces are my business."

He closed his eyes and thought hard.

The guy backed up, out from under cover of the umbrella, shuffling to get clear.

Marty's eyes snapped open. "I've seen you in a movie. Fuck,

there's too many of them in my head. But I know I've seen you in a movie."

"This is LA, man. We're all wanna-be actors, right? I was in some small parts. You must have been cruising the bargain bins."

"Yeah, maybe. Except, no. It's a stronger memory than a bit part in a movie. You ever play any leads? What was your name again?"

"No. No leads. Just bit parts, sidekicks. I gotta go, man. Good luck finding this Ellie chick." He turned and walked south on the sidewalk.

Marty watched him walk, then stood up straight. "Fuckin' hell. Hey, I know who you are. Hang on a sec." He ran after him in the rain, Nigel bringing up the rear. "You hear me? Shit."

His target picked up the pace and ducked left into an alley, Marty pulled up short. "Nige, get up here with the umbrella. I know who the kid is, and this is weird as fuck.

The killer cursed as he ducked into a doorway out of the rain and out of sight of his pursuer. Of all the shit luck in the world, he had to run in to Ellie's manager. He had to focus. He still needed to find Ellie. His schedule was going to hell in a hand basket.

He stood in the doorway for fifteen minutes, waiting, making sure he hadn't been followed. The rain abated, the storm breaking up as it moved inland. He walked out of the alley and back on to Ocean Walk, tired, hungry and pissed. She was in for the night and he had no idea where she was. He continued south along the beach looking for a place to hole up. He'd be here when she woke up in the morning. She wouldn't escape him tomorrow.

Nigel and Marty stood by the side of the car. "What the fuck's eating you, Marty? You haven't said a word since the guy took off."

Marty looked out at the beach, surf pounding on the sand, collecting his thoughts. "I know him."

"Yeah, so? You know lots of actors and pretend actors and waiters who say they're actors. It's a side-effect of your job."

"No. I know what movie I saw him in and it wasn't a bit part. It was the lead. The face is a bit beat up, but the height, weight, and he ran with that weird limp."

"Again, so what? The guy was being modest. Not a common trait among actors, but not entirely unheard of."

Marty looked at his lawyer. "He was the lead in a horror flick made in Australia, *Beast of Bondi*. Ellie was in that movie. Pretty big part." He opened the phone browser to imdb.com and entered the movie name. "What was his name again?" He scrolled down the page to the credits. "Kent Williams." He blew the head shot up to fill the screen. "Definitely him." He shook his head. "The kid must be in some kind of trouble or something."

"Why?"

"He acted like he didn't know who Ellie was and described Sweeney as "some dude" she was supposed to have killed. Sweeney directed *Beast*. He'd certainly know who he was. He's either in trouble or he's hiding something."

"Want to go back out in this crap and keep looking for him?"

"No. Lily's already going to have my nuts."

"Thought she already did."

"You like the retainer I pay you every month?" Marty leaned back against the car and closed his eyes. "I need a hot shower. And maybe an epiphany about what the hell's going on, because the more I dig into this the less sense it makes." He looked over at Nigel. "Did he look like he was afraid of something?"

"More crazed, than anything else. Probably a good idea you *didn't* catch up to him."

Marty yawned. "I could have, but I'm saving my energy for Lily."

"Right."

"Seriously, to run from her, because she's going to be so pissed."

Chapter Twenty-Nine

I sat in the container for about an hour, trying to figure out why Kent was trying to kill me. The more I thought about it, the less sense it made. We were buddies on set. Thick as thieves. Running in to him and Charlie was like getting the team back together. This was a betrayal of the worse kind.

I wish now I had caught a look at his face under the pier. It would be conclusive. Ann had seen him, but she was sleeping and I didn't have the heart to wake her.

Shit needed to be sorted. I needed to get proof and needed a little bit of space to get it.

I slipped outside. The rain had almost stopped, but the wind was still brisk. I tucked in behind, in the lee and called my old friend Jacob

Sampson. Of all the cops in all the world, he was the one who I thought I could trust the most.

"Sampson."

"Yes you are."

"Ellie?"

"Yes I am."

"Jesus, Ellie, you really need to come in. Your life is in danger."

I smiled. The perennial big brother. "It certainly is. And I know who, but I can't prove it. Get me some space so I can flush this guy out, okay?"

"No way. For God's sake, Ell, you're a kid."

"And a girl, right? That's what you were going to say?"

I heard him sigh, and the tinkling noise of his dog's collar. "I'm concerned about you, worried you are once again going to dive in way over your head."

"I'm a good swimmer. I can handle it."

"I was speaking metaphorically."

"So was I. You going to give me some space?"

"What's this guy's name? I'll pick him up."

I shook my head. "No way. You'll spook him. And I might be wrong, but I don't think so. You won't have enough to hold him and I'll be screwed when you inevitably have to release him. Let me draw him into a trap and then you can grab him."

"Absolutely not. You need to come in and let us know everything you know and let *us* track him down. If what you're saying is correct, this guy has already killed once and seems willing to kill again. I can't let you do this."

"Your big brotherly concern is noted and appreciated, but I can't run the risk of Perkins fucking this one up too. I had to spoon feed him before and I'm going to have to spoon feed him now."

"It's not big brotherly concern. I'm a sworn officer of the law. I am *ordering* you to come in."

I laughed. "Right. How's Lisa?"

I heard the collar jangle again. He must have been giving her a scratch behind the ear. "The old girl is slowing down, but she's fine. Stop changing the subject. Where are you? I can track this number, so you're just delaying the inevitable."

"This number will be history in about an hour. When I want you to find me, I'll let you know."

"That's not how it works."

I hated keeping him in the dark, but I had little choice. "It's going to have to be. Twenty-four hours, I promise. If I haven't accomplished what I want to accomplish by this time tomorrow I'll go to the nearest station and turn myself in."

"If you're still alive."

I closed my eyes and leaned my head against the side of the container. "I will be. Before you say anything else, you'll be wasting your time trying to stop me. I'll send you a way to find me in the morning, okay? I need to make another call and get some sleep. It's going to be a hell of a day tomorrow. Give Lisa a scratch for me and I'll talk to you tomorrow."

I hung up and cursed, softly. I hated leaving him out of this, but I didn't have any other choice. There would be no grey area. I didn't want a trial. I wanted this finished.

But I had a couple of more calls to make before I crashed for the night.

I took a deep breath and dialed my manager's number. I owed him an explanation.

"Marty speaking."

"Hey, Mar. How's it going?" I could hear the surf behind him. "Out on your deck? Hell of a storm today."

"Ellie? I'm on the beach here at Venice. Looking for you. What the hell is going on? Do you realize I just spent time behind bars because of you?"

"Lily told me, yeah. Sorry about that, chief. How'd you get out?"

"Nigel sprung me and in my efforts to save my most favorite client from herself I made him take me right here to the beach. To try and find you. So come out, come out, wherever you are and let's get back to my place where I can ply you with expensive scotch and get you to tell me what the fuck it is you're trying to prove."

"As tempting as that sounds, I'm just calling to apologize for putting you through what you went through. All will be sorted by this time tomorrow."

"More Warshawski shit? You don't have to keep trying. The part is yours. Come back. Lily will have the cook make something warm for you. You must be incredibly uncomfortable out in the rough for the past couple of days."

I thought of Ann, and her last two years. "It's nothing. I've been worse off on camping trips. Thanks for all you do for me Marty. I forget sometimes how supportive you are. Give Lily my best. After she beats on you for coming down here to the beach."

"Down *here* to the beach? So you are down here?"

"Forget it, Marty. I've got to go."

"Hang on, wait. Don't hang up yet. I saw one of your friends down here. Keep an eye out for him. He might be able to give you some back up."

"A friend? Who?"

"That kid from the *Beast* movie. Kent. Looking a little rough. Maybe the two of you can team up."

I stood straight and looked around the corner of the container. Stupid, actually, because if he was anywhere near me he would have heard me talking. "Stay away from him," I whispered. Again, stupid, but ingrained.

"Why? He seemed a little skittish. But I thought you two got along."

"I did too. Just keep clear of him. And don't bother calling me back on this number. I'm burning it after the next call."

"How will I reach you?"

"You won't. If everything works out I'll call you."

"If? What the hell?"

"Gotta go Mar. My love to Lily." I hung up. That call had gone on too long.

I slid down the wall of the container and sat on the ground, head on my knees. Marty had a run in with Kent, and came out of it alive. Some people had all the luck. I was putting too many of my friends in danger. I needed to end this. A plan was starting to gel. A good night's sleep and I'd be gold. And he'd be under my heel.

One call before I slept. I dialed from memory

"Ellie, what the hell are you doing?"

"Nice talking to you too, Cath. What's going on? Anything new and exciting in your life? You start rehearsals yet?"

"Forget about me. The news is painting a very confusing picture about you. They're saying your life is in danger and you should turn yourself in."

I combed my short hair back with my fingers. "Have I been exonerated for Sweeney's death yet?"

"I don't think so. It's not really clear. Like I said, confusing." I heard her take a deep breath. "They're right, you know."

"Cath, you're the steadiest girlfriend I've ever had. I'm really, really sorry to put you through this. I know who's behind the bullshit and I promise you it'll be beer and pizza, my treat, tomorrow night."

"Why? What's going to be different tomorrow? How do you know you'll even be alive tomorrow?"

"I can't let that ass win."

"So call the police. Jesus you're stubborn."

"He'll get out of it. He's covered his tracks pretty well and even a half decent lawyer could keep him out of jail. I'm going to set him up."

"You're playing with fire."

"I don't have a choice. I'm not going to get wrapped up in some long, never-ending legal pile of bullshit. Or would that be a pile of legal bullshit? Whatever. I'm doing it."

"Well let Bernie and I help you. When are you doing this?"

Oh, Christ. That's all I needed. I'd already caused enough hassle for my friends. "Stay out of it. Seriously stay out of it. Promise me."

"I can't. You're too good of a friend to abandon."

I banged the back of my head against the container in frustration. "Fuck no. Just stay out of it. Please, stay out of it. This guy is insane. I couldn't live with myself if you got hurt."

"And I couldn't live with myself if *you* got hurt. No arguments. Now do you have a safe place for tonight?"

"Yes. I think. Don't let me see you down here."

"Get a good sleep Ellie. And if there's anything I can do to help, yell."

And then she hung up. I looked at my phone, tempted to call her back and decided I'd be wasting my breath.

At least the rain had let up. The clouds were breaking up and the full moon popped through once in a while. It would be sunny tomorrow. Maybe I'd finally be dry. I was going to grow fungus soon at this rate.

I turned off that pre-pay and turned on the other. I called the voicemail. Nothing. Nobody had been leaving messages on this number. And no text messages. Odds were good it was still clean.

I yawned. A shiver swept across me like was in the early stages of an epileptic seizure. The cold and tired was catching up to me. I eased around the back of the container, ready if necessary to split some asshole's head open.

But it was clear. I pulled open the door and ducked as a piece of wood swung at my head. I hit the ground and rolled as Ann took another swing at me.

"Ann, Ann. It's me. Ellie. Hang on. Don't hit me." I rolled again just as she checked her swing and threw the stick to one side. "What the fuck, Ann?"

She covered her face with her hands and sobbed. "Oh, shit, I'm so sorry. I heard a bang on the outside of the box and thought he got you. I was too afraid to go out. And then you opened the door and I thought the worse."

I pulled her to me and hugged her tight. I got a bit of the sniffles myself. "It's okay. He hasn't got me and he's not going to get me. I know who it is and tomorrow I'm going to lay a trap for him. I want you to get as far away from here as you can tomorrow."

"Why? What are you going to do?"

"I need to get his sorry ass and me and the cops all in the same place at the same time. You don't need to be there. In fact, I really don't want you anywhere near. It's too dangerous and I don't want you anywhere near it when it goes down."

"But you're just a - "

"Just a what? Girl? Kid? I'm both and I don't want you messed up in this anymore."

"Why, because I'm crazy? I bag lady? Psychologically unbalanced?" She had a small smile on her face. "I'm a lot tougher than I look. I've survived out here almost two years without life-threatening injury." She touched her split lip with her tongue. "This isn't life-threatening, and I'd love to repay him the favor."

"It was the same guy?"

"The same guy who popped me in the face was the same guy who tried to drown you." She smiled and took my hands. "I never did thank you for making him bleed." Her smile got wider. "I think you really pissed him off."

"Even better reason for you to keep your head down. Okay?

Promise me."

She frowned and pulled into herself.

"Oh, come on, Ann. I just want you to be safe. I want to help you after all this is over, and I can't do that if you're in a hole in the ground, can I?"

She grunted and dropped on to her thin mattress and scowled.

I shook my head. "I don't want you to take it personally. I've come to care for you very much. You've helped me a couple of times and I probably wouldn't be here without it. I owe you. And I want to pay you back." I sat beside her and pulled her close. "Ann, honey, you're the best. You've only known me for two days and you're already prepared to fight for me. There aren't enough people in the world like you." I sat back and moved to my side of the container. "I'll be back here tomorrow night. It'll all be finished by then. You're coming to my place for a nice hot tub and a quiet dinner at my friends' restaurant. Just stay clear of me tomorrow morning. Deal?"

She grunted and pulled her blanket over her and faced the wall. I couldn't be sure if she had sunk back into her mental fugue or was just pissed at me. Didn't really matter. I was going to sneak out tomorrow morning without her and this discussion would end up being moot.

And if I lived through tomorrow I would make sure she didn't spend another night on the streets.

Chapter Thirty

Ann woke with a start. She froze and listened. A noise had woken her. Weak light filtered through the cracks near the top of the container. She estimated it to be between 6:00 and 7:00 in the morning. She rolled back to go back to sleep and heard it again. A whimper and a grunt.

She looked over and saw Ellie through the dim light, tattered blanket pulled tight around her and having a nightmare.

Ann slid across the floor dragging her blanket with her. She tucked in behind Ellie and put an arm around her and pulled her blanket over the both of them. She hugged her tight and rested her head on Ellie's back. She could feel the young girl's heart pounding and her muscles twitching. She was in the middle of a really bad dream. "There, there. Ann's here. You'll be okay. You'll be fine." She snugged her in close and closed her eyes. Ellie seemed to relax, to her feeling, and she slowly drifted off.

Charlie woke, swiveled out of bed and woke up the laptop sitting on his bedside table. A couple of key-clicks later and he was in the billing system. He entered her mobile number in the trace program and saw calls to three different people. He shook his head. She still wasn't keeping a low profile. He couldn't afford to help her any more. He stood and stretched. He knew roughly where she was. And he knew a bad thing was coming her way. What he didn't know yet was if he was going to do anything about it.

Cathy lay in bed staring at the ceiling. She'd been awake since Ellie's call, and she certainly couldn't sleep after the fight with Bernie. He was on the sofa. His refusal to entertain helping Ellie was almost the last straw. He argued that she didn't want them to help so he was actually acceding to her wishes.

Cathy thought different.

She got up, pulled a robe on and padded out to the living room. "You change your mind yet?"

Bernie groaned, his feet hanging over the end of the sofa. He swung his arm off his eyes and knocked an almost empty bottle of red wine on the floor.

"Oh, you fucking asshole." Cathy dove and grabbed it before the few remaining drops could spill on the carpet. "You're not even sober yet, are you?"

"Cath." He covered his eyes against the early morning sunlight.

"Jeez, can you keep it down? My head is killing me."

"Are coming to the beach with me?"

"We've already had this fight. You're crazy to go."

"You're a spineless lazy asshole *not* to go. She's our friend. She's in trouble. We're obligated to help."

He rolled over and faced the back of the sofa. His voice was muffled. "Don't get involved, I say. And the trouble she's in is of her own making. Let her sort it out herself."

Cathy stormed the sofa and punched him on the back of the neck. "You cowardly piece of shit. I'm going to find her and help her. I may not be back."

He tucked, his hands covering the back of his neck. "Shit. Spousal abuse."

"No. Not spousal. And I'm glad we didn't get married." She stalked out of the house as her phone started ringing.

Sampson held the phone between his shoulder and his ear as he navigated the surface streets. He was ready to abandon the call when Cathy finally answered.

"Cathy, this is Jacob Sampson. We met a few times a year or so ago."

"Yeah. The cop. Joel's brother. I'm kind of busy right now Jacob. Call you back later, okay?"

"Wait. You're one of Ellie's best friends. She talks about you all the time. I was hoping you might know where she was. She's in trouble. I want to find her and help her. Can you help me?"

"You're a cop. You all want to arrest her for something she hasn't done."

Sampson sighed. "I know she didn't do it. I'm not sure who did, but I've *never* thought she did. If you know anything, you've got to let me know. For Ellie's sake."

"Look, I don't know where she is, specifically. I know she's still near Venice Beach somewhere. Something she said the last time I was talked with her."

"When was that?"

"Last night. Late. I would have been out there last night but my asshole boyfriend refused to go. Ex-boyfriend, now."

"Sorry to hear."

"Sorry it took so long. So I'm on my way to Venice. I'm not sure where exactly she is, but if I can find her, I'm going to help her. If that means you have to arrest me, so be it."

"I'm on the same side you are." Sampson pulled off Pacific Highway on to N. Venice. "I'll see you there. I'll be looking for her too. Maybe we join forces."

He listened to silence. Then she said, "If I see you, I see you. I'll be there in about twenty."

The dream was a frantic patchwork of colors and sounds and a dread feeling of immeasurable fear. It felt like icy-cold fire licked at his feet. Shadows of something threatening played at the corners of his eyes. He sat upright, a scream throttled in his throat as the incoming tide lapped around his feet.

"Fuck." Kent rubbed his eyes and flinched at the searing pain on his left cheek. He touched it lightly and inhaled sharply. "That fucking bitch." He looked at the approaching water and scrambled out from under the pier.

"Son of a bitch. I need food and then I need to kill me a bitch." He opened the Altoids tin. Two left. "And one of these." He tossed it in his mouth and dry swallowed. He tightened all the muscles in his torso, flexing his pecs, shoulder and arms and let out a yell. "It's fucking great to be alive."

He staggered north on Ocean Walk. The sun was barely up. He squinted at his watch. "6:30? Shit. Too early." Rattling around in his head was a free meal he caged a couple of days ago - a lifetime ago it felt. He tried to remember where.

Shops were setting up, inventory placed on outside shelves and fresh food shuttled into the cafes and fast food outlets along the strip. Kent stared at every food outlet he passed, trying to remember the friendly one. He was hungry and had no idea where his wallet was. It probably fell from his pants in the fight with Ellie. He touched his nose again. The swelling had subsided but the pain remained. "She'll pay for it."

"What's that, pal?" An old Mexican-looking guy was hanging t-shirts in front of his stall. "You talking to me?"

"Get lost."

"Nah, I don't think so. I'm here for the day. You, on the other hand, would do well to get lost. You look like shit, pal. Clean up a bit. We've got standards, even here. Take a shower. You're disgusting. Did you piss yourself?"

Kent snarled and made to swing at him, then backed off and continued up the walk. He didn't need to get picked up this close to his goal.

He passed Emily and Henry's cafe a good ten paces before he remembered that was where he and Charlie got the free meal. He backtracked and wandered in to the cafe.

"Hey there. Remember me? Ellie's friend? She said she'd be joining me for breakfast here and I should start without her if I got here early."

Henry wiped his hands on his apron and came out from behind the counter. "Do I know you?"

"Hey, old man, I'm Ellie's friend. She said it was cool."

Henry placed a hand on the center of Kent's chest and gently pushed him toward the door. "I don't think so, Ellie's friend. We have a dress code and you fall short. Considerably short. Go get cleaned up and we'll talk again." He gave him a final push and closed the door behind him.

Kent stood on the sidewalk, clenched his jaw and threw one of the restaurant's patio chairs at the front window, shattering it and spraying the inside with glass. "Go fuck yourself you fucking dick-wad." He picked up a second and threw it through the hole, just missing Henry.

Kent continued north. Hunger fueled the rage, and the rage fueled his hunger. He was quickly devolving to a ball of psychotic nervous energy. He had no idea where he was going. It was random walking. The odds of finding Ellie increased with every minute he was on the street, his logic told him. He licked his lips, parched. His tongue felt thick. His lips were caked with dried spittle, salt spray and old blood. He rubbed his hand over his chin. The stubble was soft. "I'm going to grow a beard."

He heard yelling behind him. He slowly turned and smiled. The old guy and his wife were out on the sidewalk yelling at him. He shook his head and turned back north, looking for Ellie. They couldn't touch him. He was invincible.

Sampson pulled into the long term parking lot at the north end of Venice Beach. He hopped out of his car and opened the back door. Lisa, his eight-year old Golden Lab, lifted her head and thumped her tail against the back of the seat. He clipped a lead on her collar. "Let's go, old girl. Let's go find our friend Ellie."

At the sound of Ellie's name Lisa's tail beat faster and she hopped out of the car. He laughed and started walking. He called the last number he had for Ellie, not bothering to leave a message when he got her voicemail. "No joy, girl. We're going to have to do some hard work here." They strolled south. If he had something of Ellie's it would be a lot easier. Lisa was a trained sniffer. Retired, but one of the best in her prime. "Ellie will be hanging out with some of the less advantaged residents of this little burg." He scrolled through the pictures on his phone, stopping when he got to a headshot. "That'll do."

The population along the boardwalk was still thin. The majority of the people were still setting up stalls and cleaning up the mess from the previous night's storm. Those not working were skating or walking along the boardwalk getting an early start to the day.

He scanned the people looking for someone of the right socio-economic class and spotted one almost immediately. A tall man, dark hair, unshaven and younger than he would have expected was walking toward him, slightly off-center.

"Excuse me, can I have a minute?"

The man stood and cocked his head. "Who the fuck are you? Never mind. Don't matter who you are. Outta my way."

"Hang on, pal. Detective Sampson." He lifted the side of his jacket and realized he didn't have his gun and badge with him. "Currently off-duty. It'll only take a minute and you could be saving a life. What's your name?"

"Kent Williams." He closed his eyes and inhaled deeply through his nose.

Sampson smiled at the whistling sound. "You break that in a fight?"

"Fell off my bike. What do you want?"

Sampson held out his phone and showed Kent the picture. "I'm looking for this girl. Her name is -"

"Ellie Bourke. Every sentient being on the face of the earth knows who she is. Why do you think I'd know where she is?"

Sampson stowed his phone. "Maybe not you specifically, but I believe Ellie is in danger and she knows it. She's been located around here a couple of times now, so I think she's staying in the area, but gone to ground. Living with homeless people trying to stay below the radar."

"So?" He stepped away from Lisa, who was sniffing around his feet. "Hey, call the dog off."

"She's a little baby. Wouldn't hurt a fly unless it was wrapped in sausages and barbecue sauce." He scratched the corner of his eye. "Look, I'm just thinking, seeing as you appear to be living on the streets too, you may have seen her, maybe point me in her general direction since you've probably crossed paths with her."

Kent squared off, feet shoulder width, hands at his sides and fists clenched. "What the fuck? You think I'm homeless?"

Lisa backed up, hackles raised. Sampson did pretty much the same, sans hackles. "Back it up, son. You don't want to go where you're thinking. Have you seen her?"

"I'm not homeless. I am not a failure. I'm not a crazy fucking bat-shit loser who can't manage to keep it together."

Sampson automatically reach back to unclip the restraint on his holster to find it not there. He left his hand on his hip. "Relax Mr. Williams. You're not homeless. Great. Fantastic for you to be paying rent. I'm impressed. Now let's just get past that and you tell me when and where you've seen Miss Bourke." He held up the phone again, showing him the picture.

"Yeah, fine." He was breathing heavily. "I saw her on the TV. She was doing that red carpet thing for her next movie. And then after when the news put her picture up." His cheek throbbed. His blood pressure was rising and the increased blood flow to the cut on his cheek caused pain. "Is that all? I need to find somewhere to eat."

"Thank you so much for your time, Mr. Williams. You've been a great help." He watched Kent walking away and shook his head. "What do you think, Lisa? Whack job?"

She woofed. A whack job.

Chapter Thirty-One

I was snug in bed, twelve-years old, cuddled up with my mother on a cold winter's night. It was July. We were talking about heading up to the Blue Mountains for a Christmas in July dinner. Cold wind blew through the house. A window must have been left open. Dad would be pissed.

I tried to snuggle in closer, but my mother had put on weight and when I took her hand it was hard and calloused, not the soft I knew it should be. The hand squeezed back and a voice not my mother's whispered in my ear.

"It's all right. You had a nightmare."

I pushed her away and tried to stand, falling into the side of the container, cracking the side of my head against the wall.

The previous two days came screaming back at me and I retched. My head hurt. Not just from the growing lump above my right eye, but also from a deep, behind-the-eyes pervasive headache.

And I had to pee.

I steadied myself against the wall, standing on the thin mattress and blankets and looked around. The light was poor, thin shafts of sunlight forcing themselves in wherever they could find a crack.

"Ann."

She scowled and pulled her coats tighter.

"Sorry, Ann. I was in the middle of a dream when I woke. My mother and I. Years ago. I was a little disoriented. Are you okay?"

She grumbled something and stood there, looking at me like I just kicked her puppy.

"Really sorry. And I really need to pee. Where do you go to the bathroom around here? Do I have to walk down to the public toilets on the beach? That's got to be almost a mile away."

She reached into one of her pockets and gave me a small plastic package of tissue. "Around the back."

"Of the container?"

She nodded and sat down on her bed.

"You mean around the back where I've been standing, and sometimes sitting while I've been making phone calls?"

She cracked a small smile and nodded again.

"Well, thanks for letting me know. Although a heads up yesterday would have been brilliant. I'll be right back."

She grabbed my arm. "Be careful. It's not safe out there."

I gave her a hand a reassuring pat. "I'm always careful. And I know it's not safe. Let me relieve the pressure and I'll tell you what I've got planned."

I peered around the edge of the door, made sure the coast was clear and slipped around to the back. The storm was well and truly gone. The sky was blue and the sun promised a very warm day. In the daylight I could barely see where Ann and others had peed. But I could see I'd been sitting in one of those places last night.

I'd been out here on the streets too long. I didn't even notice the smell.

When I went back in, Ann was sitting up and staring at the wall. I wasn't sure if she had slipped off to some private world of her own or was just trying to think things through. I'd been in that vacant stare space many times myself. Almost missed auditions a couple of times.

Regardless which state she was in, it was time to go. I needed to find some food and needed to find a place suitable for a final standoff. I was pretty sure how I was going to do it; I just needed to stay alive until I did.

I placed the remaining tissue beside her and quietly collected my phones, battery pack and tried to slip out the door.

"I'm coming with you." Ann stood and stretched. "Sorry for startling you this morning, but you were having a nightmare earlier and some strange motherly instinct came over me." She smiled. "Very foreign feeling, trust me."

I peered closely in her eyes. "You're home?"

She tapped her head. "Up here? Yeah. As home as I've been in a long time. It's you, I think."

"How is it me?"

"I don't know. You've been kind. You're concerned about my welfare. You treat me like a real human being instead of an aberration messing up the streets."

"It's the least I could do for all the help you've given me."

"Let's not get all lovey-dovey. What are we up to now?"

I didn't like this. I shook my head. "This is going to be dangerous. I need to set this guy up and lure him into a trap at the same time I lure the police to the same place. I don't want you getting in the middle of it."

"Honey, I'm in the middle of it. I saw his face. He knows me. He knows my haunts. If he gets you, he's coming after me next. I've got as much invested in taking this guy down as you do."

"That's where I have an advantage, Ann. He knows you know him. He doesn't know I know who it is. I didn't get a look at his face when he was attacking me. I've got a leg up. If he sees you with me, he'll know his anonymity is blown."

She sighed, thinking about something. "Look, I'll hang back a bit. I'm feeling really protective right now and I can't let you go on your own. Look at it this way: either I come with you and we work together, or I skulk around in the shadows and you're never really sure what I'm up to." She smiled. "Easy decision to make now, isn't it?"

She had me there. "Okay. First things, first. We need food."

"I could eat."

"You never eat. You're like a bird. How do you keep from passing out?"

She laughed. "Spend enough time out here and you'll develop the same skill. I can go quite awhile without food. Water I need every day, but food is as I can get it." She chuckled. "All this talk now has me hungry."

"I've got a treat for you."

"Breakfast at Tiffany's?"

I laughed. "A movie buff. Perfect. I've got friends. We'll sneak around the back way."

I led her down side roads, past two houses partially constructed and abandoned, past an empty lot with a couple of abandoned cars and to the back of Emily and Henry's place and rapped on the door.

"You sure this is okay?"

I nodded. "These people are okay." I waited another couple of minutes and knocked again.

Emily opened the door. "We aren't expecting any deliveries, Henry. How would I know who it - oh."

She stopped in mid-sentence and looked at me, then at Ann, and then at me again. "You look like hell."

I grinned. "Excellent. My disguise is working. Emily, this is my good friend Ann. Ann, Emily. She and her husband run a very nice cafe. I hope one day to enjoy a sit-down meal with you there. In the mean time, Em, you wouldn't have some fruit or rolls you could spare?"

She looked up and down the alley. "Get the hell in here. Both of you." She pulled door closed behind us and snapped on the light. "Explain?"

We were squeezed in pretty tight. I'm sure we didn't smell that great, but Emily made no mention of it. "Ann has been a fantastic help keeping me below the radar. There's a guy trying to kill me, the police want to arrest me and I'd love nothing more than to get them all in the same room and duke it out. That's my plan, anyway." My stomach growled. "But first, food. I can pay you if you want. I've still got a couple of hundred dollars on me." I fished in my pocket and took out a couple of twenties. "That should cover it."

"First you take off and we think you're maybe dead and now you insult me with money? I thought we were friends." She looked at Ann. "And any friend of Ellie's is a friend of ours. I'll get you some food." She stopped herself as she was opening the door to the restaurant. "One exception to that "friend of a friend" thing. You know those guys you brought over for breakfast? The taller one? He's not so much a friend. He came by here earlier today looking for free food. Looked terrible. Henry asked if he'd mind sitting outside and the lanky asshole threw one of the chairs though the front window."

Kent. I looked at Ann and gave her a small shake of the head. "Is he still here?"

"No. He marched up the beach on the hunt for something. The guy's crazy."

Ann finally spoke up. "I've seen crazy. Hell, I've *been* crazy and *that* guy is so far beyond crazy he's scary."

"She speaks the truth. Wait here and I'll get you some grub. On the house."

"And I'll pay for your window."

"Oh, don't worry about it. It's drawing a paying crowd and the insurance will cover it. Everyone thinks the storm was worse than it really was. I'm not going to set them straight. Stay here and stay quiet."

She closed the door and Ann turned to me. "You trust her?"

"With my life."

"Yeah, you just did. I hope you're right."

We stood in silence for a couple of minutes, my nerves stretching to the breaking point. You never really knew someone and while I thought I knew Emily, there was a small sliver of concern.

Unfounded, it turned out. She came through the door, opening it just wide enough to let herself through with two bags of food.

"You might want to hightail it out of here." She handed a bag to Ann and then one to me. I liked that. Ann looked like every caricature of a bag lady you've ever seen, and by giving her the food first she was telling her she considered her an equal to me. I'd never doubt her again.

"What's going on?"

"Your old friend Sampson is out there, with his pooch. Doing a door to door search for you."

"The cops are here looking for us? Shit. That's too early."

"No, he's not identifying himself as police. Just a concerned friend. You've got a lot of them."

I took her by the arm. "Em, he is a friend, but he's also a cop. He'll do what he has to do as a cop if he finds us, so please don't let him know. Which way is he traveling?"

"Your secret's safe with me. He's going south, toward the pier. How long is this going to go on?"

"It'll be finished tonight, one way or another."

"I certainly don't like the sound of that."

"It'll be good. Ann here's going to help me out." I hefted the bag of food. "And you've helped also. Immensely. We've got to go so you don't get into any trouble. And if the insurance people take too long,

I'm serious, I'll pay for the window."

I reached for the back door and she intercepted me. "Let me check first." She poked her nose out and looked both ways before opening the door all the way. "It's clear. Come back when all this shit is settled, will you? Henry's come up with this fantastic warm chicken salad with rocket, avocado and balsamic vinegar that is to die for."

I smiled. "We will. It's a date. The both of us will be back, a little less worse for wear." I stepped out and closed the door behind us.

"Dig in Ann, they make good stuff there."

I looked over and she was finishing her first roll and digging out a banana. She smiled and nodded. "Very good."

So part "A" was accomplished. We had enough food to last us the day. Emily had been very generous. We walked slowly north up the alley until we reached a cross street, about half a mile away from the cafe. Safe enough to get back out on the main thoroughfare. Ann was dragging her heels, a few yards behind me when I turned the corner.

I stopped and backtracked. "Stay here."

"What?"

"Stay here. He's just around the corner. You don't want him to see you."

"Is he coming this way?"

I shook my head. "Sitting on a bench. I'll just be a minute. I'll come back for you." I saw the look in her eyes. She'd been lied to non-stop for the last two years. "Honest. Here, you hang on to my food." I handed her the bag and walked around the corner like it was any other day of my life.

Kent was sitting on a bench, facing away from the beach, looking at skaters and boarders pass in front of him. I slipped through the foot traffic and sat beside him. I don't think he saw me coming. He started and stared at me.

"Hey, mate. What are you doing down here?" I was shaking. I wanted to drop him right there, but there were too many people around now, and I still didn't have enough proof to back up my claims.

"I thought you were on the run." He sniffed and shivered. "Where you been hanging out?"

"Here and there." I leaned in close. He stunk worse than either Ann or I. And he was radiating heat. I rested a hand on his arm. "You're burning up. You should see a doctor."

His hand started moving toward his face and he stopped. The cut on his cheek looked inflamed. It was harsh red a good half-inch either side of the cut and it looked like there was pus in it.

"That looks nasty. You really should see a doctor. How did it happen?" This would be good. He looked like he wanted nothing more than to throttle me, but he couldn't.

"My bike. Stupid fucking piece of shit bike." His voice rose in a crescendo, spittle building up in the corners of his mouth. He leaned forward and grabbed my wrist. "I'm going to find that fucking bike and I'm going to dismantle it until it's in its smallest component parts, then I'm going to throw it, one piece at a time, into the ocean. I'm really going to enjoy doing that."

His grip tightened to the point of being painful. I tried to wrench it free and he squeezed tighter, pulling my hand toward him. "Do you understand what I'm saying?"

I twisted my arm free and stood. "You don't like your bike? You don't like all bikes? You're fucking bat shit crazy? I don't know. Listen, do me a favor and don't tell any of the cops I'm around, okay? The place is swarming with them."

He scowled and rubbed his arms. The fever was getting to him.

"And look, be a mate, I might need some help later today. If I text you where I am, can you come and help out? I've got some stuff to do. Nothing definite. Might not need it, just would like to know it's there if I do."

"Tell me know where you're going to be and when you want me there. I'll be sure I'm there."

"I thought you had a bike to kill." I laughed and shook my head. "Not sure where it's going to be yet, and not sure if I'm going to need your assistance. Your number is the same, right?"

He nodded. "I tried calling you earlier and it went to voice mail."

"Any message you left is in the hands of the coppers now." I laughed at the expression on his face. "Oh, relax. They're looking for me, not you. And they haven't found me so far. Just keep your phone on, in case, okay?"

"Want I go with?"

"Oh, no, mate. I don't want you messed up in the middle of this." As if. "Just stay in the shadows, okay? Cops are hot on my tail."

I winked and ran back the way I came. Ann was leaning against the wall with her eyes closed. "Let's go, princess. Got to get a few blocks between us and him, just in case he comes looking."

"Do you think he knows you know?"

I shrugged as I picked up the pace. "Hard to say and it really doesn't matter now, does it?"

Chapter Thirty-Two

Kent stood from the park bench too fast. The head rush disoriented him, keeping him from following Ellie immediately. By the time he regained his equilibrium she was nowhere to be seen.

"Fuck. Fuck, fuckity fuck. Does she realize how lucky she is?" He rubbed his scalp, the hair matted with sand and salt water. "I feel like crap."

He swayed a bit. His eyes watered and his nose ran. An instinctive sniff brought more tears to his eyes. "Ah, shit." He carefully wiped his eyes, flinching as he brushed his hand across his split cheek.

He stood straight, took a deep breath - through his mouth - and took stock of his situation. She was around. He could still probably con Charlie to help him find her phone and, unbelievably, she didn't seem to realize he was the guy who attacked her under the pier. "How fucking lucky can I be?"

He'd use that knowledge.

Finding Ellie was the first challenge. She turned right at the alley after running from him. That would be south. If he were to walk south, though, he'd pass by that shitty cafe and probably run into the cop with the dog.

So he looped out on the beach, walking up the sand stepping over people and walking on towels. Two kids kicking a soccer ball were on the receiving end of his wrath. It would take them fifteen minutes to recover the ball from the surf.

"Flanking maneuver. Classic military strategy. *Call of Duty* pays off. She'll be expecting me from the North and I'll sneak in from the South." He walked over a beach towel, dragging sand, ignoring the yelling mother and the three crying kids.

He was lost in thought, imagining what he was going to do to Ellie. Before he realized it he was back at the Venice Fish Pier. He looked up and smiled. "Classic pincher movement. I'll head down to del Rey and swing back and trap her."

Perkins sat at his desk, large coffee in one hand and the morning paper in another. When Stanfield showed up they'd hit Venice again. Maybe.

There were phone records to run down and a reinvestigation of the scene now that it appeared Ellie was framed. He was willing to concede that, but it didn't make it any clearer who actually did kill Sweeney.

He sighed and dropped the paper on his desk and opened the Sweeney file. He looked up as his young partner walked in. "Stanfield, what do you think?"

"About what?"

"Venice Beach or Sweeney's place?"

"No brainer, partner. There's no bikinis at Sweeney's."

"I'm kinda on the same page, but we need to review everything from Sweeney's murder. Seems like Ellie wasn't involved. Actually, that's a definite now. But we don't know who *did* kill him. You run his phone records?"

"Again. And again. His lawyer, the two kids we already talked to and the food place. None others."

"Ellie. Check her phone?"

"She keeps bouncing the number. We're still working with the phone company. Should get something later today."

Perkins looked up from the file. "Should? Later today? Give them a call and tell them a killer is still at large and if another person dies because of their recalcitrance I'll be looking to see if it's possible to charge a company with manslaughter."

"You can't."

"I know and you know, but maybe the ass-wick working this request doesn't. Might scare him in to action."

Stanfield shrugged. "I'll let him know."

"Good man. You're the second best." He returned to reviewing the interview notes when his phone rang. He answered without looking up from the papers.

"Perkins."

"Hey old man. Sampson here. Comfy at your desk?"

"What's up Sampson? Lose your dog?"

"Nope. The old girl is walking with me as I speak. Down here at Venice. Where you and your partner should be."

"We already had that debate. Sweeney's won. Need to revisit the crime scene and find what we missed."

"Nah, that can wait."

"Really? How do you figure?" Perkins leaned back and put his feet up on the desk. "You on this case now? I thought you were dog squad."

"She's a friend, Perkins. I'm off duty right now, just taking a walk, looking for a friend. She's in trouble. She told me it was all coming down today and she'd reach out to me if she needed help. Can you imagine? *If* she needed help. Get down here and help me find her before she does something stupid."

Perkins closed his eyes. "My case, pal. My decision. And I've decided we're going to Sweeney's to re check the house."

"You never were good at snap decisions, I recall. This is going to be yet another in your large collection of mistakes. Sweeney is dead. He can wait. His killer may very well be down here tracking her. So, yes. Your decision. You can drag your over-fed ass a few blocks west of where you are now, putter around in a crime scene three days old and accomplish almost nothing today. Or you can haul that same over-fed ass down to Venice, bring the kid with you if you feel it's necessary, and help me find her. She's around here somewhere. You owe her."

Perkins shook his head and hung up the phone without replying. "Fuck."

"What now?"

"Dog-squad has almost convinced me we should go meet him at

Venice and look for Miss Bourke."

"Almost? What'll it take to push you over the edge?"

"Funny guy. Get your stuff. We're going. I'm going to regret this at some point, I know."

Sampson pocketed his phone and continued walking south. He slowed as he passed a couple of bike cops talking to the Henry about his broken front window. Lisa sniffed the air and let out a small whine.

"Not good for you old girl. Your food is at home." He hovered in the background until they finished talking. When they were about to mount their bikes and leave he signaled them over.

"Got a minute guys? Detective Sampson, K-9 unit. Off duty."

The older cop leaned against his bike and the younger straddled his. "What can we do for you?"

Sampson nodded toward the window. "Henry tell you who did it?"

"We grabbed an image off the security camera next door. We'll canvas. The usual stuff. Why?"

Sampson took out his phone and opened Ellie's picture. "They tried to brush the whole incident, and me, off when I was by here about an hour ago. Curious, their change of heart. Especially since I kind of know them." He held up the picture. "I'm looking around for Ellie Bourke. Intelligence says she's in the area."

"We know the face. We were told to back off on her though. Has that changed?"

He shook his head. "No. Her life's been threatened by the person who killed Sweeney. In order to find the killer I've got to find her. Can you keep an eye out?"

"Sure. Transfer the photo."

Sampson bumped the picture to the others. "So, quid pro quo, show me the picture of the person responsible for the window."

The bicycle cop showed Sampson the grainy shots taken straight from the security camera at the entrance to the apartment next to Henry and Emily's cafe.

Sampson nodded. "I talked to him about two hours ago. Looked like hell. Told me his name was Kent Williams."

"Where?"

Sampson pointed north. "About a mile that way. Not sure where he is now. It was early and I think he was scrounging around for food. Looked homeless to me but he assured me on no uncertain terms he wasn't."

They transferred the picture to Sampson's phone. "Fantastic. Witnesses have described him as off-his-meds whack job."

"Just what we said, right Lisa? Whack job."

She woofed and wagged her tail.

"Good luck guys." He handed his card to the both of them. "If you see Ellie, don't spook her, okay? Just give me a call and I'll swing by and have a chat with her."

They slid the cards in their shirt pockets and mounted their bikes. "You got it. Likewise for this Williams asshole, okay?"

Samson nodded and watched them bike north. "Too much work for me. I'll stick to the car." He waved at Emily and Henry in the cafe and continued south.

Lisa uncharacteristically strained at her lead as they passed a busker resetting his juggling act. "Lisa, behave. What's got in to you?"

He stopped in front of the act and laughed when a small Black Lab popped out of the man's equipment bag. It waddled over and stuck its nose in Lisa face. "Ah, motherhood urges. Too old for kids, girl." He squatted and scratched the puppy behind the ears. "Nice dog you've got. What's its name?"

The surfer dude busker stopped his set up and sat on the ground near his dog. "Damien. This is Lisa, is it?"

"On the nose."

"Damien here is the star of the show. Gets a better reaction than anything I've ever done. You should stay and check out the next show. I'll be starting in about fifteen."

"Love to, but I'm looking for a friend. My name's Sampson, by the way. Jacob Sampson. You're down here most of the day, right?"

"Pretty much, yeah."

Sampson showed the busker the picture of Ellie. "I'm looking for her. Have you seen her around?" Sampson sensed a wall erect almost immediately after the busker saw the picture. "And what's your name?"

The guy cleared his throat. "Patrick Fitzpatrick." He pointed at the picture. "Anyone you ask around here will tell you she lives in the apartment just over there." He pointed in the direction of the cafe with no front window. "So have you checked her apartment?"

"Actually, no I haven't. But you haven't answered the question. Have you seen her lately?"

The busker sighed. "I don't know where she is, man. The cops are looking for her too. I think she's in a bit of trouble, if you want to know the truth. Sampson, right? Jacob Sampson? If I see her I'll let her know you're looking."

"Again, *man*, you haven't told me when it was you last saw her."

He shook his head. "Can't remember, *man*. Too much weed."

"Of course." Sampson stood from his squat and looked down at the puppy trying to chew the tail off his dog. "Thanks for your help, Pat."

"Who?"

"Your name's Patrick, right?"

"Right, right. No problem. Good luck, and tell her hi if you see her."

Samson separated Lisa and the puppy and continued the stroll. He watched the display at muscle beach for a few minutes trying to guess how much HGH he'd pick up if he busted them all.

"You thinking what I'm thinking?"

He turned and saw Perkins and Stanfield. "I don't know. Depends on your sexual orientation, I would guess. There's a lot of meat up there if you're so inclined."

"You're implying they're gay? That's not nice."

"No, I'm just saying the average gay guy would probably be salivating all over them."

Stanfield pointed to the lone woman. "Not all guys up there."

Sampson shook his head. "Never date a girl who can bench press you."

"Words of experience?"

"Just common sense, kid. You guys see anything yet?"

"No. Just got here. Gramps drives like an old man. Probably because he *is* an old man."

Perkins looked at Stanfield and cocked his head. "Performance reviews are coming up in a couple of months. Soon enough that my feeble mind won't forget these types of comments when I'm asked to give my input." He narrowed his eyes, going for a young Clint Eastwood look. "Don't forget that." He switched his gaze to Sampson. "What about you?"

"Nothing so far. The bike cops have her picture now and will give me a call if they see her."

"That's mighty nice of them, helping out us Valley cops and all."

"Quid pro quo, of course, we're also keeping an eye out for a nut job who trashed a cafe just up the way earlier this morning." He showed Perkins and Stanfield the photo. "Kent Williams. A bit on the rough side. I ran into him this morning and thought he was homeless."

Stanfield took the phone and examined the picture closer. "Kent Williams? Perk, correct me if I'm wrong, but wasn't one of the people of interest in the Sweeney thing a Kent Williams? He looked something like this, right?"

Perkins took the phone, nodding. "Not exactly 'person of interest' status. He was one of the last to see Sweeney alive. Him and this Charlie guy. What's his last name again?"

"Bates. Master Bates. How could you forget?"

Sampson looked at the two of them. "Regular vaudeville act you guys got going. So let me get this straight. The guy down here terrorizing the friendly locals is one of the guys who saw Sweeney alive last. Ellie is here, somewhere, trying to track down the person or persons responsible for setting her up, just like a Nancy Drew. You guys believe in coincidence?"

"Not hardly." Stanfield handed the phone back to Sampson. "You thinking what I'm thinking?"

"We find this Williams kid and finish this once and for all."

"I'm thinking it's going to be hot as hell out here today, but that was a close second. Where'd you say you saw him last?"

"I didn't say. It was north of here. Past the line of shops and getting into residential territory. Or close to it. Shit. The bike cops are approaching him like he's a vandal. We need to get a message to them that he's probably armed and dangerous."

He called his station and instructed the desk sergeant to put out an alert for Kent, particularly in the Venice Beach area. "Make sure they know to tell the bike cops too, okay?"

He slid the phone in his back pocket. "You guys look really cop. You may as well be wearing uniforms. We need to head back to the cafe Williams trashed and interview them."

"What did he do?"

"Sounds like he tossed a chair through their front window. Maybe two. It wasn't really clear to me and I wasn't really listening. At that time I was more interested in finding Ellie."

Perkins adjusted his pants, giving them a slight tug up. "How much walking are we talking about here?"

"You got comfortable shoes on, I hope. It'll be a couple of miles today, at least, with a good chance of some running before the day is out."

Lisa perked up her ears at the word 'run' and let out another one of her quiet 'woofs'. "Yeah, yeah. We'll get a run in Lisa. If you're lucky we'll have to chase the guy across the beach."

Perkins groaned. "If we're really lucky, the hump has a bad leg or something so we *don't* have to run."

Sampson sobered. "He's a loose cannon. If we're lucky, honestly, we find him before he does any harm to Ellie."

Chapter Thirty-Three

We sat in a delivery doorway for about an hour. Long enough to make sure Kent wasn't following me.

"He scares me, Ellie."

"As well he should. He's nuts. This is why you need to stay away from me for a little while. I don't want you caught up in the crossfire." I pulled my knees up and rested my head on them. "It's going to be hairy for a bit today. You've had enough hairy in your life. Shouldn't have to go through any more."

"I'm not weak."

"I'm not saying you are. I just think it would be prudent if you didn't get yourself killed today. Today is *not* a good day to die."

She open her coats and muttered something.

"You must be sweltering. It's almost 80 degrees already and it's not even noon yet. You're going to die of heat stroke. Take them all the way off."

She shook her head and closed her eyes. "Why don't you trust me?"

"Oh, Jesus, Ann. It's got nothing to do with trust and everything to do with my concern for your well being. Just go back to a safe place and wait for me to get in contact with you, okay? I promise, seriously promise, I will come back for you."

Ann shook her head. "Not safe, young lady. Not safe at all. I think *you* think I'm incapable of doing anything for myself. Well you're flat out wrong. Flat out wrong. And your wrongness is going to get you hurt."

"I'm pretty sure I can handle myself. But I can't protect you, so please, do me a favor and keep your head down for the next twelve hours. It can't be *that* hard, can it?"

"I'll keep an eye out. But I'm not going completely to ground. If I do, it means the terrorists have won."

She was fully sane this morning and that was a good sign. "Just stay far enough away I don't need to worry about your safety and we'll be all good. Deal?"

"Deal."

We stood there and looked at each other for a minute and started talking at the same time.

As she said, "Where are you going to trap him?" I said, "Where are you going to go?"

I shook my head. "No way." I smiled and shook my finger at her.

"Not falling for that trick. I want you to stay clear of me. Got it?"

"Yeah, yeah. You're super-girl. Powerful. Invincible."

"And I want you to be invisible." I gave her a hug and turned my back on her, making a point, I hoped.

I had a plan.

Well, I think I had a plan. Certain things needed to happen at the right time, in the right place, and with the right people. I could control the time, I think. And I had an idea for the place.

There were a couple of half-finished houses near the container we shacked up in. One had the outside walls up. Good place to bring everyone together.

The killer would be easy. The police, maybe not so much.

I wasn't completely convinced Kent didn't know I knew. There was always the danger he was pulling one on me. He was a reasonable guy when I knew him in Australia. He even seemed kinda nice when he ran into me at the cafe. Pretty sure it wasn't luck, now that I think of it. When he was trying to drown my ass under the pier, though, that's when I was convinced he wasn't Mr. Nice Guy.

But he still had a brain in his head. And like any guy, he could be manipulated.

I was so deep in thought as I walked that I almost walked around a corner and straight in to Cathy. I recognized her voice before I saw her or I would have flattened her. I pulled up just shy of the corner and peeked around. I was shielded by a rack of tourist t-shirts. They looked great, but they wouldn't last past the first washing.

She and Sampson were talking.

About me. Of course, I listened.

"Listen Detective, what are you doing to keep Ellie safe? She's in a lot of trouble right now."

"I know. And I know you're good friends with her, but this is a matter for the police. Stay out of it. It's not a matter for a young lady such as yourself."

Oh, that was a mistake.

"Listen, you pig. I'm not something if I don't have a dick? I've been her good friend longer than you've known her. Would you be talking like this to Bernie?"

"Where is he? I would have thought he'd come with you."

"He's an asshole. I'm not sure he has balls anymore."

Oh, shit. Not because of me, I hope. I fought the urge to reveal myself and give her a hug. She was on fire. Sampson was about an inch shorter than her and was out of his depth.

"Well, I'm sorry to hear that. I'm sure you'll work things out with him."

"I doubt we will. He thinks, much like you, I shouldn't be out here looking for my best friend and, like you, he can go fuck himself."

Ouch. I heard enough. They were both looking for me. Sampson I'd need when I needed him. Cathy, bless her, needed to stay out of this. I needed to get clear of the both of them. If they split up and I was in the area I'd be toast.

I turned to leave and bumped into Kent. Literally.

"Ellie."

"Shit, you scared the crap out of me. You're not looking so good. You okay?"

He squinted and gently touched his cheek. I fought the smile which would give me away.

"That looks painful, mate. You really should see a doctor."

"In good time. It won't kill me."

"Are you sure? It's just screaming infection. I suspect if I touch it *you'll* be screaming." I raised my hand and he flinched and took a step back. "Yeah. There's got to be a hospital or a clinic around here somewhere."

He shook his head and wagged his finger. "No, no, no. I've got something I've got to show you."

Really? He was going to try that line? "I've got no interest in seeing your dick, buddy boy."

He took my arm. "No, nothing like that. Just come back to my place and let me show you some stuff I found. Might clear you of the Sweeney killing."

I gently retrieved my arm. "I'm doing just fine on that front. Appreciate the offer but I'm afraid I'm going to have to pass." I looked over my shoulder. Cathy and Sampson had left, searching for me. Where's a cop when you need one?

He took my arm again and dragged me into the alley. "Come on, Ellie. Seriously. I've got some information on this guy. My girl inside the police station has passed on some info."

"Sammie, right?"

"Yeah." He held his head. "No. Stevie. Stevie." He took a breath. "Apparently this guy is a stone cold killer and what he's going to do to you when he catches up to you," he shuddered, "it's just horrible."

"I bet."

"You think I'm kidding?"

"No, I'm sure you're dead on." I twisted my arm free. "Stop grabbing me, okay? It's starting to freak me out." I was getting a little loud.

He backed up a bit and smiled. "Don't want that. Keep your voice down. There are people looking."

"Yeah. Don't want an audience." I rubbed my wrist. The asshole was strong. "So what is this information? Why can't you tell me here?" I had a brilliant idea. "You just want to take me off somewhere. Alone. Don't you? To put the moves on me."

"Well." He shook his head. "No. No, not at all, as tempting as that may be. For reals. You'll regret this, you know."

I backed away through the t-shirts on hangers and waved him off. "I'll catch up with you later." I turned and started jogging, trying to blend in. I needed to get space between him and me and he wasn't very fast with his bum foot.

Danny and his puppy were sitting on the ground. He was playing tug-o-war with Damien, and the puppy appeared to be winning most of the time. He stood when he saw me jogging toward him.

"You okay?"

I slowed and looked over my shoulder. No sign of Kent. "Yeah." I squatted and gave Damien a pat. "Can't stay and chat. I've got a couple of things to do real quick."

Danny sat back down on the ground. "Hey, this older dude with a great looking Golden Lab was by looking for you. Said he was your friend. I didn't tell him anything."

"A cop, right?"

Danny shook his head and frowned. "He didn't identify himself as a cop. What an asshole. He needs to identify himself as an officer of the law when he's questioning me."

"He is a friend, so maybe he was off duty. Don't worry about it. He's a good guy." I stood. "Really got to run. Anyone asks—"

"You're in Oxnard," he interrupted.

I laughed. "No, not this time. Just say you saw me around here somewhere this morning, but you can't remember where."

"You know what you're doing?"

"I hope so. Take care, Danny. And be good to Damien."

I jogged down to the pier and rested for a minute on the south side, concealed by one of the concrete pylons. My first hiding place three days ago. It would end today, or I'd die trying.

Literally. Enough was enough.

I was fed up with being pushed around. Kent was strong, but I was stronger. And he was sick.

But first the house. I needed to check it out. I backtracked toward the container. Past it, by about half a mile, the two houses were side-by-side and abandoned in mid-construction. The economy was shit.

The first was just a frame. Beams and studs and a real skeleton look to it. Not much point in trying to hide and lay a trap in that. The next one, a two story, had the outside walls built. Temporary stairs led to the front door which was, fortunately, just hanging on the hinges. No lock. Not even a knob. Weather damage made the place a total write-off. The beams were warped and the floor had buckled in places. A rat scurried out the back. A big sucker. If I was lucky I wouldn't run into it again.

The place would do.

The largest room, probably going to be the living room, gave me plenty of space. I would have the space to do what I needed to do. He caught me by surprise before and couldn't close the deal. I'd catch him by surprise and finish his ass, then collect the cops.

Boards, some wiring and general refuse needed to be cleaned away. I pushed the small stuff to the edges and dropped a load of the large crap on the front yard, turned and plowed into Ann.

"Shit. I told you to stay clear. Come on, girl. This is serious shit."

She pulled her coat tight and said nothing.

I took her by the shoulders, pointed her in the general direction of the container and gave her a bit of a push. "That way. Home. Hide and be safe. I'll find you later."

She stumbled forward a couple of steps and turned. The look on her face was heart-breaking. Tears streamed down her face, etching tracks through the dirt. I ran toward her and gathered her in a hug. She was completely non-responsive, physically, but the tears kept flowing. "Ann, Ann. I'll be fine. We'll be fine. Let me get this one thing out of the way and I'll make everything right."

"Not if you're dead."

I held her at arm's length and looked into her eyes. "That chump? The punk who hit you in the face? He's nothing. I know his sore spots and I don't fight fair."

"He's psychotic. You never know what he's going to do. He could have a gun."

"He would have shot me by now. Don't worry. I hung out with some pretty tough guys in Australia and learned how to fight there. And I got some excellent hand-to-hand combat training for this movie.

He doesn't have a chance." I pointed at her lip. "I have extra motivation. I need to pay him back for that. Very ungentlemanly of him, hitting a lady."

She sniffled and hugged me again. "You don't have to do this. The police can -"

"The police don't have enough evidence. I'm going to record him bragging about what he did. I'll use my phone." I held up the phone and external battery pack.

"You have enough battery?"

I checked and swore. "Shit. Less than 10%."

She pulled a fist full of batteries from one of her pockets and smiled.

"You're a lifesaver, Ann. You've done more than enough for me. I owe you now. Please get clear. I've got a thing with a guy." I smiled and pointed past her toward the container. "Make sure you lock it from the inside."

She turned and shuffled away. I watched her go until she was out of sight and returned to the house.

I was ready. I set the arena. Now I just needed to draw the opponent.

I loaded the battery extender with fresh batteries and watched the power bar go up to 100%. Perfect.

I opened the settings and turned on location services and toggled the "Find my iPhone" switch. If I was right it would be like a clarion alarm to Kent.

I placed the phone on the floor in the corner, well away from any potential ruckus. I dialed Sampson's number and left the screen open. I wanted him to hear what eventuated.

If I lived or died, he'd know what the score was. This was ending today.

Chapter Thirty-Four

Kent's phone buzzed and warbled. He looked at the display. He had a new email. Rare. He received a notification that Ellie's iPhone had been located. He scrolled through his apps and opened the "Find my Phone" App.

"Shit, shit, shit." He squeezed his eyes shut and tried to remember her email and password. Not right on the first attempt. Not right on the second attempt. Third time lucky. The timer icon spun for a couple of seconds and the map resolved to a green dot almost a mile north of where he was, south of the Venice Pier. He'd guessed wrong. Not as far as del Rey then. "So much for her being smart."

He mapped out a route keeping him out of the heavily populated areas. The map told him it would take fifteen minutes. "Do you have a gimp factor, you fucking piece of shit? More like twenty minutes with this foot."

He took a deep satisfied breath. Twenty minutes to getting rid of the traitorous bitch.

Cathy pulled her ponytail through the hole of her baseball cap and continued looking south of Ellie's apartment. Arbitrary decision. No reason to go either direction, really. She'd been on the beach for almost five hours and so far no sign. She saw a perfectly horrible juggling act with a small dog. She came about five seconds away from popping the guy in the nose and rescuing the dog before it dawned on her the dog he was juggling with was not real. The puppy must have been put back in the equipment bag. Clever trick. Didn't make her any happier.

She looked at her watch. After noon. "I'm getting hungry. What is she doing for food out here?" She stopped at a food cart and grabbed a sausage and coke.

She was close to where the juggling act has pissed her off. She went over to see how the puppy was doing. She squatted and he came running over, back half wagging and front half trying to get a piece of her lunch.

The juggler looked up from his bag at what his dog was interested in and did a double take. "Ellie?"

Cathy looked up. "Excuse me?"

"Nothing. Thought you were someone else. You're too big. And your hair is still long."

"Ellie Bourke? You know her?"

"I think she's in Oxnard. For the berries"

"Bullshit, pal. What do you know?"

"How do you know I know anything?"

"I'm going to call animal control and tell them you're putting the life of a tiny, harmless puppy in danger."

"I'm not really juggling it. Honest. It's a sleight of hand thing and I'm really throwing a stuffed dog around. Believe me."

"Doesn't matter if I do or not, they'll make your life hell. Tell me what you know about Ellie or I call them."

"Man, you're a hard bitch. She's around here somewhere and half the freakin' beach is looking for her. I've had I don't know how many cops, a younger dude with a gorgeous lab - "

"Jacob Sampson."

"Yeah, that's it. And some other people. I'm telling them what she told me to tell them. She's in -" He paused, a confused look on his face. "No, wait. The last time we talked she said to say she was in the area. She didn't want anyone leaving this area."

Cathy pressed. "When was that? When did you talk to her last?"

He scratched his head. "Couple hours ago. Maybe longer." He screwed up his face. "Hell, I don't know. It was today. I don't have a watch or a phone or any other way of telling the time."

"You're a waste of fucking space. How do you know her?"

He shrugged. "You know. Local. I make her laugh. She buys me breakfast once in a while. She's a really nice person, for a famous movie star."

"Yeah. You're still useless. If she happens to pop by tell her Cathy is down here looking for her."

"Are you related? 'Cause you're like sisters. Thought you were her at first."

"I've heard that before. We're not, no. We really don't look that much alike. Very superficial." Cathy gave the puppy one more scratch behind the ear. "It's terrible what you're doing to this puppy. I still have half a mind to call."

"It'd be really cool if you didn't. I'll let Ellie know, if I see her."

"If your drug-addled brain remembers."

"That too."

Cathy left, shaking her head. "Fucking hippies down here."

Ann hated the feeling she was having right now. Danger loomed and she couldn't do anything to avert it. Hiding in the container with the door barred wasn't an option. She had to do something to help Ellie. She found a vantage point about two blocks away. She could see both access roads to the houses. If the attacker came in through other yard and over fences she wouldn't see him, and that was a possibility, but this was better than nothing.

She settled in for a wait when she saw Ellie. Different clothes and different ball cap, but from a distance it was her.

She jumped to her feet and ran out on the street. "You're finished? It's all okay?"

Kent found progress slow. He had to detour three times to avoid crowds. The end was in sight and he didn't want to be sidetracked. If anyone recognized him, it would delay things. He wasn't in the best of moods. This was far more difficult than he ever imagined it to be.

He turned left on a small side street, a one-way lane with minimal traffic, when he saw the bag lady talking to Ellie. He looked around. Vacant. Nobody was around. This would be as good as any. He looked at his phone. The dot representing Ellie's phone was still a quarter mile away. *She must have dropped it and not realized it,* he thought. "Fucking lucky running in to her." The tide was turning.

As he approached the two he started experiencing cognitive dissonance. His brain was insisting the tall blonde in front of him was his target, but his eyes betrayed that thought. It was Ellie, but it wasn't Ellie. As he got closer she flicked her eyes up at him a couple of times and didn't display any signs of recognition, then continued talking to the bag lady.

Ann caught the blonde's glances and turned and let out a scream. "That's him. That's him. That's the guy trying to kill Ellie."

He lashed out and punched her in the side of his head, dropping her like a sack of rice. "Fuck, she's got a hard head." He looked at her companion. "It's you. Fuck. You're not Ellie. That's twice you've fooled me."

"Kent?" Cathy back-pedaled. "What did she mean?"

"What in the fuck do you think she meant?" he approached slowly, limping on his now very sore foot. "I'm the guy trying to kill Ellie. And now, since you know, I'm going to have to shut you up, too." He lunged forward and grabbed her by the throat with his left hand and swung his right fist at her face.

Cathy shied away at the last second, turning her face enough that he hit her on the side of the head, stunning her.

"*Fuck* that hurt my hand." He squeezed tighter. Cathy grabbed at his hand with both of hers, tearing at the skin with her nails as consciousness slowly faded. She was a big girl, and as she dropped he had to follow, not strong enough to hold her up. He dropped her in the alley and looked around. No witnesses. The luck was definitely turning. He wiped the blood off his hand on her shirt then dragged her behind a dumpster. He flipped the lid open, grunted as he picked up the bag lady and tossed her inside and dropped the lid shut. "I'll deal with you later."

He wiped the sweat off his forehead. Some had trickled down his cheek to the cut and the sting was driving him crazy. He dabbed at it with his sleeve and blinked a couple of times, organizing his thoughts.

The phone.

He checked the location. Unchanged. "So you *are* there." About a ten minute walk.

His hand still bled. His DNA would be under her nails, but after he dumped her in the ocean no one would find it. He rolled his shoulders. "This killing shit is a good workout. I could do an exercise DVD. *Burn calories and the annoying people in your life at the same time.* It'll sell like hotcakes." He laughed, giddy. Nothing could stop him now.

Perkins wiped sweat off his brow with his handkerchief.

"I would have bet you were a hanky guy. Stanfield, what's it like working with a guy who keeps his old snot in his pocket."

"Oh, fucking gross. I hadn't thought of that."

Perkins pointedly ignored them. "We need to eat and get something to drink or we're going to suffer from heat stroke."

"It's March. The temperature hasn't hit 80 degrees." Sampson pointed ahead. "But since you're old and have a gut to support, let's let

Emily and Henry feed us."

"Who?"

Sampson pointed. "There. Friends of Ellie. Let's see what they've got to say."

They parked themselves at one of the outdoor tables and waved at Emily who came out with an order pad.

"Gents, you find Ellie yet?"

They looked up at her, surprised.

"Come on, guys. Why else would two Valley cops and a dog patrol guy be down here on the beach? How's my little Lisa? Can I get her something too?"

"Emily, you're too smart for your own good. Nothing for Lisa. She's on a diet. Special food at home."

"So she's going to go all day without eating?"

Sampson looked down at Lisa who looked up at him, her tail thumping on the floor. "Fine. Do you have some lean meat? A couple of pounds." He scratched Lisa behind the ears. "An extra walk for you today, pooch."

"We can do that. What'll you boys have? Or is the raw lean meat for you?"

"Chicken Caesar for me and a lemonade. The meat's for the pooch."

Perkins and Stanfield ordered and waited for Emily to return inside before they continued talking.

"Sampson, this is a waste of time. She's not down here." Stanfield nudged Perkins. "We head back to Sweeney's place after lunch."

Sampson adjusted himself in the chair. "Everyone seems to think she's around here somewhere."

Perkins cocked an eyebrow. "Like everyone was telling us she was in Oxnard before? She certainly has a lot of friends willing to help her."

"Weird, right? In this day and age? A celebrity with real friends?" Sampson shook his head. "Says a lot."

Emily delivered the drinks and promised food shortly.

Perkins sipped at his iced tea and nodded. "Yeah. Very peculiar. And more the reason to not believe what anyone is saying."

"Well you guys can head back to the banality of the Valley if you want. Lisa and I will stick it out. Right Lisa?"

She woofed and rested her head on her paws.

"See, even Lisa agrees, and she's a dog. A pretty smart dog, but still a dog. Smarter than you two boys."

Stanfield shrugged. "What can I say? She's a smart dog."

"Better looking than you, too." Perkins laughed. "By a long short."

Emily returned with sandwiches and Sampson's salad. "Boys, your food. Lisa's meat will be out shortly. Henry is trimming the fat."

"And we're just chewing it." Sampson picked up a fork and rested it on the edge of his bowl. "Listen, Em, you had Ellie in the back of your place this morning when I dropped by, didn't you?"

"I don't know what you're talking about."

"Oh, come on. You were trying to get rid of me like I was an old, fat guy at Club Med. Spill it."

She chewed the inside of her mouth for a minute. "Look, she's always been good to us. And she's as down to earth as they come. She may have dropped by with a friend, and I may have given her a bit of something to eat. That's not a crime."

"What friend?"

Emily hesitated.

"It's not a crime. Don't worry about that. Ellie's in some spot of trouble and we're here to help her. Was she with a guy, looks like this?" Sampson showed her the picture of Kent.

"That asshole? Hell no. He wouldn't dare come back around here. Henry would cleave his skill like a watermelon. It was an older woman, homeless. I've seen her around scavenging for bottles and loose change on the beach. Ellie's adopted her. Or she's adopted Ellie. Her name is Ann. They took their food and lit out." She crossed her arms. "If you guys are really here to help her, then what are you doing sitting on your asses, stuffing your faces?"

Henry brought out a bowl with cut up beef and placed it in front of Lisa. "What's the conversation about?"

"These guys are supposed to be looking for Ellie. I say they're a little bit late. She needed their help a couple of days ago."

Kent checked the map. The dot on his phone indicated he was less than a block away. The only possible candidates were two partially built houses. The dot was located between them. One was still all open frame. He walked through it. It wasn't this one. There was no place to hide. "Like a bloody skeleton."

He heard a scuffle noise in the other house and smiled. "Stupid, stupid bitch."

Ann regained consciousness and opened her eyes. It was dark and it stunk. She banged against the wall of the dumpster and thought, for a second, she was back in the container.

Her nose throbbed and she had a blinding pain behind her eyes. She struggled to get to her feet and pushed the lid up. "Damn it." It flipped back against the alley wall with a clang. She grabbed the edge and crawled over garbage until she could lift herself over the lip. She swung her legs to the ground and heard a groan as she landed. She crabbed around to the back, leaning on the dumpster for support. The girl she thought was Ellie held her head, looking up at her.

Ann squatted in front of her. "You okay?"

"Stay the fuck away from me."

"Relax, lady who looks like Ellie. I'm her friend."

Cathy squinted against the pain and looked up and the middle-aged woman. "You know Ellie? My name is Cathy. What's yours?"

"Ann. The asshole who punched us is going to kill her, then come back here and try and kill us. I suggest we get the hell out of here."

Cathy pushed herself up and looked around. "What asshole? Kent?"

"If that's his name. I don't know. Ellie knows him and she's setting some kind of a trap for him, but I don't think she's going to be successful."

Cathy held the side of her head and leaned against the alley wall. "I'm a bit scattered. Why?"

"Because you were punched in the head."

"No, why is he trying to kill her?"

"Because he's bat shit crazy and I think that's all the reason he needs. Come on. We need to help her."

Cathy closed her eyes and took a deep breath through her nose and winced. "Good plan. There's a cop on the beach. He's a good friend of hers. I'll go find him. Come with me so you can let him know where she is. You do know where she is. Right?"

Ann shook her head. "I'm not going to the police. I'm going to house she's in. I do know where it is. Come with me and help her."

"I don't do bat shit crazy well. Tell me where it is and I'll tell the cops. You shouldn't go on your own. It's clearly dangerous."

"I'll do anything for her. You go. I'll be fine. Tell the policeman friend it's the unfinished house two blocks west of here."

Kent stepped in through the front door to the half built house. Ellie was bent over in the corner doing something on the floor. "Do you know how long I've been waiting for this?" He smiled. "It's going to be beautiful."

Sampson looked at his phone. There was an incoming call from a number he didn't recognize. He held up his finger to get the other two to be quiet and held the phone to his head. "Shush. I can hear Ellie talking." He frowned in concentration. "Shit. It doesn't sound good."

Chapter Thirty-Five

I stood from the phone and turned.

"Did you hear me?" Kent smiled. "This is going to be beautiful."

"You found me."

He held up his phone, map app open, dot blinking in the middle of the screen. "Wasn't that hard. You do that on purpose or was it a mistake?" He shuffled a couple of steps closer.

"I had an idea you were tracking me with my phone. Charlie tipped me off and I closed down the location services. Best way to draw you to me would be to turn them back on."

"Draw me to you? What, like some sort of trap or something?" He laughed. "You've got balls."

I tried to stay close to the phone on the floor. "You need my email address and password to do that. How did you get them?"

"You're not very bright. On your desk on a sticky note."

I smiled. "Oh yeah. The yellow note on the top of my laptop screen." That better do it. "Why'd you kill Sweeney? I mean, I agree he was a bit of a douche and of all the people in the world, I was the last to mourn him, but why?"

Kent shook his head. "Dumb blonde. I'm not going to stand around talking. He fucked up my foot. You knew about it and didn't say anything to me. Charlie too. When I'm finished making you hurt I'm going to kill you and then I'm going after Charlie." He smirked. "He'll never see it coming."

"You got it wrong. I didn't know about your foot until recently. It came out in the trial. The prosecution dug it up but the judge wouldn't let it be used as evidence, so almost no one knew."

He shrugged. "Don't believe you. I fucked up Sweeney and now I'm going to fuck up you." He took another couple of steps toward me.

I slid to one side, trying to keep a good distance between us. "I do have to say I'm impressed though."

He frowned. "About what?"

"You set me up pretty good. A poorly executed staged suicide followed up with evidence pointing to me. How'd you manage that?"

"I've been around movies for*ever*. Wasn't hard. Surprised more people don't do it."

"But my gun? When in the hell did you have time to break into my place and take my gun?"

He laughed hard enough snot ran out of his nose. He wiped it on his sleeve. "I didn't break in. You invited me in. You told that putz,

Pollak, you had a gun. You even said it was in the set of drawers by your bed. When you and Charlie were on the balcony and I had to use the bathroom I got everything I needed. The bedside table? Really? I was hoping for more of a challenge."

I had to admit, it was good. "That kind of imagination you should be writing screenplays. They'd be better than most of the stuff out there now."

"Don't try and change the fucking subject. My life is fucked because Sweeney broke my foot and you knew about it and didn't stop him."

He was literally foaming at the mouth. Spittle built up in the corners of his mouth and he had a feverish gleam in his eyes. "You're not looking well, pal. You need to get yourself checked out. In a psych ward, maybe. I already told you I didn't know he did it."

"And I already told you I don't believe you." He lunged at me and as I tried to side step him I stubbed the side of my foot on a raised floor board, falling hard on my side. He was on top of me like a rat on a cheese wheel, grabbing at my throat.

He had a strong grip. I tried to pry his fingers, even just one, to use as a pain lever. It wasn't the lack of oxygen in my lungs, it was the reduction of blood to my brain. He had a good clamp on the carotid arteries. I tried to blink away the redness. As I was starting to slip I saw the cut on his cheek and slammed it with the heel of my hand, splitting it open.

He roared and fell back, releasing my neck and grabbing at his face. "Bitch. You fucking bitch."

I could have run. That wasn't the plan though. He had to go down.

I needed to keep him talking and revealing until the cavalry showed up.

"Hurts, does it? Told you. You need to have it checked out. Looks really infected."

Blood flowed down his cheek on to his hand. He looked at it and flicked it in my direction. "I'm going to keep you alive a bit longer because of that. What doesn't kill you isn't going to make you stronger. It's going to make you long for death. I got some fantastic ideas from our movie. *I'm going to slice you from ear to ear.*"

My chest heaved, trying to fill my lungs with air and my brain with blood. I clenched my teeth and replied: *"You've got to catch me first, you miserable fuck."*

"It was a classic, wasn't it? Such fantastic dialog. And so fitting to right fucking now."

His back was to the front door and I had my back to the stairway to the unfinished upstairs. I may be blonde, but I'm not *that* blonde. Running upstairs was not in my plans. He shifted his weight like he was going to run at me when out of nowhere a whirling dervish landed on his back. Ann screamed something horrific, legs wrapped around his torso and both hands full of his hair, twisting his head back and forth.

He staggered sideways under the onslaught, caught off guard and off balance. "What the fuck?" He grabbed her wrists and pulled. He was wide open and if I was a bit more on the ball I would have kicked him in the nuts while he spun, trying to dislodge her. I missed the opportunity. He banged her off the walls a couple of times and finally managed to fling her across the room and into an inside corner. She hit with a sickening crunch and lay still on the floor.

He looked at her while sucking deep breaths. "You're next, pretty.

But you won't be so lucky."

I rushed to her and dropped to the floor beside her. Her breathing was ragged, but she was breathing. Better than the alternative. She didn't look too good. And she was in this state because she felt she had to help me. Something she wouldn't have had to do if this ass-hat hadn't stuck his nose in to my life. I pushed myself to my feet.

He was more concerned with adjusting his shirt. A couple of buttons had been ripped off and it was hanging loose on his body. He looked pretty skinny. Not at all healthy.

"I can't believe she did that." He spit in her general direction. "This'll be the third time I've knocked her out. Maybe she'll get the fucking hint and stay down this time."

"Third?"

"Yeah, you believe it? I ran in to her and this chick who looked kinda-sorta like you on the way here. Dropped them both." He pointed at Ann. "Dumped her in a, well, dumpster. The other one dropped like a sack of spuds. She's behind the dumpster. Too big to lift in. I'll go back for her when I'm finished with you." He smiled. "Going to be a busy afternoon."

I had enough of this. "The other person is one of my best friends. Cathy. That was the last straw."

He had the gall to laugh. "What are you going to do?" He slowly advanced on me. His limp was more pronounced than when I first ran in to him three days ago. Blood caked on his jaw. His smile added an air of psychosis.

If he thought I was going to run from him, he was mistaken. This is where I wanted him.

I let him advance one more step.

They say everyone has a plan until they're punched in the nose. I wanted to test that aphorism. He seemed awfully confident. I had about an inch or so reach on him. He wasn't that tall. An inch or so shorter than me. I had great hand-to-hand training during *Blood Thunder*. I knew exactly my reach. I spent six months making sure I didn't hit my fellow actors. Time to switch it up a bit.

I faked with my right and snapped with my left catching him on the end of the snout. His head popped and he staggered backwards.

"Fuck." He held his hand in front of his nose. "You bitch. That hurt."

"I wasn't kissing, you asshole. I've got more."

He charged at me, trying to catch me off guard. No more.

I met his oncoming rush with a classic side kick, my leg sharply extending my foot into his gut as he ran toward me. Impact velocity was around sixty miles an hour.

I was on one leg, the other one firmly planted in his gut. His momentum both knocked the wind out of him and knocked me on my ass. He continued forward out of control and landed on top of me, gasping for air. He had the presence of mind to grab me around the throat again and at that point I was pretty sure he didn't have any grand plan to torture me. He was winging it. I stuck my thumb in the cut on his cheek and pushed as hard as I could while I brought my knee up between his legs.

I think the male nervous system has an automatic response to anything heading toward their sack. Even though he was splitting his concentration between trying to choke me and the pain I was inflicting on his cheek he managed to twist enough to one side so I only glanced my knee off one testicle.

It was enough, though. He loosened his grip on my throat. I twisted my arm around and caught him in the jaw with my elbow, rolling with him and kneeling hard on his nuts. I wasn't heavy enough to hold him down and he pushed me off. I added a couple of extra rolls to keep out of his reach. I scrambled to my feet.

He got up almost as quickly. He coughed and gingerly moved his jaw around. "You're a devious little bitch. I owe you another one." He held his hand against his jaw. "That hurt." Blood flowed freely down his cheek, off the edge of his jaw and on to his shirt and chest. "You've really given me the shits now."

"You're not getting out of here." I was feeling good. He'd tried three times now and didn't have whatever was needed to finish me off. Time to go on the offensive.

I trotted toward him. The last thing he expected. He made a mistake and took a half step backward and I lunged and swung.

I'm not stupid enough to punch his head with my fist. There are tons of tiny bones in my hand, and smashing him in the skull would break most of them. So I hit him with my right elbow across the bridge of his nose.

His head snapped to his right and he spun with it. When his back was to me I brought my elbow back and caught him at the base of the skull. He fell forward with a grunt, landing hard on his knees. I stuck a foot on his back, between the shoulder blades and pushed. He must have been stunned by the shot to the neck. His hands stayed by his side and he landed on the wooden floor face first with a soggy crack. If I hadn't broken his nose before, I had now.

I placed my left foot on the back of his neck and pressed. "Stay still, jerk-wad. The cops are on their way."

He started shaking. I thought at first he was crying and was about to lay into him about being a pussy when I realized he was laughing. At me.

I pressed a little harder, grinding my heel into his neck. I really hated this guy and it was only the knowledge the police might be here soon that kept me from killing him.

Yet he laughed harder. "What's so funny, shit-dick?"

"You think," he gasped, trying to talk through the laughter. "You think you've won."

"Who's foot is on who's neck?"

He tried to turn his head. He was smiling. What the fuck? "I know something you don't know, bitch."

"What's that?"

"I've got a knife." He twisted to the right and swung his hand back, Ann's blue-handled knife in his hand. It entered my right calf muscle and tore and I collapsed with the knife stuck in my leg. "Who's winning now?

I swallowed, trying to keep my head straight. There were no major arteries where he stuck me, I don't think. The pain was almost unbearable. I fought the urge to spew. I looked down at the incongruous blue handle of the knife sticking out of my leg. The amount of blood on my jeans was disturbing.

Kent struggled, pushing himself up off the floor. Blood and snot poured out of his nose mixing with the blood from his infected, cut cheek.

He leaned over and pulled out the knife, slowly. I clenched my teeth. I wouldn't give him the pleasure of hearing me scream, although I almost passed out. He stood and walked around, flipping the knife like it was a baton, or a drum stick. My blood flicked off the end of the blade.

I supported myself against the wall and pushed myself to my feet, putting all my weight on my left leg. Blood dripped off my foot on to the floor.

Kent circled, flipping the knife. "Not so shit hot now, are you?"

I put my hands up, surrender-like. "You're the man, Kent. What do you want from me?"

"I want you to die. I'm going to cut your throat. I'm going to do that last. You'll have so many holes in you the Swiss will induct you in the cheese hall of fame." He flipped the knife again. "You'll have so many holes in you, you'll be mistaken for a colander." He sniffed and wiped the bloody snot off his nose with his arm.

He took another step toward me and flipped the knife one last time. I reached out and grabbed it, cutting a finger in the process. He grabbed at me and we struggled for the knife. He ended up holding me from behind and started squeezing, hard. I couldn't breathe. I felt that tingling feeling you get at the end of your nose just before you pass out. My vision was reduced to spots. I was fading fast. With the last of my strength I adjusted my grip and drove the knife into his groin as hard as I could, and collapsed on the ground on top of him. The last conscious words I remember, just as I was passing out, came from Perkins.

"Fucking hell, Sampson. What the fuck is all this?"

A very handsome young man had my pants off.

I surfaced to the land of the aware while Studly McParamedic applied a compression bandage to my calf. I let out a whimper. It still hurt like hell.

"You're awake. Excellent." I tried to sit up. "No, no. Don't move. I've got some pain relief." He ripped the paper packaging off a plastic, green whistle shaped tube. "Do you have asthma or any other breathing difficulties?"

I shook my head and raised myself up on my elbows. "You've got those things here, too?"

"You've used them before?"

"Dislocated a collarbone surfing when I was much younger. Tastes like crap. But I thought they were only in Australia."

"We've had these for a while now. So you know how to use it?"

I nodded and stuck it in my mouth and took a sharp inhale. "After I dislocated my collarbone this green plastic baby kept me from going nuts on the ambulance ride."

It was about six or seven inches long and had a flattened tube on one end I had to breath through. The taste hadn't improved, but the efficacy had. A general numbness poured over my body after three or four breaths. I seemed to remember it took more than six before, but maybe it was because this time I hadn't eaten since morning. I licked my lips trying to get rid of the taste. "What's going on?"

"I'm taking care of your leg. It looks like you'll be hobbling around on crutches while this heals, but I don't think you'll have permanent damage. You might have a bit of a scar when it's all healed up."

I croaked, licked my lips and tried again. "Something to remember this by. How is Ann?" I looked around and couldn't see her. A pair of medics were working on an unconscious Kent, his pants also cut off and a fair bit of blood on the floor around him.

"Ann?"

"The homeless-looking lady. She was on the floor over there. Wasn't doing too well."

"She's on the way to the hospital with your friend, I think she said her name was Cathy. Are you related to Ann?"

"Let's say she's my Aunt, okay?"

He raised an eyebrow but had the decency to not question me. "Your Aunt has a slightly fractured skull, a couple of broken ribs and a possible punctured lung. But I think she'll be fine. She was conscious and lucid when we put her in the ambulance."

I sat up. "Whatever it costs, I'll pay for it. Top quality care. You make sure people know okay?"

"Lie back down. You're making this more difficult than it needs to be. And yes, I'll pass the info on. But you can, too. You'll be in the same hospital."

I slumped back. Perkins poked his head in. "You okay?"

"You believe me now?"

"Believed you for a bit more than a day. You should have listened."

"You wouldn't have had the evidence you needed to convict this asshole if I turned myself in when you wanted me to. You should thank me."

He laughed. "Maybe. We'll see if the guy lives."

"Really?"

"He's missing a testicle, and lost a lot of blood. You did a good number on him."

I leaned back and closed my eyes. "What took you guys so long. Samson got the phone call, right?"

"Getting in to your apartment to get the password. We couldn't just kick the door down. We needed a warrant. And then the building Super took his own sweet time getting the key. Another minute and Sampson would have put his size twelves through the door. Thank God Stanfield was with us, because both Jacob and I didn't have the slightest idea you could track your phone. That's going to come in handy."

I opened my eyes and took another puff of magic dust. I looked around and took stock. My last stand. Fighting in real life was nothing like in the movies. I hardly used anything the Seal taught me. No chance.

An army of CSI type people, none of them looking like they were from a TV show, swarmed into the house doing their techie stuff. Kent was still flat on his back to my right, paramedics stabilizing him before transport to the hospital where, I hoped, he would be handcuffed to the bed and kept under constant guard. I could see the blue handle of Ann's knife, covered in his and my blood, on the far side of his prone form. "Don't you think you should secure his knife?"

Perkins looked up from his notebook. The never ending flipping of pages. "What'd you say?"

"The knife."

"Needs to be processed. That's for the crime scene boys and girls. I'll take your statement about what happened and it will of course involve the knife, but I'm not touching it."

Sampson walked in. No Lisa.

"Where's the pooch?"

"I can't bring her in here. She'll contaminate the scene. You doing okay?"

I held up the green whistle. "Fan-fucking-tastic. You?"

"I've had better days." He took Perkins by the arm. "I overheard most of what went on over the phone. I can help you with the statement and Ellie can fill in the blanks when she's ready."

I smiled and put my head back down. I was tired. "Thanks Jacob. Much appreciated." I lifted it up again. "Make sure Ann is okay, right? After the medical stuff is sorted there's some mental stuff she needs help with. I'm her insurance program. Whatever it costs I'll pay. I owe her so much."

"I'll make sure." Jacob nodded at Perkins. "You want the statement now?"

I heard a groan and looked over at Kent. His eyelids fluttered. And he inhaled a sharp breath. The paramedics scrambled to check vitals. He opened his eyes, looked to his left, stared at me straight in the eyes and bellowed something incomprehensible. He scrambled for the knife and swung it at me.

Time dilation is real. Everything shifted to slow motion, like my life was suddenly a John Woo movie. Doves should have flown by.

Sampson scrambled for a gun he didn't have, him being off duty. Perkins struggled to remove his; the restraining strap on the holster was still clipped and he was losing valuable time.

I gripped the green painkilling whistle, thumb over the end and swung it with every fiber of my strength, driving the tube end into Kent's left eye. It squished and bounced off his eye socket and his clear eyeball fluid mixed with blood. His follow through with the knife had no strength behind it. It hit me on the boney part of my chest, which many will tell you is the entire chest, but didn't do more than scratch.

I looked at the stunned paramedic. "Can I have another one of those green whistles? Mine's kind of icky."

Chapter Thirty-Six

The waves curled nice at Warriewood. Not huge, but big enough for Ellie. She was glad to be back on the Northern Beaches, just north of Sydney.

Late May was kind, the temperature in the high twenties and not a cloud in the sky. An onshore wind added to the fun.

Cathy, Charlie and Ann sat around a table at the beachside cafe, eating their lunch, drinking beer and watching Ellie surf.

Ann picked at her chicken Caesar. "A world away from reality. I can't believe it's been almost three months." She took a deep breath. "I never knew Australia was so beautiful."

Cathy took Ann's hands in hers. "You feeling okay?"

"Never better, really. Is she always like this?"

Charlie watched Ellie catch a particularly good wave and ride it in. "Like what? Carefree, not a problem she can't handle just taking life as it comes? Pretty much."

"Not that. She's virtually adopted me. Paid all my med bills, got me some fantastic mental health help, and has brought me to this beautiful place."

Cathy nodded. "Yeah, that's her."

Ellie walked up the beach, board under her arm, wetsuit stuck to her body. Charlie smiled. Life was indeed good.

"What are you guys looking at?" She parked the board against the railing and sat with her friends. She pulled a towel over her shoulders, kissed Charlie and looked at Ann and Cathy. "Everything okay?"

Ann nodded and Cathy held up a finger. "I've got a couple of questions."

Ellie opened a beer and sat back. "Fire away."

"I still don't get it. What the fuck was wrong with Kent?" Ann slapped her lightly on the arm. "Sorry, what the *heck* was wrong with Kent?"

Ellie took a deep pull of beer. Surfing worked up a thirst. "Aside from the deep-seated pathological sociopathic tendencies? Sweeney intentionally broke his foot to get him to limp properly in *Beast of Bondi*. He'd thought it was an accident for the last three years. He heard about it on my interview with Kevin Pollak. Sorry, my "conversation" with Kevin Pollak. Something snapped. He thought I knew and I'm pretty sure he thought Charlie knew, too."

Charlie stopped his beer halfway to his mouth. "Yup. No idea why he'd think that."

"He told me he was going after you once he finished with me."

"Fu - " he looked at Ann. "Damn."

"Not much better, young man." She smiled. "But thanks."

Cathy winked at Charlie. "I've got a follow-up, Ell. What's the deal with you and Charlie here?"

"It's a thing. We'll see how the thing goes. He's apparently had a crush on me since he first met me years ago. That kind of devotion a girl could get used to."

Charlie blushed, to the amusement of the ladies around the table.

Ann yawned. "My clock is completely out of sync. What time is it in LA?"

Cathy looked at her watch, squinted and counted off on her fingers. "5:00 pm. But I'm not sure if it's today, yesterday or tomorrow."

"It doesn't matter, people. You'll be adjusted in a couple of days and it'll be like you've been here all your life. Beautiful, isn't it?"

"Isn't it coming up on winter? When does it get cold?"

"This is a bit warmer than usual. Wait until July, though. It'll get pretty cold."

Cathy picked at the label on her bottle. "So why are we here? I mean, the vacation away to get clear of the paparazzi is all well and good, but why do I think there's an ulterior motive?"

Ellie looked at Charlie and smiled. "There is. I've got a small script. Friend of mine just up the road wrote it. We'll stop by and have a chat with him after lunch. It's about two sisters," she pointed at Cathy and then herself, "in a coming of age story. Cathy, you're finished with the Shakespeare thing, Charlie here is a hell of a director and Ann is,

I'm told, a financial wizard. We're all also producers and I've got some local financing lined up. We're going to make a movie."

She looked around the table at her friends. This was what she wanted to do. She wanted to make movies to tell stories. No big blockbusters. Just some friends getting together to tell a good story.

ABOUT THE AUTHOR

Tony McFadden is a Canadian now happily living in Australia, a land with very little snow, writing near the beach whenever possible.

You can find him on the interwebs at www.TonyMcFadden.net,

Also by Tony McFadden

Matt's War
Daly Battles: The Fall of PyongYang
Target: Australia

G'Day LA

Book 'Em
Family Matters
Unprotected Sax
(with Charles McFadden)

Have Wormhole, Will Travel
Killing Time

Mac D: Private Investigator
A Step Too Far (A Mac-D Mystery)
Hunter / Prey
·
The Murder of Jeremy Brookes
Number Fifteen

Batteries Not Included
Broken
Dead Tomorrow
Under the Shadows